# THE OCTOBER FILM HAUNT

## MICHAEL WEHUNT

St. Martin's Press / New York

This is a work of fiction. All of the characters, organizations, and events portrayed in this novel are either products of the author's imagination or are used fictitiously.

First published in the United States by St. Martin's Press,
an imprint of St. Martin's Publishing Group

*EU Representative:* Macmillan Publishers Ireland Ltd, 1st Floor, The Liffey Trust Centre, 117–126 Sheriff Street Upper, Dublin 1, D01 YC43

THE OCTOBER FILM HAUNT. Copyright © 2025 by Michael Wehunt. All rights reserved. Printed in the United States of America. For information, address St. Martin's Publishing Group, 120 Broadway, New York, NY 10271.

www.stmartins.com

Design by Jonathan Bennett

Library of Congress Cataloging-in-Publication Data

Names: Wehunt, Michael, 1952- author
Title: The October film haunt / Michael Wehunt.
Description: First edition. | New York : St. Martin's Press, 2025.
Identifiers: LCCN 2025012338 | ISBN 9781250333698 hardcover | ISBN 9781250333704 ebook
Subjects: LCGFT: Horror fiction | Novels
Classification: LCC PS3623.E42275 O28 2025
LC record available at https://lccn.loc.gov/2025012338

The publisher of this book does not authorize the use or reproduction of any part of this book in any manner for the purpose of training artificial intelligence technologies or systems. The publisher of this book expressly reserves this book from the Text and Data Mining exception in accordance with Article 4(3) of the European Union Digital Single Market Directive 2019/790.

Our books may be purchased in bulk for specialty retail/wholesale, literacy, corporate/premium, educational, and subscription box use. Please contact MacmillanSpecialMarkets@macmillan.com.

First Edition: 2025

10 9 8 7 6 5 4 3 2 1

*To Natalia.*

*For encouraging, for believing,
for understanding,
for giving light to it all.*

TAPE 1
FUNERAL WATCHING
VIDEO CASSETTE

But there is your tired Abrahamic view. Jesus and the swine. Wicked angels tumbling from heaven. The Bible is no place to look for demons. The church knows of them like a child knows, peeking from under its blanket. You may find demons with the small light in a child's room, but not with the light of any Christ.

—ROGER EILERTSEN,
*PROOF OF DEMONS*

# CHAPTER ONE

## Jorie

▶▶ The package fills half the mailbox. Before Jorie even touches it, before she hears the rattle of the spools inside the plastic housing, some part of her knows it's a VHS tape. The shape of it, the corners sharp beneath the padding. Her mind has its own muscle memory.

She slides the envelope out, the thick yellow paper stark among the bills and a red-stamped collection notice. For a full minute, she stands in her gravel driveway by High Rock Road, in the lowering chilled dusk, and stares at the western edge of her little Vermont acre. The knitted quilt of it all. The bleached bone trunks of the paper birches, green crowns turning buttery in September. The maples ruddy, blushing behind them.

Personal mail is rare for Jorie up here. Her life is small now, filled with earnest words instead of creeping images. There is not a single videocassette inside her home. A few of her editing clients have sent her things in the mail, retirees who want to be authors the way it was done when they were young and their dreams were only glimmers. Jorie remembers the ink smudging under her fingers on one of the home-printed manuscripts.

Most of that is digital these days, zipped Scrivener files, Word docs. When she has clients.

This has nothing to do with her freelance work, she feels it at once. Jorie hears the faint clicking when she shakes the package. She held hundreds of VHS tapes in her past life, she knows the weight and the percussion they make.

The mailbox door scrapes its lip as she closes it.

It's almost warm inside her house. She hangs her jacket on the back of the chair at the table, sets the mail down, and listens to the silence. Her son is with his cousins for the weekend because she has a manuscript to finish editing and an

3

author to invoice. This memoir has made her so tired. The traumas in it weigh so much they've almost become her own.

Jorie glances down at the yellow envelope. She imagines what is waiting inside, imagines not opening it. Her client's book is the kind of story she wants to live in now. It's not made up, it tells the world about real things that happened to a real person. The monster is human, and best of all, a soft and bright thread of hope is woven through the ending.

She sits down and places her hands on her computer. She slides her hips across the seat until she finds the comfortable broken-in spot. Her office is a dining nook in the corner of the house, tucked between the kitchen and what Oli calls the den, a residue of when they moved in last year and he pretended for weeks that he was part-wolf.

"A sad wolf, Mom," he told her once, and she still hasn't gotten all the way over that. She's still a sad wolf mom herself, whenever she catches him sitting on his bed, wishing his father would call.

Without Oli here, she doesn't have to listen to him murmuring to Agatha, the Victorian doll he found in the attic a few months ago. Agatha is the closest thing to a horror film allowed in the house, Oli's voice filling the rooms in spite of—or because of—how softly he speaks to the doll. Worse, he likes to tap Agatha's faded porcelain face against everything in his bedroom in some secret code.

She misses the two of them already.

It's the end of a month without any shifts at the market, and she can't decide if she's happy about going back next week. Stocking shelves and scanning barcodes and feeling like a struggling single mom in a movie, even if thirty-eight is too old for the role. She's okay with making ends meet in a grocery store, but she only glances at other people's stories there.

One day she hopes to make all her money right from this nook, this table. She gets to dig into stories here. They get under her fingernails. She bends their frames so that the blood soaks into the words in beautiful, sharper ways.

It suits her quiet, hidden life.

Vermont does, too. She loves the cathedral light that pours in around the table on certain clear afternoons, slanting toward winter as the mountains reach up to drag the sun behind them, earlier every day. The angle this time of year, the light feels thick as honey. She seems most like her real self, what's left of it that she still wants, when she is held in it.

The spare room has her grandmother's big pine desk and the vintage filing cabinet, but it doesn't have the paper birches outside the window. Here in the nook, Jorie can lift her eyes from the laptop and get lost in the tree line.

She should be pulling up the final chapters in her author's sad story. Instead she turns the yellow envelope over. J STROUD is printed in rough black marker. There is no return address, just a postmark from Arden, North Carolina.

The first small bell of recognition goes off in her mind.

The black tape slides out onto the table when she tears the envelope open. It shows its age, scuffs and a chipped corner. FUNERAL WATCHING fills the white label across the spine in faded print, as though it has stood on a shelf in years of its own cathedral sun.

Who is left to think she would want something called *Funeral Watching*, tucked out here in her rural pocket? Ten-plus years are supposed to add up to a new start, with room to spare. She hasn't traded obscure horror movies since Hannah Kim, before Oli, a lifetime before Vermont.

Jorie vanished from the scene, from the entire internet. Her connections, her film production and book deal, the screenplay she sold, her agent, the October Film Haunt brand, the two hundred thousand followers scattered across social media—everything drained out of her life a long time ago. She hasn't so much as watched a trailer for a scary movie since.

Much harder to answer: Who would know where she lives now?

Here is the second bell, a faint dark ring in her thoughts. Muffled inside the old excitement.

It's second nature to assume a horror film is on this tape, one she's never heard of, and the title's unfamiliarity exposes the phantom limb, a gap in her knowledge that begins to itch again. *You have to check this out*, Colin says from a warmer past where the sun set later in the day.

She misses Colin first because he's been dead for almost nine years, then Beth because Jorie's been dead to her even longer. She misses the late nights watching *Mulholland Drive* and *Proboscis* and *A Nightmare on Elm Street* and the only thing to do the next day was serve coffee for seven hours. Colin holding up a bootleg VHS. *This one's by Orrin Grey, before he did Campbell's* Incarnate. *It took me ages to find it.*

She misses their film haunts, too. Staying up until dawn with the two of them in places where movie magic happened, absorbing the whispers of fiction and wishing they were real. For that alone, she feels something like hate for the person who sent this tape.

With the empty house to herself, and the itch, she unearths the VHS/DVD player in the utility closet and thanks her neurotic past self for hoarding the machine, lugging it all the way up here with the RCA cable taped to it. She curses that past self, too, but five minutes later she's sliding the tape into the player in her son's old wolf den and sitting down with the grimy remote.

Tracking lines scroll on the TV screen, a moment of distortion and muddy warping that still feels like home to Jorie, and before the picture clears she recognizes what she's watching. The trees filling the top right corner of the shot, the people facing the bottom left, the swath of green lawn between.

It's Pinewood Cemetery, in North Carolina, where a scene near the beginning of Hélène Enriquez's *Proof of Demons* was filmed. The site of their last film haunt.

Where a girl named Hannah Kim would later die instead of finishing high school.

All the heat in Jorie seems to rise to her face. She feels a nostalgia that is almost nausea. The hundreds of hours she spent thinking and talking and writing about *Proof of Demons* and its mysterious director. The night she visited this very graveyard with Colin and Beth. For a moment she's twenty-seven again, her little Oliver a distant mote in a life she never would have lived if they'd chosen a different film that year.

The images stabilize as well as they can. *Proof of Demons* was made and released long after the VHS era, but here it seems to have been rendered with analog effects, as though it's pretending to be a low-budget production from the 1980s. The colors are saturated. She can't quite tell where the digital transference ends and the original medium begins.

A static shot unravels itself slowly, dark-clothed mourners at a funeral, someone delivering a eulogy off-screen in a voice that has been muddled just beyond comprehension. A woman holds a black cloth to her eyes before hunching forward, in grief, just as Jorie remembers from the thirty or forty times she saw her do it, when watching a movie for the thirtieth or fortieth time was the best kind of homework.

But she begins to feel real excitement as she realizes this is some sort of extended scene. More than the famous six minutes have passed, the unmoving camera marking the first of the peculiar segments that supposedly form a ritual opening the door to hell. The iconic Pine Arch Creature should have come out of the trees by now, from under the boughs fans named it after. She waits for it, feeling the anticipation draw a chill up her back, and starts noticing other differences. Her hand creeps up to cover her mouth.

The trees aren't pines, they're paper birches, bright trunks like quills in the earth. There are no limbs to stretch across into an arch, their foliage is cut off by the frame, but in the background there's the suggestion of green that hasn't begun to rust yet. She sees dead leaves scattered across the band of grass, not pine needles. The tenor of the light is different, too, lower and closer to sunset, more able to be poured into a glass.

These are details her mind only plugs in now because it has insisted on seeing the original scene, darkening the bark of the trees, needling their crowns, moving the late-day sun south, where it would roll slower across the sky above the graves. But these trees are etched in her mind for a more recent reason.

This was filmed in Vermont. Jorie thinks a few stands of white birches may grow high in the Smoky Mountains in Tennessee, or the Blue Ridge, but never down at this elevation in the South. She nearly turns to look through the picture window above her nook, across her own swath of lawn. The paper birch is a beautiful tree, and she never saw one until she moved up here.

With nearly eight minutes on the VCR's counter, two huge, skinny shapes emerge from the birches on the TV screen, and her thoughts of the trees behind her are gone. In a scene soaked in too much of the color scale, the creatures are desaturated lumps. The smudged figures move, hunched over, elastic and arrhythmic, quietly toward the mourners. They look identical to the thing from the original *Proof of Demons*, strangely difficult to see and even more inscrutable in the VHS haze, their torsos seeming to open up half like curtains, half like ink spreading in water.

But there shouldn't be two of them.

The first of the blurred things crosses the lawn and reaches its misshapen arms toward a child, and the scene cuts to a scrolling lull of greenish static with no sound. Jorie's heart is pounding. Her first thought is to call Beth, and to wish she could call Colin. She'll wonder who sent her the tape later. She'll let the scab of guilt break open in just a moment. Whatever this is, it's brought back the old skin-crawling tingle of why she loved horror movies so much for so long.

Beth hasn't spoken to her in a decade. Jorie's phone is on the table by her laptop, under the window with its view of the birches, and she's still deciding whether to go get it when she lifts the remote and presses rewind instead. Even the wasp whine of the VCR ejecting the tape rolls back the years. It's one of those old late nights again, Colin bursting into giddy commentary the second the credits are rolling.

But her phone chirps, saving her from the memories. She goes to it and smiles when Oli's face fills her screen. The text is from her cousin, Sam. Sonic the Hedgehog viewing #37 before bed, under a photo of Oli stretching his mouth into a grimace with finger hooks. Samantha's twins are in the background trying to copy him.

Getting close to Sam has been the best thing about moving up here, more life-affirming than all the gorgeous foliage and more comforting than every cozy woolen pair of socks she's splurged on for her and Oli. She and Sam didn't see each other much as kids, and even if Jorie had other friends in this miniature life, the two of them would have clicked.

The text is exactly what Jorie needed. Better you than me, she types back, tell the little rodent I love him. And the twins. And you. Thank you.

When she wakes just past two A.M., cold rain is pattering on her bedroom window. Her heart is trying to catch up from a skipped beat, and she wonders if she has dreamed of the figures from the videotape creeping out of the trees. She pictures them approaching the house—are their skins glossy in the rain, or do they remain an obscured matte darkness?

This tendency to pretend horrors in the middle of the night is almost atavistic in her, stretching back to childhood stories she made up to scare herself under the covers. The vampire in the glow of the streetlamp, the thing bracing itself just below the foot of the bed. Some presence behind her where her eyes couldn't go. She's never been able to turn it all the way off. For most of her life, she didn't want to.

Oli thumps his bedroom wall, turning over in his sleep.

Of course the tape has brought Hannah Kim back into Jorie's mind. The death threats tapered off sometime in 2015, but someone could have tracked her down, someone who can't let go. She pictures Hannah's broken father, and the dead eyes of Hannah's mother staring into TV cameras. Anyone seeing those faces would want Jorie to hurt.

She hasn't thought of them in months, at least not on the surface of her mind. All the images and articles she once forced herself to stare at have been fading slowly over time, finally reaching a place where that long year is more scar tissue than open wound. Now she thinks of Hannah's school photo that hung in the corner of news reports before and during the trial. *Teen Ritual Slaying. 'Pine Arch' Trial Continues. Occult Film Creator Unknown. Popular Horror Website Under Fire.*

Close behind Hannah is Colin, the shy live wire of the October Film Haunt. He would have ended up a brilliant writer with a fan base following him into strange shadows, but he was hit even harder by the guilt of what came out of those North Carolina woods with them.

Some nights, there's the thought that she killed him, too. And what that did to Beth, who had more empathy than anyone Jorie ever knew, who loved stray dogs intensely and horror movies almost as much. She's had thousands of nights to relive it all, some of them can't help but reach this level of bleak.

Like so many bad things, the October Film Haunt began with love. There was no other ingredient, least of all expectation. Jorie met Beth, they met Colin, soon they had the idea to visit the filming locations of cult horror movies. They wanted to capture the essence of the art form they cherished, and hopefully pick up some of the lingering spirit of the casts and crews, like ectoplasm at a séance. Write it all down. Transfer that love to others like them. There was something almost paranormal about it.

Their blog posts and social media clips resonated. They were just a blog with a modest following for a while, with more passion and insight and savvy than most. But after Guillermo del Toro tweeted about them and Jamie Lee Curtis was photographed dozens of times wearing an October Film Haunt shirt under a blazer, Jorie and Beth and Colin were suddenly everywhere. The spotlight snapped on with all its oily heat, social media management became a full-time job, and they were somehow tastemakers.

*BuzzFeed* even did a piece on future film haunt suggestions. Colin scoffed at nearly the whole list.

All three of them were going places, especially after the final haunt went viral. Jorie optioned her script *Dead People's Things*, it had a director attached, the holy green light. Her book about found-footage horror films had sold on proposal, the advance money two years of what she made at the old coffee shop in Atlanta. She was ascendant.

Beth's film agent had strong feelers out, too. Colin finally started a novel. All three of them were getting writer and producer credits on the *Proof of Demons/October Film Haunt* documentary. They were signing deals and creating content that wasn't disposable, that would be talked about. They had so much road ahead of them, until Jorie—

An elbow or knee bumps against the wall in Oli's room again, the comforting sound she's used to from his restless sleeping body. A series of soft, solid knocks follow it, Oli tapping Agatha's face against his headboard. These are less comforting, since Agatha is usually quiet after bedtime. Jorie waits to hear his sleepy voice mumbling to the doll.

And she comes fully awake now because Oli is with his cousins tonight.

The window is a smear of rain. The alarm clock bleeds red onto the bookshelf near the bed. She sees the dim outline of herself under the blanket, the September cold that seeps into her grandparents' house—her house, she still has to remind herself, ever since Gram's will cleared probate—trying to find its way into the cocoon she's made.

These bleary images are all that surround her in the dark room, in the resonance of that thump on the wall. It sounded so much like her son.

As so many have done in her favorite films, Jorie slides out of bed to investigate. The floorboards creak under her socks, the cold breath of the house wraps around her. She almost shivers. She can check Oli's room or wait for quiet to fill the world back up, but she won't let herself call out, *Hello?* At the doorway her resolve falters, on a hinge, but she pushes forward to the hall light switch, and stands in the cone of light that wedges into his small bedroom.

The sheets are a swirl on the mattress only because neither of them made his bed. Nothing is crouching at the headboard against the wall. The wad of Oli's unicorn comforter isn't shaped like something hiding from her. There's no Agatha to stare glass-eyed across the room at her.

But Oli's window is open. She can't say for sure if it was closed earlier.

She sees only herself inside the mirror that hangs on his open closet door. Her eyes are black in the faint light reaching her reflection. She flips the light back off and watches her ghost for a moment. There's a part of her that savors the rough hum of adrenaline in her blood, the trip of her heart.

It's that same part of her, maybe, young Jorie, that imagines someone standing beside the mirror, inside the mouth of the closet doorway. A pale blurred face stretched and making the shapes of frantic words, round eyes, the suggestions of clothes and arms in the shadows. It's pleading with her. She starts whispering, "Bloody Mary," and it's gone by the second incantation. The glimpse was as insubstantial as a projected spirit in an old silent film, like Dreyer's *Vampyr*, the kind of effect that looks primitive but is all the more entrancing for its low-res aesthetics.

She closes Oli's window, then the adrenaline forces her into the kitchen, where she weighs making coffee and editing another chapter against reading until she fades back toward sleep. Instead she turns the TV on in the living room and pushes the *Funeral Watching* tape back into the VCR.

When the creatures have come out of the trees, and static eats the scene, she leaves it running and fetches her laptop. She finds *Proof of Demons* on Wikipedia and reads the bare-bones plot summary, with all the nuance stripped away, not to refresh her memory but to refresh a previous self that would have wanted this tape in the mail. Before the hyperlinks *Controversy* and *Kim death and trial* were needed down the list from *Plot*.

The movie plays fast-forwarded in Jorie's head as she reads, nearly all the strange visuals intact after a decade of avoidance, its particular atmosphere still within the reach of her mind. From the opening shot of the naked people crawling across a ceiling like spiders, to the end, the hole opening above the floor of the crypt, the eye rolling within the hole to find the audience, it's still with her.

She remembers late-night arguments about the four Transfigurations, and she can almost smell the cigarette smoke that clouded living rooms and diner parking lots. The three of them agreed that the film resisted a complete understanding, but that the mathematical arrangement of the weird six-minute shots formed a would-be occult ritual. The repeated incantation of "I belong" and "You belong," the demon summoned by a cult, the door to hell, the huge eye opening in that doorway—the structure was clearly there to be mapped out. Of course they mapped it out.

But unlike the ripples they saw spreading across internet forums, she and her friends never believed it was more than a movie during all those conversations leading up to the last film haunt. They felt only the high of fandom.

Jorie misses Beth and Colin with a fierce cresting ache. She remembers it all. Throwing the DVD in the trash was never more than a gesture.

She starts clicking other links and teetering on the edge of real research. At some point, the silent VHS snow is interrupted by a color shift in the light falling across her legs, and she looks up from the laptop to see a room full of people, a police officer facing the camera in the background. A voice says, "But what are we doing about these murders?" and a new scene begins.

# INTERLUDE

[Excerpt from "Proof of Demons," *Wikipedia*]

## Contents

Plot
Cast
    Use of amateurs
    Roger Eilertsen
Release
Reception
Controversy
    Kim death and trial
    Occult hysteria
Popular culture
    The Pine Arch Creature
    Reddit mythology
    October Film Haunt claims
    Hélène Enriquez rumors
References
External links

## Plot [edit]

Márcia and Jackson Smith attend an elementary school play in Whisper, North Carolina. Their daughter, Alma, is part of a production. Two nude figures of advanced age crawl slowly across the theater ceiling behind the unknowing crowd. On stage, the students act out a story involving a fawn stealing children.

The man and woman from the ceiling approach the Smiths afterward. The same night, Alma wakes to find the old couple standing at the end of her bed. A figure is behind them in the dark, much taller and only faintly visible.

The next morning, the Smiths report Alma's disappearance. Outside the police station, they are approached by a different elderly man and woman, residents of a local retirement home, who tell them the man who took their daughter is attending the graveside service across the street. Jackson runs to Pinewood Cemetery but sees no one fitting the description the man and woman provided him. After a six-minute static shot,[1] a giant but indistinct figure (known by fans as the Pine Arch Creature) emerges from between two pines that form an arch and carries a young boy back into the trees. Jackson is gone when the POV cuts to where he was watching.

Ashley Brown and David Blake, whose son also performed in the play, are asleep that night. The camera moves to the closet, where a voice says from inside, "I belong with you," before someone comes out and kills them with a butcher knife. The figure, draped in a pale blue bedsheet that's torn by wooden horns or points on its head, kneels and watches their bodies for six minutes. A voice-over says, "You belong," as a child begins screaming from another room. Fans refer to these six minutes as the First Transfiguration.[2]

Jackson spends the next day visiting local nursing homes, looking for the old couple from the police station. A Whisper Pines resident shows him a vertical line the couple allegedly drew in blood on her wall, representing the closed door of hell and its unnamed keeper. In a confessional booth in the local Catholic church, Jackson speaks of Alma and references demons. The hidden priest tells him demons have nothing to do with Christianity. A hole appears in the air next to Jackson, with a large eye pressed against it. Just as he notices it, someone in a blue sheet enters and stabs Jackson in the side.

Later, a blue-sheeted figure appears with a knife and attacks Márcia, but she escapes and drives away. Thinking she sees Alma running down a gravel road to Murmur Lake, she follows to the beach. Unable to find her, Márcia, in a trance state, watches blue bedsheets floating on the water for six minutes. An unidentifiable child's voice says, "I belong with you," followed by a much deeper voice saying, "You belong." This is known as the Second Transfiguration. A small opening appears in the air above the lake.[3] The same eye is peering out of it. Márcia flees, shouting for her daughter.

A town hall meeting is held to discuss the escalating child abductions and the killings. The lights go out, and the sound warps for six minutes—the Third Transfiguration—with the only clear words being a high voice saying, "I belong with you" near the beginning and a deep distorted "You belong" at the end. A large humanoid shape appears in the foreground, and screaming can be heard.

Jackson is arrested after being seen in the church near a murder weapon and sheet. Released due to a lack of evidence, he argues with Márcia about the possible supernatural element of their daughter's disappearance. Márcia goes out searching and sees a small girl run into a neighbor's house. Márcia enters, calling for Alma, and finds a sheeted figure and two more victims in a blood-spattered room. The figure leaves Márcia alive after stopping to stare closely into her face and leaving behind a crudely drawn map of a cemetery, two trees with touching limbs, and a line leading to a box near a blue circle.

Márcia and Jackson walk through the "pine arch" in Pinewood Cemetery and follow the map to a crypt in the woods near Murmur Lake. Descending underground, they encounter eleven people wearing blue sheets, a coven of witches attempting to open a hole into hell. As the sheets are removed, revealing nude figures wearing wooden crowns, Márcia and Jackson recognize the four elderly people they spoke to previously. Márcia asks what they plan to bring out of hell. One of them laughs and says that "hell" is just a word, and they plan to enter, not bring something out. It is another green world,[4] where Alma and the other children are "transfiguring."

The coven leader reveals that Márcia has been chosen and guided here because she is a powerful mother. Jackson is covered with all the sheets and stands for six minutes in the Final Transfiguration. He says, "I belong with you." No one moves for an uncomfortably long time, then the coven members chant, "You belong," and stab Jackson repeatedly with knives. Half-glimpsed in the throng is a much larger figure moving toward and seemingly onto Jackson. As a wooden crown is placed on Márcia's head, a hole opens in the air, in which a large eye rolls toward the camera. The perspective shifts to a close-up of Márcia, who stares at whatever is revealed until her face softens into relief, joy, then perhaps the beginning of horror.

# CHAPTER TWO

## Jorie

*Beth. I know it's been a while but someone is messing with me. Pretty sure it has to do with OFH. I almost called but you not answering would just add to this feeling of*

▶▶ Two hours, give or take, switching back and forth from the memoir edits, restless, and this is all Jorie has managed to say to her old friend. Wired and edgy after too much coffee, she keeps passing by Oli's room to glance into the closet, into the mirror. She keeps getting creeped out by the smooth surface of the comforter, until she remembers again that she made the bed this morning.

The house still feels like she's not alone in it. She calls her father, who's been in a care facility outside Atlanta since the osteoporosis took him off his feet, and the brightness in his voice means there is a brightness to Jorie's morning. They talk about her mom, Anne, sharing old stories and wondering how they've made it through fourteen years without her.

His energy starts to flag, and she promises again to bring Oli down to see him at Christmas. When she hangs up, there is the usual guilt that she moved up here, so far from him, but it melts away, and there is only the grim taste the videotape has left in her mouth.

Last night there was an undercurrent of enjoyment to the feeling, a sentimental thrill. The thread of it is still there, but it's weaker now. She's driving herself to distraction over this tape and a phantom thump on the wall. It's a long way from a haunted house she has to talk herself into staying in.

She checks her email again to verify that Eric hasn't responded to her child support request, worried she might let it slide and ashamed that she might not ever take him to court over it. There's nothing. She closes the laptop and goes outside, pulling her puffy blue jacket on.

The clouds of her breath are picked apart on the air. The birches stand sixty feet away, like bones in the great green flesh of the pines and firs around them. Already their crowns are starting to blot her landscape with mustard stains, joining the scattered red chorus of maples, until the evergreens seem like intruders out of time. After leaving Eric last year, new to Vermont and used to the modest fall foliage south of the Appalachians, she would stand out here and take it all in, amazed she owned this land and the modest brown Cape Cod sitting on it. She lived in a postcard.

Now she is watching for faces in the trees.

There were three more scenes on the videotape, each the traditional six minutes, and each was separated by—she should have guessed it from the start—a twelve-minute wash of static, the same structure surrounding the Transfigurations from *Proof of Demons*. They were all variations on the cemetery scene, deviating from the original plot in disturbing ways. Only the story was missing.

The tape's second scene started in the town hall, with someone asking about the murders. But then the camera dissolved into the same long take from the first scene, birches and pines crowding the top right of the frame, the graveside service in the opposite corner.

But not the same—the characters had changed. This time, the funeral attendees were draped in the bedsheets made famous by *Proof of Demons*. The sheets were a muddy shade of green, not the soft blue from Enriquez's film. They seemed to wear the movie's familiar crowns under the sheets, though, elongating their heads, the wooden tines tearing through the fabric.

Somehow, seeing the costumes in this calm, mournful frame was worse. Creepier, more loathsome. The story's slasher element had been brought in a couple of scenes too early, diluting the shock of the original's closet scene, which felt like horror genre sacrilege.

Not all of them wore the sheets. A pale man in a dark gray suit near the back, and an older woman in a black dress sat on the left edge of the frame. She looked a little like Mrs. Compton, who lives a three-minute walk through Jorie's northern wedge of trees. A nice woman. A bit young for a retiree, and even newer in Hinesburg than Jorie.

Mrs. Compton went about retirement backward—sold the consignment shop she owned for twenty years on the Gulf Coast and moved back home to this almost-Canada corner of Vermont. She missed the cold, she told Jorie once, and had grown weary of the sun and humidity.

She's watched Oliver several times when Sam couldn't, and there's a remoteness to her, but it's rounder and sweeter than the woman at the funeral. The face on the tape looked dead, somehow, as though she had climbed out of the casket to find out what had disturbed her burial.

Thirty more awful seconds crawled by in the scene, trembling between tension and parody. The dozen sheeted figures sat in their chairs, still as wax figures in a slasher movie museum, the crowns horrible and corrupt just like she remembered from *Proof of Demons*. But Jorie sensed that each was a moment away from raising a butcher knife from their lap.

The woman who resembled Mrs. Compton shifted her face and looked nothing like her now, it was an older woman, with sharper angles to her profile. The priest or minister continued droning his almost discernible eulogy. Finally, the towering things from the first scene—the two Pine Arch creatures, plural—came out of the birches like smudges on the landscape. Cut to static.

Twelve fast-forwarded minutes later, the same funeral, and the greenish sheets were gone. Instead, the fourteen people in the corner of the frame turned their heads slowly, over the course of ninety seconds, toward the camera.

Jorie had never seen anyone turn to look at something with such slowness, who would even imagine it as a concept, but it was nauseating. It was against nature, somehow. It spoke of Hélène Enriquez's love of unsettling anticipation, the opposite of a jump scare. When their eyes reached hers at last, there was so much weight in the connection, enough to crawl through the lens and onto the spool of the tape.

The small crowd stared out of the screen at her, their faces blank but stern. The vacant disdain seemed to ask how she could dare peek in at such a somber rite as a funeral. Four minutes of eyes, the fourth wall crumbling with mute horror.

When the creatures came out of the trees, they seemed more like flickering background actors that had nothing to do with the tension. The tone of the scene had been upended by those dreadful staring faces. Jorie barely registered the Pine Arch creatures until they abruptly changed course and lumbered toward the camera instead of the funeral attendees.

Frustratingly, thankfully, the tape warped before they came into sharper focus. She had time to see cavities flexing open from what passed for their heads to their torsos. They looked like the corpses of old giants pulled out of a fire. Like ink drawings a dirty eraser had tried to rub out.

Then static ate into the images until the final clip.

It was almost identical to the first, but instead of coming out of the birches and moving across the grass, their unreadable shapes like cigarette burns, the creatures beckoned from their shadows. Long blurred arms with joints in the wrong places drooped out and curled back. Jorie paused the frame and counted at least six of the arms.

Somehow the boy from the first scene sensed them and turned and walked toward the trees, reaching out as though to be picked up as he passed out of view. The boy's mother stood and began to shriek. The eulogist stopped speaking. The veils of reality and traditional narrative held this time, and the shouts were cut off by the scene ending, like some kind of mercy.

A final touch came crawling out of the static just before the tape ran out and Jorie ejected it. "You killed her," something whispered, pitched low and high at the same time, at least two voices layered over each other.

"Hannah?" Jorie said, then clamped her hand over her mouth, clawing the name back inside.

But she's ready to be done thinking about the tape. It's drawing her back to that night with Colin and Beth. The cemetery, the film haunt. The creeping sense that someone out there is punishing her for Hannah's death—elaborately, in the way that would hurt most.

Maybe she would succumb to the old addiction with a different horror movie, but not this one. Not this baggage. She wants to push it off on Beth, who always had a bit more wisdom. Jorie was the face of the October Film Haunt, but it was also Jorie who wrote the blog post that caused everything to fall apart.

Beth would have never written that. She shouldn't have to talk to Jorie about *Proof of Demons*, not after the night in North Carolina. After what Jorie did a week later. Beth has the right to not even read whatever email Jorie finally comes up with.

Under these thoughts, climbing to the surface—*Was what's on the tape filmed in Vermont?* There are the birches. The right camera angle would allow someone to re-create the composition of the *Proof of Demons* scene in a lot of cemeteries.

And the style and the ability suggest it's Hélène Enriquez. The director, somewhere close by. This is what she can't get around. This is why she's been wandering the house, pretending there are ghosts. Ghosts are less messy.

She's grateful to have had a client with some talent and a story worth telling. This deeply sad memoir, beautiful in places. The author, a woman named Lucy Dendrich who came into Lantman's one morning while Jorie was working, is brave for pouring all her trauma onto paper. Lucy has earned the empowerment in the narrative, and so will the readers she finds.

At Lucky Coffee in Hinesburg, she gets into a long groove, finishes the last chapters and all her notes. Over eight thousand words of mostly assured suggestions, hundreds of comments. A weight lifts off her shoulders, replaced by a faint sense of loss.

Jorie thinks she's helped Lucy broaden some brushstrokes here, press a finer point there, move paragraphs and strike blocks of lines that might slow the reader down. Jorie even recommended cutting a chapter out and repurposing bits of it later on.

She's never been inside the gilded houses of Manhattan, but something in her knows how to make a big picture more intimate. The bits of memoir that started to creep into the found-footage book she never finished writing, the October Film Haunt blog, even the screenplay she sold—something in Jorie's fingers was able to find the emotional chords of an audience. Everything she ever wrote, really. Her ability to see all the moving parts, but more than this, she saw her way into the hearts of things.

Eventually, when the past scabbed over, she realized she was able to give this sight to the words of others. At bargain-basement rates for a while, yes, but each manuscript is a step.

The work drains her, too. Lucy's grandfather was a monster, a man-shape creeping into a little girl's bedroom at night. Using his fists when the sun was out. Some of the abuse Lucy relives in these pages, it's been dragging Eric through Jorie's mind for the past six weeks. His hands clenching. The orbital bones he broke around her eye, the warning bass of his voice, her skull fracture, the sudden flight up here early last year when the house was finally hers.

At first she wouldn't tell Eric where they were, but still, too many of the old horror films slipped into her thoughts after she and Oli left. One quiet evening while they were watching TV, the second week in Vermont, a dish fell out of the drying rack and shattered on the kitchen floor. Jorie couldn't stop shaking for half an hour. Oli cried because he didn't know how to help, and because everything made him cry in that first month. A few days later, she was sure she saw someone peering through the glass in the back door.

But the ugliness of Eric ended up mundane. Gaslighting turned into nasty voicemails turned into a quick divorce. A single trip to Atlanta to sign her name a dozen times in real ink. Hospital records and photographs from the night he hit her were enough to justify moving half a dozen states away and keeping Oli this far away from his dad. She only saw Eric with her lawyer—and all those billable hours—present, and his calm only seemed hurt, not scheming or hiding something.

Distance and time were apparently enough. Eric seemed made to be an absentee father.

It's only been a challenge to keep Eric's child support payments current, though soon—very soon, if Oli has his way—she's going to have to deal with visitation. For now, even the weekly phone calls with his son seem too much for Eric to handle.

When Sam brings it up, Jorie reminds her that he only really hurt her once. And there was never anything close to violence with Oli. She's not making excuses, she's saying that Eric is not that scary in the end.

The book is done now, though. She can wish Lucy the best and be a devoted mom for a week or two, here in their quiet corner of the world. Oli can get some clothes for the new school year that's a month old already.

She pulls her backpack over to dig out the Advil for her screen-induced headache, and there it is again, the yellow envelope with the VHS tape inside.

She didn't want to leave it at home, near where her son sleeps, near that ghost she didn't see in his closet, and her thoughts turn to movies again. In a movie, she would toss the tape in the garbage out on the sidewalk and feel an apprehensive, post-exorcism sort of reprieve. But the itch is still there, the mystery to dig into—and there's the fact that someone would have to put some real effort into finding her. If a stalker situation escalates, the tape could be Exhibit A in a courtroom.

Something else is in the envelope, a lump she can just feel under her fingers. She slides the cassette out onto the table, and a small thumb drive comes with it. It has a rough texture, she has to tilt it in the light to read the words PINE ARCH RESEARCH scratched into the plastic casing.

"This is just wonderful," she whispers, her voice toneless and unbelieving. She puts her face in her hands for a moment, the café noises swelling and receding around her. A picture forms in her mind, of someone sealing this envelope—sharp bones, long greasy hair, a film villain face—and dropping it into a mailbox on a North Carolina street corner. The face smiles around its black eyes.

Jorie slots the thumb drive into the laptop's USB port. Relief and disappointment flood out of her in a sigh when she sees the filenames: funeral_watching1 through funeral_watching4. She opens each and clicks near the beginning and near the end to make sure they all match what she's already seen on the tape. The only difference is the lack of nostalgic VHS flaws—no odd color grade or image degradation. She was right that the clips had been tweaked to fit the medium.

The "You killed her" waits at the very end of the fourth clip, but she doesn't look for it. Even in the constant noise of a coffee shop, hearing it might push her over some edge. She transfers the files into a new folder named PRANK on her desktop. There's now both more and less of a reason to contact Beth. How insensitive is she willing to be?

Instead of email, she opens her notes app and tries to wrap her mind around the differences between the original film and whatever these new scenes are.

*Original—Pine Arch Creature*

*New—multiple Pine Arch creatures*

*Original—pines, North Carolina*

*New—also birches, Vermont?*

*Original—blue sheets*

*New—green sheets*

*Original—6-minute Transfigurations*

*New—2 extra minutes (only first scene)*

*Original—funeral was just a funeral*

*New—funeral was participant in creepiness*

What else? The sheets in the second scene, green now for some reason, remind her of Márcia Smith staring at their floating blue counterparts halfway through *Proof of Demons*. Jorie used to want to know Márcia's thoughts when her daughter, or just a ghost or revenant-like projection, lures her to the lake and the supernatural begins to really open up around her.

She always felt Márcia in her bones, she ached when Márcia ached, but she was that way with so many protagonists, final girls, half the victims in those movies. So much of Jorie's empathy was felt on theater screens or laptops that ran hot enough to nearly burn her crossed legs. It powered her writing, it helped keep the October Film Haunt strong and vital in the horror community. It was where her heart lived.

Some fans argued that an entity enters Márcia Smith in this scene. The Pine Arch Creature or something else. That Enriquez needed to write a possession into the film to subtly bolster the *Proof* in the title. There were even those who claimed the title was literal, that this was an actual demon. Jorie never read the scene that way, but she remembers when she had the chance to commune with the idea of Márcia, standing on the shore of the very lake from the movie, but couldn't get close to an answer.

For a few seconds, Jorie tries to read Márcia's mind again, on the other side of a decade. But she doesn't want to know what it was like for her, she doesn't want to be her, there's nothing of that left. She wants to keep horror and tragedy at arm's length.

\* \* \*

> Beth. I know it's been a while but someone is messing with me. Pretty sure it has to do with OFH. Maybe they also mailed you a VHS tape labeled Funeral Watching with four versions of the Pine Arch Creature scene in THAT movie. All different, like a sequel . . . or a reboot. But in a way, the biggest difference is I think they were shot up here in Vermont, near me. I don't know what that means, or if I should be worried, or who's still angry with us. (If people are still holding grudges, I hope they're all for me.)
>
> I hope you're doing well. I google you from time to time, and I know you've edited some real actual movies. I'm endlessly proud. Do you have kids? I got pregnant not long after I last saw you. Oli (short for Oliver) turned 8 last month. He's smart and kind and perceptive, such a truly great kid—MY WHOLE WORLD BASICALLY—but he's been struggling with our move up here. Missing his dad, blaming me, etc. But he still doesn't know his dad punched his mom a few times (though he never touched Oli, thank God). I'm sorry if you don't want to know these things. I hope you can find it in your heart to at least be ambivalent about my continued existence.
>
> There was a USB drive with the same scenes, so if you (fingers crossed) didn't get a tape but want to know about this probably harmless but still kind of troubling thing, get the files out of [my Dropbox](). You know better than anyone to keep them to yourself. I'm feeling nervous. I'm thinking about Hannah a lot again. I could use your advice. About the tape. I don't really deserve advice about Hannah.
>
> I'm still so sorry.

Her finger rests on the trackpad a full minute before she clicks send.

She and Beth were seventeen when they met. They were the type of friends who shrink the contours of each other's lives because there's no need to meet other people and experiment with different social groups. They fit. Their personalities and dreams and passions had come out of the same box.

Colin would come along and make them even better, especially for Beth, but before, it was just the two of them, Jorie and Beth scouring the southern states for the perfect horror. Jorie has missed her far more than she's missed the genre.

A tray of dirty dishes—spoons, mugs, a carafe of milk—clatters to the floor, the sound of breaking crockery and metal ringing up to the high ceiling's exposed pipes. Jorie jumps and turns in her chair. Beyond the crouching barista picking up the mess, sunlight washes across the huge glass window. Her brain tries to put a looming shape in the light.

# CHAPTER THREE

## Coleman

▶▶ He pictures a funeral home—maybe Corddry & Son, down the street—with the lights turned out, what is left of him a lump of shadow in a casket. The director or an assistant has forgotten to close the lid on him for the night, to get his body used to the darkness of the earth. He looks like he is made of a heavy, dense wax. Gravity pulls at him, slow enough that he will be put in the hole in the churchyard before he loses the shape he carried for fifty-eight years.

His blood will have been sucked out through a murmuring tube and replaced with preservatives. Someone will have packed his mouth and sealed his lips shut. He read yesterday that even the fingers are glued together. Someone will have punctured every organ, deflated them, emptied out his stomach. His back will be a mess, pooled black with all the fluids they weren't able to suction out of him, swollen against the casket's velvet lining. His eyeballs will have been capped, tape beneath the lids so they don't creep open during the viewing. He is glad his grandchildren won't be allowed to come.

Coleman blinks, opens his mouth wide, splays his fingers until the skin between them hurts. He tries to want to be cremated instead.

It has only been two weeks, but he has started visiting funerals. He reads the local obituaries. He pretends he needs to practice being laid to rest, as though it will be imperative for him to lie perfectly still and stiff while the people in his life stare down at him, desperately glad lung cancer didn't eat them, and feeling a flush of shame at the thought. *Never smoked a day in his life,* he can almost hear them say. *What a terrible thing, isn't it?*

*What are you doing?* he scolds himself. *You are still alive!*

*Go hug your wife. Go call Evie, ask to see the kids. Visit your mother at the home, tell her what's coming.*

*Or walk into those trees. Find a trail, smell the pines, feel the sunshine coming through the branches.*

He looks out past the cluster of people in ties and dark dresses to the wedge of trees, like an arrowhead angling back toward the bow of the state park and the pond everyone calls Lake Julian. Two of the trees on the far edge of the lawn form a sort of archway with their limbs, almost a fairy-tale door, if he squints.

He can't go home. He finds himself wanting Gloria to drift away from him, there are small moments when he wishes she never loved him. But she is always reattaching to him, forbidding him to die. He hasn't told anyone else about the diagnosis, after the cough and the back pain passed beyond ignorance, the way weight started siphoning off his body these past six months.

He is terrified of his daughter because she won't be able to handle this. Evie isn't able to detach or retract. It's easier for him to stand here, somehow, and imagine his only child crumbling with sorrow when it's too late. When he's escaped the look in her eyes and the soft hugs to avoid breaking him. When she can't plead anymore for the poison he would have to put into his body.

Evie isn't the type to see the other cancer in her father, the decision growing in his mind.

For a moment the woman nearest the grave, behind the black veil, is Gloria, she's carved herself into a pillar of strength. She'll feel she has to be strong for Evie and, back at the house, Charlotte and Liam. He imagines a sudden stain of clouds over the flat lawn—it is always raining in this picture of his own funeral—and Gloria has gone under the steep black curve of an umbrella. Evie is out in the open air of her grief, hair soaked dark, her partner's arm a tourniquet around her.

A hum drifts toward him and he watches the maroon casket grind its way down into the grave. Eugene Beckman, seventy-nine, father, grandfather, begins to rot inside his box. Coleman doesn't know what he'll do now, this is the only funeral in town today, and he is too tired already to drive over to Asheville.

A young family drifts away from the mourners, the father tall and vibrating with health, the mother's head down to speak to their little girl, their small feet disappearing in the soft grass. The girl is around Liam's age, one of Evie's best ages, seven or so, her long black hair in a French braid.

The three of them ache with life. Coleman decides to follow them. He wants to be close to their vigor and to move in the same direction they're moving, toward all those open years.

The sun is hot on his head, the bald spot like a stove eye, his neck is sweating behind the knot of his tie. He walks between graves, cutting a diagonal toward the family, who are crossing the street in their gray and white clothes and turning east on the sidewalk along the shops of Meridian Street. They blend with the Saturday morning families who haven't been brushed with death this week. Their body language loosens.

He gets closer to them, hears the daughter suggest ice cream. They must not have known Eugene Beckman well.

He's walking, he tells himself, he's still alive. He's managing the pain. During the first appointment with the oncologist, they gazed at the night sky of his backlit lungs in the CT scans. The constellations of tumors. Hungry stars glimmering through him. He made a joke about stage 5 cancer as an option, explaining that he meant suicide. It's just that there are chemo and radiation or there are sleeping pills, he told the doctor. Whatever leaves the smallest mess behind. The joke got him a palliative counseling recommendation.

It wasn't quite a joke, though. Coleman just needs to come to a decision and find a way to do it that leaves Gloria with some insurance money.

Part of him wants to speed up, reach out and touch the young father, feel the easy clockwork under his skin. He wants to tell him he could be listening to an oncologist's death words before he knows it. But Coleman realizes he's being followed, too, there's the prickle of eyes behind him, like insects caught in the fine hairs on the back of his neck. He turns and sees a grinning man with black holes for eyes, but—maybe Coleman's imagination is metastasizing along with the tumors that have already spread out beyond his lungs—it's only a man with dark sunglasses laughing into a phone.

When he turns back, the young family has stopped to look in the ice cream shop's window. Coleman nearly knocks the girl over, and as he stumbles around them with a muttered apology, the mother says, "Not everything is so nice. When I was your age, witches would get you if you couldn't sleep. There was supposed to be a coven back in the woods behind the cemetery."

The father is the demure one. "Honey, let's not," he says. "She's seven."

"I'm eight soon!" the girl almost shouts. "What's a coven?"

The mother laughs, and Coleman slows down just enough to hear her answer. "They practiced witchcraft underground, where the colonial cemetery used to be. There was a crypt and they would . . ."

They are pulled out of earshot, their voices fading into the gentle crowd. The crypt tugs at him for another moment, unresolved. He thinks he hears the girl raise her voice and say, "I belong with you." Will she ask what witchcraft is?

But he lets them go. He faces forward and sees a man going into a shop holding a long knife smeared with sunlight. The glare is so warm, it's like the blade is dripping butter. The man is not much younger than Coleman, short with pale hair down to his faded blue polo collar, and the knife is angled out from his waist, where his belly hangs over his belt. It's heavy and made for cutting through meat. A blue swath of fabric is folded over the man's other arm. A sign over the doorway, above his head, reads VIDEO SPOT.

Coleman turns to check on the family, hoping they'll get to safety, but they've gone into the ice cream shop. He imagines the knife going into his own chest, the man in the blue polo shirt sweating, wheezing with ugly excitement as he pushes it in. The knife would pierce one of Coleman's lungs. Would the cancer cells stream out like spores, dying in the air without him?

If he's murdered, his body will be given to a forensic medical examiner at the city morgue, which is probably in Asheville because Arden is so small. They'll have to cut him up more thoroughly, take all the ropes and heavy bags out of him for tests. He will be a gaping cavity. They'll snip the strings that tie his organs together. A saw will whine through his skull to expose his brain and the last of its running, whirling thoughts of mortality.

He checks his pockets. He's been forgetting to bring his phone with him, likely because it's full of the world he's leaving behind, the beauty and violence and grim unendingness.

"Go back toward the trees," he mutters to himself, "smell the pines, pretend you're looking for the crypt that lady talked about." He half-remembers an old French poet's line about the living pillars in nature's temple. It was on a picture of a forest Gloria printed out and taped beside the desktop computer in the home office.

But he's at Video Spot now, and only silence is seeping out of it. The cemetery is reflected in the storefront window and the door's nine small panes. He sees his face parceled out into four of the squares, his trim hair that has lost so much of the orange he loathed as a child. He sees his hand reaching out to the scratched brass doorknob.

A matching brass bell jangles as he steps inside. The place looks careworn, from another era, and dim except for the early sun straining in after him. He turns the dead bolt in case the man with the knife flees the store in the same moment the girl and her parents walk by with their ice creams. He'll warn someone, call the police, do something other than watch funerals.

But the store is empty. Rows of DVD and Blu-ray cases line three of the walls and the freestanding shelves set at angles throughout the interior. Handmade signs divide the shop into categories like ACTION and PERIOD PIECES. A gray disc lies on the floor in the section marked HORROR in bloody capital letters, the sun stretching far enough to gleam a thin rainbow off the edge of it.

The man must have slipped through a door in the back, like a man with a knife would do in one of these films. Or he's in the restroom, working up his courage. Coleman isn't sure, he's never cared much for scary movies. He prefers courtroom dramas and cozy mysteries, where cool, fierce minds slot all the puzzle pieces together.

On his way to the register to use the phone or call out for an employee, he's not sure yet, he stops and picks up the DVD from the floor. The title is printed across the gray in a white, artfully faded font, and it takes him a moment to make it out as *PROOF OF DEMONS*. In smaller but bolder print are the words *An Hélène Enriquez Film*. At least it's in the right section, probably, but when he scans the rows in front of him, he sees empty spaces but no matching box.

He turns and the guy with the knife is standing beside him, suddenly there. Coleman's senses gave him no clues. The man is still holding the blue bedsheet or soft curtain, and up close he's younger than Coleman had thought, not much past thirty.

"That's a special one," the man says, looking down at the DVD. His lips are full and pink. The blond hair seems to float in humid wisps around his forehead, veiling the green eyes. His breath is warm and sour. "You can actually see into hell when you watch it."

"What do you mean?" Coleman says, the world slowing down, going syrupy around him.

"Literally see," the man says. "Sorry, I'm improvising right now. We're meeting each other between drafts. I was in town to put something in the mail and stuck around to watch you. This is a casting call."

The knife slides into Coleman's left side. The metal is cold, and there's a distant fire that can't reach the cold. The blade has gone in low, Coleman thinks it's scraping the top of his belt—what's there, the spleen, a kidney? Nowhere near his diseased lungs.

He collapses to the floor. His lungs seem to be filling with water. His breaths sound to him like two hands slowly tearing sheets of paper. From this new vantage, he sees someone else, who must have been standing behind the door when he came inside. A phone is blocking this second person's face, its black lenses watching Coleman from across the room.

Filming him, maybe.

Then the second person is gone as the man with the knife moves into Coleman's field of vision, black boots with black eyes, shaking out the blue sheet as though making a bed. There is even the soft crack of thunder as the fabric snaps in the air. He bends at the waist and settles the sheet over Coleman.

"Watch *Proof of Demons*," a voice says, and Coleman feels a tug in the seat of his pants, an object jammed into a back pocket. "See into hell."

"Help." Coleman thinks he groans this, low and wet instead of his intended shout. He closes his eyes. The bell rattles at the front of the shop, and he hopes the ice cream family went the other way, into the woods to look for the devil.

# CHAPTER FOUR

## Jorie

▶▶ A memory comes after she sends the email to Beth, of not knowing she was pregnant at first because she thought the morning sickness was just guilt residue. So many nights the year before Oli, she would wake at three or four and hunch over the toilet. She'd have to pace the apartment before her body would let her sleep again.

The trial had been over for months. Two of Hannah's friends were already halfway through their prison sentences for daring her into the grave in the woods. Hannah was still dead, and here was fidgeting, pacing Jorie Stroud, still not quite at rock bottom.

For her, Hannah Kim was a vengeful spirit made of lines Jorie had drawn herself, blurs in photographs, dark smudges of shame that haunted her periphery like the auras of migraines. Hannah was coming for her. Hannah was a ruined thing crawling out of a well. Hannah was the swirl of black hair in the water draining from the bathtub. Hannah was a proboscis sucking all the horror movies out of Jorie, she was a wave that crested on the third night of 2015, when Jorie's throat narrowed to a straw and the breaths wouldn't come and Eric called an ambulance.

The doctors told her about the pregnancy, there in the eleventh week. She didn't want to be a mom, but it was the greatest excuse she could have asked for. Eric wanted the excuse, too. She started moving on during those twenty days in the hospital, as they made sure Jorie wasn't going to lose the baby. Therapy sessions, survivor's guilt, fluids and IVs full of sleep. Exhaustion, slowly waking up and breathing. Something new and enormous needed her to think about it all the time and worry about herself in the future tense.

She and Oli pushed each other into life.

Eric insisted they get married, and there wasn't enough of a reason to say no.

They had been together only a year, but he would doze beside her hospital bed. He saw the worst of her, and he didn't leave. He was good for her, he was another excuse, until the first time he left a mark on her and she started making different kinds of excuses. They seemed to always start with, *Well, I deserve this, right?* She had fallen from grace, and Eric was a cushion between her and the ground.

Jorie wipes her eyes and pulls up a list of local cemeteries, but of course there are so many, people have been dying every day for centuries, even in rural postcards. She can't shake the thought of the scenes on the tape being filmed up here. Her laptop tells her the paper birch is common throughout the northeastern states, across the brow of the country into Oregon. Canada, too.

The tape in her mailbox, the clips on the thumb drive, they could have been shot anywhere colder than the South. Jorie had nothing to do with the production of *Proof of Demons*. She never had a clue who Hélène Enriquez was. This is just a cruel joke. A years-delayed prank. There's nothing else to it.

She gathers her things to leave the café. As she's standing and turning toward the door, a figure pulls away from the window outside. It was shaped like someone looking in at her, but it's gone now, bright leaves swirling down the sidewalk after it. One of them sticks to the glass, still wet from last night's rain.

Just someone walking by, glancing in, and Jorie picked the exact two moments that would make her think the person was pressed against the glass, peering through the shade of their hands directly at her, the morning sun a crown.

She steps outside but there's nothing, just a mother halfway through packing her three young kids into a minivan. But Jorie feels herself being watched. From a car in one of the slanted spaces, from the bank across the street. From somewhere close. A stooped old man walks toward her, his arms hanging at his sides. He looks like he's mourning someone as another breeze of dead leaves parts around him.

Jorie sees herself reflected in the window, imagines all nine of her gray hairs are glinting in the sun as the round-faced man from Oli's closet rises over her shoulder. But it's just her, the same messy boy haircut she's had for fifteen years, everything else in her face nearly unrecognizable to her sometimes.

"How's my little Oliver?" someone says, and Jorie sees a real face move into the reflection. She almost screams but is able to turn it into a laugh as she turns around.

"Mrs. Compton!" Jorie says, nearly gasps. "I was just thinking about you this morning."

The woman watches her with clear amber eyes. One corner of her thin mouth smiles. Jorie doesn't know how old her neighbor is, there are aspects of her that say sixties, but her skin doesn't have those sorts of creases and lines. She could still be just on the downside of fifty. Tall and birdlike, but a softened, plump bird, a dove or pigeon. The hair that falls onto her shoulders is a dull gray.

"Why would you be thinking of me?" Mrs. Compton says, her thick eyebrows raising. Something close to a grimace twists her mouth. Her hands fold into each other at the waist of her linen blouse, peeking out from dark blue cardigan sleeves. But there, all at once, is the bloom in her cheeks, the storybook old-lady roses Jorie has seen before. A grandmother promising sweets. It's cozy on this winter-hinted morning.

"No, just something I saw in a movie," Jorie tells her. "Someone reminded me of you."

"Well, too bad for that someone!" Her laugh is as rosy as her cheeks. "My life is full of shadows. I've lamented not having Oliver around the empty house. You let me know if you need someone to watch him."

Jorie smiles at the strange poetic turn. Mrs. Compton likes to use words like *lamented*, and she speaks with the trace of an accent, Italian or German, that has been washed away by time, or by the salty ocean air she breathed for so long.

"He would like that," Jorie says. "My cousin Sam's had some free time, and he loves her kids, or I would've brought him over to see you more." An inexplicable relief wells in Jorie, unpinning the stress of last night, and she steps forward and hugs the woman. She has to raise onto tiptoes to do it. She feels tears brimming in her eyes. Vermont has been lonely.

"Thank you," Jorie says. "Thanks for making us feel welcome."

"Anytime. He's a sweet thing." Mrs. Compton pulls back and hugs herself in a lifting breeze, her hands—as young-old as the rest of her—slipping back into their sleeves. She pats Jorie's arm, the knowing look of a mother, and walks off. When she reaches the corner of Silver Street, she stops and peers back over her shoulder.

Jorie watches for a moment, waiting for a final wave that doesn't come, a pause that grows uncomfortable. Mrs. Compton looks much older from a distance, and Jorie wonders if the expression on her face is pity. They're too far apart to tell. Finally, Jorie tilts her hand up and waves.

She thinks of graveyards again, her grandparents, maybe because of how diminished her neighbor seems as she finally turns and disappears around the brick building. It's nearly October, and Jorie hasn't been to Maple Walk Cemetery recently, where Gram and Granddad are buried, a small resting place in a pocket of forest off Mechanicsville Road, not far from Sam. Jorie tries to visit their graves every month.

Oregon or Canada. All those cemeteries, all the ones between them and here. All those paper birches. The thought of having another reason to go to Maple Walk brings a flush of heat into her face. The stirring of anger. It turns the idea into a decision.

Maple Walk. The symmetry—pine, maple—is ringing in her mind. She almost pulls her phone out to google "Birchwood Cemetery" just to be sure, but nothing could be that perfect, or that awful.

Sam's Honda isn't in front of her house. Jorie wonders if she took the kids to the Hinesburg Festival—the unofficial one before the foliage tourists show up. She hopes Jeff is with them to give Oli some time with a stable adult male. It hurts to need that.

Oli's been asking for a phone, and she's planning on caving this Christmas with some of the editing money. She has another manuscript lined up, they'll be okay for a while. He'll probably scroll himself into oblivion instead of playing in the snow, become obsessed with TikTok, or whatever the next trend will be, but it might loosen Agatha's hold on him. A week ago, walking past his bedroom, she heard him tell the doll, "What if Dad dies and I never find out until I'm grown up?" Jorie's heart was in her throat the rest of the day.

She takes a right onto Mechanicsville and sees the open wrought iron gate with MAPLE WALK CEMETERY arching above. Time has worn the scrolled metal lettering a little rusty. "The Maple Arch Creature," she says as she pulls in, and for one delicate second, Beth and Colin are in the car, they're all laughing at her joke.

She parks and walks through the gate and winds her way to the right, skirting the first section of graves toward Gram and Granddad Ames on the east side. She's not actively looking across the lawn to her left, but a part of her is focused on it, feeling the angles change, her eyes a camera. As she reaches the corner, a crossroads of concrete walkways in the middle of the grounds, her breath catches. Spread out in front of her is the setting of the VHS tape's four scenes.

The light's all wrong. It's still caught in the trees this early in the day. But she walks forward ten paces, then fifteen, and stops, maybe in the same spot the camera operator stood. Shooting footage only for Jorie's eyes.

Once upon a time, there was a Jorie who signed a deal to cowrite and produce a documentary based on her group and Hélène Enriquez's film. This new twist, the tape and the cemetery all these years later, would provide a stunning meta angle, says that Jorie, and incredible visuals.

The pathetic itch deepens. Sometimes she is awed by the audacity of her former self.

The paper birches are more clearly outnumbered by maples, a scattering of pines and cedars and oaks, than it seemed in the video, but they're at the same diagonal, ahead and to the right. There are fewer of them than on her property, so the trunks stand out even more like gnawed bones. Their leaves are turning earlier than her own. But there they are, two of the trees reaching across to join limbs, making a doorway. *Birch Arch* doesn't exactly roll off the tongue.

She hasn't moved, and she wonders how many minutes have gone by. How close to six. There's a quick knot of panic in her throat, but she forces herself to stand under the open sky, the scent of rain still sweet in the air, as though nothing at all can hurt her. There's no feeling of eyes on her. She can pretend there was never a blog post at the end of 2012, no talk of occult transfigurations, no *Proof of Demons* at all. She's only visiting her grandparents, whose deaths can't press on her conscience.

Still, her eyes are filming, she can't help but admit this. They still know how to look and frame. How can some part of her, even now, want to step into a horror movie? She already lived one, in her own way, the true crime variety that wounds and grieves and must scab over gradually. She's the worst kind of final girl, the one who survives because she pointed the main characters into the woods, and the camera followed after them.

*[x6:00x]*

She waits two more minutes because one of the new scenes on the tape has a longer static lull than the original film. Closer to ten, she breathes out at the empty trees. She can hardly see her breath now that some warmth has softened the edges of the morning.

For a moment she thinks she's about to walk forward to the birches, and she's telling herself not to when her phone buzzes in her pocket. It's a New York number. She was hoping it would be Sam, and her son's voice would bring her back to the last eight years. She says hello and scans the trees.

"You still have the same number," a voice says, and Beth sounds the same, too, her words carrying a bright roundness. Jorie pictures her pulling her hair back because she's lost the ten thousandth elastic band of her life. Her hair was always dense and lovely, with a mind of its own.

Jorie is about to say yes, she doesn't like change, and besides, nearly all the death threats back then were online. But across the sweep of lawn that needs its last cut of the year, she thinks someone is standing in the paper birches. "Jorie?" Beth says in her ear. "Hello?"

"Help me" is all she can say back. "I need your help." And she does, she's pinned to the grass waiting to see if her life will take its old shape.

"What is it?" Beth says, and her voice, it's an astonishing thing to hear, the simple fact of it.

"There's someone watching me right now," Jorie says. Except there isn't. The trees are empty. There's just a breeze combing through them and rippling the long grass out toward her.

It's a classic first-act assurance in a horror movie, to tell herself she imagined someone following and watching. But she does, even as she stands where the images on the tape were filmed. "They're not mutually exclusive, Jorie," she says out loud.

"Who are you talking to?" Beth says in her ear. "Where are you?"

"Nothing. I'm being jumpy." Jorie keeps searching the trees. "Did you watch those clips I sent you? I'm at the cemetery where they were shot."

"Well, stop snooping around the scene of the crime and go home, Velma. I did watch them. Nobody sent me a tape, but I'm coming up there." Jorie clenches her jaw as Beth says something about taking a couple of days off work, she wants to see the foliage, not because she thinks Jorie is in danger. It's a weak joke, and they don't laugh. The leaves have only just started to turn, and they wouldn't be enough of an excuse even in October, not enough to bridge the long hole stretching back from now to the awful thing Jorie did.

"Beth, I don't even know what to say." Jorie hears the tremor in her voice and arches her back to get rid of it, knifes her eyes harder at the trees.

"Just be safe," Beth tells her. "A friend of mine owns an Airbnb somewhere up near Burlington. Look, I haven't been holding on to all this resentment, exactly, but I've held on to something. It would be nice to try to let go of it. Go home. I'll call you tomorrow."

Jorie takes a first step toward the stand of birches, and the rest of the steps are easy, a resolute line into the dim shade, where the temperature drops ten degrees and the sounds of rural Vermont are muffled behind her. She would go home, but she's angry, this is an intrusion into the new life she's cobbled together, the borderline reclusiveness, the half-formed penance she's tried to do.

Up close she can see that the two birch limbs have been tied together into an arch, forcing their embrace. Just a bit of rough thin rope that would never show up on camera.

"Who's out here?" she almost yells. She's barely five feet tall, but she's in the trees and her fingers are curled into fists, tight enough to dig her chewed nails into her palms. "If you sent that fucking tape, I'm calling the police."

Only the leaf-skittering of a small animal answers. Behind it, the faint thread of a car that needs a new muffler.

Some part of her is back in North Carolina in 2012, scaling another cemetery's walls at midnight in October, and Colin and Beth are young ghosts beside her. Colin is breathing deep and saying he can smell the shadows of the trees, not caring if no one outside their trio could understand. Beth is quietly sketching camera angles for future scripts.

Any wisdom Jorie's earned is lost in the years ahead. There's only a growing ambition, like heat on her skin.

She wouldn't make the swap now, she wouldn't go back into those southern trees unless she could take the knowledge of the consequences with her. Surely she wouldn't. But the old thrilling electricity does touch her again, rising through the fear and feeding on it.

The sense of Hélène Enriquez is with her as she listens for footsteps, or the whisper of leaves. The squirrel or whatever it was is gone. She imagines the gauzy blur of the director's face emerging from deeper in the woods, the unknowability of her fading, pixels evaporating, some truth approaching. Her proof of demons, perhaps, finally, or simply the answer to what her movie means to her and to Jorie.

She wants to leave this place before she imagines Hannah Kim here, too, and the drunken laughter of the boys who dug the hole. She wants to pick Oli up and keep him next to her, figure something out that will make taking him away from his father okay. She wants to go home and crawl into bed.

She looks out toward the graves, from the creature's point of view, as she did the night of the last film haunt. The images of *Proof of Demons* play out from this alternate vantage point.

Would she find a lake if she walked far enough into the trees?

As she steps out into the open, of course there will be a sound, a sliding step or a low chuckle, something to turn the dial to the next notch of tension. The silence gains another fold, there's the horn of a big truck half a mile away. Her horror is still on the periphery, testing the membrane around her life.

The tape in the mailbox has made her start thinking like an aspiring filmmaker again. Like a fan. Her mind jumping ahead to the next beat. She hates it. It cuts almost as deep as the worry that someone will show up at her home when Oli is there.

Only at the last moment does she remember to visit her grandparents' graves, and all these mind-fogging distractions add to her anger. She goes back to the path toward the eastern corner, to the plots that were purchased before she was born. Robert and Modean Ames, beloved—

Jorie stops as their graves come into view, under a spreading sugar maple. Something has been left for her.

Two blue sheets drape across the low humps of earth as though to comfort Gram and Granddad in their rest. Jorie approaches and stares down at them, her skin tightening all over. Maple leaves have blown across the sheets. *Who would do this, why now, why ever?* Her thoughts are like little holes in the air.

A sign is propped against her grandfather's headstone. Cardboard, like a flap torn off a box. Thick letters scraped on with black paint, smeared by the recent rain: HANNAH.

A breeze sighs out of some cheap 1980s movie, dragging more leaves scratching along the sidewalk. Jorie can feel the lo-fi production values of her life. The grainy thing crawling toward her. She stands there with the cardboard shouting the whisper she's carried through these years.

There was someone in the trees, watching her as she talked to Beth. She's now sure there was someone looking in at her through Lucky Coffee's window. She imagines feeling a camera lens burning the back of her neck now, as fear soaks into her. She can't turn around, away from Hannah's name.

At some point she begins to worry that six more minutes have gone by, that someone's Enriquez timer is about to go off. Silly, yes, she doesn't believe the door to hell will open if she stands still, but right now it's the only thing capable of getting her moving again. She grabs both of the sheets, wads them up as tight as she can, adds the sign, and stuffs them in the trash can on her way to the car, turning back one last time to replace the fallen metal lid that rings and scrapes against the concrete walk.

She calls Sam and has her put Oli on. "Hey, buddy," she says. "How about I come get you a day early? I'm done working on the book. We'll treat Sam to dinner because she deserves it and I miss her, then we'll watch a movie at home and go to bed late."

"Yeah!" he says, and Jorie loves being the reason for that upturned note of joy. She hopes she can hold on to it until middle school, at least. "Can we watch *Monsters, Inc.* again?"

His voice is so warm, it makes everything okay. She'll allow a few monsters tonight, if they're Pixar's idea of them. Because this place is nothing like North Carolina. She says this to herself all the way to her cousin's house.

# INTERLUDE

[Excerpt from "October Film Haunt: *Proof of Demons*," by Jorie Stroud, *The October Film Haunt* (archived webpage), November 2012]

The first surprise was that none of us had ever spent a night among the dead.

Yes, dear Film Haunters, it's true. Please don't let this tarnish our True Fandom Seal of Approval in your hearts. Maybe camping out in a cemetery was so cliché—not to mention a bit disrespectful to the dearly departed—that we just never got to it before now. Of course, after years of movies full of graveyards both quiet and unquiet, our horror skins were thick enough to feel at home in one.

Then again, we'd all seen *Proof of Demons* multiple times. We knew its reputation. We knew how uniquely unsettling the film was.

And we knew the rumors. That following the independent 2009 release, the nine-foot-tall "Pine Arch Creature" began to creep out of the filmed trees, across the filmed cemetery lawn, through 4chan's creepypastas and the message board pixels of Reddit, and into the real and living world. How dozens of people claim to have seen it and felt its strange and palpable menace.

If you've been living in a no-horror-allowed cave the last few years and don't know the Pine Arch Creature, picture the Slender Man lore crossed with *Ringu* (or *The Ring*, if you prefer to Americanize this comparison). Not the videotape in *Ringu*, but the film itself. Now imagine the entire movie serving the same purpose as the videotape within it—to transfer a demonic entity out of media (film) into the real world (the place you actually wake up in every morning). *Proof of Demons* is that certifiably eerie—and possibly REAL.

Along certain strands of the web, this lumpy half-seen monster has shown up in photographs and a few blurry videos and a hundred streams of debate about digital mythologizing. The film, they say, isn't there to entertain or stand alone as art. It is a document. It may be a doorway. *Proof of Demons* is now as much urban legend as it is one of the most effective horror movies ever made. That its director, Hélène Enriquez, seems to be a ghost or a pseudonym only adds to the enduring power of this occult hearsay.

Soooo . . . your humble October Film Haunt trio set out for North Carolina, to the cemetery where one of its most famous scenes was shot. The pretty, village-y town of Whisper in the movie, the slightly bigger, slightly closer to bland suburbia town of Arden, NC, in reality. It was, naturally, only a matter of time before we chose *Proof of Demons* for our yearly homage. It's an understatement to say it's in our dark wheelhouse.

We camped in the thin, manicured trees two hundred yards from the gravestones—just far enough away for a hint of forest—and soaked ourselves in the atmosphere. Nearly all the insects had gone for the year, and the highway traffic was too distant to reach us.

We spoke the words—"I belong with you"—into the textured quiet. We let the idea of terror run cold on our skin. The moon was packed away in woolen clouds.

Never fear, dear Haunter—or, if you're like us since that night, *constantly fear*—for we visited other scenes beyond the pine arch. And we kept most of our eyes out for what fans call "the moving hole." After all, it's the likely origin of the film's title, this supposed keyhole to hell, and what primarily elevates the production even beyond a murderous cult and some terrible summoned thing lurking in the woods.

But an eye was being kept out for us, too.

There's something about the tangled density of nature in the South. There's a wildness you can feel, trees swallowed by vines, puddles of pine needles, old pollen, acorns, with the Appalachians hemming much of the land. They're some of the oldest mountains on earth, gorgeous but worn down to nubs by relentless age, laid out like a horizon line God traced with an arthritic hand. There is no sense of youth here. You expect the ghosts to be bony and withered.

Even just inside the arch, still on the cemetery's property and under the watch of groundskeepers, nature is in its slow bursting hurry to reclaim the land. If given a few weeks, the poison ivy might wind its way to the graves like evil garlands. That feeling of ancient breath is in the air, full of dust and pine resin.

As we've described before, we keep supplies to a minimum on film haunts because we want the faintest possible intrusion into the spirit of a location. It doesn't matter if there were trailers lined up on the fringes during the film's production. It doesn't matter if set designers once tromped all over the scene. It may not even matter if the public still uses a space. It's important to respect the purity of where magic happened. Most of the movies we seek out were shot on small budgets anyway, with skeleton crews.

The vibe is intact, if you know how to tap into its vein. But even if we haunted the Maryland state park where *The Blair Witch Project* was filmed with no sets or scene slates, we would aim to leave even fewer footprints than Heather, Mike, and Josh did. (*BWP* isn't off the table for a future haunt, but, well, it *is* kind of obvious.)

Occult or make-believe, Enriquez struck a rich mine of dread here in these trees, at the lake, in the stone crypt. We were especially hesitant to muddy this particular essence, however much of it was in the soil and not in editing software.

Each of the four so-called Transfigurations in Enriquez's film lasts six minutes and is separated by twelve minutes of narrative. Some fans—and a handful of film scholars who have written about it, including our own Colin—claim that this explains the odd structure of the movie, the patchwork Frankenstein that's half unsettling surrealist experiment, half giallo-esque slasher fest. Those numbers are the kind of math that could only be deliberate, much like Enriquez's decision to fill just under a *third* of her total running time with five static shots in which only atmosphere does any heavy lifting.

I was as intrigued as anyone by the possibility of an arcane ritual encoded in film, a movie made specifically for an occult purpose, but I'd always preferred to look at it as a weird little masterpiece that didn't answer any of my questions. I left it at that. That's where it got its power, I figured, it was the reason I'd watched it who knows how many times even before we chose it for this year's trip.

We found the plot fascinating. Enriquez mixed small town and nature set pieces with the fluid imagery and framing of a master coming into her own (and God and the Devil both know we need more women horror directors). The final product stood on its own strange legs. But ultimately, that was all it was: a product.

Now, after our night there, I have to rewrite all those thoughts.

To preserve the atmosphere of the site, we brought no sleeping bags, and certainly no cameras. It wasn't supposed to rain, but if it did, we would get wet. Those are the rules. We planned to stay up all night, eat at a greasy diner on our way out of North Carolina, and crash at my place before we went our separate ways, back to our regularly scheduled programming talking about horror with all of you.

Tonight was about us three sponges soaking up what we could of whatever *Proof of Demons* spilled here.

The first two hours were spent discussing the Transfigurations, transcribing impressions and thoughts in our journals—sponging—by flashlight, listening to what must have been frogs out by the lake. They sounded like old door hinges in a haunted house.

There we were, just before the night's second surprise. Our brilliant Colin with his bad posture, folded over a blue Moleskine, his hair hanging in curtains over his face, an *In the Mouth of Kronos* T-shirt under his corduroy jacket. Beth rooting in her backpack with the John Carpenter and Shirley Jackson and Joe Pulver patches, pulling out a new journal already because her handwriting is both huge and rapid, not quite aware yet that her dark curls had lost their second hair tie of the day. And finally me, hair much too short to get in the way, a battered dollar-store spiral notebook in my lap, plain brown sweater, no Freddy Krueger stripes, nothing to mark me as a member of our precious fellowship.

Three cultural archaeologists digging to the heart of another legend.

We heard something moving around in the dark just after three a.m. It was much closer than the lake, back in the woods behind our little cross-legged triangle. We swept our lights across the ground, up into leaves and needled limbs. Red hints came out of the dark from the scattered maple foliage, the evergreen pines and live oaks melting back into the dark quickly.

A local roaming the night? A fellow horror fanatic seeking out these demonic vibes? Or a vicious killer with a hook for a hand???

Colin started to say something and was hushed by Beth's stage whisper. It was that moment all three of us long for, in October and every other month: to be, if only for an instant we could try to stretch out, in a horror movie. To feel the rush of horror movie cold across our bodies. To feel the brain lock up, paused, as some atavistic impulse prepares to take over. That moment before the moment.

In other words, we were unnerved, spooked, transported by the possibility of something that was Other.

But not terrified, yet.

Something moved again, a dragging sound followed by a low, wet breath. Beth's light came to rest in an open area. There was nothing there, but she had an impulse to hold her light steady, a yellow tunnel cutting through the dark several feet above the ground. We'd all seen the Reddit claims about creating your own Transfiguration to summon the Pine Arch Creature, and the usual discussion of why its first appearance in the movie doesn't qualify as a Transfiguration even though a six-minute continuous take precedes it.

I was proud of Beth for daring to hold herself so still in a place where stillness led to horror. An urban legend has at least the chance of being true. Nothing in me screamed out at her to stop.

I checked the time on my cell phone somewhere around the sixth crawling minute, and when I looked back out to the path of Beth's light, I saw it was somehow corrupted. A glossy black texture was blocking the beam, both like and unlike a slow-moving shape. Or an opening, since the light disappeared into it, leaving the faint silhouettes of trees in the background. Colin added his flashlight and we saw that the black had a red tinge as he traced the edges of it in a rough circle. The opening seemed to squirm, and suddenly within it, a horrible huge eye rolled in its socket to find us.

"The moving hole," I said, that horror movie moment deepening into a colder tightness across my skin. Colin said something reverent, his voice not far from worshipful, but I didn't hear it over the wooden snap that came from behind me.

# CHAPTER FIVE
## Coleman

▶▶ Four, maybe five good months, the oncologist told him. If treatment isn't successful. His first thought that afternoon, with the CT scans clipped against the light, was of 1979, when he and his brother fell out of a tree. Coleman was twelve. Jackson went missing three mornings later.

Coleman thought he saw heaven that day, so of course an angel had come for his brother. He spent years lost in thoughts of dying, drawing in the margins of school notebook pages. He didn't sleep enough, afraid he wouldn't wake up, or that Jackson would come back and loom over his bed in the dark.

He was the kid whose brother ran away from home. Whose mother did her best to move on for the son she still had. He likes to think he helped her, but even all these years later, it's hard to know if he did.

Jackson and the obsession with death followed him into adulthood. When Evie was a baby, he would stand by her crib and keep watch until Gloria asked him to get help.

He finally grew up, the thoughts faded, but there have always been certain moments. When his grandchildren cry. When he reads about a child abduction, or a murder victim's eyes glass over on a TV show, or the pandemic swept through the world like a calm gray pestilence.

Now the old fascination—what will come in the moments after the end—has returned. What will happen to him when the cancer is finished and he takes his last clogged breath? Where will the specks of him go when they dissipate? He's been an accountant for thirty-four years, he likes to keep things in order, and science says that matter cannot be created or destroyed.

The knife the blond man stuck into Coleman's side missed all his organs. A shallow wound, not meant to damage. He is at home on bed rest, watching *Proof of*

*Demons* on his laptop. The credits are scrolling to the end of his fourth viewing in three days, such a small list of production designers and actors and effects artists, hardly a short film's worth.

Coleman doesn't remember much after the attack, no matter how gentle the knife was. His focus had been on the pain. He imagined the soggy weight of the cancer in his lungs as he lay on his back, and he thought of the afternoon in 1979 then, too. Square ceiling tiles above him, none of them opening to a glimpse of a strange world.

A nurse or a doctor—or it could have been Gloria—found the *Proof of Demons* DVD tucked into the back pocket of his pants after he was brought to the ER. They sealed the disc in a box with his wallet and keys and a handwritten list of last week's funerals, neat lines drawn through nearly all of them in ink.

So he watched it.

Gloria winces whenever she comes into the guest room to check on him and sees what is playing on his laptop, usually the screen is paused on the first man under the blue sheet, the red splashes of blood. The butcher knife he's holding, muted in the bedside lamp glow in such a different way than the blond man's knife caught the fluorescent ceiling light in the video store. He pauses at the other murders, too, stares at the other knives. Sometimes it's the cemetery, as the long human-shaped smudge comes out of the trees.

"Turn that off, I don't like it," she tells him.

"It's not my kind of thing either, is it?" he says, and closes the computer until she leaves. She wouldn't understand how the movie is echoing his life.

When he thinks of death, so continuously now, he's twelve again, staring up at branches and leaves latticing the sky. Jackson is fourteen, and the big limb that held them all their lives in the oak tree behind their Greensboro house, straight and stout and perfect between their forked legs, breaks from disease or their growing weight.

The fall was so quick. They lay in the dirt for several minutes, Coleman's voice knocked out of his chest. Was he dying? He thought of heaven and its angels and couldn't remember where his mother was. His brother's left arm was broken in two places, but Coleman didn't know it yet.

For a long moment, a wound opened up in the air above him, and he saw—or dreamed—silken shrouded angels among the crosshatched limbs. The angels he was just thinking of, as though he had called them. He looked through the misshapen window.

It was the afterlife, he felt it in his chest and in his throat. The figures were wrapped like mummies by the creamy light, a kind of light that could not have come through the half-closed lid of clouds above. It was the light of some other day. He was young enough to know it wasn't this world.

He remembers a shoulder turning, a dense shadowed face lowering into the opening to watch him—and the hole seemed to pulse down toward Coleman as an eye filled it. There was the warm promise of that eye, green and black, until it slid away and the busy heaven returned, full of nearly distinct figures and blur. All in that creamy constant light, and a feeling of sharp, painful calm.

Coleman was diagnosed with a concussion. He tried telling a nurse about the eye that had looked at him from heaven. She called him "sweetie" and said he'd sure had himself a heck of a dream. The next day, when he tried to tell his mother what had really happened, she stared at him. He didn't hear her voice again for hours.

Jackson refused to say if he had seen anything as they lay in the dirt, he acted confused and secretive, and two and a half days later, he was gone. Ultimately, the vision became something wondrous to attach to that loss, a cause and an effect of Coleman's fading hope. He can still hear the deep murmur of words through his bedroom wall, Jackson's voice answering. A vibration that seemed to travel through the floor, up into the frame of Coleman's bed.

"I belong with you!" a voice called out, Jackson or someone or something. Coleman was never able to decide. Sharp and clear, as though from a speaker.

More words were spoken, then a heavy thump. A long, small groan. The house trembled one last time.

When Coleman went to his brother's room, Jackson wasn't there, he wasn't in the bathroom or the kitchen, and he wasn't in any of the months and years that followed. He vanished with the cast on his arm and nothing else.

A single line of blood had been smeared down the wall over his bed.

Gloria was the only other person Coleman told about the vision until 2005. She urged him to set up a blog, which he titled *Missing Jackson Smith*, because maybe his brother would see it and, well, strange things happened in the world. At least an attempt would be out there on the expanding internet. He could post photos of them as children, memories and updates about Coleman's life, Evie and any grandkids she might give them. A package of consolations.

He didn't want a blog, the format was too public and he was too awkward, but he enjoyed it at first. There was a tenderness. He's still not sure why he opened up about the vision on the blog, describing it in detail, except that Jackson was the only one he imagined reading it, and he wanted him to know. How believing an angel had come into their home that awful morning added something sweet to the poison of losing him.

He was careful to never use his own name, only Jackson's. It gave him more honesty. He wrote five or six half-pleading letters before the roaring silence made him delete the story of the alien light and the eye a year or so later. He left the rest of it to molder.

These three weeks after the diagnosis, though, he's been reading through it. The attack in the video store, too, he knows it's the natural thing to grasp at his childhood in the face of death. He wishes he could curl up in his mother's lap, but he's avoided her since sitting in the tomb of the oncologist's office.

Now this horror movie is mixing itself up with Coleman's life. There are coincidences in every scene. One of the main characters is named Jackson Smith. There are killers with kitchen knives. It was filmed here in Arden, Coleman recognized several streets and landmarks, he saw the very trees the horrible smudge came out of just before he was stabbed with a similar knife. And the young mother he saw that day spoke of a crypt back in the woods, and inside what must be the same crypt, inside the film, an empty cold space opens up. And there is a hole filled by an eye.

How did some screenwriter come so close to him?

The man who stuck the knife into Coleman a week ago, the man the police haven't found yet, said *Proof of Demons* lets you look into hell. But Coleman can't decide whether to be chilled by the childhood echo of recognition or heartened by the fact that it's only an echo. It is a different eye turning to find the camera. It's been cast in the light of fear, not a milky benevolence.

But what does a man who won't live to see his sixtieth birthday—a quiet accountant with tie clips and pleats in his pants, a soft man who used to polish his shoes religiously—what does he think he's doing, fixating on these things?

He closes the laptop again and rubs his eyes. These are not coincidences. He knows the man in the video store stabbed him because of the movie, and that the ice cream family—he only assumes they ended up getting ice cream—were involved somehow. Why is another matter. Coleman is too mild to have enemies.

Gloria comes into the room again, towel wrapped around her wet hair, floral bathrobe clinging to her curves. He feels a stirring, and wonders how soon the last time he takes his wife to bed will be. In stage 4, it could be soon. If he handles his ending himself, it could be any day now.

But his thoughts click back to the man under the sheet, the first killing in the movie, and the way the crude wooden thing on his head tears holes in the blue cotton. It's revealed to be a crown later in the film, not some bestial head on a man's body. For a second, or even less than a second, he imagines something like a crown beneath Gloria's towel. A butcher knife behind her back.

"Have you called her yet?" she asks him, standing beside the guest room bed, looming. He ascribes tension and sourness to her, but really she's only scared, as she works her way toward losing him.

"Not yet," he says, and he can't hold her gaze. If he doesn't tell Evie about the cancer, Gloria will. She first made the threat this morning. He got a reprieve because of the attack, because they did tell Evie about that, but he knows she means it now.

"Today's the weekend. It would be best to tell her when she has some time alone with her thoughts, away from work." Gloria slips her hand beneath his head to force him to lift it, then plumps his pillow for the third time since he woke up. "She'll have Charlotte and Liam and Darius to hold on to."

"You think I don't know that?" he almost snaps. "You think I'm going to call her office Monday and pull her out of a meeting to tell her?" Irritation brings heat to his face. Now that he's dying, his wife seems to think his common sense has cancer, too. The wound in his side throbs once, as though he's twisting in the bed. He wonders if he'll be cruel to Gloria in the painful months ahead, when he's near the end and in and out of a narcotic fog. If he lets the months come.

"That's not what I meant." She touches his shoulder, and her words come out in a rush. "Is it even right to do this over the phone? Can't we ask her to come home for a couple of days? She can just come by herself. But then she'd know it was something like this if we said to leave the kids, wouldn't she? We'd have to make something up just to get her here. And here you are stabbed by some maniac in town, and that's already got her scared. Coleman, I don't know how to do this."

He shakes his head because he doesn't know either.

"I don't think you're going to tell her at all," Gloria says, interpreting the movement of his head as a refusal. She begins to cry, her voice goes hoarse with sobs. It's the kind of crying she never used to do. "I don't want to hear her being scared from so far away. Not on the phone."

"I'll tell her." His voice is softer now, back in its usual cadence. He puts a hand on her cheek and uses a thumb to swipe some of her tears away. "I don't know if it'll be here or over the phone. I guess I'll have to feel it out."

But she sinks onto the bed beside him and doesn't answer. Her tough exterior has broken open again. He pulls her over to him, and the shifting of her body causes some envelopes to slip down between her body and his laptop. He didn't notice her bringing the mail in. His name is written in smeared capital letters on one of them.

He knows he shouldn't give any of his attention to it now, so he holds the person who has held him for thirty-two good years—serviceable years, haunted years, beautiful and quiet and tender years—as she rocks against him and lets awful noises out because there won't be any more years.

"I don't want you to go, honey," she whispers, tucked under his chin. Then she slips off the bed and leaves the room, not looking at him, as though it's forever and they have agreed, after much discussion, that it's best this way.

Coleman tears the hand-addressed envelope open and pulls out a single sheet of thin white paper, nearly tissue-thin like the mimeograph paper his office still used occasionally when he was starting out. Typed in the center is a string of words in quotation marks. "The Demon Can Answer Many Wonders And Knowledge As You Glimpsed As A Child As A Curious Eye." He can't quite find surprise that the message, if that's what it is, seems to have read his wandering cycle of thoughts.

Or that he doesn't feel terror.

There's no return address, but that would make it even stranger, he thinks. The postmark reads Hinesburg VT 05461. He has never been to Vermont, Gloria always wanted to go see the foliage and drive through the mountains there, and he sighs the last week and the impossibility of that vacation out of his lungs. He turns the page over to see a final line typed on the back: "Walk In The Woods & The Crypt. You Have Always Belonged Here."

All his life he has wondered if he saw heaven the last day he and Jackson were normal brothers with an exhausted mother and a father who died much too young. It's an obscenity to suggest it was hell, a demon rather than an angel. But whoever sent him this note, they're just referencing the film, surely. The man who stabbed him must have mailed it to him after fleeing up to Vermont and the endless forests. What does he want with Coleman?

He opens his laptop, where the movie is waiting, paused on blood-splashed walls. His finger brushes the touchpad, but he decides not to click the play icon.

There is a peripheral change in the bedroom's light. Outside, a shape walks up to the window and stops, the sun casts it onto the rich green curtains that are almost completely closed. A bit of Gloria's garden runs along the house here.

Coleman waits for movement, for his wife to stoop down and fuss with her day lilies and verbenas, or for the shadow of the blond man's knife to lift against the light. But the shape stands there, with the body language of looking in, except that it couldn't possibly see through the fabric.

"I belong with you," a faint voice says. Coleman jerks back, but it's only *Proof of Demons*, it's started playing again on the computer screen. The man in the blue sheet and the crown kneels next to his victims. The thin wails of a child leak out of the speakers. Coleman presses the mute button and closes the laptop.

The right curtain twitches and begins to draw back from the center along the rod. The shape grows larger. The sun strains through the window, dimming to a shapeless, pearly light that for only a moment reminds him of the day he fell out of the oak tree. Then it shifts into the quality of an eclipse, not night and not day and not either of the seams that join them.

The air in the room darkens. Coleman gasps at it, unable to breathe it in. A picture of his brother enters his mind so clearly, Jackson, fourteen in that last year and a stunning blur on his bike. His hair raked back by the wind he made. Down the hill in front of their home and into the terrible future.

His memory of Jackson breaks apart as the person shape appears again. It's inside the room now, dragging toward the bed. It reaches him, for a long, deep second it's in front of his face. A dark non-color, the cold smudge of it on his skin.

Coleman claws at his neck. A knot slides down his throat, slow and wet, ending with a rupture of bright black pain in his lungs. He coughs, coughs again, twists the knob inside the bedside lampshade and nearly screams when the bulb blows in a cracking flash.

He turns back to see the leaning shape, but in the same moment it's gone. It doesn't shift away from him or duck down below the mattress. It doesn't fade or blink out of his imagination. It's just not there anymore. The curtain drops back and stills.

"Who's there?" he tries to shout, risking Gloria running into the room. The green-filtered sunlight returns. A plane flies over the house, on its way to Asheville or maybe across the ocean.

He stares at the window for at least five minutes, the gap of the partly opened curtain that was closed a minute ago. His breaths come easier. The obstruction in his throat is gone. Only the cancer sits in his lungs now. He ejects the DVD and sits there with his eyes shut tight, propped up in the bed, then picks up his phone from Gloria's grandmother's bedspread to call Evie in Colorado.

# INTERLUDE

[Excerpt from *Missing Jackson Smith* (archived webpage), February 2005]

It's Valentine's Day and I'm writing to you instead of getting ready to go out. Gloria would understand. I was halfway through putting my tie on, and I thought of something.

A firecracker went off near my head when I was in college. No permanent damage but for a while I would hear you screaming from your broken arm. A high-pitched whine. I would lie in bed at night and hear it. Sometimes even now I hear you when someone goes quiet on the phone line. Moments when I notice the quiet. When I write in this blog.

That isn't what I thought just now. What I thought of was hell because of that line of blood you drew on the wall before you left me and Mama. Was it your blood? Did someone hurt you? Did a serial killer come through town? That is an awful thing to think all these years. The front door was open that morning. The police said maybe you hurt yourself and ran away. But I thought the blood on the wall was a door closed up. A door that had an eye in it, and it was open when your voice woke me up. You must have gone through it. But into heaven, not hell. I believed that for a long time. I was a kid.

Why would an angel come out of hell? You should have told me if you saw the window into HEAVEN when we fell. If you saw the angel's eye. I hope you are somehow out there in the world. If you are married I hope you have a nice romantic night. You deserve it. You belong.

# CHAPTER SIX
## Jorie

▶▶ "Mom?" Oli comes up behind her but not close, unsure what to do or how to act. Jorie was distracted, ragged all night, and today has been more of the same. One minute she's smothering him, tucking him too tight into bed, or trying to get him to eat an extra pancake. The next she's ignoring him, hovering at every window like a distraught sentinel.

It rained for most of seventeen hours, cold and sharp as the temperature dipped near freezing during the night. Sleet tapped on the windows, just loud enough to hear, like soft fingernails. More hesitant than the sound of Oli rapping Agatha's face against a pane, but somehow more demanding, too. The sound kept waking her with its creeping shyness.

Old houses weren't quiet, she told herself. There was no one outside.

The sun has crawled back out this afternoon, weak and trembly, and she hasn't seen anyone watching from the trees. No crazed Enriquez fan—Rickies, that's what they call themselves, she keeps reminding herself—with a vendetta skulking around under a bedsheet with no holes cut out for the eyes. There's still a little absurdity in the image, and it helps break the skin of Jorie's anxiety. Some of the overworked thoughts can leak out.

But Oli being home still has the rest of her on a fine edge. To think there was a time when she dreamed of living in a haunted house. Would have paid extra.

The two of them did manage to escape Jorie's tension for a while this morning. Her author sent her another chunk of the editing money, so she bought Oli a cartful of shirts and pants at Target. They stopped by a boutique thrift store and got lucky with a light jacket and a thick down parka that fits him almost perfectly. Now he only needs shoes and winter boots and galoshes.

Another way it's expensive to live up here, especially with a child. Every part of him is stretching an inch a day, she could swear, and barely eight years old. She got a laugh earlier by saying she can hear his bones creaking in his bed as they grow.

But now he's behind her, subdued instead of laughing. She turns and looks at him, the raft that carried her to shore when she was adrift and aching and sinking. He's holding Agatha by one of her legs, her lacy maroon dress and petticoats hanging down over her face.

"Is there something scary?" he says. "Why won't you stop looking outside?"

He's tall for his age, he'll sprout past her by the time he's ten at this rate. "Sorry, buddy," she says. "These wet days feel lonely. That's why I snatched you from Sam's house a day early. I owe it to you to cheer up, I guess." She offers a wan smile that Oli doesn't return. He just stands there, and she sees that he's picking up on her fear. Mom's bothered, so he's bothered.

And he's lonely, too, she shouldn't have used that word and opened that window between them. She gathers him up in a hug. "What should we order for takeout tonight? Your pick." She kisses his head above the ear. Even his hair is warm and vital. For a second she can detect—or imagine—that thriving milky smell he had as a baby. She remembers it lasting until he started walking on his own.

"I don't know," he says, and she feels his face tilt down toward the floor.

She steps back but lowers herself to her knees. "What's wrong, honey?" Brushing one side of his bangs out of his eye. He also needs a haircut, his entire life runs on a high metabolism even though he's such a quiet little guy. "Feeling the rain, too?"

He tries to decide whether to be honest, his eyes going glassy as he stares somewhere near her chin. Eric hasn't called him in over a month, and it was at least that long before the last time. She sees his father in the shapes of his eyes that make him look intense when lines crease his forehead. The flare of his nose, the dusky fineness of his hair, the small cherub mouth that helps him pout so beautifully. This strange alien child she feels she hasn't gotten to know well enough.

She raises her eyebrows at him, waiting, and he finally says, "Yeah. A little. Agatha says she doesn't like the damp." Then, getting it in because he thinks there could be plenty of planning time to spare: "Do you think Daddy could come for Christmas?"

"Oh, buddy." Her vision blurs with the warning of tears. She hates this, easily as much as she hated Eric when she left him. "I don't know. But I'm going to be honest and say that's very unlikely."

His eyes are wet, too. "You're scared of something outside, because you keep looking out the windows. And Daddy's so far away, and he can't help us. He doesn't like me, and it's—" He looks down at the floor. He flips Agatha up so that she's facing him. He stares at the doll's face. A part of him closes itself off to Jorie.

"And it's my fault? Is that the rest of what you were going to say? I brought you up here with me? It's okay if you think that, you know. It wouldn't be mean of you to say."

But this time her raised eyebrows don't get him to answer because he's pretending not to see them. "Someone I used to know is bothering me a bit," she goes on, which isn't true but she has no idea how to phrase it. "Someone from work, kind of, before you were born. But it's no big deal. We just have to be careful and tell each other if we see anything weird, and we can't talk to people we don't know, no matter what. And it'll be fine. Okay?"

Her voice is a little too bright, but it's not false. There's not much of a tremor in it because there's not much of a tremor in her. She still feels the assurance she needs. Talking to Beth helped.

She holds out a hand, and after a moment he takes it with a half-smile that goes right through her sternum and scrapes her heart. "Okay," he says, and he's somehow sadder and happier than he was earlier. He is her beloved heartache. She'll just have to keep wondering how to do this whole parenting thing until she figures it out.

He goes into his den with full movie privileges until dinner, and she wanders over to the dining nook, where her laptop sits in its bag. Soon she hears him murmuring to his doll. The sun reaches the house through a strainer, its light like tea on the third steeping. Far from a cathedral sun, and the skin around Jorie's left eye tightens with the ghost of the last time Eric punched her, and her head hit the coffee table on the way down, and the wash of black stars.

He only hit her six times. Only three of them were terrifying. He only broke something once. And she realizes that the *only* is still there in her thoughts, corroding the stark facts into an excuse. It's an albatross of a word. She wants to get *only*—and the man it's still growing on like mold—out of her mind. Along with the look in her son's eyes.

She needs to be proactive, and she was always good at researching horror movies.

Typing *pine arch creature* into Google drags her back into a murky, pained nostalgia. The last time she climbed into this hole, Oli wasn't even a thought.

Subreddit threads clutter the first page of search results, a handful from the last few years. It seems the urban legend is still alive, though the bonfire she set off might only be embers now. Her eyes pick out the words *October Film Haunt* as instantly as they ever did back when their blog was nearing half a million visitors a month and the three of them were mentioned all over Twitter.

Her original film haunt post about *Proof of Demons* has been archived in more than one place, of course, and it still makes her face burn and clenches a knot in her chest. She wonders again if she should have changed her identity, or at least muddied it by switching to Anne, her middle name. She can't scrub the internet of Jorie Stroud, but she's done a fair job of erasing that Jorie from herself.

She clicks to the second page of results, and a headline she's never seen before lashes out and reminds her why her past self is past. "Monster or Monster: When Online Influencers Bring Horror Into the Real World." It was published by *Vice*, which means it would have had who knows how many thousands of eyes on it since 2018, making sure the world remembered Jorie.

The title is a shocking string of words, and she doesn't need to pull up the article, doesn't need to see her name in the first few words of Google's snippet to know it's about the October Film Haunt and Hannah Kim, at least in part. The Slender Man stabbing is surely discussed in the article, too, the trial and verdict were big topics in 2017. She doesn't know if she can face any of this, not yet.

Old memes are still littered across the web in ugly posterity. The internet never forgets the ashes of old outrages. She hovers over the *Vice* link and is surprised to see a tear land on the laptop's trackpad. The old helpless ache is welling up.

But Beth saves her, like she used to, more than anyone other than Oli. Jorie's phone vibrates across the table, toward the fogged window and the trees across the yard, lighting up with Beth's name.

Pulled some strings and left town early. Want to meet in the morning for breakfast? I cook now. A second text follows with an address in St. George, not quite five miles from Jorie's home on the way to Burlington.

Yes. Not scared of your cooking one bit, even though I still have nightmares about those turkey burgers you used to make. She sends the text, then adds another: Thank you thank you.

Jorie can't really believe, not all the way, that she just texted Beth. Joked with her. That she'll see her tomorrow.

When she and Beth were young, from seventeen most of the way to twenty-seven, more a stretch of effortless bright blurs than years, they would take Jorie's old Civic, Dave, and drive for hours. Half a tank of gas just to pull over at a roadside diner or truck stop, maybe a lake found on a road atlas if they wanted nature, and write stories in each other's company. Then back to wherever home was.

They had gone to different high schools in different North Georgia towns, and Beth had been a grade younger, but their affinity for scary movies and the few theaters that played them made sure they found each other. They drank pots of coffee and riffed on themes, collaborated on outlines for horror spec scripts, laughed at their characters' choices and imminent grisly murders. Serious about their craft but still on their way to being serious enough.

And they both loved the sense of untethering, something easier but also rarer, in a way, in those final years before social media swallowed everyone. They loved driving out to anonymous places, even if—especially if—they were mundane. Dave had no air-conditioning, so they got used to having all four of his windows down, and it was like always being in a wind tunnel, the pressure building and easing in their ears, a companionable roar like a physical presence around their seats. They never listened to music if it was warm out. They were aimless but almost never listless.

They met Colin in their early twenties, the October Film Haunt led off with *Phantasm*'s Morningside Mortuary in California a few years later, and soon there were actual people, people they didn't know, reading their blog. Blue checkmarks on Twitter, long before that stopped meaning something. Mentions in *Variety*, *BuzzFeed*, tweets from John Carpenter and Robert Englund and Jamie Lee Curtis, all these things around the next curve in their lives.

And all that time, the broken record speaks up in her mind, while they were waiting for those amazing things, a little girl named Hannah was growing up and waiting for her own life to begin. And a grave Jorie might as well have dug herself was waiting, too.

She closes the laptop. The sounds of car engines drift from the living room, bright cartoon voices, at a low volume because Oli is usually considerate. He told her once that Agatha doesn't like loud noises, just like Jorie. A smile softens her face. A weight slips from her. Research, if there's any to do, will have to wait until she can handle it. If she has Beth back after all this time, she thinks she can.

Now she just has to figure out how to not look out the windows until tomorrow.

But she forgets about Oli's closet. Jorie glances into his room on the way to her own, and something makes her stop. The door is half-open, the mirror tilted inside so that she sees herself at an angle. Her hair is a bit matted on the right side of the mirror self's head, but she has to lean back a few inches to see the reflection of the closet interior.

And the face peering out of it.

A faint round shape, the face she glimpsed two nights ago. Pale with shadowed eye sockets, something like the frame-quick glimpse of Pazuzu in *The Exorcist*. A man, she thinks, his mouth opening to speak or scream.

There's a subtle light inside the center of the doorway, creating the sense of a hole, but the face is gone now. It was like the eye in Enriquez's movie, if it pulled back to reveal the face that Márcia Smith must see in the final moments, after the screen cuts to black and the brief trail of credits.

Two seconds, probably closer to one, everything else like she's pausing, rewinding, playing it back in hazy slow motion.

She used to agonize over whether to let herself backtrack to watch some film's creepy moment again, to savor it, or to keep going at the pace the director intended. Sometimes she would, sometimes she'd wait until the second viewing. There was never a perfect way of going about it.

The image was so subtle and brief and indistinct. Her mind is ready with a list of excuses, brief flares of relief. It's stress, it's the angle of reflected light catching the patterned sleeves of Oli's shirts on their hangers.

Or the trauma of old actions and desires. Why wouldn't she see things after the tape?

She turns to check behind her in the hallway. Of course there's only a wall, a blank space for her mind to project tricks, between a photo of Jorie around Oli's age with her grandparents right outside this house and a larger photo of Gram and Granddad with Jorie's mother before the lymphoma diagnosis—nearly everyone hanging here is no longer in the world.

And she looks back at the open mouth of the closet. Only she is in it now, her eyes wide and shocked with some of the blood drained away for her own manic *Ju-On* look. All she needs is a wig and a bloodied dress.

There's no thickness to the air, nothing charged in the atmosphere. She doesn't feel a presence or a chill. But her heart jolts when she turns back toward the front of the house and sees Oli, his backlit silhouette seeming to stretch along the hallway floor toward her. Her little jump scare.

"Decided on dinner yet?" she says, putting her brave face on.

"Can we have pizza?" he says, lifting Agatha to show the other half of *we*. Not for the first time, she wants to take the doll away from him. She wants to make sure there is no horror in his life, not even the fictional kind.

But Agatha is a stand-in for Eric, it's how Oli has chosen to cope. She pulls her phone from her pocket to order their usual from Good Times on Earth, which may be the perfect name for a pizza restaurant.

She's not about to beg Samantha to take Oli again, not when it's so easy to slip what she thought she saw into a shoebox back in her cluttered mind. Not on a school night, even if he can catch the bus with Cara and Carter. She's leaned on Sam so much lately. Oli seemed to enjoy the one night he stayed over at Mrs. Compton's a few months ago—Jorie had to drive to Montpelier late to meet Lucy Dendrich about her memoir—but she doesn't feel comfortable asking her on short notice.

She grabs onto her thoughts and pulls them to a stop. No one is in danger here. Both of them are safe. She'll just have him sleep in her room tonight.

Oli turns and taps Agatha's face against the wall, and Jorie nearly jumps. She's not sure if it's a compromise or a stubborn gesture, but she goes into his room and takes the mirror down. She closes the closet door with her foot. It's something a character would do, like putting the TV outside at the end of *Poltergeist*.

Except this isn't an ending, and will she please stop finding similarities with scary movies and attaching them to every small moment? She's emptied herself of horror. She's learned to prefer herself without it.

If Jorie were writing this scene, if she still had that in her, the protagonist would carry the mirror down the hall and outside where it could fill up with gray clouds. An anti-séance. The opposite of inviting a vampire inside.

Oli is back in his den as she opens the front door and steps out into a cold that digs into her skin, the air nearly moist enough to call rain. She props the mirror against the wall and steps back to watch the paper birches reflected in it. A ground fog has begun to spill out from the trees, a movie set with dry ice, and of course she thinks she sees the hint of someone out there watching her, someone standing up from a crouch between two trunks.

But she will not turn from the mirror to look. She knows it's nothing. She won't look. Already she can see it's just a trick of the dying light.

"Hello, neighbor!"

Jorie screams and nearly slips off the front stoop. She turns and sees Mrs. Compton standing beside Jorie's car in her long cardigan. Half of her is in shadow because the drowning sun can't reach her over the house.

"You scared me again," Jorie says, and forces a laugh. "What brings you over?"

"Just this." Mrs. Compton steps forward into the light that swells out from the front door. She's holding out two glossy apples in the palms of her hands. "I went picking and wanted to share. Well, that's not entirely true. What I really wanted was for you to let Oliver know I'm baking a pie with them." She smiles, and Jorie thinks it looks sad, a little haggard.

"Are you okay?" Jorie asks her. "Want to come in and tell him? We're about to order pizza."

"I'm just tired. A very full plate just now." Mrs. Compton turns and looks behind her, as though checking her house through two acres of woods. "It is so ravishing this time of year, and usually a bit lonely. I won't have any of your pizza, but I will come in and see my favorite boy, thank you."

As her neighbor steps into the house, Jorie thinks she's aged just in the short time since she saw her outside Lucky Coffee. Bruised flesh under the eyes, lines beginning to carve down from her mouth. A slight stoop diminishing the regal height she normally carries.

"Hello, Oliver Twist!" Mrs. Compton's voice calls from inside, and Jorie pauses and looks out at the trees to see what the mirror is seeing. She can't stop herself, and if she stared long enough, it would start to feel like a Transfiguration. But there are only trees and the evening's stain.

# INTERLUDE

[Excerpt from "October Film Haunt: *Proof of Demons*," by Jorie Stroud, *The October Film Haunt* (archived webpage), November 2012]

Friends, close your eyes and imagine your favorite horror moment, the one that drops your body temperature in an instant. Your skin tingles. It's the moment that taps into your soul-deep sense of awe and wonder. The one that tricks your brain into setting off those ancestral fight-or-flight alarm bells.

Now dial that up by 10. Or more like 100.

I fell as I turned around—and dropped my flashlight, which further proved that your heroic October Film Haunters were in a horror movie, because it went dark as it hit the ground. In that blinked-out moment of light, something approached.

It was thin and huge and difficult to pick apart from the darkness, like a shadow the mind insists is a human shape, gray and mottled. I saw an elongated head but can't say whether I saw eyes, I'd change my answer from yes to no and back again and never settle on either. Don't ask! The thing was too strange.

As though to drive this point home, its chest opened in a great mouth that would have cracked its sternum, if it was something encumbered with bones.

I scrabbled backward until I collided with Colin's legs, and he pulled me to my feet. The Pine Arch Creature—the *freaking Pine Arch Creature*—came toward us. It blurred, it shivered in and out of our ability to see it. Fiction became Reality.

Enriquez had been a documentarian, not a dreamer of monsters.

Another light found it, we saw the curved torso, long and horrible and bent open, unfolding arms reaching down. We ran into the trees whimpering and screaming. In the direction of the moving hole, which we couldn't see without direct light. It wasn't until morning that Beth realized she had a burn across one of her jacket sleeves, like a coffee stain. She must have grazed the edge of the hole, and we all pictured that rolling eye, its wet membrane pressed against her.

Running, weaving between the blurs of tree trunks, until we came to the lake, and I swear I expected to see blue sheets rippling on the surface of the water, just like Márcia Smith did in the film. I think some distant part of me almost believed I *was* Márcia Smith in that moment. All three of us could have been.

The shore was a ribbon of sand dotted with wet pine cones and needles. The water smelled like a chlorinated pool, a false lake on a movie set. Across the surface, imprinted above the trees, were the spectral lines of the mountains to the west.

We caught our breath, and Colin stabbed his light at the cluster of red maples we'd come out of. Somehow, silence returned to the world as we stood there. If those were frogs we'd heard earlier, they were quiet now, waiting to see what would happen. I finally knew all the different layers of the word *breathless*.

Adrenaline looped through me, and in this rubbery, time-frozen, brain-fizzing moment, I remembered the first time I watched *Proof of Demons*. I was in Beth's apartment. It had been raining all day. Something lifted and turned over in my gut when the Pine Arch Creature came out of the trees, like a cord that was light and heavy at the same time, a kind of nausea.

It had seemed at the time like striking gold, a feeling in the same family as that chill brushing your arms when a movie executes a scare really effectively, but more rarefied for people like you and me, a real dread that crawls up into the throat.

I believe what made me love the film was the six minutes of stillness spooling out before the creature's appearance. You know it isn't right, all that stillness, the moment is much too late in its arrival, why is the camera not moving, and it's just so awful when it comes. Someone is playing outside the rules of storytelling.

You love it. This is what you chase after as a fan, as an appreciator. It makes you feel the way lesser horror films make the casual viewer feel, those people who have to weigh the risk of watching scary movies because of a deep and visceral impact you've always tried to understand. You feel an itching envy, you wish you could suspend your disbelief just a little more, you would dial back your addiction to horror a bit if you could trade it for whatever chemical reaction keeps those non-fanatics from falling asleep or makes them check behind the shower curtain when they get up in the night.

*Proof of Demons* stripped the jaded varnish from me a few times over that hour and a half. I had that shower curtain feeling.

Those were my thoughts, all in a spiky jumble I couldn't pull apart then, as my heart slowed down and let the rest of me catch up. What we had just experienced, the fight or flight—THE HORROR MOVIE FILMED HERE HAD JUST COME TO LIFE—left me petrified and elated, like my first viewing of the film if you amplified it until the knob broke. "What a rush" is a cliché for a reason. Neurons sizzling in the middle of that Venn diagram—fright and joy. I looked at Beth and Colin and tried to see it glinting in their eyes, too. The lake water sloshed behind us.

"What the fuck was that?" Colin said, still panting. "That wasn't—there is just no way—"

"The title," Beth cut in when Colin kept stammering. "It's right there in the title. *Proof*. That was always a bit, I don't know, stilted for a title. Not catchy. Enriquez named it something academic, like a paper you'd give at a symposium." She laughed and pulled her hair behind her neck and held it there. "Because maybe it really *is* proof."

"So does that mean there are *five* Transfigurations?" I asked them. "If that was the Pine Arch Creature, the six minutes before it actually opened something. We saw the hole. We saw the *eye*."

Beth pointed out that we hadn't heard a voice say, *I belong with you*, as is the case with the four accepted Transfigurations. I reminded her that we ourselves had said it.

"Why are you two talking about the *movie*?" Colin leaned toward me, staring into my face wide-eyed. "We're in actual danger, if you hadn't noticed. There's no *film* in our name anymore."

I couldn't explain how I felt, though we all felt it. So we debated. I wanted to find the crypt. You're probably yelling, "Don't go in there!" at your screen right now, but . . . I wanted to go in there. If we backtracked just a smidge—not nearly as far as where we'd started running—I thought we could use the copy of Márcia's map that lived in our heads. If the Pine Arch Creature was real, then why not the crypt? Beth agreed. Colin did not.

But it seemed there was a fourth vote. We heard a thin voice repeating what sounded like, *You belong*, growing closer. *You belong, you belong*, with each *long* drawn out more like the sound of a dying speaker, full of raspy clicks. The maples at the edge of the narrow beach began to tremble as a shape pushed through them.

I turned and looked out over the water—and saw the eye again, hovering two feet above the surface of the lake within its impossible hole in the air. It was fixed on me, calm and unblinking. The moon managed to gleam off the white of it from behind the clouds. I thought the iris might have been green, though it's an indeterminate dark color when seen inside the crypt at the end of *Proof of Demons*. Would an eye looking out from hell be green? How long had we been standing out here deciding what to do? Six minutes, maybe?

Beth shouted and before I could turn back and see, we were running again, this time along the shore. Somewhere ahead was the town, behind us a nature preserve. I heard our breaths tearing out of us, and a huge and distant splash, followed by a sound like a car horn drowning. We ran and I saw every spray of sand kicked back at me by Colin's shoes, even in the dark I thought I could make out each grain.

Like so many horror fans and old movie tagline brags, I had never known True Terror. Not this life-and-death kind. It felt like I was half lizard brain bent on survival and half TED Talk about how scary movies might train us to process the inexplicable in real time. I was fully engaged in my immediate surroundings, yet I was cold and detached from it at the same time.

The beach widened to the size mothers could sun themselves on as the kids played in the water. We came to a lake house not long after, its windows dark, and cut up its lawn to the street in front. A sodium lamp burned in the near distance like a beacon, a halo of salvation blurring around it. Civilization had been this close all along, but it was like we had been gone for days, not two and a half hours. To hell and back, Colin would phrase it on the drive home, after a long drone of highway silence had rolled out behind us.

Beth's cell phone had a weak signal. We called a cab because we were only mostly sure we knew how to get back to the car through the trees, and completely sure we didn't want to risk it. As its doors clunked shut, we stared at each other and started examining what we had witnessed, what had pursued us, the breach in the wall between what is real and what is made up.

Every spool of brown tape in a VHS cassette, every cigarette burn on a theater reel, every streaming one and zero—the bare atoms of every movie we'd loved seemed suddenly to be infected, or at least rewritten. Hélène Enriquez was a true occultist, tuned into a real supernatural frequency that changed everything.

We waited in a diner until first light before retrieving our journals and backpacks from the cemetery. We sat there with our coffee mugs and thought about how the night might reshape us.

And how we'll ever come close to topping this year's haunt.

# CHAPTER SEVEN

## Jorie

▶▶ She pulls onto the gravel driveway that hopefully wraps around to Beth's Airbnb, the little hatchback jostling between polite rows of spiny red pines. The gravel mutters under her tires, and she wishes she could have Dave back for just a few hours.

And Colin, of course. The two of them after a long drive full of earnest talk, the easy catharsis of a horror marathon waiting with Beth at the end of the lane. This feels like the one day she would let herself fall back into her old life.

Jorie tops a small rise and the property opens out on the rim of a soft valley, another postcard, like a vineyard with ten thousand trees instead of grapes. It's the blanket of foliage laid out at the beginning of a film, waking fall colors muted by the morning's rain. A drone camera would be tracking the shot from above.

Something awful could happen in those trees, or in the cabin nestled against them, in the approaching swell of cellos.

It seems vulgar that Lake Champlain is too far to the west to see from here, but she can sense it. There are splotches of white matchstick trunks and yellowed crowns across the acreage, paper birches a week or more ahead of their deciduous neighbors. The red maples are trying to catch up, and the color tide is turning against the evergreens. It's almost October, and she still hasn't found a month to replace it as her favorite.

A low ridge of mountains sits above the trees to the right, looming over the cabin.

Beth is standing on the porch. It takes Jorie a second to recognize her, but not because of the years. Her hair is short now, barely reaching her chin, still willful and jet black but reined in at last. She's ten years more beautiful, from the red-and-black lumberjack flannel to the black jeans, even the leather sandals with dark green socks. She could have stepped out of some Manhattan wilderness.

Jorie gets out of the car and just looks at Beth for a moment. "Dave gave up the ghost in 2017," she finally says, and pats the warm hood of the nameless Nissan hatchback. Beth smiles at that, but her eyes close as she does it. Jorie cries first, though, before she even gets to the three steps leading up to her lost friend.

"Have you *really* not seen any horror movies this whole time?" Beth says.

Jorie stiffens, her gait even changes, making her feet drag louder through the leaves. The trees quiver everywhere in a breeze, in a long sigh.

"No, I haven't," Jorie says, and clears her throat to get above a whisper. "I looked up a few because they broke through the barriers into my boring mainstream life. Making myself want to see new movies felt like a... I guess it was a penance I deserved. I know so many good films have been made. New directors I've never heard of. It's weird knowing there are *Scream* sequels I'll never see, and sometimes I would start to *ache* for them. But I always put myself in a dark place when I let my brain go there, like stomach cramps and mental spiraling. So I stopped."

"I'm sorry," Beth says. "I'm out of the loop, trust me. I lost most of my appetite for scary stuff. But I still miss how it used to feel. I wish we could curl up tonight and start an Argento marathon."

"I miss that, too." A new sob surprises Jorie, crawling up her throat, but she swallows it and goes back to picking the maples out of the gathered trees. Their leaves are just beginning to stain with their beautiful dying.

After their awkward hug that tried to bridge such a long gap, the forest inspired enough awe in them, the kind of majesty that would sneer at the word *woods*, that they found a path and wandered. Breakfast could wait. Beth didn't even change out of her sandals.

At first they talked about Beth's wife, Monse, an assistant director who has finally accepted the *assistant* part and begun to thrive, happier downgrading her dreams in an industry that still belongs to men. And Oli, his difficulties adjusting to the slow semi-reclusive life Jorie's made for them up here, the burden she's placed on him, to be her world, the shame of that and how she's tried to use it to replace all the older shame. The trauma and hindsight of Eric.

But then a silence that slowly changed color like the leaves.

"I hated you, I know you know that," Beth finally says, walking a few feet ahead in the trees so that Jorie can't see her face. "I was crushed and I didn't know how to deal with it."

It's not easy for Jorie to keep up. Beth's legs have maybe six inches on hers. The morning is a wet cold, clinging, soaked in the smells of resin and clean mint. "I know you hated me," she says, "and I wanted to reach out so many times."

Beth goes on, needing to get over this hurdle. "But I didn't come up here to hash it out. I'm letting go of the last of it. I think I can." She stops and turns to face Jorie, brushes a maple leaf out of her hair and the hair out of her eyes. "I came because you made my life so good until then, and because those files you sent are disturbing. They're awesome, sure. I want to know what their deal is from a filmmaking perspective, I want to know if it's Enriquez, I want more, I'll admit all that. I'm not immune even if you sort of killed that part of me."

"I feel the same way." Jorie makes herself turn fully toward Beth and look right at her face. "I almost feel like the old me, the one who did so many stupid things, is haunting my house ever since I watched that tape."

Beth reaches out and comes close to taking Jorie's hand, but reconsiders and lets her arm drop. "If Enriquez is the one who shot that stuff," she says, "do you see what that means? That she's zeroed in on *you*. She could have it in her head that you ruined her career."

"It just—sounds so unlikely when you say it out loud like that." Jorie pauses and takes in the endless quiet of the trees. "What if it's a fan? She never made another movie, so maybe somebody took it upon themselves to, I don't know, do their own version. I didn't even tell you what happened after we hung up the other day. There were blue sheets laid over my grandparents' graves. And a sign propped up next to them with Hannah's name on it. That's terrifying. But I keep telling myself it's like a movie. That feels less like danger, right?"

Beth groans at that. "I don't know if it's danger in a police way, but it still counts. Do you think an amateur could have made those scenes so good? What does it mean that she, or whoever, filmed them *here* and wanted to make it personal?"

"If it was a threat or something, wouldn't there be . . ." Jorie doesn't want to say it. "Wouldn't they have put someone playing Hannah in the footage? Like, pan over to the coffin and it's her funeral? Or put me in it with the creature coming after me? Why are they just rewritten versions of that one scene?"

"Jorie—" Beth stops and shakes her head. She looks up at the treetops, the tips of them like an optical illusion, extending miles into the sky. Jorie knows what's coming next. It's a question Beth asked her more than once, back then, but it will be different now. Jorie will be expected to have the wisdom of hindsight.

"Why did I do it?" she says before Beth can find the words and look back down at her. "Why did I take a perfectly normal film haunt about *Proof of Demons* and make up a giant lie about it?" She's trembling, her soul is shaking loose its oldest troubles.

"No," Beth says. She's still watching the trees spear the bright after-rain sky, and she sighs a brief white cloud that's just visible above her face. Either the cold or the memories have made her eyes wet. "I told you I didn't come to rehash all that. I'm just worried. I don't like what was on that tape."

"But you *should* rehash. That whole year, I wanted something *bigger*, I wanted meta and edgy, and I was too stupid to think—" Jorie stops. Something is moving in the forest, a few hundred feet from them. A smudge of green stepping—maybe—behind the trunk of a birch that's too skinny to hide it. It's almost the color of the pines. And there's a gleam of light, like someone holding a mirror.

Or a camera.

She takes a few steps forward, leaning to her left, then right, but she can't see anything now. There's no crunch of leaves. No one could hide that well or that quickly.

"What is it?" Beth says, and in the same instant, from the depths of the trees, a voice calls out, "You killed her!" Not close, but held by every wet atom of the air.

"I belong with you!" a second voice shouts, young and rough and male, somewhere near the first.

Then Beth spins to her right, as though catching someone else watching them from the south, and runs after whatever she's seen. Jorie follows her, and even here in this moment, her mind is flicking through images and aching flashbacks of actors abruptly racing through trees, clumsy with panic and doomed to be separated and devoured by the entity that's been dreamed up for them.

But soon Beth stops and leans down to put her hands on her thighs. "Fucking hell," she gasps. "I am so out of shape."

Jorie needs a minute, too, and so they listen to at least one person crashing through nature. The noises fade until they can only hear their own struggling breaths. Jorie thinks she hears a laugh, and then there's nothing.

"Did you hear that shit?" Beth says. "'I belong with you.' Jesus. What is this, a *September* film haunt?" She spits on the ground and wipes her mouth with one of her lumberjack sleeves.

"I can't decide if that was really immature or creepy," Jorie says. "But either way, that's something a fan would yell out."

"Probably. It was too childish, too . . . I don't know what."

"Too Reddit?" Once Jorie would have laughed as she said this. It does feel like something from an online forum, but it's still frightening. And she deserves it. If Beth won't dredge it all up, maybe someone else should.

"Yeah, that." Beth straightens up and looks around. "Otherwise, this is a beautiful place, if I didn't mention it before. Is it even necessary to say Vermont's beautiful, though?"

"It's inferred this time of year." Jorie smiles but it's shaky. "I'm glad someone was out here."

Beth gives her a bemused look, raised eyebrows and exaggerated shock.

"No, really," Jorie says. "It means you don't have to decide whether or not to believe me." It takes her a moment to realize she's crying. It's wonderful and awful to have someone here who knows what she did. "But maybe their point is that Hannah should be alive and those kids' lives shouldn't have been ruined. Colin should be in these trees with us."

"Don't put the weight of the whole internet on your shoulders," Beth says. "I would have hoped that ten years would let you accept that much. We need a new Jorie, a strong mama bear Jorie who's a long way past putting herself in the hospital. Yes, I read about that. Let's go back to the cabin, and you can rehash if you want. I'll listen." Beth's face goes dark, their easy togetherness fracturing for a second. Her voice cracks a little, too. "And it will suck, but we never really talked about Colin."

"I'd like that. It would be nice to talk about him. You can get out of those wet socks, too."

Beth turns back the way they came. "My feet are freezing. Whose idea was it to wear sandals in a forest?"

Two old hands at the craft of horror, jaded by a thousand films, walking through the damp pocket of wilderness. The sky flat and white, the dark fairy tale dissipating to leave regular, difficult life behind. There's even a moment to laugh at the start of a forgotten anecdote.

But someone is waiting for them on the cabin's porch. The present comes back with a jolt. The person Jorie glimpsed in the trees earlier is standing there, draped in a pale green bedsheet. It's identical to the ones on the videotape.

Beth puts her arm out across Jorie's chest, like Jorie used to do when she had to abruptly step on Dave's brake pedal. An inherent, half-maternal instinct. "That's not a person," she says, and she's right, there are no feet or ankles below the hem of the sheet. It's been hung from a hook in the ceiling of the porch.

Beth walks up and yanks it down, tearing a long hole that turns the sheet into more of a cape. She wads it up and throws it out into the yard, and it opens like a horrific bird, like something waiting to be filled with physical intent. Jorie watches it flatten and settle on the gravel of the driveway.

It's only fair, Jorie thinks, that someone would make up their own October Film Haunt story and put her in the middle of it.

Her first day back at Lantman's Market is tomorrow. She needs the thirty-odd hours a week to help with the stunning property taxes up here. The scraping-by life of a single mom pushing forty doesn't have a pause button. Her boss, Chip, will keep hitting on her with his carefully chosen comments—*It's so good to have you back*—and Jorie will keep feeling guilty for asking so much of Sam and Mrs. Compton. There's another manuscript to edit, waiting to be put off until she starts to panic about delivering it on time.

But that's tomorrow. She wants the breakfast Beth promised. She wants to talk to her friend. About Hannah, yes, and Colin, too, but then maybe it can be like it used to be for a few minutes, with Dave and the open road. Thoughts on what it's like to get older. Beth's film-editing work, and Jorie won't even let herself be jealous. They'll figure out what to do about the sequel they seem to be in.

*You deserve this*, her mind whispers again. *It's not the weight of the internet, it's only your share of it.*

"Jorie? You okay?" Beth is still standing where she tore the sheet down. "Hey. It's just fans, like you said. They call themselves Rickies, right?"

"But they know where you are," Jorie says. She isn't scared, not quite. She's unsettled. Reminded of the past, when everything had a tinge of unpleasant revelation.

"You heard them laughing," Beth says. "They're kids, probably film school guys. What are they going to do, scamper off to their online Enriquez altar? They just want Pine Arch content. A shitty student film—okay, we'll make it really boring for them. Act one, Beth goes out to buy eggs. Jorie closes her curtains."

"I don't know. Guys with guns came to your apartment once." Jorie looks out at the trees before turning back to Beth. "I have an actual kid. He's only eight."

"The guys with guns got bored pretty quick, too," Beth says, coming down the steps onto the gravel. "And all these years later, no one has died. There's no outcry, no one cares who we are anymore. Look, we want to know why and how these guys followed us here. But we're not in danger. We'll lock our doors. Don't go cemetery wandering."

*Funeral watching*, Jorie thinks. "Beth, I can't put either of you in a bad situation."

"You're not. I don't want to speak for Oli, but I'm pretty sure we both want to be by your side through whatever prank this is."

Jorie looks at the dead green sheet on the ground. The new ugly color of it itches at her, insisting that something has changed. But Beth is surely right, they're Enriquez worshipers putting their spin on things.

"Okay, we're on the same page," Jorie says. "Now I want to see the inside of this hipster cabin." She finds something like a smile for Beth, still a little awed that she's here. Really here.

# INTERLUDE

[Excerpt from "Monster or Monster: When Online Influencers Bring Horror Into the Real World," by Salma Trabelsi, *Vice*, October 25, 2018]

[But] precedent is everywhere on the internet—or will come along soon enough in our increasingly polarized, screen-driven lives. Some seem to seek out precedent simply for the purpose of setting it, staking a claim on some piece of the mental landscape of America, those amber waves of memes. With algorithms monetizing propaganda and misinformation, even the internet is running out of unlit corners. And when everything is out in the light, anything can feel true.

This was the case almost exactly a year before the Slender Man stabbings, 800 miles away in Arden, North Carolina, when 17-year-old Hannah Kim died in a botched occult ritual. Though less manic and murderous than what transpired in Wisconsin in 2014, it was no less misguided, no less a row of dominoes trailing back to that blurring of fact and fiction.

In fact, stories of the Pine Arch Creature seem to have been constructed for reasons beyond a new fiction paradigm. It was an online effort—a scary movie Pizzagate, if you will. What strikes Dr. Amanda Pitro, professor of cultural studies at the University of Virginia, as insidiously different about the Pine Arch Creature legend is "the intent, almost from the start, to convince fans that it wasn't a myth at all."

Originally appearing in the 2009 cult horror film *Proof of Demons* (written, directed, and produced by the [possibly pseudonymous Hélène Enriquez](#)), the tall, amorphous figure skipped its origin story and proceeded directly to true horror message boards. This postfiction growth was possible because the movie was rumored to be a documentary hiding in plain sight within a fictional framework. Literally a haunted film. It gave fans enough creepy details, clues, and patterns to build a supernatural conspiracy theory.

"Certain online communities," says Dr. Pitro, "exist as a sort of virtual campfire, and people have always told each other spooky stories around campfires. There's a camaraderie to it, a collaborative nature of adding to the narrative. In a vacuum, it could be an interesting exercise in meta-folklore. Like Slender Man, the Pine Arch Creature was a new round-robin species of creepypasta, as these online fictions are often called. But once someone claimed to have summoned it and suggested dangerous activities to replicate this experience, the fandom began to cross the line of culpability."

Late on a warm May night, Hannah Kim, a high school student who had recently been accepted to Duke University, was buried in a shallow grave dug by her friends and left there for a length of time corresponding with a supposed "transfiguration" ritual inspired by *Proof of Demons*. This particular effort to summon the Pine Arch Creature did not originate in the film itself but from a Reddit claim. According to details revealed in the ensuing trial, the young woman panicked and suffocated within a few agonizing minutes.

True responsibility on the internet is a slippery slope, whether you ask legal experts or ethics professors or the president's most ardent, believe-anything supporters. Two of Hannah Kim's friends, both 18 on the night they urged her into the grave, were convicted of involuntary manslaughter and endangering a minor. The anonymous Redditors, meanwhile, remain free and presumably ambivalent behind their keyboards, hundreds or thousands of miles away from those pine woods.

Two prominent names that popularized the claim were Jorie Stroud and her October Film Haunt blog group. While Stroud and her partners Beth Kowalczyk and Colin Davies—the latter of whom passed away less than a year after Hannah Kim from a drug overdose—weren't directly involved in the first accounts of *Proof of Demons* featuring genuine occult activity, they helped it go viral. Stroud's blog post about their visit to the North Carolina cemetery—where a key scene of the movie was filmed—and the group's summoning of the Pine Arch Creature spilled over the walls of Reddit onto Twitter and Facebook thanks to her large following. It's worth noting, after all, that Kim died wearing an October Film Haunt T-shirt.

Stroud, who could not be reached for comment for this article, admitted that she fabricated the narrative of the October Film Haunt's visit to the site where Hannah Kim would later die. Crucially, her fateful blog post even included a hyperlink to the Reddit post detailing the supposed burial ritual.

But perhaps more than drawing attention to potential danger, Stroud's impassioned writing about experiencing real horror rather than watching it on a screen was influential. It spoke to readers, and she had many of them at the time. She presented it as something rapturous and profound, adding a resonant chord to what others had already invented about the legend. It's no surprise that younger fans wanted to take that next step and feel what she claimed to feel. Horror is, in some ways, a genre of transcendence.

That Enriquez cast Academy Award–nominated Roger Eilertsen (1978's *Came Down the Mountain*) as the cult leader seemed to lend even more weight to these imaginings, as the character actor had once garnered a reputation for his esoteric lifestyle. Fans pointed to his involvement as yet more "proof" to echo the film's title.

Popular artist Trevor Henderson—maker of his own urban legends, most recently Siren Head, a massive, eerie humanoid creature whose head is a fleshy, yes, siren full of strange noises—was a prominent catalyst for the online proliferation of the Pine Arch Creature. He created it, in fact. Henderson was credited as a creative consultant for *Proof of Demons* and has since described his commission to design the creature. He cheered the modern legend leaking out of the film—but soon became uncomfortable and spoke out against it.

"It was a really cool folklore for a minute there," Henderson says. "A great monster that lingered with you. The movie has a unique way of blending the occult and slasher subgenres. But then people were pushing these rituals. Some of them were like self-harm. It wasn't just for fun anymore, so I checked out, which was easy because I never had any of the rights to the Pine Arch Creature. Looking back, I can see the root of that kind of thinking that's everywhere now, that sort of desperation to believe anything you want even when the reality is right there. There's a difference between make-believe and post-truth. One of them isn't dangerous."

Stroud had been driven from social media by the time the trial began. A particularly vicious Twitter account (since suspended) named Slander Man helped generate death threats against the members of the October Film Haunt. I'll emphasize that the online influencers mentioned here have done nothing that can be categorized as legally wrong, but the debate about responsibility in a digital world rages on.

Meanwhile, luckily, the Pine Arch Creature seems to have faded back to the furthest strands of the web here in 2018, cloaked in shadows once more. The niches can have it. Through tragedy and perspective, perhaps we have learned not to give these urban legends so much daylight.

*Jorie Stroud, Beth Kowalczyk, Roger Eilertsen, and various Reddit users could not be reached for comment for this article.*

# CHAPTER EIGHT

## Beth

▶▶ Her second day up here is brilliant and crisp and almost cold. Beth can't believe how late she slept in, and the sun has a thread of summer in it as she sits with her coffee on the little deck that juts out from the cabin's attic loft. She's surrounded by calm beauty and freshness and all the metaphors she could want for healing. Redemption, even.

It was good to see her friend, and kind of stunning to think they were separated longer than they were inseparable. Stunning, too, that Jorie spent nearly three hours here before going home to her son, and that it felt okay. Just hugging her, feeling her warmth, standing in the forest with her, talking about darkness and light with her, it all made a through line for Beth, something hinging the parts of her life together the way she used to think they might end up fitting.

That's too dramatic a way to think of it, but she doesn't care.

Not a complete line, though. The thing in Beth's way, the only roadblock left, is the belief that Colin would be alive if Jorie hadn't turned their film haunts into lies. There might have been no ruin at all. Jorie said it out loud herself yesterday, and her anguish was still raw after all this time. Her eyes wide and glassy, the look of someone going into shock.

Beth has always shared the blame around. Someone else made up the burial rite to summon a fictional monster out of a fictional movie. Others had already built up the road that led Hannah Kim and her friends into such foolishness—Jorie only added the biggest sign pointing to that road.

Hannah died in a pointless grave chasing the high that Jorie sold to her. She died wearing an October Film Haunt shirt that Jorie designed herself. It was an easy complicity to fixate on. Beth understands. She's always understood that.

Except Colin is still there, an aching wall in Beth's mind. He wasn't a stranger to chemicals before Hannah died, but he had waded deeper into them by the time the trial started. Jorie was the reason he got into a fight when three guys showed up at his apartment.

Someone had doxxed him on Twitter just a week earlier. An oxycodone prescription helped him through two broken ribs and kept helping him until he joined the tide of the opioid crisis and died in his bed with a spoon, traces of fentanyl in the heroin in his blood.

She was always a moment or two away from being in love with him. It didn't matter that she was already mostly dating women. She knows he felt the same. But he crumbled too fast for her to help, at least from a state away. None of them knew how to handle the ruins of that last blog post. Beth has carried her own guilt.

She was the one who found his body, tucked into bed, a crust of foam around his mouth that had dried while creeping down his left cheek toward the pillow. She'd driven up to Knoxville to spend the weekend with him, convinced he had a serious problem. She was going to get through to him, she was a third of the October Film Haunt, she had her own death threats, they could share the burden.

A syringe and a spoon lay on his nightstand, as they had in endless other tableaus. Colin was already cold on the bed. The late-evening sun lay on him in stripes from the blinds, and she'd gone to the window and watched the fading light glow in the distant Tennessee River while she gathered the resolve she needed to call for an ambulance.

In the days after, abuse and memes kept swirling in the online ether, and Beth's future kept breaking into pieces she didn't recognize. Before long she was doxxed, too. She once saw two young men with rifles across their camouflaged chests in her apartment building's parking lot, their legs spread in some macho combat pose as they scanned the row of windows on the third floor.

She had trouble getting film work for a while, but as her connection to Jorie severed and she left the horror genre behind, the skin of it all began to slough off her. She was tender underneath, but it mostly healed. There was new skin.

Yesterday she told Jorie most of the truth about wanting to let it go, and being ready to. She's talked it over with her wife. She feels the rest of it softening, and she's glad she came up here, where maybe the ache of losing Colin can start to soften, too.

Jorie wanted her to go back to Brooklyn—just in case, she said—but Beth refused. She's between film jobs. They'll keep each other safe, if they need to be kept safe.

This is her first time in Vermont. Her parents took her to Maine once, she was thirteen and it was the summer before her dad's heart attack, the last summer that felt entirely good. She begged them to drive inland to Bangor to see where Stephen King lived. She remembers the wonderfully Gothic Halloween fence surrounding his house, she remembers her joyful yell when she saw the statue of Paul Bunyan, the water tower, Pennywise's sewer drain. It had started raining, and she'd felt like she was another blessed loser in his books. Maybe that was the start of what led her to this cabin.

But this place feels so different. The Maine in her memory is the craggy face of a giant, all broken rock and harsh beauty, the pitted cheeks of land, and Vermont is something like being lost in the giant's wild, soft beard.

The sun spreads across the trees crowding the cabin, the mountains burnished with coming fall if she cranes her neck around to her left. There are no smells of exhaust or hints of garbage in the air. New York could drift away like a new continent if she let it.

And that tape scares her. She feels like she dreamed about it all night.

She pushes aside the book she brought out with her but never opened and wakes her laptop up. Each of the four funeral scenes is still open in its preview window on the desktop. Yesterday she called them the *Proof of Demons* remix album, because they're more than deleted scenes but, she's pretty sure, less than parts of a sequel. This was somewhere in a conversation that ended with a tentative decision, that a fan, a Rickie—surely no more than two or three Rickies—had somehow tracked Jorie down to refresh the Enriquez urban legend.

But something nagged at Beth the whole time, while they were watching the scenes and dissecting them after. Talking about Colin, how he had died and what they missed about him, had made the feeling stronger. It had something to do with the porch below. A connection somewhere. She tries to let her mind fade back from it, hoping it will come on its own.

She opens a web browser and goes to octoberfilmhaunt.com just to verify that it doesn't exist, that its ghost is still lost under a decade of digital dust. The domain name is for sale. She doesn't realize she was holding her breath until half-frozen wisps of it drift over the deck railing.

Next is Twitter, or whatever it's called now. While deciding what to search for, assuming she'll have to go to Reddit to find anything new about Enriquez or the Pine Arch Creature, she clicks on the bell icon to check her notifications. She's been mentioned in something from an account named The *Original* October Film Haunt: "Will @kowalczykfilm join the Proof of Demons reboot?"

She stares at her name, the blue-gray coffee mug trembling in her hand, until her heart slows down.

The post and presumably the account itself are less than an hour old, and even though there are fewer than fifty followers, the tweet already has thirty-one likes, twenty retweets, and a dozen or so comments alternating between "Yessss so here for this" and "seriously how dare you." She stops reading when she gets to "y'all belong in a grave not that poor girl."

Of course the person who sent the tape to Jorie would drag all this onto social media. It's where everything went wrong in the first place, so where else would phase two of the harassment begin? Jorie was right—she and Beth shouldn't engage with this anywhere online. Angry GIFs blink in Beth's face. One of them features a cartoon ghost shaking a fist, and the rippling white of its arm makes it click in her mind, somehow, in a way that the gift left for them could not.

The blue sheets from the film changing to that yellowed green yesterday. Colin's death. The exact color of the bedsheet pooled on his chest when she found him. Half her attention is stuck on Michael Myers raising a knife over and over in a two-second loop beneath The *Original* October Film Haunt's post, the other half is trying to find her phone to call Jorie and tell her. But it's the one thing she didn't bring out here.

She starts to go back inside and sees the phone lying on the deck, where it must have fallen from the pocket of her pajamas. Her face unlocks the screen as she bends and picks it up, and when she stands, there's movement out on the periphery of her vision. She looks down.

Only the trees look back up at her. The melting crayon box of them, shadowed gaps between clusters of trunks. If Jorie were here, she'd ask her what she saw, already out of her chair. Both of them remembering more *Who's there?* movie moments than they could ever count. But there's no horror fan skulking in there, nothing more than a bird or a breath of wind.

A booming thump comes from the main room of the cabin. It's heavy enough to shake everything, she feels it through her feet out here on the deck. The refrigerator tipping over, someone with a sledgehammer.

She told Jorie to lock her doors, then went ahead and forgot to follow her own advice.

She turns to run through the loft and down the stairs but instead goes to the railing and stares at the short roof of the porch. Most of her waiting for someone to come sprinting out of the cabin, a smaller part trained behind her for footsteps.

More nothing, just corrugated tin, white dusty gravel, fading grass, the tree line. Yesterday Jorie confessed to feeling the residue of the old thrill when she was at the cemetery, when the two of them were out in these trees. The hunger for fear. Beth isn't immune to it, either, but it's still sleeping in the past. It hardly stirs now.

After no one makes a dash for the trees, she goes back into the attic. Around an old desk with a chair pushed under it, past a tall wardrobe with a pale green bedsheet standing just inside the parted doors, not seeing any of it. Down the plank stairs, and she nearly stumbles into the empty living space.

The room looks just like it did when she woke up. Or almost—a black VHS cassette is on the coffee table. FUNERAL WATCHING—COPY is printed along the white spine sticker.

Beth doesn't bother with the tape. She runs straight through the front door, down the steps, across the lawn into the gloom of the trees.

# CHAPTER NINE

## Jorie

▶▶ The mirror from Oli's closet is still leaning against the house, beside the front door, when she comes home in the already west-leaning sun. Jorie is tired, full-shift tired even though she only worked late morning to afternoon. She ignores the mirror, doesn't even look to see the trees reflected within its frame, and goes straight out back to tend her dying garden.

This was her grandfather's modest pride, but now it's a sad piece of the yard, nothing more than the latest way she's been trying to fill the decade-wide hole in her.

In Jorie's worse moments, she thinks of this hole as something she's buried in, as though she shares a kinship with Hannah. A dreadful, wistful thing to imagine. But it's also something to trigger the guilt and bring it to the surface. Like using a finger to make herself throw up.

Her New England asters, the coneflowers and black-eyed Susans, all her googled Vermont-proof choices have been wilting almost since they came up and bloomed in the spring. It's the second time she's made gardening a forced hobby, and like before, every petal seems to sense her lack of passion. This round she's been having better luck with the indoor houseplants, especially the rubber tree, which loves the dresser in her bedroom.

She would have preferred not to work the meat counter on her first day back at Lantman's, but that was where Chip put her. Maybe it kept her enclosed for him. Her arms ache from the slicer, it even hurts a little to lift the watering can.

But what she really wants is to hear from Beth. Even an acknowledgment of the two texts Jorie sent her after the lunch rush. She knows Beth wouldn't have a change of heart and go back to New York, so she must be busy. Some unexpected work might have come up.

Only one corner of her mind has the crawling sort of thoughts, the anxious what-if tangents she's gotten better about not following. Beth is fine. But Jorie keeps thinking of the two people who were in the forest with them near the cabin yesterday.

She checks her phone—nothing—and waters her failing plants. Probably too much after the recent rain. There's an hour or so to decide when she'll pick Oli up from Sam's, so she'll do a bit of research on the Rickies, read the Reddit posts she saw in the search results the other day. Gather up some forward motion, anything to drag her brain back toward its happy place, where the biggest problem is watching bad TV when she should be editing.

Most of the day it was easy. She's been so light on her feet, the simple joy of Beth like caffeine in her blood.

When the watering's done, she wakes her laptop in the cathedral light that pours faithfully through the dining nook window. Still nothing from Eric about child support. He hasn't always had steady work, and it's made getting help tricky. As far as Jorie knows, he's been living with his parents the last several months.

Shaking the thought of him away, she lets Google lead her down the dim holes of Reddit, where she finds something.

"Get this waste of time out of our faces"

"But enriquez/the pine arch/verified irl sightings all coming ***SEQUEL*** stay tuned"

The photo itself is nothing. Not a fake, just wishful thinking. She finds it in /r/Scarymovies with the heading "New Pine Arch Creature sighting in Providence RI?" It looks like it was taken with one of those old Nokia cell phones, washed out by a flashlight, scoured by digital grain. Impossible to guess at what the shape in it might be, or if the columns to the left of it are even trees.

But that ***SEQUEL*** comment almost blinking like an old flash animation. This is what her internet detective skills, amateur as they are, have been looking for. The trouble is that there's nothing else in the thread.

Next is /r/CultWeird, where she comes across "POD 2 casting wish list," a thread that's less than three months old. She clicks into it, and one of the comments stands out as though the text has been highlighted. In early August, a user named helenelives wrote "Someone needs to take the Márcia torch with *authenticity* right?" Jorie is certain the reply—from the handle pinedemon—is a reference to her: "JS in VT confirmed." There's no elaboration, nothing around it to provide context.

Cold crawls all over Jorie. Her hands twist at each other in her lap.

The last comment is from yesterday and seemingly innocent—"Florence

Pugh would be a great Marcia type imo"—but beneath it, helenelives responded with "BK with JS." Beth Kowalczyk with Jorie Stroud. She's sure of it. And with real initials being used, they don't mind her knowing. She can't decide if that makes it worse or not.

The first of those thoughts she doesn't want to have crawls out of its corner, into the light.

Beth doesn't answer when she calls. Jorie taps the end button before voicemail picks up and opens Twitter—she'll never be able to think of it as any other name—on her phone. There's a 3 hovering over the notification icon. Nothing on her account links her to Jorie Stroud or the October Film Haunt or anything else from when she had a future. Her name online, in the few places she lets herself go, is Wilt Flowers. A handful of followers, nothing horror-related anywhere. She's anonymous.

Something bad is happening here, something with momentum is moving toward her, and she sits by the window and looks out at the paper birches across the lawn for a full minute before her hands clench into fists. She will not be fucked with, and neither will Beth.

Beth not answering her calls is nothing. She's just not around for a few hours. She mentioned meeting up with her friend, the one who owns the cabin, at some point while she's up here. It's nothing.

Is someone making a movie and putting them in it?

She imagines pulling Oli out of school and going back to Georgia for a few weeks, letting him stay with Eric at his parents' house. An awful thought, but no matter what her history with Eric is, she knows he would never raise anything more than his voice to Oli.

And she'll spend that time doing what? She doesn't know. Hide. Borrow money for a hotel. Force these people to find someone else for the Márcia Smith character, someone who's given a choice and a script.

What she does know is that something connected to those Reddit comments is waiting for her in these notifications. She clicks the bell and sees a reply that's just her handle, @notaredemptionarc, tagged by The *Original* October Film Haunt. She stares at that account name until her eyes go dry and she starts blinking, then taps the post.

One of the scenes from the VHS tape pops up on her screen, the final segment, with the arms of several Pine Arch creatures beckoning from the birch trees. She lets it play out, the voice of the off-screen eulogist tinny in her phone's speaker. It's a short clip, chopped off not long after the blond boy turns and looks toward the woods, as he slips off his chair and starts walking toward the waving, lumpy arms.

Something, some minor element, is different in this version, but she can't tell what it is. Then lines of pale yellow text appear on the screen like subtitles: *Proof of demons?* and then *#funeralwatching tell the trees you belong with them* and ending with *Record 6 minutes of stillness to be film haunted.*

It jumps to a new scene, different light and different trees, the view from what might be the attic deck on Beth's Airbnb. The gaps between all those trunks. White gravel edging the frame. Three seconds later, the video ends.

The clip and the tag of Jorie were also shared by Beth an hour ago.

Jorie stares at what Beth wrote to accompany the video, sickened by her words but still not sure if she's really seeing them. "Excited to have a supporting role in the next and final chapter of PROOF OF DEMONS, currently in production. #dontcallitacomeback #thisishowitfeltjorie"

Scrolling back down, tapping the profile picture of The *Original* October Film Haunt's profile—a simple "OFH" stylized so that the letters begin to merge, the avatar they always used because it matched the shirts in the online store. She wipes tears from her cheeks, but they're replaced within seconds. She sees the "Will @kowalczykfilm join the Proof of Demons reboot?" post from two hours before Beth shared the video, and her confusion is swarming now, it itches and has sound and weight and too much texture in her head.

She goes back to Beth's post. A thousand views in four hours. How could Beth do this to her? How could she do it to Hannah's family and Colin's memory? A moment ago she was cold, but now heat is flaring in her face. She wants this anger to replace the deep shock of hurt.

When she first pulled the VHS tape out of the envelope, she wondered who was left to know there was ever a Jorie who would want it. She should have realized then, back in the opening scene of this. It was Beth all along, a classic horror twist.

She swipes the app closed before she loses what breath she has left. Before her eyes linger on any replies. There were nights, the longest nights before the hospital, when she would hyperventilate in her apartment. The pacing would help most of the time. She doesn't think she's had an episode like that since a few weeks after Colin's memorial service.

Her phone rings while it's still in her hand, making her jump, but she answers it without looking at the screen. "Beth?"

"Hey, it's me," Sam says. Her voice is so bright and normal and unworried that Jorie doesn't recognize it for a second. "I was wondering when you're coming over to get your wolf. Wait until you hear what the head of marketing did in the Zoom today. Disciplinary meeting, minimum."

The tree line across the yard is still. There's nothing in those birches. She'll go see Beth on her way to get Oli, because it will only get harder to do it later. She stands up and paces with the phone, for the first time in so long, her lungs wanting to squeeze shut, thoughts falling off shelves in her memory.

Maybe she won't go. She and Oli will have a quiet evening and she'll look into cheap airline tickets after he goes to bed. "I'm leaving now," she tells Sam, "but I have a stop to make first. I have to deal with someone."

"Is everything okay?"

"I don't know." Another urge to cry comes, how could Beth do this, but she shoves it to the back of her mind at once. "I'm sorry, Sam. I'll be there soon."

The world is hushed in front of the house, the sky blushing a jaundiced rose color. Streaks of clouds. A memory of Beth pushes at her, the two of them hiking a mile and a half of the Appalachian Trail back in 2006, turning around and coming back. They asked someone to take a photo of them at the sign marking the beginning. They flexed their biceps, as though to claim they started in Maine and did all two thousand miles. There's probably some symbolism in there.

When she reaches the gravel driveway, she can hear how hard the anger is making her steps. The stones squeal under her feet as she gets in the car.

Jorie reaches the turnoff for Beth's cabin as the sun grazes the soft felt of the mountains. The crowding spindled shadows of the red pines have turned the driveway into a throat. She's had trouble breathing the whole way here, her skin is flushed and her hands feel numb on the wheel.

She almost talked herself out of coming. If Beth has any sense, she's gone. There's no reason for her to still be in Vermont. She drew Jorie in with the warmth of reunion and hope, all to make her betrayal—her revenge, Jorie supposes—wound more.

Unless she's waiting for Jorie at the end of this driveway with a camera.

In a horror film, the Beth character would have nursed all this bitterness, carried the resentment around with her since Colin died. She would see an opportunity for the Jorie character to get her comeuppance. There's a reason so many plot synopses are about the past catching up with someone. Old sins like to come home.

Did someone contact Beth about a *Proof of Demons* project? Is it too coincidental that Jorie reached out to her, too? Is this really just for some movie? There are too many questions. None of the answers seem possible. She makes a choked screaming noise at everything she can only guess at and accelerates the car, changing the timbre of the gravel under her tires. It rattles her undercarriage.

And where is Hélène Enriquez in all this? Jorie thinks Enriquez isn't involved at all—it's both reassuring and terrifying if she's the one behind it, the mysterious director stepping forward from the murk of controversy and conspiracy. But the thought has no origin point. There's nothing to hang it on.

Jorie is at the top of the low hill now, descending into the vista bookmarked by the hipster cabin. She sees Beth's car and pushes the questions away.

The scene has the look of an abandoned film set. Of course her mind would insist on seeing it this way. The cabin is dark and the front door is open. She wants to slam her own door shut when she stops the car, righteous and inflamed, but she leaves it open to match the cabin, only reaching inside to take the keys out and stop the maddening chime.

She glances to the left and sees something moving inside the dimness of the forest, a daub of red slipping between trees. "Beth!" she shouts. There is no thought yet of something darker waiting for her, nothing firm enough to push through the membrane of what she thinks Beth has done.

But she does remind herself that in a film, the music would drop into the soundtrack right now—a thick buzzing tone building up from the threshold of hearing, warning the audience. The kind of sound that seems to vibrate the camera lens, hum in the air like a nest of disturbed wasps.

The thing about movies, though, is that the characters don't get to hear the musical cues.

Real darkness is creeping in now. The figure in the trees seems to linger. Wanting to be glimpsed. She's sure she can see Beth's lumberjack shirt, the one she wore yesterday. A curve of red shoulder, the rim of a pale face.

"Beth?" she says again, her voice smaller this time.

"Jorie?" A low murmur, and it *is* Beth, coming out of the gloom. Beth puts her hand on a paper birch, leans into it and wipes her forehead with her other arm. "What are you doing here?" She's out of breath. Her hair is wild enough to remind Jorie of the old days, when it was longer and never behaved.

"I came to ask you the same thing." Jorie doesn't like how easily her anger has dissipated, how she feels only relief to see her friend whole and safe and full of their complicated nostalgia. But the hurt is still here, just beneath her surface, and she tries to pull it back out.

"What?" Beth straightens and removes her hand from the birch. "You know why I'm here. Is something wrong? What happened?"

"Yes, something is wrong." Jorie slips her phone from a back pocket and navigates to the teaser clip Beth posted earlier. "Something *happened*." She notices her hand is trembling as she hands the phone over.

"What is it?" But then Beth's eyes widen as she looks. Her finger taps the screen and the dim light changes on her face.

Jorie watches her. She can tell when Beth's eyebrows knit together, tucking downward, that the playback has stopped. That's all she's waiting for. "What the fuck, Beth? What in the fuck is that?" Her voice breaks but Jorie forces it together with all her will. She will not cry here.

"I—" Beth glances at Jorie but goes right back to the screen. She moves her finger as though to play the clip again but drops her hand. The moment is caught in the spreading dark.

"Why?" Jorie is frozen, too, unable to push past that word for a few seconds. "How could you? You can hate me, fine, but you can't do this to Oli. Did you even check to see if I had kids when they hired you?"

"Jorie, I didn't do this." Beth touches the screen again, scrolling down, scrolling back up. "I've never seen this before. This new October Film Haunt account. It tagged me in something else today. Someone was messing with me, but I didn't see this video."

"Pretty sure that's your account, though." Jorie hears her voice thinning, turning into half-whispers, as though her lungs won't let her go on. "Pretty sure you shared the video you didn't see."

"Yeah, that's me," Beth says. "But it wasn't *me*, Jorie. Someone was here earlier. One of those creepers with a sheet and a wooden crown, inside the cabin. They left a tape like the one you got. I chased them into the woods. I got lost. I got really lost, actually, it's like the wilderness out there. I dropped my phone, or I can't remember if I had it when I came out here. I—Jorie, I did not post that."

Beth stops, now she's the one remembering to take a breath. Jorie thinks she can see the shimmer of tears about to spill onto Beth's face as she hands the phone back. Her eyes are huge. The last pink light of the day is reflected in each of them.

Jorie is trapped between instant belief and the hot itch of rage on her skin. Even the old allure of fear is there, picking at the seam of guilt. She's a mother. It's the only thing that's supposed to matter. An image of Oli burns in her, three years old and screaming after tearing open his knee on a sidewalk, Jorie running in slow underwater motion to get to him.

Her next decision has to carry a lot of weight.

"You're saying a Rickie broke into the cabin. They're stalking you out here with their knives. They lured you into the forest and—what? Doubled back and stole your phone and posted this shit from your account?" She can't see Beth's face well enough to read it.

"Yes. Well, maybe not my phone. My MacBook was on the deck." Beth points up above the two cars. "It was open and everything was logged in. I think there were two of them here. Jorie, please. I know you must be scared, but I would never."

Beth is actually crying now, and Jorie doesn't know if these puzzle pieces fit together or if she just wants them to. She steps forward, lifts onto her tiptoes, and hugs her friend.

"You can't stay here," Jorie says, turning her face on Beth's shoulder. "Come stay with me and Oli. He'll love you and we'll figure all this out."

Maybe believing her is the easy thing to do. She's isolated up here, and she's tired of being alone in a deeper way for the last ten years. The soft warmth of Beth is a joy. She decides not to let go of it.

# CHAPTER TEN

## Coleman

▶▶ He has to limp a little through the woods. There are shallow flares of pain in the wound the doctor sewed up in his side, like feeling the ghost of the blond man's knife twisting in him with every few steps. The bandage is still strapped around his belly, the mouth of the cut scabbed over.

He's had the most awful cabin fever—and he has to know if there's a crypt back in these trees. Why he got that strange note in the mail. He wants to see the lake, too, before he tells Evie the news, somehow he must follow this fixation through before then. These are all the reasons he gave himself for leaving the house.

"There's that sicko out there who might finish the job," Gloria reminded him this morning. As though he hadn't thought of him a hundred times since she last brought him up.

There was such hurt in her eyes as she said it, trying to keep him home, Coleman felt it even more than the idea of the knife. It was easy to guess the rest of what she would never say, something like, *If I can keep a murderer from taking you, maybe the cancer won't either.*

"You have to get used to me being gone," he told her, and hated himself for it the whole drive into town.

He parked the car on Meridian Street, just two doors down from Video Spot, and waited to see if some post-traumatic shock would set in. If he would see knives in the hands of the shoppers and pedestrians. One of the mannequins in a clothing store window, next to the ice cream shop, was draped in a pale blue sheet, an arm beneath it lifted and pointing right at him.

Seeing it out in the world and not on his laptop screen, it came to him that his mind associated the sheets in *Proof of Demons* with hospital gowns sliding over his body, the flow of loose air and bad news. The one on the mannequin was almost the same shade.

Gorgeous pipe smoke clouds drifted across the shop window. The other two mannequins, one to either side of the blue ghost, gleamed like pearl in their swimsuits, sunglasses on their blank faces. A sign reading CLEARANCE sat below the three of them on a crumpled rug.

Evie will be here tomorrow. He already has the flight details in an email. The conversation, the tears, the way she'll look, they're weights on him, getting heavier every hour. It will be harder than telling Gloria because Evie doesn't have any armor. And she'll be one more person he'll have to lie to about when he's starting treatment. If he decides not to. If he lets his mind keep tipping in that direction.

"It's no big deal," he told her on the phone yesterday. "Just something your mom and I want to discuss in person."

"Daddy, this isn't like you," she said. And she was right. She knew one of life's trapdoors was about to open under her. Her voice had that clipped, panicky quality he remembers so well from when she was little and too upset to control her breathing. She didn't even mention bringing Charlotte and Liam.

"Just tell me," she said at the end.

"It's nothing," he insisted, the heat of the lie spreading like a fever across his face. "Well, it's not nothing, but it can wait."

It's almost funny, he thinks as he fades deeper into the woods. Fathers lie to their children from the day they're born, from Santa Claus to the thousand assurances that everything will get better or easier or clearer, but he's not sure he can do that to Evie now. Which makes him scared of her.

He's always hated lying to his wife, too, but he did it without thinking. The first round of chemo starts on October third, he told her. He even let her mark it on the kitchen calendar.

He quit his job yesterday, too, only a formality since his two partners already knew about the prognosis. All his affairs, one by one, lined up and with the sense of order he has always appreciated. He's getting ready to die. He just hasn't decided when, or on whose terms.

"Suicide," he says to the trees. "If you can't say the word, you won't actually do it. Suicide, suicide."

Half an hour ago, he passed under the archway between two pines, their branches not as beautifully entwined as they are in the movie—fifteen years have made them start growing in other directions, like falling out of love—and he hasn't been able to find the crypt. Either the monument was demolished while those limbs were slowly untangling themselves, or it was never more than a film set. Márcia Smith's map showed the crypt close to a path, but he doesn't think there's a second trail back here, this part of the woods is too narrow.

But then he sees the lake glitter through the trees ahead. He limps—slightly—the rest of the way and sits on the gritty strip of beach. A breeze lifts his thinning hair, which has grown less red and more an indeterminate blond with every year that brought him closer to this final one.

A few children play on the far shore below a house that has cedar shakes, he thinks, their voices piercing into high registers that almost carry across the water.

He doesn't know he's sitting where dozens of fans of *Proof of Demons* have communed, but at the same time, the thought isn't distant from his mind. The Transfigurations, the strict timing of the film's structure, he hasn't looked into these things yet. They are merely sensory itches, the recognition of math without the affinity for genre.

He does scold himself, because this would be the perfect place for someone, maybe a devil worshiper like the rumored old days, to emerge from the trees with a knife to open him back up. Maybe his week-old dried blood would still be on the blade.

It's quiet, though, and peaceful, with green trees clogging the horizon on the mountains. The lake water smells faintly of rot. He lets a memory of his brother settle around him, drape his shoulders. There is such a bright clear heft to it. He can smell the Irish Spring soap he and Jackson used for a few years, back when it was first on the market. They loved the scent, their mother said it was the only thing that could make them want to bathe.

His brother was eight or nine, years before they fell out of the oak tree. They were at Lake Townsend with their aunt June, both of them sunburned, and Jackson dared Coleman to dare him to swim out to the canoe Sarah Layton and her father were in. Coleman was too addled with worship not to, and soon his brother was cutting a line across the water that looked like a tear in a plastic bag.

He could tell Jackson was tiring because his hands started slapping the surface, too far away for Coleman to hear the flat bursts of water erupting from his hands with each stroke. His head had gone under twice before Mr. Layton jumped in and got him.

It was only fifteen, twenty seconds. But Coleman can remember the absence of him, the lake closing up over where he had been, almost as well as the day Jackson broke his arm. The day of the window in the air and the face staring through.

Coleman stays for a while, pretending this is more than just a small lake, or a large pond. He pretends it's Lake Townsend and finally says something. "I belong with you." The film isn't near his mind now. He's thinking of Jackson's head, a silhouette as indistinct as an acorn, distant in the melting gold of the sun on the surface of the water. He's thinking of what his daughter's eyes will look like that first second after he tells her he's dying. He'll say the right things to her, and he can decide later if those will be lies.

He wanders off the path on the way back after seeing what looks like an arrow painted in green on the trail. His strength is beginning to drain away from him on the uneven ground. His lungs feel heavy, and he's already learning to overfocus on them, to sense them hanging in his chest, separate from his ribs and his angry heart and all the other organs. The malignant, alien mass of them.

He hears the whisper of feet behind him, too rhythmic and heavy to be animals. Steps dragging through pine needles, breaking dead leaves. The trees close off the light of the sky above the lake, deepening the gloom. He stops moving. It takes a full minute for the wheeze in his lungs to clear and let him listen to the woods.

The footsteps stop and wait with him. He hears a cough, then a voice hissing, "Shut up." Coleman turns and looks through the pines, trying to peer between hundreds of trunks, the maze of pieces of sunlight and meaningless silhouettes. He counts to a hundred, giving his breathing more time to normalize. The chatter of a squirrel scratching high in a tree. The spiritual depth of the woods swells around him, even here with the town so close.

Passing through a dense grouping of red and longleaf pines, he comes across a clearing. A large square has been marked off with four stakes connected by muddy ropes, a crime scene or illicit construction site. The earth is undisturbed here except for a scrap of paper half-covered in pine needles, but his mind insists on seeing the square as the shape of a crypt. It looks enough like a grave.

He steps over a rope and picks up the paper, a business card with the name HÉLÈNE ENRIQUEZ embossed in a simple black font. Below this, smaller, is ANOTHER GREEN WORLD PROD. Then a phone number with an area code he doesn't know.

He's seen the words *An Hélène Enriquez Film* and *Written and Directed by Hélène Enriquez* too many times by now. Is the director making a sequel in Arden?

This thought falls away as he turns the card over and sees something more personal, handwritten in a green ink pale enough to force him to bring the card close to his face: *a beautiful cure/for cancer in the paper/birches of Vermont.* Is it a haiku? The man who stabbed him, or someone, mailed the note about the demon from Vermont.

Finally, under the haiku—he tallies up the syllables and yes, it's a haiku, the westernized kind, some things from childhood are never forgotten—is the command, *Wait 6 minutes.*

His fatigue deepens. If this is how he feels now, what would chemo be like? Or, as he remembers the oncologist saying, the concurrent chemo and radiation, "to get in there and throw everything we have at it." The stuff that will make him nearly as dead as the cancer will, from what he's read.

Maybe a quarter of a mile from where he's standing is where the smudged thing came out of the trees in the movie. Coldness creeps over his skin. Why would someone try to take this film Coleman had never heard of two weeks ago, the kind of thing he has never had an interest in, and bring it into his life so resolutely?

He imagines Gloria being here, whimpering in terror and shrieking at him to go home, because surely there is some sort of plot—he winces at the unlikely nature of that word, and at how it fits with this roped-off piece of earth—against him.

He'll go back home. He'll go back to bed and let her fuss over him and calm down. But he stays, vaguely counting off six minutes, staring in a glazed way at the square of rope, the card in his hand blurring in his foreground. [x6:00x]

And when he's waited long enough, he turns and looks behind him and sees three people standing in the pine cluster, close together, each draped in a light green bedsheet. For a few elastic seconds, a long shape looms behind them. It's like the thing that steals the child in *Proof of Demons*, but it isn't really there, it's more a flaw in his vision than a presence. Flickering.

He blinks and there are only the three figures playing ghost. The green of their sheets is a sick shade, somehow, the color of pea soup, and they're all wearing something on their heads, like in the movie. Wooden crowns that tear through the fabric, rough spear points peeking out through the holes. Their heads look like strange boxes.

One of them is filming Coleman, a small camera held up beside its covered face. The lack of eyes and mouths is subtly horrifying.

Any moment now three arms will be raised, the sheets will fall away along the forearms to reveal butcher knives. But they only watch him. He wonders how well they can see through the sheets. "You guys got the color wrong," he tells them without knowing he's going to say anything at all. His voice breaks the stasis of the moment apart, and they begin walking toward him, fanning out.

He nearly trips on one of the ropes, almost falls in the very first moment of pursuit, but he's off into the trees and dodging between trunks. His feet slide on years of pine needles in his unsensible business casual shoes. The wound in his side throbs like a shout. His lungs rasp in their cage. He's not sure how far he's gone when he starts coughing, violent and gasping hacks, and he only makes it another few seconds before he collapses.

He hears feet running. Branches snapping. A low, urgent muttering. He curls himself up in a wash of pain and waits for them to find him. The business card is still clenched in his right hand, and he sees that it's misted in blood from his coughs. He rolls over on his back and watches a hawk looping far above him, its circles broken by treetops.

"Mr. Smith?" The voice is rough, male, and close. Coleman cranes his neck toward it but sees nothing. "Mr. Smith, do you have the card?"

The card? He looks down at his hand and sees it. He nods because he can't possibly speak yet.

"Mr. Smith?" Closer now. Different, younger, maybe.

"Yes," he manages, a whisper that carries none of his voice's color.

Someone laughs. This, too, sounds young somehow.

"Good," the first voice says. "Wait for your brother. Soon, you will be a part of something wonderful."

"Jackson?" he asks them. "Is he alive?" But he can only rasp the words, and the people wearing the sheets are leaving, moving away toward the lake. Their bedsheets sigh along the ground, over the clumsy rhythm of their feet.

"Will you believe in what you made?" one of them calls back to him. The voice sounds so far away already.

Something stays, though. It stains the trees for a moment before coming toward him. The same long smudge in the air from the clearing, laced with static. It pauses and Coleman realizes it is the shape from his bedroom, too, the thing he saw before something awful caught in his throat.

The half-thing lowers to the ground, shifting the dry leaves and pine needles, and crawls to Coleman. The world starts to blur, and he raises his head a few inches and sees his body grow indistinct, blackened and edgeless, as the smudge covers him.

His face goes cold. There is the block in his throat again, something creeping into his mouth. He can't breathe, and he fumbles at his neck, clawing. He tries to scream, but he can only get out a glob of foamy saliva that slides down his left cheek, to the leaves under his head.

Moments pass. Coleman can breathe again, his lungs ease their drowning and their ill pulsing. Strength returns. The air clears and the details come back into the trees above him. The sounds of animals crackle and chitter. When he is calm, he rereads the haiku on the back of the card, *a beautiful cure/for cancer in the paper/birches of Vermont.*

He thinks of what Evie will say, and he feels her hand in his hand.

The presence is gone. He watches a plump red ant crawl up onto his knee and seem to regard him. The kneecap is a tight knob that could break through the skin at any moment. He can see the bones of his legs so clearly these days, he's lost so much weight, and it occurs to him that the hawk may be a buzzard, patient and curious about the possibility of Coleman. He reads the haiku again.

# INTERLUDE

[Excerpt from "Cinematography,"
www.reddit.com/r/CultWeird]

Posted by u/helenelives 2 hours ago

Lake Ontario appears, the last hopes of summer still aching in clear waters. The sun drowns across its surface. A ribbon of empty sandy beach, and the lake is gone. A sheer stone wall, mountain-shaped, then the green fur of treetops that slope down and end at a park, concrete paths littered with joggers and extras wearing sweaters.

Toronto's light is fading. Beyond, a roadway, cars, a wide brick wafer of a building sweeping closer. Arms and faces move on balconies. Someone shakes out a green sail of fabric, drapes it over a red railing, then slips around a glass door pasted with clouds.

The drone camera is mindless, steady and tunnel-visioned. It does not pause to observe or differentiate, it draws itself through a small open window on the eighth floor of the Markham Road Apartments. It is only gathering footage.

The camera turns left into a longer hallway. A figure is standing at the end of it, peeking around a corner.

A recessed light flickers in the ceiling, a yellow tinge that drains into the indoor dusk again and again, and now the view slows to a stop. The camera begins to tremble almost imperceptibly. In the footage it records, lines of distortion crawl across the frame and make the image impure—electrical interference, the drone's thinning radio signal range, or something less scrutable.

There is no music, for now, only a child crying somewhere nearby.

The watching figure does not move. It is wearing a robe or sheet, a diluted brown or green color pooling on the floor, difficult to see back in the shadows that flutter from dimness to darkness. The corner of the wall, which cuts right toward another hallway, bisects the figure, only half of its enormous head visible above the sheet—one staring circle of an eye, part of a pained, straight-toothed grin, chalky white skin.

Beneath the inconstant light, along the hall, wooden tines lie on the floor beside a large ring or band and strewn splinters. A crown has been broken. The figure shifts, as though stepping fully into view, but seems to change its mind and withdraws farther into the proceeding corridor than before.

When the trailer is released, some will say—even with only the few frames bridging other horrors—that the largely static scene looks remarkably like an image created by Trevor Henderson, the renowned artist and urban legend enthusiast. It's in the figure's oversized round head and indistinct, shadowed features. The slight surreal blur that distorts trust. The peripheral positioning designed to tell the eyes that something is wrong before the shape settles into definition.

It is an homage, perhaps.

Even when the artist himself appears in the trailer, pursued through these broken seams of light.

Suddenly the drone jars into movement and drifts down the hall, slower than the line it drew through the sky above the lake and the trees. The half-mouth of the figure at the end of the hall seems to stretch and open. The dark begins to shrink from it, but the view stops again above the wooden shards and rotates to the left, dragging along the wall, to a door marked 857.

Posted by u/weirderfiction 1 hour ago

Wait Trevor Henderson the Siren Head guy is in your screenplay??

# CHAPTER ELEVEN

## Trevor

▶▶ He sits at a raw wood desk, staring at a monitor through heavy black glasses. He scratches his beard. The white letters on his black shirt read KEEP ONTARIO WEIRD. A matching black and white cat sits ten feet away, watching him, her tail curled around her paws.

The cat is unsure about him because he is not her human. This is not Trevor's home. Four days ago a fire burned through the vacant apartment next door to his own, on the other side of the city. A heavy blanket of smoke through the old ductwork, packing itself down from the ceilings and filling the hallway. He was trapped inside just long enough to begin coughing, thinking he might die.

The fire services arrived moments after he collapsed on the floor at the farthest end of the farthest room, as the smoke crawled around him. Jenn was at work, thank all the arcane gods sitting on Trevor's display shelves.

His own cat, Boo, is staying with a neighbor because this is Calloway's kingdom, and she doesn't play well with other animals. The same neighbor told him arson is suspected, but Trevor hasn't heard anything since. Nils, a musician friend on his first long tour since the pandemic, is letting Trevor and Jenn stay in his place at Markham Road until whatever comes next.

Trevor is listless and uncomfortable. His desk at home is set up just so, with each monster crouched or creeping at a specific angle. He's used to vampires eyeing him as he works.

On the monitor is an enlarged high-resolution photo of a house exterior, dark red siding, a utility pole with thick wires trailing at a diagonal across the screen. Two windows, a slight tilt to the house. The edge of another building, brown and blurry, is in the extreme foreground. Trevor likes that edge and doesn't crop it out. He chooses not to straighten the photo's axis and create a pleasing symmetry, either.

He inserts an unpleasant, almost human figure into a smudge of alley between the brown building and the red house, then wreathes it in gloom. There is a suggestion of a torso and unsettling long legs, but the face is allowed to ease out of the murk. A pinched white face, elongated, an indistinct black mouth and two coal ember eyes.

He spends several minutes on the face, dialing it to the right frequency with the cursor. Thickening the mouth he painted earlier. Dulling the eyes to a disposable camera sheen. He adds shadows and takes other shadows away. He leans closer to the screen, clicking tools and brushes.

A low thud shakes the wall over by the door to the hallway. Trevor jumps in his chair, and the cat runs out of the office area to hide under the yellow L-shaped sofa. The thud comes again, almost certainly on this apartment's wall. He goes to the door and looks through the fisheye lens of its peephole. Nothing but the door across the hall bending toward him in flickering light. The image could be from his dreams or his work. It's Trevor's kind of ambiance.

He leaves the door to find Calloway, gets on his hands and knees to coax her from under the sofa. It's almost dinnertime, he tells her, and coughs twice. The smoke from the apartment fire still has a few tendrils in his throat. The cat's eyes are flat lamps in the dimness, milky and mirrored.

He misses taking pictures of Boo in the near-dark, right before bed with the camera flash turned off, and zooming in on those same strange lantern flares on his phone screen. Calloway's eyes have more iridescence to them. He tries to memorize the alien way they hold light.

Back at the desk he takes a break and opens the corpse of Twitter, ignoring the usual notification flood, to check for news about the supposed *Proof of Demons* sequel. The hashtag #funeralwatching is still slowly expanding. He first noticed it yesterday when he was tagged several times in mentions.

Now #proofofdemons is starting to trend, too, and his own name appears in a few hashtags.

Text at the top of the screen reads, A NEW TREND INVOLVES RUMORS THAT THE 'PINE ARCH CREATURE' FROM A CULT HORROR FILM HAUNTS THOSE WHO FILM VIDEOS OF FUNERALS.

Nearly three thousand people "are posting about this," and Trevor's gut clenches. He hopes there's not another video like the one he saw this morning, but a small corner of his heart, where a colder and passionate horror fan is huddled with sharp teeth, wants to see where this could go.

It feels like crowdsourcing a found-footage film.

It's less certain how the involvement of real cops will help sell a movie, though.

A bit too guerrilla style. He sees a post by the Providence Police Department in Rhode Island: "Recording communications without consent of contributors is illegal. The PPD is following leads regarding threats from and to those using video devices at funerals. We ask that this #funeralwatching trend cease out of safety and respect."

Trevor wonders what a threat is in this context, whether it's even close to true that someone disappeared after posting a TikTok video of a "demon" showing up in their bedroom.

A minute later he's reading a Providence news report about Brandon Mares, a nineteen-year-old who has been missing for two days, and emotions swirl up in his chest, concern and fear and a reluctant thread of giddiness. The horror itch is never far from his skin, and this approach to marketing is something else.

He sees "@slimyswampghost whats your take on this?" and "this is creepy af @slimyswampghost got to be in on it" and a scattering of other assumptions. There's a link to a Bloody Disgusting article about the new #funeralwatching trend and the possibility of it being banned on some social media platforms. Good. Just in case.

The problem he's seeing here, on Reddit, and across a couple of Discord channels he frequents is that this *Proof of Demons* revival is already being treated like more than a movie, just like the original was. And the high school student who died in 2013, she's being wielded as a weapon in comments and replies instead of as a cautionary tale.

He types "original october film haunt" into the search bar. The account is still there, but it's been temporarily restricted. This is probably good, too, to overreact on the safe side.

He sifts through several videos of graveside services shot with shaky smartphones. There are gray skies, sun-glare skies, a sky of drizzling clouds blurred by water droplets on the camera lens. Funerals with a handful of mourners, gatherings of a hundred or more.

Trevor watches one clip through to the end and hears a voice, maybe a teenage girl, yelling, "I belong with you, trees!" Nothing comes out of said trees, there's only the girl's laughter. Someone else, presumably with their own phone camera raised, repeats the words.

The posts accompanying these scenes range from "ok admit this was a little creepy" to "Um 6 min now what?" and he says aloud, "This is really catching on." He rakes his fingers through the short fur of his beard.

Is he surprised? Yes, because horror has trouble entrenching itself in the mainstream, which is how he likes it. And . . . no, because people will believe anything.

They used to believe in demons so easily. Get them to hate science, and demons suddenly don't seem so—

A small noise comes from the door, something between a knock and a click. Trevor turns and stares at it, as though he can see the sound. It could be the apartment across the hall, but then the steel doorknob begins to shake.

Trevor rolls the chair back from the desk, swivels it until he's facing the door, his hands expectant in his lap. A moment passes and he laughs at himself. All the scary story ingredients snap into place. Analog horror on social media, a possible sequel to one of his favorite indie horror films, rumors of occult activity... he's made a career in this wheelhouse.

But to start creeping himself out in the real world—who does he think is standing out there, rattling the doorknob in an echo of ten thousand wonderful cheap movies? Roger Eilertsen, if he's even alive, wearing his *Proof of Demons* bedsheet?

The Pine Arch Creature?

That is a strange image, the stretched-out creepy thing he designed himself trying to get into his friend's apartment. The prodigal demon. He was never involved with Hélène Enriquez before or after that concept art commission in 2007, he knows nothing about her, he never met her or the crew or any of the actors. But he knows the Pine Arch Creature's contours. There is still this responsibility he feels about it all, if that's the right word.

The doorknob rattles again.

"Hello?" he calls out, and the door opens. He's up from the chair, sending its wheels clacking across the floorboards behind him.

"Um, hello," Jenn says, almost uncertain as she comes in. One hand is holding two paper bags, close to dropping them if she doesn't get to the kitchen counter soon. "Sushi rolls, remember?"

"Hey." He walks over to her, away from the monsters on his screen and away from disrespectful kids videoing funerals, and takes the bags. He sets them down safely and turns back and pulls her into a hug that confuses her even more. "God. You weren't messing with me just now, right? Pushing on the door, jiggling the knob?"

"Excuse me? No, of course not." Jenn pulls away from him and studies his face. "Did something happen? I told you you'd go too far and traumatize yourself one day."

"That's actually not super untrue today," Trevor says, and laughs at himself again. "Let me wrap up and let's eat. How was work?"

"I brought the panels I finished inking for you to see." She's on the other side of the open living space now, in the laundry room, so she almost has to shout. The acoustics here are strange, like there's soundproofing material in the walls. Their conversations have felt different because of it. "New issue should be ready in two days."

Trevor raises his voice, too. "I can't wait. You should still let me put a creepy-crawly guy in there, though." He glides the chair back in front of the monitor and sits down. "Mostly, though, I just miss Boo. Calloway was hiding under the sofa earlier when someone—"

The rest of his sentence dies in his mouth as he nudges his phone to wake it up. An email notification box is on the lock screen, just the name **Hélène Enriquez** in bold.

Jenn says something, but her voice is far out on the periphery of the world.

At first he thinks the email is blank, but he scrolls down and sees the text, tiny agoraphobic paragraphs buried under lines and lines of white space. *So that none of it would show up in the notification snippet*, he thinks.

> *Tell me something, Trevor. What happens when we don't believe?*
> *When proof fails?*
> *The demon has to evolve. The demon has to speak louder.*
> *A film has to speak louder.*
> *So, answer another question. Will you believe in what you made?*
> *Warmest regards,*
> **H. Enriquez**

"Is something wrong?" Jenn asks, back in the same room. The ringing clunk of two plates on the counter, the rustle of paper bags.

"No," Trevor says. He sits there for a long moment before pushing his phone away. "No, it's fine, let's eat."

# INTERLUDE

[Excerpt from "Funeral Watching,"
www.reddit.com/r/CultWeird]

Posted by u/helenelives 3 hours ago

You all may remember me from my post here called What Proof of Demons Means to My Brain that sort of blew up in 2012. There were hundreds of us in that thread. I wasn't the first person to say you could summon the Pine Arch Creature (thank God) but I know I helped make more people believe it was real. I'm not proud of it.

There's a part of that old post I want to bring up real quick before I write about what's going on now with the funerals:

*So I got to see my professor react to Proof of Demons and it showed we're right. I picked two scenes for a 20 minute presentation, the cemetery and the town meeting, with a couple of minutes on each side to show the more regular parts of the movie too. He had never seen it, no one had. I watched my classmates but mostly I watched him wanting to dismiss it because it broke all these film rules or something. He went pale and under his eyes got all dark. He told me it was just using "experimental techniques in a mainstream mode" and it reminded him a bit of Dogme 95, which I guess is fair enough if you haven't seen all of it. But his voice was hoarse, sort of out of breath, then he ended class early. I already knew the power of this film but now I REALLY knew it.*

*I tried to explain to him about the Four Transfigurations and the moving hole and he said there's a "precedent of haunted images throughout history" including still photography and early moving pictures. "Like spirit photography?" I said and he said that's not a great example because it was debunked. "Do you think these images are haunted?" I said. He wouldn't answer me but he was going to watch the whole thing. Well, he took a leave of absence and someone else had to finish the class. That was last year and no one has heard from him since.*

Other people lied about Proof of Demons as you all know. I shared that to remind us just how much we WANTED it to be real. It was my favorite movie for a long time. When people started talking about it more and the October Film Haunt people said it was real and then that girl died, I felt just terrible.

My professor did talk to me about haunted images, but I made up the part about him quitting his job. He was back for the next class. I saw it in his eyes, like a new Rickie being born, and I told him about how Enriquez was probably anonymous so no one knew if any other work existed. (Though I did turn him onto Under the House since some of us think Enriquez made it.)

Since I told an important lie inside all that truth, I owned a little part of it all. I started to see how the Pine Arch stuff was inside me. I was a Rickie who spent hundreds of hours talking online about the Creature and was there really a moving hole that would let you look into hell. I wanted to know its secrets. Even after that girl died in the fake ritual, I kept going to the woods and trying to commune with Something.

I felt like I was so close to what I wanted to feel. There was this Calm deeper than I ever had anywhere else. This thing and this place where everything didn't have to hurt. But awful too because I kept thinking it COULD be real. It was a fever like worship. But so much better than church. Even if nothing ever happened for me.

And [now the movie is back](). With multiple Pine Arch Creatures and instructions on how to get haunted by one. We're in this weird situation where a tragedy made us admit it was fake, but now this #funeralwatching hashtag is trending a little with people filming funerals and yelling out "I belong with you." I've been able to find 14 of them already in a couple days.

So it looks like Enriquez is making something else like we all hoped. We don't know if it's a sequel or a reboot. Some crazy marketing thing, right?

BUT then I saw the [video of this teenage guy's bedroom](#) today. He says he filmed a funeral for 6 minutes and he has felt haunted ever since. Faces hiding. Something in the mirror with the light off. Then he jerks around suddenly and there's this huge skinny thing with long arms bent over at the ceiling, all smudgy like what you can see of the Pine Arch Creature in Proof of Demons. This creepy voice says "You belong" and the thing gets harder to see the closer the guy gets. He's mumbling, then he like climbs into the thing and the phone moves to show his face. He looks peaceful? I don't know. And the video ends. I belong, you belong, I think the words open and close the Transfiguration.

It's been shared online a lot already. Then the same thing happened to a woman in California. Her Instagram clip is shorter and doesn't show much because the Creature or whatever is much closer to the camera when you see it. There's a line of blood or something dripping down the wall.

So now we could have real proof. But also maybe real danger.

Sorry this is so long but I think we have a responsibility to make sure this is true this time. No lies. Some of us have made Proof of Demons our whole lives in the past. We have loved this with all our love. We need to warn people to only Funeral Watch if they are committed and know what they are doing. I hope these two people are found soon and it turns out they were fine. I'm excited too but we don't want someone else to die, do we?

**TAPE 2**

**PROOF OF DEMONS**
**OCTOBER FILM HAUNT**

HI–FI VIDEO

> The candle flame gutters. Its little pool of light trembles. Darkness gathers. The demons begin to stir.
>
> —CARL SAGAN,
> *THE DEMON-HAUNTED WORLD: SCIENCE AS A CANDLE IN THE DARK*

# CHAPTER TWELVE

## Roger

▶▶ For two days, he hasn't been alone in the house.

The estate is rarely empty, but he thinks of *alone* in the sense of his staff having left the house for the day, those few still on his payroll. The housekeeper and chef. Two of the four security contractors are strictly outdoors, patrolling the tree line that could be accessed if any fanatics managed to scale the wrought iron perimeter. Draped in their silly blue sheets, they are twenty or thirty strong outside Roger's front gates with rumors flying about a sequel.

The worst of them are still convinced he wasn't just pretending to lead a cult. Why else would someone of his stature—Roger Eilertsen, reclusive Oscar nominee, rumored agoraphobe, ascending star of the 1970s—have deigned to appear in an independent horror debut in 2009? Detestable swarming flies, they'll believe anything. Combine that anything with film and it's stronger than religion. The police had to be called once already.

His nurse, Beatriz, was the last to finish her duties this evening. She has retired to her guest house in the southwest corner of the property, in the shade of an enormous sycamore tree. He likes her very much and will try not to ring for her again. There are various pills on his nightstand if he needs them.

Now he is the only one left in the house, and he is not alone.

The high ceilings of the dining room and parlor and entrance hall gather up Roger's footsteps and cane, send them back in muted echoes. These rooms have not served their purposes in years. He walks slowly, with his slow bones, to make sure the security system is still armed.

It's only a feeling, the residue of his middle years, this sense knitting in the air of something that is on its way. He pauses in each room and waits for it to arrive, disappointed and profoundly relieved when it does not, and shuffles on.

He still has a full head of white hair, though it is finally thinning. Faded blue eyes, too rawboned his whole life, stooping a bit more each year. Skin a strange burnished yellow from his UV lamps. His hand trembles on the worn bone grip of his cane, which once pressed against the learned hand of the alchemist Richard Bonbridge as he recovered from fever in Wales in 1781, three years before the same hand committed murder.

Too many of his things were once touched by wicked hands. In his eighty-third year, he has accepted that no energies are left behind in trinkets. He has seen precious little of Hélène's proof.

All these ways he finds to think of Hélène.

The first time he noticed someone was with him in the house, it was a laugh. A deep flat sound that looped—"haha ha, haha ha"—for several seconds before it cut off abruptly as it reached his ears down the main staircase. A thumb pressing a phone app, he mused. A door boomed up there. The four-hundred-year-old tapestry depicting the Black Death lifted and fell back against the wall just past the top riser.

Then silence, so profound that he could hear the tumble of the ice maker in the kitchen, five rooms away. He climbed the steps, giving the laugher all the time in the world to find a hiding place, as he rarely puts himself through the hell of the staircase. He always feels the ache in his legs and hips the next day.

The second floor was its usual tomb—open parquet floors, plastic and cotton sheeting over furniture in rooms that no longer remembered the sound or step of life. He, too, was beginning to forget where he sourced many of his pieces, or why they called out to him at the time. Which tables had the supposed stain of ectoplasm and which were rigged for tipping and ghostly knocks. He once had personal assistants to handle those matters.

Roger slept well in the not-aloneness, with his usual black wall of dreamless rest. He hasn't remembered a dream in fifteen years, even as his sleep slowly thins along with his hair. The security detail found nothing this morning when he asked them to search the property and review the exterior footage.

Tonight the intruder is tracking him irregularly from room to room. Thumps, scratches along the walls, an occasional laugh in that same maddening, almost familiar motif. "Haha ha, haha ha."

He's agitated, which always gives him heartburn. More of the movie idiots have been creeping down his street like poison ivy throughout the day. It must be one of them inside the house, he knows this. But he is thrilled by old possibilities, in a way he hasn't felt in a very long time.

Because Hélène reached out to him. And now this, just weeks later.

Young Roger's blood would have sung with adrenaline: an empty house, a presence. One that isn't here to rob him. Old Roger's blood is leaner, but he lights tall candles in his library, which is filled with tomes he hasn't leafed through in longer than he cares to admit. The candles are placed in a wide circle on the floor. He draws a pentagram inside of them with black chalk, one of its sides untrue with arthritis, smears rendered chicken fat from an ancient mason jar at each point, and speaks certain incantations still buried in his mind.

He doesn't believe in any of the words, or in the cliché of the pentagram, and nothing happens.

He is still thinking of the occult when he wakes in the morning. He gave it up, he supposes, but it was more like it sloughed off him. Hélène's film was his last chance for a rekindling, but a wry sort of resignation loosened like dead skin not long after *Proof of Demons* came out. No festivals, no features, just stacks of DVDs and the chattering internet to give it a reception.

Almost a million dollars of his money to produce the movie, this final delicate ripple on the pond of his life. He was intrigued by the reputation it garnered, rumors and muttered legend, but none of it was real. None of it happened for *him*, its seeker.

The thing is—he felt *something* during the filming. In his other, younger life, before the open vat of the world closed itself off to him, he had traveled much farther than North Carolina to experience fainter residues of darkness. The *something* was there in the frames, he grants Hélène that, but diluted. That was her problem, the obsession with translating through diodes or pixels or however sniveling people watched movies in 2009.

But she got closer than he ever had. All because a missing persons blog reminded her of a ritual she had once come across in a nondescript book. She was convinced that anyone could summon an entity because a lost child had done it in the 1970s. He doesn't remember the particulars, but she wanted her film to be a sort of window for it.

On the set, all three days he was involved in shooting, he kept sensing a hidden aura around the cameras, something trying to get into the lenses. Movement in the air of the crypt Hélène commissioned inside a plywood set in the woods, in the confession booth of the church they had broken into, even in the little girl's bedroom in the first take they shot.

He remembers wandering about in a state of acute energy, a prescription of Zoloft to keep the agoraphobia humming in its flimsy container. He was convinced something was going to happen, sure Hélène had a veil to part. Some kind of realness pressed against his skin, they had to do a dozen takes in the crypt because he felt like the inside of his mouth was burning. He was finally on the cusp of what he had given up acting for.

But they wrapped, Hélène withdrew even further, and he was back here in Lake Placid the next day.

Hélène was on set those three days in North Carolina, but Roger never saw her. He was busy being eaten alive by his fear of every gaping space he found himself in, the graveyard and woods and streets of the town. A man who uncannily resembled Philip Seymour Hoffman in *Boogie Nights* ran the scenes, shrewd at playing dumb. He told them his name wasn't important, that he was merely a proxy.

The Hoffman doppelgänger as director of cinematography, one cameraman, one gaffer, the location sound engineer/boom operator, the almost emaciated man in charge of costumes and hair and makeup—the set felt like a library the night before finals. That was how small the crew was, and how blank and quiet they all were most of the time.

Hélène did not grace them with her presence, even during the occult interlude of her film. The pudgy blond man was on the phone as they set it up, clearly taking direction: *Stare slack-faced at Kip until the camera moves. Slack with awe. Emilia, stand as though you'll flee up into the woods, but as though you are a moment from tearing the sheets away and saving your husband. But also, you will soon pick up a knife. There is a war inside you.*

The other actors came to think of him as the director.

Roger almost did, too. He listened closely to the character of the man's words, the tonal lifts and falls, wondering if the voice he had heard through the phone was disguised—if this man was, in fact, Hélène. It nearly soured Roger on the entire project, but he was still just hungry enough then. Still willing to swallow his phobia for his oblique love.

Subterfuge or no, Hélène only seemed to care about the long static scenes that ate up the film. Roger was involved in shooting just one of them. The last, before the ending when the camera finally turned to swim in Emilia's tender horror. The only time Emilia Ramos brought Márcia Smith truly to life, he would think later when he watched the film from the beginning.

Roger felt the *something* most keenly during that scene, as he stood nude in the crypt, the wooden crown too tight against his forehead as they all stared at the shape of Kip Corliss beneath the heaped bedsheets. Six minutes in a trembling stasis. The presence was almost dense. A knot around the single camera, a bending glare on the lens. A seam sewn into the air.

It's right there on the DVD, one second, flickering out, then nearly two seconds a moment later. A tall thin hint. The shape of it pressing among Roger and the others as they stab the blood packs strapped to Kip's chest.

He didn't see the *something* then, in the moment, and this absence has gained weight in the years since. He has given up convincing himself the presence—the entity, the demon in her title—wasn't added in editing. But the sinking chill on his naked skin, he remembers his breath catching in his throat. His heart galloping.

Irritation rises again at all these memories, during breakfast, his morning walk through the house, waiting for Beatriz to come check on him, stock the week's groceries, start today's hour of physical therapy. The temperature has dropped into the forties. He loves this time of year, when he doesn't have to wish he could stroll in the grounds instead.

One of the men calls to tell him that several of the movie's fans are returning to his gates for another vigil.

Now that he has declined Hélène's invitation to reprise his last role, and he is not alone inside his home, he is tempted to reply to one of the handful of new press emails in his computer. *Former Oscar Nominee Opens Up About Unhinged Horror Film Director*. Show her what happens when she coddles him and tosses him aside, unsated. Not even showing her face.

No press, that had been in Hélène's original contract, and he had signed it, intrigued by the phone calls they shared before convening down south. He relished saying no to journalists in the months and years after. The worst of those turkey vultures gathered when the high school girl died in the film's cemetery.

But he still thinks of all those drowning hours he spent on the phone with her in the months before her film. Like teenagers in the throes of lust, but tasting each other's minds. Her deep unknowable voice like rich chocolate waking on the tongue as it melts. Sexless, languid, strangely lilting.

Seven nights spread across a year, filled with Cabbalism, the Golden Dawn, John Dee, all the greatest hits. Minds like Helena Blavatsky and Jinarajadasa. A slow spiral into the deep cuts. Braucherei, Appalachian granny magic, Navajo skin-walkers, Mesopotamian gallu demons. Div and jinn and a hundred other entities across the seas.

And God, the Bible, Abrahamic sects. The Western mainstream. Most occultists diminish the role of God, but Hélène saw it as much more fundamental than simply anti-God. She mused to him that the Christian God was essentially a demon himself—or itself, as she preferred—and that only a musty cobbled-together book claimed otherwise. If it existed, God was as likely to tremble the planchette on a Ouija board as any spirit.

*Occult, "to conceal" from the Latin, we learn that on day one, dear Roger,* he can still hear that rich voice saying, *Who would claim that God is in the light?* Her words would sometimes thicken, sink even deeper in these moments. She had ideas about the practical application of demonology that made academic study of it seem as juvenile as the way Roger's pulse danced on the rare occasions his phone vibrated in his pocket. Hoping it would be her.

*The occult is everywhere, Roger.* That was a favorite line. *It creates, rather than exists. Worthy artworks always contain a trace of the esoteric, for what else is creation? What is spirituality but a yearning for a dream to be real?*

She wanted it all to be real. Hélène was much younger, she claimed, she had done less, but genuine contact already seemed more possible for her. Her light dwarfed his light like a star.

Those calls ached in him. He misses them even now.

There is no faith without proof, not in his old heart. She never gave him that, whatever she decided to call her film. Though he finds that he still loves her, not with any romantic ardor, but with the reluctant worship of someone who is weary when a god rises again.

The thought comes for the first time, that it is not a mindless fan sneaking into the house. Hélène is trying to scare him into doing her film.

Sleep comes close, but not as close as other nights. The sound of something dragging down the hallway toward the main bedroom keeps pulling him back. Then a fingernail tapping the wall. It starts just past one in the morning, and he spends forty minutes brushing enough courage into a little heap in his chest to get out of bed and creak open the door to check.

But as his first foot leaves the warmth of the comforter and sinks into the deep wool rug, the quality of the room changes. A dimming. He looks at the door and sees that the line of weak light has been cut in half along the bottom. As though a shape is standing out there, on the other side, summoned.

"Get out or I'll call the police!" But his voice seems to be mostly air, a wet rasp far from the shout he wanted. He clutches at his chest. He's completed eight decades without a whisper of a heart attack. Please not now, not like this.

He waits, his ears full of the absence of sound. His pulse slackens to its old-man rhythm. The visitor steps away, and the light under the bedroom door stretches back out.

In the same moment, the "haha ha, haha ha," but farther off in the depths of the house.

Dr. Petrarch tells him he's in good health for an elderly man who gets so little sun. There's no pressing need to keep a caregiver on a leash out in the guest house. His bones are dense enough, his arthritis is moderate, there's no reason to think he won't see ninety. But he has felt for months that he is brittle. The end trails after him, biding its time. As faint as his shadow just before the sun falls behind the trees.

Maybe all men who reach his vaulted, decrepit age feel this cloud of ending hover at their backs. But he is sure that soon there will be nothing left of him to block the light. He will be only the shadow itself.

He thinks repeatedly of his childhood in southern Tennessee, tucked in the pocket of the Smoky Mountains and poor enough to have only two sets of clothes, neither fit for Sundays. He thinks of shining like a light in school even though he was always bored to tears. Fleeing west at sixteen, living with groups on their way to becoming communes, older women, men not much younger than he is now.

His first screen role as a gutshot louse on an episode of *Gunsmoke*. His first motion picture, six lines in Billy Wilder's *The Apartment*. The tired, frantic sex with dozens of partners who all melted into an amorphous blur of limbs and drugs and staring out of clean windows at dark streets, the Academy Award nomination and the red carpet and the Halston tuxedo still hanging in a closet somewhere around here, the two or three years of directors practically on their knees, lines of coke on glass tables, pouring champagne off the Empire State Building, erasing half the skin from his left calf in a bike crash and getting up and walking away like only the young could, moons and flashbulbs, long cars, the eyes of coyotes in the Hollywood Hills.

Everything slowly lost its luster. Life dulled like silverware in a drawer.

Until he met Simeon Gott in a windowless basement illuminated by a single naked light hanging from a cord of human hair. The heart of a black goat sitting on Gott's palm, blood leaking between the fingers. May of 1983, still two years before he really felt the teeth of the word *agoraphobic*. A friend, a fellow dabbler, had talked Roger into descending grimy stairs into the bowels of an apartment building on the Lower East Side of Manhattan, where Gott ruled in splendorous filth.

The next twenty years opened like a lotus flower. Strange masks. Black-market 8mm reels and VHS tapes of forests and villages, grainy exorcisms, entrails hanging from vines. Wooden crowns, intricately carved or crudely hacked. The imported blood of animals smeared on his skin. Once, the blood of a woman who had died moments earlier of a heroin overdose, upstairs in this very house. Roger's huge white eyes in a mask of blood in a mirror.

Every failed summoning, every sealed door led him deeper into the search for the arcane, though all he found along the walls of the maze was the profane. Like LaVey's Satanism or Crowley's Thelema, it was an excuse for people to be animals, to do what they wilt.

Roger has been in cults. They create nothing.

Hélène Enriquez took away that excuse. She got his email from an assistant nearly twenty years ago after couching esoteric hints in a fan letter. Before long, Roger was the fan, not her. Since Hélène, he has stopped collecting, stopped poring over books. Strange how, in the end, she was the one who let him stop caring.

Another sun has been raked open to bleed into the trees. Roger is alone again, in his new not-alone way, and instead of wandering the house to listen for the laugh and the fingernails on the walls, he goes into his study. The thought of emails has made him want to read Hélène's message from early August.

He turns his Mac on and navigates to the email app. Her message is marked unread, so it's waiting at the top for him to click on it for the twentieth time: Will we finish, dear Roger? Will we believe in what we made? Say it. "I belong with you." Give me six lovely minutes of silence on your camera.

No context, no reminiscence. Just that *dear* before his name. An *H.* at the bottom and the gulf of the years that have passed. But he said it aloud in his study, that day, *I belong with you*, because he still did. He sat at his desk for six minutes, frozen in the eye of his webcam, because he still did.

"Will we finish," he whispers now. "What is there to finish?"

Something thumps in the hall outside the study.

He stiffens in the chair, staring through the open door. An old revolver is in one of the drawers by his knees, he thinks. It should be loaded, but who knows if it works. Someone left it behind at a party Roger threw in the abyss of the seventies. He remembers the man quoting *Dirty Harry* and waving it around.

The thump comes again, but from farther away. It's the front door, not someone creeping down the hallway with a knife.

Still, he waits another moment, until two knocks that sound more like knocks echo through the entrance hall, before getting up and moving his bones through the house. His cane adds its own knocks against the floor. The soles of his slippers shush them.

He peers through the tall sidelight window and sees nothing on the length of porch. Two pillars, yellow light that dies long before it reaches the bottom of the fourteen steps he hasn't descended in years. His heartbeat is steady. He taps a code into the security panel, opens the door, stares out into the night. The cane taps on the threshold. Roger feels the first note of breathless outside panic rising in his throat.

"Who's there?" he says, and flips all the switches on the wall to his left. Islands of light bloom: two making a soft white sheet across the length of the porch, a floodlight on either corner fifty yards away, the dead fountain in the center of the crushed gravel ring, a string of electric lamps hiding in the grass along the driveway and diminishing toward the gates. How many of Hélène's ardent goth kids are huddled out in that dark?

But nothing is skulking or so much as crawling along the edges of all these islands. The crickets die out slower each year in the warming world, and there are only a handful of players left in the coda. They stitch the deep quiet blanket. The dark smells like dry mint, as it always does here at the end of summer. He'll ask Faber and his security men to watch all the camera footage again in the morning.

He's about to turn and close the door when a voice calls back, "I belong with you!" A high barking shout off to the right, in the black sea between the lights.

From the film. Of course. And from Hélène's email.

"Hell is just a word," a second voice says, somewhere to the left. Closer. Lower, almost as though it doesn't want to be heard.

"Go have a movie night and leave me alone," Roger says, a boldness edging his fear now. His voice cracked with disuse but strong and projected, the ghost of the young actor. "I'm going to bed."

The laugh comes from behind him, inside the house: "Haha ha, haha ha." Followed by a sharp click.

He spins around, pain flaring in his left hip. There's nothing in the entrance hall. The high ceiling and dark slate tiles play with the acoustics, so the voice might not have been as close as it seemed. It wasn't brushing against his shoulder.

A faint odor, grease and an unwashed body. It could be one of Faber's people he smells. Or even himself. It strikes him that he's been too afraid to bathe. Hearing the strange laugh while standing vulnerable in the shower, his withered body clinging to the safety rails all over the main bathroom, would feel too much like the crypt in Hélène's film.

His focus is so bent toward his too many silent rooms that he almost forgets someone could be creeping up behind him from outside. He steps back, raises his cane like a foolish club as he closes and locks the door. He presses the stay button on the alarm system. *Stay*, the word he knows more intimately than any other.

"Haha ha, haha ha." Click. Distant, upstairs again. He swears he knows that laugh.

Roger goes back to his study to call the police for a second time.

# CHAPTER THIRTEEN
## Beth

▶▶ She hears Oli tell his mom, "Beth is up!" His voice like Christmas morning. Her first day as their guest and he's already pulled her into their tiny family.

Beth's heart hurts, though, thinking of how lonely the kid must be.

It took about an hour with Oli yesterday, past his usual bedtime, before they were a bit obsessed with each other. The way he giggles, she'd call it a cackle because of how it bursts out of him, but it's so soft and close to melody. Loose and free and without the need for thought. The way he shifts into serious, too, his eyes getting big and watchful, taking her in.

She washes her sleep away in the house's one bathroom, then dries her face with a small towel patterned with oyster shells as something taps its way along the wall from the bedrooms to the kitchen. The doll. Beth can't remember the creepy thing's name.

His mom is lonely, too. Beth can tell with every glance Jorie darts at her, the hope flickering between guarded and naked. Jorie takes up so little space in the house, not wanting to intrude even in her own life. Her shoulders drawn in. The last ten years written all over her.

In that amazing forest surrounding the cabin, a million leaves getting ready to fall, Beth told her to be a mama bear. It was good to see some bear energy when Jorie confronted her about the October Film Haunt post yesterday, and it's good to see glimpses of it here in her home.

The three of them eat breakfast in the dining nook, Jorie's office. Scrambled eggs, toast, vegan sausage cooked in a cast-iron skillet by Oli on a small stepstool, flannel pajamas getting too short for his arms and legs. His hair is sleep-matted on the left side. The cold morning creeps up and breathes on the windows. The trees are lovely ghosts caught in ground fog.

Oli talks about school, his cousins, how his breath froze in his lungs some mornings last winter and how this year will be easier because he'll be ready for it. Agatha—Beth swears she won't forget the name again—sits on the table next to his plate, staring off into her Victorian past. Beth tells Oli about *The Favorite Pants*, a short animated film she edited two years ago, and promises to show it to him on YouTube later.

He goes quiet after he cleans his plate, and raised eyebrows from his mom tell him to get ready for school. Beth is sure he's going to hug her, he takes a sliding step toward her chair, but he runs down the hall instead. Agatha's face taps a secret code along the hallway and into his room.

It feels good, sitting here, watching the two of them. But sad, too. Ten years ticking away, and she and Jorie were always this close to finding each other again.

Jorie lifts her eyebrows at Beth now. *The movie*, they're saying. *The October Film Haunt, the cabin, the Rickies.* Too nervous to bring horror into the house with words while her son is here.

"Will this be the montage?" Beth asks her. "Where we make a plan?"

Jorie watches the piece of hallway she can see from the nook. "I don't know," she says, then drops her voice. "What would we even plan? When it comes to ghostly pranks, even Velma and Daphne had more to go on than we do."

Beth smiles and looks around the room. "Okay, so coming into the cabin—*breaking* into the cabin, even if I did leave the door unlocked. That puts us at police involvement level. It wouldn't go anywhere, but it would be on the record." She pauses, reaches back for the storm of hair she had in her twenties. She catches Jorie grinning at that. "You know, I got used to not having twenty-five pounds of hair anymore, but you're making me all nostalgic. Like my muscle memory is haunting me."

"I love it," Jorie says. "Don't stop. Grow it back out."

"It got in the way once I had a real job and had to get up early. I'm getting my first gray hairs, too." Beth pushes her bangs away from her eyes. "Anyway, after a police report, I think we look at social media, Reddit, maybe even 4chan and the uglier corners of the internet."

Jorie sits back in her chair. "I was thinking of sending Oli down to his dad in Georgia, but . . ." Her eyes close for a moment, her lips press into a line, holding the anxiety back. When she comes back to the moment, there's a grimness to her, and a light like a stove eye heating up. "I want him here with me. I'm not ready to trust his dad with anything."

"Done!" Oli comes skidding down the floorboards into the room, wearing socks and holding blue sneakers that have seen better days. He almost tumbles forward but catches himself and laughs again, that infectious, half-wild sound Beth already loves.

"Okay, let's go," Jorie says. She gets up and grabs her coat from the hook by the front door, bends—but not much—to kiss the top of Oli's head. Plucks her keys out of the brown glass dish, then looks back and smiles at Beth. Her expression is almost timid, but her eyes narrow for a second, the smile hardens again.

Good. If this is a movie, it opens with Jorie. Maybe there's a thrilling death before the title screen, or something that calls back to the original *Proof of Demons*, but it really begins with Jorie, signaling to the audience that she's the final girl. In the editing bay, Beth would start with the VHS tape in the mailbox, a piece of cheap plastic from an era that still has weight in so many hearts. A close-up of Jorie's face. The tape, an old sorrow coming into her eyes, a breeze scraping leaves across the gravel driveway.

Now they're out here, in the cloud-building hush of the second act. She and Jorie need to roll the credits, name the names, before those clouds open up. Thinking in terms of final girls is a bit much, but Beth doesn't care. It has to be on their list.

Oli waves at her, more love in his face than she has any right to after thirteen hours. She blows him a kiss back.

Jorie leads her cub outside.

Beth is fidgety while Jorie drives Oli to school, picking up the few framed photographs off the mantel, the side tables, and placing them back perfectly along their pristine lines in the fine dust. There's a recent picture of Jorie holding up a pumpkin that's bigger than her head. Oli is mid-laugh with his arms around her waist. Beth can already recognize Vermont around them and in their snug knit caps, the thickness of their coats.

Another is of foliage like paint swirled in a tray, deep reds and vivid yellows and burning oranges spattered across the world from the rise of a road in the mountains. It was taken from inside a car, the passenger side, probably by Oli. The windshield wasn't quite clean, and he caught a faint reflection on the glass.

One photo contains Eric, to match the one of Oli and his dad on his bedside bookshelf. His hair is sandy, kind of feathered like a frat boy's. He has Jorie and Oli pulled into one-armed hugs that feel uncomfortable, too proprietary, but maybe Beth is projecting because she would enjoy punching his face. She had to stop herself from turning the other picture face down last night when Jorie insisted on moving her son into her room, so Beth wouldn't have to take the sofa.

Crazy fans, icky exes, a sequel she never wanted. She feels balanced on an edge.

She calls Monse just to hear her voice. "I miss you," they say at the same time, followed by "Jinx!" in perfect stereo. The laughter feels even better than reconciling with Jorie.

"Is it cold up there?" Monse asks. Her voice recedes for a moment. "My phone said it was touching the thirties this morning."

"It's coldish." But Beth feels warm, talking to her wife. "I was wearing the plaid flannel you gave me. That thing's more of a quilt than a shirt. I look kind of silly in it."

"Pics or it didn't happen—do people still say that?" But the pining small talk doesn't last long. "You got a package yesterday. From some place called Pine Arch Research. Want me to open it?"

Beth sighs, but she can suddenly feel her heart. "I called you to get away from Pine Arch anything, but sure."

There's some rattling, the sound goes muddy. Then Monse comes back on. "It's an old videocassette. Label just has *casting call* written on it. Oh, wait, one side of it's gone. It's hollowed out."

"Anything inside?" Beth can't help it, chills break out everywhere on her, as though all her blood is hiding. She also can't help guessing, because that's what she used to do when watching horror movies. "A piece of fabric, cut out of a bedsheet?"

"No." Monse pauses. "It's just a postcard with mountains. And GREETINGS FROM VERMONT, big letters. This has something to do with why you're up there, I'm guessing?"

"Basically. I don't know much yet. I'm staying at Jorie's and . . ." A trembling movement in the corner of her eye. Beth turns and sees a pale green sheet through the kitchen window. An eyeless ghost looking in at her.

"I thought you were staying at Nancy's Airbnb—"

"I have to go. I'll call you back. I love you." Beth ends the call and stares at the window. Several seconds go by before she lets herself believe it's just a sheet, with no one inside it. Just like at the cabin.

She steps into the kitchen, pulls a knife from the block on the counter, and squeezes the handle in a fist, absorbing the heft and the grain of the fake wood. Silence pours into the room. She goes outside through the back door, stands in the sunlight struggling its way toward warmth.

Someone laughs. She thinks she hears a second person join them, there's the sound of someone running on the left side of the house, already too distant to be sure.

"You want your movie?" she calls out, and walks to the sheet hanging over the window. "Come get it!" She pulls it off a small hook, this time without tearing it, and notices the glossy brown ribbon trailing out of it and across the grass. The innards pulled out of a VHS cassette, probably the one Monse was just holding, the light making the tape look wet as it disappears between two pines.

But the trees stand apart. There's no arch of touching boughs.

Beth follows the ribbon through the yard, straining her ears to pick something out of the silence. Distant cars, the single rusty caw of a crow. She stops at the hemline of the trees, where a skirt of damp gloom is laid out toward another road, more houses, the rest of the world. All the properties around here must have these brief hollows of wildness between them.

Behind the two pines, a wooden crown sits on a bed of needles, nestled at the base of a paper birch. Three cruel spikes rise seven inches at least, tapering to points that could draw blood. The space between them nearly symmetrical.

In *Proof of Demons*, the crowns look roughly carved, but there's still a strange majesty to them. An intent. This one is amateurish, like someone just learning to whittle on a front porch. It fits what she and Jorie have been assuming—fans with cameras, too much free time but not quite enough patience. Most of all, a shoestring budget.

But she's staring at the crown. The longer she does, the more she thinks the clumsiness of it might be more effective, there's something that feels rustic and even more pagan. It could work as a clever aesthetic choice for a horror sequel, to make the props rougher. To go grittier.

"A comment on the dialogue between creator and fan," Beth says, rolling her eyes. She can see the film-snob rant now, as though it's already posted on some message board. Even as a sliver of her wants to read it.

So the crown tells her nothing. Is she supposed to put it on, pull the sheet over her body, run into the trees laughing? She already has the requisite knife. It's growing heavy in her hand.

She listens to the woods for a long time but turns in slow circles, watching the back door of the house, watching the rest of the tree line. In the end she takes one step into the gloom and stomps on the crown, bringing her foot down from an angle in case it could pierce her shoe. All three of the spikes break off, and the snaps sound clean and crunching and therapeutic.

"*Fuck* you!" she screams. The world is too far away to hear her.

Jorie is silent as Beth shows her the sheet, the shattered crown, the puddle of brown tape behind the house. Her cheeks are flushed and the rest of her is too pale. She pulls out her phone and calls Lantman's to tell them she can't come in today, as the sun burns the clouds down to scattered threads.

"This is just a couple of guys trying to scare us," Beth says when Jorie hangs up. "If it's Enriquez, we must be a side plot. It's too amateur."

"Or they're making found footage. They'd shoot way more than they need." Jorie stares into the trees. She's clenching her teeth, making the muscles in her jaw jump. "They were at my house. My *house*. You could have been hurt."

"They were laughing again as they ran off," Beth says. "I think they really are just Reddit kids. It's a prank. It might be on TikTok already."

"You're probably right." Jorie says it like she's giving up. "I want more coffee."

Jorie gets the pot brewing while Beth turns on the VCR. They queue up the *Funeral Watching* tape Beth found in the cabin.

It's identical to the one left in Jorie's mailbox. The two of them sip from Jorie's grandparents' mugs. They don't speak as the funeral scenes play, there's none of the old commentary or the wash of inspiration. As the last clip nears its end, Beth raises the remote to turn it off.

Jorie grabs her arm and pulls it down. "Something was different," she says. "They changed it. It was different when I saw it online, too. I just don't know how." Beth lets it play out, the small blond boy entering the birch trees, the mouth of cool darkness, where the waiting creatures beckon with their arms like corrupted cartoon figures. The minister murmurs in the background.

"What is it?" Beth says.

But then an undeniable change comes, the camera retracting and jerking in segments toward the left. The group of mourners blur in their chairs until the frame stills again. Beth has time to think that they'll see the casket for the first time, and for half a second she *can* see it—someone is sitting up, a smudged face behind a veil, staring across the lawn at the camera. But this is soon blocked by a woman in the extreme foreground, inches from the lens.

The TV is six feet from where they're sitting, but Beth still shrinks back from it. The woman's great brown eye fills the lower left corner of the shot. A round, upturned nose, a dull cheekbone. Dark hair curtains her face. The eye is so close that Beth can see its pupil dilate, then narrow to a pinhole, a shutter between daze and clarity. A rill of blood collects in the woman's eyebrow, building up until it's ready to spill.

The sharp corner of a smile lifts into the frame, changing the woman's eye from terror to creepy mirth. The blood overflows the eyebrow. The clip cuts off into static.

"Okay, what the hell was that about?" Beth looks at Jorie, who seems unfocused herself. "Jorie?"

"A minute," she says. Then her head lifts up, and she turns to Beth. "That was the boy's mother, I think. The first thing that was different was she didn't scream, like she did on my tape. Before, she screams and the reverend or whoever stops speaking. The boy went into the trees here, too, but now the mom doesn't see it. She's been . . . hurt, I guess."

"Is that supposed to mean something?" Beth mutes the TV snow and sets the remote down. "I'm guessing she's not the Márcia Smith equivalent if she's happy about her kid being taken."

"I don't know," Jorie answers. "It doesn't feel nice, though."

Beth scoots closer to her friend. "And does this change our minds, could maybe Enriquez be involved? I know what I said in the backyard, but these scenes are too good for a copycat."

"Maybe. No. You and Colin studied her even more than I did. But wouldn't you agree this tape is too—too *something*, or not something enough? And why *us*?"

"I'm not really trusting myself here, Jorie. We're rusty." Beth puts her hand on Jorie's knee. "If it is her, we have to find out what she wants. Hannah's all that connects us to Enriquez, so what does Hannah mean to her?"

Jorie's eyes go distant at the name.

Beth sighs, pulls Jorie to her, and for a minute they sit with this quiet wedge between them. All the years open back up. The magic word *Hannah*, the ghost of Colin sitting next to them, his knees bouncing because he could never sit still for long.

"It's time to move forward, babe," Beth says, still pressing Jorie against her. "We have to see where we are."

They enumerate yet again. Someone is tracking them, following, sending things. Discussing them on Reddit threads, putting words in their mouths on social media. Getting off on their discomfort, probably. They decide on the paper trail of a police report. Statements on social platforms, terse and dismissive of the October Film Haunt and anything to do with *Proof of Demons*. They'll ask the world to let the past stay where it belongs. They'll reach out to anyone from their old lives who might be able to help them find Enriquez. They'll follow those dead ends.

Jorie sums it up. "If this is about contrition, we'll show ourselves to the world." She lifts Beth's hand and laces their fingers together. "But if there really is a sequel, we're staying the hell off-screen."

"Okay, how does this sound?" Beth turns in her chair, pushes her bangs out of her eyes. "'We are not involved with any *Proof of Demons* or October Film Haunt production. We ask that our privacy be respected and our online personas be removed from discussion. Sincerely, Jorie Stroud and Beth Kowalczyk.' It's short enough for all the socials."

Jorie is standing at the sink, washing a few dishes and scrubbing out the coffeepot. "It's fine," she says. "It's good enough for most people, and the rest will believe what they want, whatever makes the most noise and the worst memes."

"I'll take 'good enough for most people.'" Beth puts her phone down, crosses the kitchen, and grabs a towel to dry the plates in the rack. "So we'll each post that. I've messaged everyone I still know from back in the day and a few people I haven't talked to since before everything that happened. Some of them are still in indie horror. Maybe somebody's heard rumors about Enriquez, the original cast, a new production, whatever. *Proof of Demons* was so off the grid, especially by today's standards, so I don't know if there's much to find."

Jorie turns off the water and looks out the window at the backyard. "Whatever we can find out. And when the police come, I need to figure out how safe the house is, and if Oli can stay here. Sam could take him for a few days. That might help me. . . ."

"What's wrong?" Beth says when Jorie doesn't finish her thought. Jorie swipes her hands on a towel and half-runs out the back door. Beth follows her into the bright afternoon, across the grass. "Jorie, what is it?"

They stop at the tree line, forty or so feet to the right of where the unspooled tape led Beth to the wooden crown. "In the kitchen," Jorie says, "I saw the sun reflect off something." She points into the trees, at a metal box strapped to a maple. Textured brown paint, bark-colored, an antenna molded to look like a twig. Its camera eye peers at them and at the house.

"A trail cam," Beth says. "Like we're wildlife. Jesus." She walks over to it and swivels the antenna down. "This thing probably costs less than two hundred dollars. It's sending the footage wirelessly, no one even has to come get it. Amateur. Found-footage heaven."

Jorie pushes her aside and puts her face up against the lens. Beth thinks of the woman at the funeral on the new tape, her foregrounded eye lost in a trance until that awful smile appears. Jorie's giving them a perfect little parallel moment.

"Leave us alone. This place is going to be crawling with cops. It's done." Jorie spits on the lens. There's something violent in her face. She bends to the ground and straightens with a clump of damp earth in her hand. She smears it across the entire face of the camera.

"I don't know if it records audio," Beth says. "I can check."

But Jorie ignores her. She pulls at the box, trying to break the black straps, too angry to reach around and unclip them on the other side of the maple.

"There could be others. We should look." Beth tugs at her arm. "Jorie, we should look."

Jorie turns, but neither of them sees the drone hovering low over the roof. Wasp eyes, silent propellers, the same charcoal color as the shingles. It watches the two women, then lifts toward the newly open blue sky, retreating over the house, the gravel driveway, skimming over the woods and the road toward the endless lake.

# INTERLUDE

[Excerpt from "Proof of Demons," *Wikipedia*]

## Contents

Plot
Cast
    Use of amateurs
    Roger Eilertsen
Release
Reception
Controversy
    Kim death and trial
    Occult hysteria
Popular culture
    The Pine Arch Creature
    Reddit mythology
    October Film Haunt claims
    Hélène Enriquez rumors
References
External links

## Hélène Enriquez rumors [edit]

The name Hélène Enriquez is largely assumed to be pseudonymous, but theories purporting to unmask the director have persisted in online communities. Most common is that Enriquez also directed the 2008 YouTube film *Under the House* under the pseudonym Lecomte, primarily due to the wooden crown it shares with *Proof of Demons*. Neither director has an internet presence of any kind.

In 2017, a Reddit user claimed Enriquez was actually Eduardo Sánchez, codirector of *The Blair Witch Project* (1999).[28] It has also been rumored that the alter ego belonged to Adam Wingard, director of the 2016 *Blair Witch* reboot, paying homage to Sánchez with a more guerrilla-style filmmaking approach.[29] These claims were denied,[30] and no evidence was presented, much as when rumors persisted that *Proof of Demons* features several actual murders rather than staged scenes with actors. Several other directors' names have been floated before and since, with minimal traction, most notably Ari Aster, whose *Hereditary* (2018) is also regularly featured on lists of all-time scariest movies and said to bear a mastery of bleak intensity and atmosphere similar to that of *Proof of Demons*.

Noted horror genre figures have shared thoughts on Enriquez as well; director Michelle Garza Cervera (*Huesera: The Bone Woman*) spoke in 2022 of *Proof of Demons*' influence on the genre, citing it as an early example of the wave of "elevated horror" films.[31] In a 2015 interview with *Rue Morgue*, Orrin Grey (*Incarnate*, 1989) praised Enriquez's one known film, pointing to the mysterious director's "unequaled fearlessness in letting the camera build dread through a lack of movement." He also asked fans to stop projecting a male identity onto Enriquez: "We should be open to women of such immense talent."[32]

In 2018, the web blog Corpsehaint (now defunct) published a lengthy interview with Enriquez discussing the Transfiguration scenes, the door to hell, the film's use of static shots, and the theme of belonging, among other topics. However, the entire interview was believed to be fake,[33] merely adding another layer to the myth of Hélène Enriquez.

# CHAPTER FOURTEEN

## Coleman

▶▶ What he saw in the trees, the thing that crawled into his mouth. He feels different since the woods yesterday. If he had someone to talk to—the therapist Gloria is trying to push on him, or even a priest—he would wonder aloud if his cancer has been given the idea of a body, seeping out of his pores like tar, coming and going as it pleases. Tasting the world before it drags Coleman out of it.

There was something about the thing, the shape. He can spill words on the floor and none of them work. He feels it on him now. A familiarity, a resonant ache inside the terror. An echo, smudged. Older than his sickness.

The shape was not the angel he saw peering at him from some unknowable place as his brother lay shrieking with a broken arm. But the angel is close to the truth. It is like a nagging memory that squirms at the edges of his childhood.

The differences in him are small. He itches once or twice an hour, and his skin seems to darken for a moment when he scratches it, as though his fingernails are pushing at the rot inside his body. Faint smoke-gray bruises that fade almost as soon as he pulls his fingers away. He wonders if the cancer is everywhere now, soaking him like a sponge.

But he slept through the night and woke refreshed. He said small, unimportant things that made Gloria laugh and pause and look at him with naked hope on her face, just because of the way he said them. Unthinking, loose sentences that didn't sound exhausted.

He feels stronger this morning, at least, but there are moments when his lungs panic to find air. Before bed last night, he thought he could feel a swelling in his throat. Something was caught in it again. He went into the bathroom and pressed his hands around his neck. The sooty imprints of his fingers vanished in the mirror.

But Evie gets here today. That's all that matters for now.

Her flight lands late this afternoon, and Coleman doesn't know how to factor this new frailty, whatever it is, into what he will say to her. The three of them will sit in the living room, Gloria fidgeting, and their daughter's eyes will be crawling on him, seeing all the weight he's lost, the bruised lunar valleys under his eyes, the quick sharpening of his cheekbones.

The last time he saw her was before the pain and coughing and the doctor's calm blank voice. It was easy to shrug off as the ravages of time, his body getting ready to be an old man.

Another new thing: the pressing image of Jackson swimming out to Sarah Layton's canoe that day. When the memory slides into his mind, at odd instances that feel like the memory is having him instead of the other way around, there is a high clarity, and a sort of doubling as Coleman sees what must be himself standing on the lakeshore.

He sees the surface of the lake close up over Jackson's head, the bright rippling worm of the sun dragging across the water, and that white glimmer of a young Coleman terribly far away. The Coleman on the beach tilts away into clouds and the burning light and the blur of submersion as Jackson goes under.

The mineral taste of the lake, the thrashing of his brother's arms and legs. The endless seconds before arms drag him out and into the canoe. The little boat nearly capsizing as Jackson flops at its rear.

Did Sarah's father yell, *Whoa there, honey, we caught us a big one!* loud enough that his voice drifted across the lake, thinning and flattening as it came? What was her father's name? Why is the ghost of that day haunting him?

Memory is its own cancer.

"You have to eat something, honey," Gloria says, and for a moment her voice drowns and warps under the water, too. His wife is a stone plunked into the lake. Coleman comes out of the half-trance, somehow in the kitchen, climbing up onto the bar chair at the granite counter. Gloria, always so beautiful in the morning when sleep has just let go of her, sets a grapefruit and the top half of a bagel down in front of him, a small bowl of sugar beside the plate.

She reaches across to his hand, but he pulls it away. He can't let her touch him and see bruises shaped like her fingers.

"I'm just woolgathering," he tells her. "I'll eat. I'm hungry." He realizes it's true. Thinking of the grapefruit's sour tang, the grainy rush of sugar, his mouth floods with saliva. As sharp and metallic as the lake. He picks up the spoon.

"I don't know if you should be driving today," Gloria says. "I can leave work early and pick Evie up."

"No, it'll do me good," he says, staring down at the counter. "I want to talk to her before we tell her. This is the last time I get to be her dad as she knows me. Before I'm a ticking clock. Just a dad talking to his daughter about normal things that aren't death."

"Oh God, Coleman, don't say things like that." She closes her eyes, pushing sudden tears out. He has always felt such sadness seeing her cry, across the whole of their marriage. Her heart is never so close to his than when she is hurting. The tears are huge things rolling down her cheeks, glinting in the pendant light that hangs from the ceiling.

"Honey, please don't. The knife wound hardly hurts at all now. And I'm seeing Dr. Banchhod soon." He grimaces at the possible lie, and adds another. "We're doing what we can."

He can't admit he hasn't decided about treatment. He can't bring himself to put more dread on her shoulders. His life has become a list of things he can't do.

Gloria smiles, her eyes shine with new tears that will not quite spill over as she gets ready for work, trying to stay close to the kitchen in case he needs anything. He hears the sound of her voice as she tells him what her day will be like, but not the words themselves. His mind is filling back up now, a day when he and Jackson were in the woods behind their house in Greensboro.

Midafternoon but almost night as dark clouds packed the sky. A huge storm was coming, and the thick air squeezed the two boys with a great humid heat, a sharp cord of cold knitting through. He can feel that cold, the wrongness of it, and he can taste the stillness of the moment decades later.

It was maybe a year before they fell out of the oak and everything in his life turned bad. Jackson dared him to climb down into the fox den they'd found the week before, half-hidden in a deadfall. Coleman could just make it if he pretended he was a worm. *What if the rain comes, I could drown* he said, already knowing he had no choice.

*Those dead limbs are like a roof, you'll be drier than me. Do it, Coleman. You're littler.*

He had done it. Wriggled under that dry lattice of branches. Twigs raking the back of his T-shirt as the ground tipped down and the mouth of the den swam up to him. He placed his hands on the bottom lip of it, his breaths coming quick and shallow, then looked back at Jackson, who stood with his hands on his hips.

*Go on!*

Coleman turned back to the hole, and two eyes appeared in its gray dark, flat and full of light like coins at the bottom of a well. A low, purring growl, the faintest light falling through the lid of clouds to gleam on wet teeth.

He remembers scrambling backward and up, skinning his knees. He doesn't remember gaining his feet, but seconds later the sky was torn open by lightning. The answering thunder was immediate. The lake fell out of the sky and they ran for home.

No, not the lake. Rain. It was just a fox, but he had screamed. At ten, eleven years old, his lungs were strong enough to inhale the world. He shakes that day out of his head. It is too vivid, the sensory details stitched with too much texture.

Gloria will be back any second to make sure he's eating. He's about to dig the spoon into the grapefruit when he glimpses himself in the antique mirror above the stove. His face is bony even from ten feet away, the loose skin and sharp planes of a dying man, but it's the grin he can't look away from. It looks already dead somehow, like something holding a secret. He doesn't feel it on his face, his mouth isn't making the shape of it, but there it is.

Something begins to happen to his eyes, black holes eating into his cheeks and up toward his receding hairline. He pulls at his face with one hand, leaving dark lines that soak the skin, but his reflection keeps grinning. He stares until sparks light up in the bruised mess, the flare of tiny green lamps swallowing the dead caves of his eyes.

Suddenly he's looking at the thing that was guarding the fox den. The thing smiles back.

*Fox. It was a fox.*

He pulls his phone over, opens the camera and reverses the lens to selfie mode to get a closer look. His face is normal, his eyes are normal, a green that isn't as pure, as moss-colored as it was when he was a boy. Rimmed with red all the time now. They're not the eyes the fox gazed into, but they are his all the same.

Coleman looks back up at the mirror and sees only his face. But another face is behind him, peeking over his shoulder, blurred and grinning.

"Honey?" he says. Now his voice has changed, distant and deep, calling out from the well. The fox's voice, to match the lost lamp eyes. The sugar bowl slides across the counter on its own, and he darts his hand out to stop it just before it falls to the floor. The movement feels like the reflexes of a twenty-year-old Coleman, his lungs feel bigger, as though they're pushing against his rib cage.

He closes his eyes, squeezing them shut until he hears a faint rumble in his ears, and sits on the stool with his hand still on the sugar bowl. Gloria doesn't come back into the kitchen. She must not have heard the strange *Honey?* he croaked at her.

Only Coleman is in the mirror when he looks a final time, his spoon still pointed at the grapefruit, the kitchen around him and the living room framed by a doorway. But what was there, in his face, in the woods with him? What was in their bedroom the day he scared Evie into coming home?

"Really, Coleman?" she says. "You'll really call the therapist?"

His wife pauses in the kitchen, the door to the garage half-open. Her left hand clutches her lunch bag and keys. Her purse hangs off her shoulder. Some of her hair is caught under the strap. The sun wakes up through the window, and she is so lovely and brave. He imagines all the years she has left, the wound of his death scabbing over until she can be Gloria again. That smile he used to coax out. A hint of a dimple on the right side of her mouth.

"I promise." He stands up straighter. His lungs hang in the cavity of his body with their awful weight. They don't feel strong now, but there is no cough on its way up his throat. "I'll call in just a bit." He takes a deep breath, filling himself, wondering if she notices.

"I hope you do. You know how hard it is to get you to talk and open up." She places the side of an index finger beneath each of her eyes to catch any tears that might smudge her modest eyeliner. "I'm proud of you. I can stay, if you want."

"No, you go on. I'll be fine. Then Evie and I will be here waiting for you."

He hears her make a noise out in the garage, a sob wrapped in a laugh. The double door grinds its way up, the car backs out, the door grinds down. Coleman is alone with his haunted thoughts.

The mail brings a new envelope postmarked Hinesburg VT 05461, this time with *JORIE → 114 High Rock Road* scribbled in the top left corner. A single sheet of paper inside contains a new typed message, *I BELONG → You Will Come ← YOU BELONG*. Below this is a similar message, but handwritten: *There Is Jorie → Jackson ← Jorie Is There*.

A memory of Jackson's disappearance comes as he stares at his brother's name on this message from Vermont. He's twelve and in shock in the memory. He's telling one of the police officers that an angel took Jackson, that the red line on the wall was the door to heaven but it's closed now. That was why Coleman heard him say *I belong with you*, and why something spoke back. The officer's palm is warm against his cheek. She has black hair and a kind soft face.

Someone, the director of that movie, the man with the knife, ANOTHER GREEN WORLD Prod., has fixated on that morning. *I belong with you.* A similar red line is on the nursing home wall in the movie that keeps circling around him, finding all the holes in him and getting in. One of the old women in *Proof of Demons* calls it the door to hell. Is all of this about what took his brother, and where? Heaven or hell, which of them is wrong? How could either be right?

His fingers have made a fist around the paper. He smooths the page out on the kitchen counter and avoids looking in the mirror over the stove. He doesn't have any idea what a Jorie is, either, and having to wonder makes him tired. He loses his energy so quickly now.

The therapist's number is in the home office. Gloria has turned their old corkboard into a calendar of death with small platitudes along the edges like flowers trying to grow in waste. *Only those who will risk going too far can possibly find out how far one can go*, as T. S. Eliot allegedly put it, is printed over a desert sunset. A blurred cactus on either side of the foreground. Gloria must be trying to put a positive spin on the sickness of chemotherapy.

He pulls a tack out of a business card and stares at the simple, crisp font for a moment. EMERSON BEKKER, LMSW, PSYCHOTHERAPIST. Right here in Arden. The paper is soft, almost pulpy, maybe to signify comfort. A pillow. A long, long rest.

The haiku comes back to him, the one handwritten on the back of the card he found in the woods before the shape found him: *a beautiful cure/for cancer in the paper/birches of Vermont*. That card is in the bedroom, he thinks, in his nightstand drawer along with *Proof of Demons*. A desire to go get it flushes his face, warm as embarrassment. His throat clenches shut for a second, his vision swims.

"No," he whispers. "I don't need it." He can see normally. He takes another deep, clean breath. The moment is gone, and he sits down at the desk beside the corkboard and dials the grief therapist's number.

"Meridian Counseling Group," a bright, young voice says.

"Yes, hello," Coleman says, then stops. The warmth he felt in his face is spreading down his neck, painful now. Hot fingers dig into his throat, and he feels his Adam's apple shift. Then the fingers change to something that's on the inside, pushing against his windpipe.

"Can I help you?" the voice says when it's clear nothing more is coming.

Coleman clears his throat, coughing not because of his lungs but simply to get the terrible invasive sensation out. "Sorry," he says, "this is Coleman Smith. I need to speak with Dr. Bekker. Or make an appointment. Maybe *doctor* is the wrong word, I've never done therapy before. I'm dying of cancer." His voice is still strained, but he manages to get all these words into the receiver, and almost sinks back in the chair in relief.

"Okay, Mr. Smith, I'm so sorry to hear that. Let me pull up Emerson's schedule." The phone makes a rasping sound, as though dragged across the person's face.

"Could you tell me a little about what your goals are with therapy? I'd like to get some basic information and leave a note."

"I think there's someone inside me," Coleman says, and a second voice says it with him. In corrupted stereo, under his normal, slightly reedy tone, is the *Honey?* voice from the kitchen.

A watery moan escapes his mouth, but this time he is the only one making the sound. He presses the phone's end button and puts his face in his hands. He tries to cry but nothing will come out of his eyes. Even the sick flush of heat is gone.

*My wife wants me to talk to someone about navigating my terminal illness.* This is what he was supposed to say. The words he imagined saying a few days ago, and when he practiced them out loud to Gloria, she had to leave the room.

He digs his iPhone from his pocket, opens the camera app again. His hand trembles as it reaches out to flip the camera lens toward him. He holds the phone up.

Black ink swarms in his eyes, filling each sclera. Black irises. His pupils are gone.

Coleman blinks. He blinks again and again and again before he lets himself look a second time. Finally, his sad faded green eyes stare out of the screen at him. He breathes out until his dying lungs feel like wrung-out dishrags. He wipes a tear the color of old ash from his cheek before it can reach his mouth and force him to taste what is happening to him.

# CHAPTER FIFTEEN

## Jorie

▶▶ "Maybe it's for one of those prank shows," one of the officers says. KITZ, his nameplate gleams. He's another horror cliché, a buzz cut that looks like a million cops in ten thousand movies. "Or that TikTok, something trending."

"Yeah, maybe," Jorie says, trying not to sigh and roll her eyes at the same time. "Pretty niche, though."

The police take the original videocassette, the trail cam, the unspooled tape, the bedsheet, the broken crown. Jorie would add their statements to the list, but she's not sure the two officers write down anything in detail. She hears a lot of empty words, the occasional disbelieving *hmm* when they ask her and Beth for the third or sixth time if anyone has a reason to target them. Not enough scratching of pens in their little notebooks.

Jorie catches herself summarizing the Hannah Kim part of the backstory. Not to minimize what happened or her own role in it, but because a panic attack makes a fist around her voice when she gets to Hannah. The physical sounds of the words have trouble getting out. It's too much like picking up a remote and fast-forwarding through the boring part of the movie. Shame burns in her.

They'll have a police report, an official paper trail. But without any phone calls or intruder sightings on the property or written threats or human contact, the officers jump to the easy conclusion.

"Just local kids," the second officer muses. ARMFIELD, with a refreshing ponytail Jorie doesn't think she's ever seen on a male cop in a horror film.

Beth leaves the second tape, the one with the close-up of the horrible woman and her eyebrow full of blood, unmentioned in the VCR. An unspoken decision passes between her and Jorie as they fall back into the silent language of best friends that might never have lost each other for more than a quarter of their lives.

The officers leave in a cloud of platitudes—"Lock your doors at night" and "These kids will get bored soon enough," almost in stereo—and promise to come back and check everything for fingerprints.

Beth looks at Jorie with that half-telepathy again. "Well, we think it's kids, too," she says.

Then the school day is done. Beth's short, *The Favorite Pants*, on Jorie's laptop, the women laughing and the boy lost in some kind of awe. Salads for dinner. Movie night on the sofa, Oli falling asleep against Beth's shoulder, gradually sliding down onto her lap. His mouth hangs open. Beth smiles and pulls a fleece blanket over him. The windows grow wet fog as the temperature slides down into the forties.

A thought strikes Jorie. She whispers, "You think they're waiting for October to start?" But Beth is sleeping, too. Jorie didn't notice her holding her son's hand until now.

She wakes her phone and searches her name, looking for clues again. She comes across a blog post she's never seen before, titled "Under *Under the House*." It's from an October Film Haunt website, though Jorie, Beth, and Colin never gave that movie the OFH treatment. No one knew where the titular house was located, so they couldn't visit the filming site and record their impressions. It was unhauntable, a bizarre thing that languished on their list. *Under the House* was never released in any traditional sense, only uploaded to YouTube by a "director" even closer to anonymous than Hélène Enriquez.

Beth and Colin were convinced that Lecomte—French for "the count" and the name of the YouTube channel responsible for *Under the House*—was a pseudonym of Enriquez. There was a similar vibe in the film, an inscrutable, patient quality that could be seen as a precursor to *Proof of Demons*, which was released the following year. Most famously, Enriquez used paganish, roughly carved crowns similar to the one seen in a dog's mouth in *Under the House*. It was yet another topic fans argued about online.

Even so, Jorie never quite believed Lecomte and Enriquez were the same. She claimed the Lecomte movie was too homemade, too film school, too edging into cosmic horror, as though some Lovecraftian thing would be waiting through that hole in the cellar wall if the movie kept going. Both were deeply unsettling, but *Proof of Demons* never felt like it was made by the same eye, in the same spirit.

Colin bet her a hundred dollars that he would prove her wrong one day.

There's a creepy analogue she has to admit now, though. For at least ten minutes halfway through *Under the House*, Lecomte's companions stare into the camera without speaking. The third scene on her VHS tape echoes this, the funeral mourners turning their heads toward the viewer with such obscene slowness.

This new similarity gnaws at her for a minute as her son sleeps curled up on her friend. She wants to tell Colin that maybe she was just being stubborn back then. She feels herself sinking further into the murk of connections and meta fascinations, drawing the years back. Like finding her own body under snowmelt in the first spring thaw.

Skimming the blog post and digging through Reddit for a few minutes, she learns that a group of men appropriated the October Film Haunt name. They claimed to have found where *Under the House* was shot, but there was no follow-up, just rumors about all four of them disappearing after setting out for the site. Their OFH blog was never updated, and speculation naturally swirled about this, too.

Several online threads make connections between her original October Film Haunt and this other group that stole the name. Jorie tries to decide if she's flattered or if it could be another awful feather in her cap, but she doesn't bother exploring it now. It reminds her just how many people out there believe found footage is real if it claims to be.

In a world with enough turned-over rocks in it for things like QAnon to crawl into the light, it's not exactly surprising.

Can't the movie just die? She turns back to the TV and cries to herself, only a little, as a beautifully carved Pinocchio navigates Fascist Italy, remembering the time Guillermo del Toro retweeted her and every day was October, all year. She'd open one of her scripts on her duct-taped laptop and see all those dark words singing against the white screen. She could make anything, fear and awe and metaphor.

She could have been anything.

"I can't call out sick again," Jorie says over breakfast, after Oli leaves the table for his morning rituals. "Back to work, school pickup, home from work. Make dinner. I'll have a new manuscript to edit in a couple of weeks, too. The movies skip over real life and all the house chores."

"Unless the monster's at the market." Beth pushes her plate a few inches away. "Then your job would get a lot of screen time."

"Don't even say that. I'd prefer that Rickies not shop at Lantman's."

"No, think about it," Beth says, and Jorie recognizes the old idea-forming look in her eyes, the leaning forward, her elbows on the table. "A public place.

They don't just want footage of your house and my cabin in the middle of nowhere. They're being voyeuristic. You climbing out of your car, walking into the store, maybe you pause and look back over your shoulder. You sense something is off. Meanwhile, these guys are *getting* off. Even worse, people online are starting to believe in all this shit again."

Jorie thinks of the fake October Film Haunt group. All the creepypasta people in the cracks of Reddit. She sits back in her chair, the opposite of elbows on the table. The windows are still wet. They're double-paned—her grandparents wouldn't have lived into their eighties in Vermont with Georgia windows—but they need to be replaced. The seals are old and the winters are starting to get in. Soon she won't be able to caulk her savings account, either.

"I can see them wanting to put the market in their movie," she tells Beth. "But then what? It seems like kind of a waste of time, hanging out and hoping."

"You have to be there regardless. And you said it yourself, real life doesn't let you gloss over the mundane fact of having to pay the bills." Beth's phone screen lights up. She lifts it and a quick smile makes her glow, too. She types something out. "My point is these guys might actually show up. And I can be there waiting."

"What, with a lasso? Come on, Beth. We need to be emailing the people who might still remember me. Someone has to have some idea of who these people are."

"We will. I've got a few more on my list. Trevor Henderson designed the Pine Arch Creature, he might know something. He might know someone who knows something. But if Enriquez is involved . . ." Beth lets the rest hang over the table and checks her phone again.

"Yeah, I know. Our research montage is going to be tough." Jorie pulls her coffee mug over—a print of morning glory vines around a rustic window and the letter *A*—and takes one last sip. "When do you have to go back to New York?"

"Not for a couple more days, at least. Until I know you're safe. Oh shit." Beth sits up straight, still looking at her phone. "There's some kind of new *Proof of Demons* teaser. You have to see this."

The room goes cold and damp, Beth's voice turns wobbly, but Jorie stands and walks the five feet around the table. Her legs are steady, but her heart knocks, insistent, inside her fleece robe as she looks over her friend's shoulder.

Beth is on TikTok. Her thumb slides a video back to the beginning.

There's no sound. Just the lake from the original film, an unsettled brown-blue. A green rash of trees across the background, a barely there tracery of mountains in the blank sky. VCR tracking lines, pink and yellow and white, corrupt the frame like static frothing the water. Then the shot cuts to found-footage movement through a wooded area, red pines blurring, daylight shifting. A knife lifts into the foreground, carried by the camera operator.

The image jumps again, still in the woods but now someone is standing hunched with their back to the camera. Trees are everywhere, slivering the frame. A square of rope seems to float above the leaf-choked ground. The person turns around, an older man, thinning orange hair threaded with glinting white, and the lens slowly zooms in on a face that seems to swarm with living bruises. The pale eyes widen.

Another jump, a low-res view of Beth's cabin, a sky clogged with low clouds. Curtains twitch and a face appears at the window beside the front door, then an abrupt cut to a funeral, and Jorie immediately recognizes the cemetery from *Proof of Demons*, the two famous pine trees centered in the shot, reaching across to each other. Mourners are grouped loosely to the left, and someone dressed in black is creeping across the lawn toward them, their elbows thrust out, sharp and exaggerated like a spider.

Jorie leans down until her chin is almost touching Beth's shoulder. Is it a child? It's impossible to tell. The same text from the first teaser appears on the screen, obscuring the crawling person. *Proof of demons?* followed by *#funeralwatching tell the trees you belong with them,* ending with *Record 6 minutes of stillness to be film haunted.* A new addition appears, *SOON,* and the video cuts off.

A total of seventeen seconds.

"Was that you in the cabin?" Jorie says. She glances down the hallway to make sure Oli hasn't emerged from his room. It's almost time to leave for school.

"It could have been me." Beth tilts her face up to look at Jorie. "But it was only a few seconds. There's probably a trail cam on one of the trees there, too. I'll have to let Nancy know before her next Airbnb guests get there. And the cops."

"But I still don't get it, why use October Film Haunt for a sequel? We weren't that interesting to begin with, and now we're just a footnote about death and mistakes." Tears shine in Jorie's eyes again, but this is anger as much as sorrow. If there were something nearby to break, she would reach for it. Part of her would prefer a Rickie's neck.

"Hey. Stop." Beth touches her left wrist, a gesture that would mean nothing to nearly anyone else, but Jorie knows that was where Beth's hair ties used to live. The two of them keep falling back in time. Or being pulled back.

"Mom!" Oli's voice, flooding the hallway. "I can't find my bear sweater."

Jorie wipes her eyes and wakes her phone to check the clock. "Okay, fine.

When I get back, I'll go to work and you can play Scooby-Doo in the parking lot."

Midmorning Lantman's is quiet. Beth points out from the passenger seat that it's the perfect time to get establishing shots for a horror film. Her seat is folded back so that it looks like Jorie is alone, just borrowing the rental car. "Just enough people and movement to give a scene life without crowding the frame," Beth says, raising herself up to peek, "but not so many that moms gets creeped out by a couple of men with video cameras."

"Are you cursed to think like a movie everywhere you go?" Jorie says. But she remembers feeling that way herself half the time in another life—and it came back the other day in Maple Walk Cemetery, when she recognized where the tape's footage had been shot.

"I did have cinematographer dreams once," Beth says. "Even the director's chair, before I got stuck in editing and realized I'm happy spending all my time in a cave. Let's not linger. The coast looks clear, but I don't want the little moviemakers to see us both and get spooked."

"Right, they're the ones who are spooked." But Jorie gets out of the car. Beth follows and they walk along the left edge of the parking lot, in the shade of a row of maple trees.

"Everybody knows sequels go bigger," Beth says. "So it makes sense that there'd be multiple Pine Arch creatures, right? Stuff like that. Enriquez can change the lore, because it was such an opaque lore in the first place. There might not even be an eye this time."

"Sure," Jorie says. "But the social media angle? Trying to start some viral demon challenge or, what, crowdsource a movie? Staging disappearances on iPhone video? That doesn't sound at all like her."

"She's reclusive, remember? Neither of us is on her wavelength, so who knows? I'll text you fun Scooby-Doo updates." Beth holds up her phone. "You can text me fun cashier updates. We'll synchronize our watches."

"In the unlikely event they follow us here," Jorie says, "and you see them." She looks around at the dozen or so cars and SUVs and trucks. "What would you even do?"

"Have words. Very strong words. Call the police." She pulls a small black cylinder out of a front pocket. "Fill their dumb faces with this."

"Mace?"

"Better, it's pepper spray. Burns way more but less toxic. I guess living up here in autumn utopia land has made you soft. Now *go.*" She slips the spray back into her pocket.

Jorie goes. She does turn and look over her shoulder before stepping too close to the automatic doors. Hopefully not giving anyone a good moment of her on video. Five-one, not much stronger than a child, her two inches of hair even making her look like a kid at enough of a distance. So vulnerable in a viewfinder, to a viewer.

Beth is standing under a maple that's still the color of old blood. In a few weeks, that red will brighten to 1980s slasher blood, a freshly opened vein. Then the leaves will fall and molder and they'll all do it again next year.

Jorie wants to take Beth in, half-reluctant even now to believe she's really here. She's helping her, they're together again. The aching lack of Colin is heavier in the presence of Beth, it hurts more and it hurts less. Jorie guesses that makes sense. She guesses that's the way it should be.

But she can't just stand out here, so she runs to the maple, back across to the fringe of the lot, and hugs Beth with something that is almost violence. "Thank you," she says into the hair Beth hasn't cut off. "I've missed you and I don't even think I knew just how much."

"Hey, you're welcome." Beth pulls her close. Jorie's cheek presses against her collarbone, she can hear the tears in Beth's voice, the way it turns dusky. The lumberjack flannel is warm. "People drift apart. I'm glad we didn't have to keep being those people. Now go to work and let me pick a hiding spot."

They both have to dry their eyes first.

No sign of antagonists is Beth's first text, on the dot at half past ten. Jorie is working a register today, wearing her cheerful mask, the tall windows at the front of the store framing her in a glass case for anyone outside who wants her on display. At night it would make for a stark scene setter.

Villainless in here too, she writes back.

Chip isn't working today, and Jorie sends up a faint prayer of gratitude to whichever god is listening. She's on edge and he would be sliding in comments about everyone missing her yesterday, Lantman's needs her smile, he would hope out loud that she was feeling better.

Her last day before her short editing leave, he dropped a hint about taking her to the Hinesburg Fall Festival. He told her the market had a booth there, but since Jorie was taking some "official" time off, maybe she and her son could go and enjoy the live music and kids' activities. It was the mention of Oli, the presumption that Chip could bond with him, that had her seconds from losing her job.

But she likes it here. Lantman's lets her stack her schedule around her freelance work. The pay is generous. Nowhere near good, but enough for a single mom pushing forty who put all her dreams into a creative basket and never built a career that would be there if the bottom fell out. If the dreams were suddenly shattered eggs on the floor of her future.

Fitting that her life ended up a grocery metaphor.

A man comes up to her register with two bags of Halloween candy, baseball cap tugged low to shadow his eyes, the hood of his sweatshirt bunched up around his neck. Acne scars creep out of an almost black sideburn.

"Hi, good morning," Jorie says to him, a notch too loud, but he's staring at the magazines and doesn't answer. She looks away but her awareness stays on him, the way he might be scanning the cover of *Men's Health* or *The Atlantic* but is maybe really looking at her.

He's in his twenties, possibly thirty. He could have a friend out in the parking lot, camera panning across the store. Jorie glances at the windows but only sees a woman setting her toddler down before they come inside. A pickup truck rattles past them, an antique-looking wardrobe standing in the bed.

Unwanted regard crawls all over the back of Jorie's neck.

She crumples a receipt that was left behind—an excuse to turn around and face the baseball cap guy—and tosses it into the wastebasket. He moves his eyes back to the magazines, actually reaches out for an issue of *Archie*, but he was watching her. He stands there with the comic in his hand, unopened. A smile curls his thin lips. It curdles on his face.

She starts to ask if he's ready to check out, but her phone vibrates behind her, in the shallow nook below the register. The buzz jolts her, and she has to wrestle down the urge to say something else to the guy, *Leave us the fuck alone,* maybe. She makes herself turn and pull the phone out to see Beth's text.

> Still quiet. I have an excellent hiding spot. Velma would be proud.
> She would nod in solidarity. There's one weird thing but not a person.
> It can wait.

One of them might be standing in my checkout lane, Jorie types out. But when she looks back, the man is gone. The bags of candy and the *Archie* issue are on her conveyor belt, and a tinge of something that feels lifted from a dozen scary movies makes her open the comic book.

The message she's expecting to leer out at her, slashed with a pen, isn't there. It's only the beginning of another day with Betty and Veronica and the gang trapped in the eternity of high school and never growing up. Jorie fans through the pages but sees nothing written or hidden inside.

The automatic doors clatter open behind her, and she turns—she's going in circles today—to see the man pivot left from the exit onto the sidewalk, shoulders hunched, hands in the pockets of crisp jeans. He's gone from view almost as soon as she sees him.

She clears her text window and writes, Heads up, black cap and dark blue hoodie. Probably nothing but for a minute I thought he was a Rickie.

Almost at once, a series of one-line texts, and Jorie imagines both of Beth's thumbs a blur across her phone's screen.

> I see him.
> Seems to be alone.
> Getting into a car.
> Gone.

Jorie can't move. She feels relieved, the mundane reality of the *Archie* guy is like warm water spreading across her scalp, but there's still this itch. There's something. She's caught in a small, central moment. She wants to be out there, doing, finding, with Beth at her side.

A minute later, another text from Beth: You're done at 4? Saw something really weird but not a Rickie. Also. Watched teaser again. That car isn't mine.

Yep, Jorie sends back, you have five more hours in your stakeout. Kidding. You can always pick me up later.

She doesn't remember a car in the teaser video. But before she can ask about it, or what Beth saw that was weird, the young woman and the toddler come through Jorie's lane with a bottle of red wine. "God, these leaves, right?" the woman says, and Jorie smiles. There's no escaping the foliage here.

Her phone buzzes as the woman picks up her little girl in one arm and passes through the automatic doors. It's Beth: Another guy coming in, also alone. Maybe too old.

The doors haven't even closed yet when they shudder open again, and Jorie looks up to see Chip grinning at her. The morning sun smears on his face, highlighting him, giving him a starring role in her world. She can't bring herself to smile back, no matter how much he thinks Lantman's might need it.

# CHAPTER SIXTEEN

## Beth

▶▶ The air is so clear this far north. It's like a new lens. Beth watches the slowness of the world through it. She sits cross-legged behind a boxwood hedge that links the row of maples to the front of the market, her face hovering in a gap in the prickly branches. The cool morning drifts out across the pavement, the white lines of the parking spaces pushing everything into symmetry.

The few people she's seen are as conspicuous as extras.

She lets herself drift some, too, thoughts of bringing Monse here, dropping hints about an adorable cottage for sale somewhere in Burlington. Soon, before the trees turn to latticework bones. The world is older up here, painted with oils. She can pretend humans will last longer within this reassurance of nature, where it shushes them.

But even in the reverie, she knows they're city girls, Beth as much as her wife. Brooklyn already isn't LA in the film industry—Vermont would effectively turn her into a hermit. Her agent, Gwyn, would threaten to fly across the country to stop her.

Maybe it's Beth's tendency to splice what she's seeing into discrete moments, or just her thoughts of stillness, but the scene she's looking at changes suddenly. One moment it's a parking lot framed by glossy boxwood leaves. In the next, something has altered it, intruded upon it. She drags her eyes across the asphalt, the scattered vehicles, trees stitching the blue horizon, a tall older woman standing at the trunk of her car near the front of the store.

Nothing is out of place. Something is wrong.

As though the morning is on a hinge, creaking open. She realizes what she's reminded of—the Transfigurations from *Proof of Demons*, this sense of awful waiting and the misalignment of things. The moment before the moment, as she and Jorie used to call it.

An impulse grips her, to keep her gaze moving, to not let her point of view linger or get stuck. She watches a man on the other side of the lot get out of a small pickup. The wrongness fades, and Beth looks back toward the store and sees the woman again. A long gray dress with pale stubs of legs, a darker gray sweater hanging nearly to the hem. A vivid blue knit cap covers her head.

She hasn't moved. Her arms are at her sides. She's just staring down into the trunk of a light green sedan, almost the color of the bedsheets haunting Beth and Jorie but more pearlescent. It's a Toyota, probably a Camry from several years ago.

A minute seeps by. There's no shopping cart, nothing to load into the trunk. The world wavers again, two frames of a film overlapping in a queasy way. Here is the thing that isn't right.

The woman seems to flicker, stepping forward and back in one instant. She turns toward Beth but is still gazing down into her trunk. Something about her seems to blur and stretch. Like pausing a VCR, Beth thinks, and the comparison fits completely.

The woman's head turns again, and Beth drops down onto her belly. Quiet swells, no birds, no traffic out on the road. Finally she hears an engine start close by, a change in the mechanical tenor as the car reverses. She sits back up and watches the woman drive away. Seeing the sedan from the front, at an angle, makes an image snap into place.

She saw this car somewhere. Not long ago. An hour ago.

It was in the new teaser video for the sequel, parked in front of her friend Nancy's cabin. The front end of it nosing inches into the frame, the same shade of sea-foam green. She doesn't think she even noticed a car when the video was playing, not consciously.

Theories shutter through her mind, narrative threads that all seem disparate and tightly bound together at the same time. The woman is a Rickie. The woman is a tourist staying at the cabin, somehow, waiting for the foliage to peak, and she's being filmed. The woman is no one, she's a local who just happened to have a starring role in this weird lucid dream of a moment.

The woman is Hélène Enriquez.

This last thought sends bright adrenaline swimming through Beth. A metallic tang in her mouth, a blush in her face. She puts it on hold and pulls her phone out, opens YouTube and taps out *proof of demons teaser* into the search bar. There it is, uploaded three hours ago.

The video is so short that there's no need to fast-forward. She waits for the few seconds of the cabin, and sees what could be the same car parked on the right edge of the screen.

She swipes YouTube away and types out a message to Jorie: You're done at 4? Saw something really weird but not a Rickie. Also. Watched teaser again. That car isn't mine.

Now what? She can admit to herself that she's thinking of driving to the cabin. She could get the car's license plate number. Something that's tangible, more than just waiting for what's next in some college kid's script. The Rickies might have just stopped by the cabin to get a shot of it in good light, then moved on. But it's a lead, it can help Jorie, it will keep her moving for an hour.

A simpler idea comes, and she calls Nancy Danforth, who used to work with Gwyn until she retired. She and her wife would meet Beth and Monse when they were in New York. Beth realizes she can't remember the wife's name, she was taken by breast cancer a few years ago—*Stop it, stay on track.* She squeezes her thoughts back together, takes a deep breath.

"How's the cabin treating you?" a voice says, and Beth jumps. "Beth, is that you?"

"Yes, sorry," she says. "Hey, so I'm not at the cabin anymore. I'm fine, the cabin's fine, but I might have to ask the police to check it out and make sure it's not part of a movie. No one else is booked there, right?"

"No, you still have it for the week. Someone's checking in Sunday afternoon. What is this about a movie?"

"Okay, well, it's probably nothing." Beth can't decide how much to say, then decides to skip it all. "I'll call back and explain after the property's been checked. I hate to worry you. I'm going to head over there now and call the cops."

Beth hangs up with a guilty wince, cutting off Nancy's confusion.

"Jesus, was that Hélène Enriquez?" she says, just above a whisper. She can hear the awe in her voice. The idea, the possibility roars in her mind, like a seashell against her ear. Her arms break out in chills.

She hears two sharp chirps and looks back toward the store. A short middle-aged guy is pointing a key fob at a polished red Subaru—a kind of car that's everywhere up here, she's noticed, something to do with all-wheel drive in the snow. He bends down to fix his hair in the window reflection, brushing his fingers back from the temples.

Another guy coming in, also alone, she sends to Jorie. Maybe too old. I'm going to check something out. Back in an hour or so. Love, Velma.

Definitely too old, she convinces herself, because she really is going out to the cabin. She feels the itch to go, to do. The thought of knocking on the door and the door opening and Hélène Enriquez standing there like a myth with all those beautiful trees around them, it's too much.

She imagines the director's eyes as cold things, full of the fierce will it took to remain a secret for so long. Maybe there would be embers of warmth there, too. *Leave Jorie alone*, Beth would say to that warmth, *she's been through so much already*.

*Let me bask in you*, another Beth would say. *Let me absorb you, let me be in your presence.*

She shakes herself out of the reverie. That couldn't have been Enriquez. But she needs to know who is at the cabin. She pushes through the boxwood, pulling out the key to the rental car.

Her intention is to find a widening of the gravel drive that winds into the gentle valley, get out, and approach the cabin like some crafty movie protagonist who's a little smarter than the rest of the cast. But the drive doesn't have a shoulder that's not crowded with trees, so she just shakes her head and rolls all the way down.

There's no Camry or any other vehicle. No one parting the curtains to see who's popping gravel under tires, no green sheets skulking about. Beth turns the engine off. It ticks under the hood as she sits and watches the cabin.

The woman from Lantman's could get here any minute, if that was even the same car from the video. Beth is more than half-convinced it wasn't. She lowers the windows so she can hear anyone before they get close.

The cabin feels as vacant as she left it two nights ago. More, somehow. The great tide of color sweeping up to it, the stillness, it's like Beth never stepped out onto this porch and saw Jorie Stroud for the first time in a decade.

She wants that plate number, and in the frustration of not getting it, she recognizes what she's planning to do. The key to the cabin is still hanging on the ring from the car's ignition.

The smell inside is the first difference. Body odor, grease, a lingering hint of cigarettes. The smells of young men. She walks into the cubbyhole of a kitchen and sees a pizza box wedged into a trash can. Dishes in the sink, two white coffee mugs. She grimaces at the thought of Rickies putting their mouths on Nancy's things.

There are no knives in the wooden block beside the microwave.

The single bedroom looks like it hasn't been slept in since Beth made it, the sheets drum-tight on the mattress, topped with a russet-orange quilt, but she stops in the doorway as though it's a murder scene. A wooden crown sits on each of the two rustic nightstands, a domestic parody that almost makes her think of *Proof of Demons* from a new angle, lending it weight it likely doesn't deserve.

An occult Norman Rockwell. The darkness just beneath the American idyll. Et cetera.

If Colin were here, he would run with the concept until he had half an essay drafted in his head. Something for *The Witch Tapes* or one of the other zines he carried around. He would whisper his train of thought at her, even here on the edge of possible danger, until she hushed him sternly enough.

But touching one of the rough, hacked points of the crown on this side of the bed, feeling it push into the pad of her finger, Colin has never felt so far away. The realization of that distance is like losing him again, compressed into a single gasped breath.

Beth pushes these thoughts away and pulls open the nightstand drawer below the crown. A new-looking green Moleskine notebook is the only thing there. She picks it up, slips the elastic band off, turns back the cover. *Shooting Schedule PAR* is scrawled across the first page in blue ink, underlined twice and smeared by a clumsy finger. PAR, not POD. She doesn't know what the abbreviation means, though there's a familiarity, something Jorie told her.

For a second she thinks she hears gravel under tires. She stiffens, focuses on the front of the cabin, but only silence ripples out.

The first page of the notebook is mostly some sort of shorthand. Her initials, *BK,* a few times, several others once or twice, but she counts eleven instances of *JS* in the scrawl. *JS trail cam, JS drone (Elliot), JS market (Elliot INT), JS closet (?), OP school (John EST),* but nothing structured or linear like dates and times.

She stares down at the *OP* and the word *school.* Oli Paterson, establishing shot. They've filmed that impossibly sweet kid at school—or they're going to. They know enough about him and Jorie not to assume his last name is Stroud.

The next two pages are blank, but after that Beth comes across heavy lines scratched into the paper. ~~BLUE~~ *GREEN SHEETS—DAVIES POLICE PHOTOS/AUTOPSY.* And beneath this, jotted like a casual, horrific afterthought: *Beth found body, psychol. stress makes her more camera ready?*

On the reverse side of this, a slanted shout that sends whispers down Beth's spine: *TODAY HELENE SAID TRUE PROOF COMING WE WILL TRANSFIGURE TRANSMIGRATE TO ANOTHER GREEN WORLD WITH HER. film industry experience and godhood!!*

"Cult members with work portfolios," she says, and shakes her head. "Jesus."

Another page has nothing but a scrawled haiku: *a beautiful cure/for cancer in the paper/birches of Vermont.*

After this, another jumble of thoughts. *Viral ritual rules. "I belong"—6 min.*

*static camera shot/mental stillness—Haunting—"You belong"—Transfiguration. Doesn't need to be funeral, just for imagery + vibe.*

Beth isn't sure what most of this means in the context of a sequel, but she lets out a sigh of relief, that it really is just a movie. She and Jorie can decode this later.

The pages flutter under her thumb, an unfelt symmetry with Jorie and the *Archie* comic, until she sees something near the back. Three crude trees drawn in green ink that's clotted like old blood. Three green tombstones in a row at the bottom, *RIP* written on each. In the center of the page, a brief list.

*Beth = Forest (pg. 49)*
*Jorie = Grocery store (pg. 68)*
*Oliver = Pine arch creature (pg. ?)*

Cold prickles, silken and dry, across every inch of her skin. She twists in a shudder. It looks like both she and Jorie don't make it to the end of the script, unless the sequel is truly bare-bones. Neither of them will be the final girl.

Why this fixation? How is it strong enough to pull Jorie's little boy into its gravity? Is Monse's name somewhere in this notebook? Even the horror movie explanation, that someone in Hannah Kim's family has been simmering in grief and rage for a decade, plotting this artful vengeance, doesn't make sense. Others were more responsible than Jorie, than Beth and Colin. Than Enriquez, even.

Some would say no one was responsible except Hannah and her friends in that North Carolina graveyard. That feels wrong to Beth, but she's seen it mentioned.

The only true villain was online culture, but rage is useless against the intangible. Anger goes through the web like water in a sieve. It is archived and preserved but profoundly forgotten. Internet trolls are antagonists that can't be killed, or even condemned. A movie title trails through Beth's mind—*Final URL*—a comet of thought that mercifully burns out in an instant.

Her name. The word *grave*.

Of the few dozen threats in her social media inboxes back in 2013 and trickling into the few years after, the one she's never managed to forget went, *One day someone will make you pay for what you did and the cameras will be all over YOU. See how you like it when your dead.* She even remembers the grammatical error.

An image of Colin comes, crying on her shoulder the first time she saw him after Hannah and the October Film Haunt started trending on Twitter and they found out about the shirt she was wearing and where and why she died. A second image, Colin's eyes half-open when she stepped into his apartment and saw the crust around his dead lips, the bedsheet pulled up to his neck.

A sheet the exact weary shade of green as these men are wearing.

She looks at Oli's name again. The first thread of real fear uncurls low in her throat. Just a wisp of it, but she's been here too long. If there's a script with these corresponding page numbers, it will have to wait. She slips the notebook into a back pocket and decides to check the attic loft before getting the hell out of here.

On the stairs she recites her own list under her breath. Back to Jorie, call the police, call Monse and tell her she's coming home. She murmurs the words again, like a litany. Jorie and Oli are coming with her, they can sleep on the pull-out sofa for a couple of days.

Men with knives could be hiding in the neat clutter up here. The wardrobe to her left. The desk with a white sheet over it, a bookshelf that looks pulled out from the wall. But what she's really looking for is anything paper, a stack that could be a screenplay, a folder.

Through the open door to the deck, Beth hears the mutter of gravel again.

*Leave*, she tells herself, *go back down the stairs and out of this place.*

She creeps outside and glances down at the driveway. Only her rental car, the world sloping gently away from it in Halloween colors. A deep valley of silence, the soft rasp of her breath, a distant chevron of geese like a cursor in the sky. *Leave now*, this time she hears it in Monse's voice, but it's too late. Her heart ramps up as leaves crackle out in the trees.

Someone steps out between a maple and a pine, into the light, tall and thin and hidden beneath the same sickly green sheet Beth tore off the porch's hook two days ago. The rip she made is there, extending from the elbow to the hem, the two sides flapping above scuffed black boots.

More rips at the top of the sheet because the person is wearing something jagged, a *Proof of Demons* crown, that's tearing through with carved wooden points.

A cloud passes over the sun, causing the light to go tepid. The Rickie stops in front of the porch and looks up at her. The area over the eyes has been worn sheer, paler in a way that won't show up on camera. The figure's mouth opens and sucks the fabric into it to form an awful, skin-crawling depression. The right arm slips through the tear.

It's holding a long and tapered butcher knife.

She holds the blank gaze as she takes out her phone and taps 9 and 1 and 1. Her thumb squeezes the call button. She feels a coldness, almost a calm. The man in the bedsheet—she would bet anything it's a man—runs forward onto the porch and she hears the door creak and slam open below her.

Beth sprints back inside but stops just past the sliding glass door. There are only open stairs leading up here, it's like she completely forgot this simple fact, and the boots are already pounding up them. She steps back and starts to slide the glass panel shut, then looks around in a panic, knowing the only way out is to go down the hard way. Then she moves to the left and puts her back against the wall.

The hand not holding the phone digs the pepper spray out of her front pocket.

She holds Monse in her mind, their wedding, how happy about it her parents were in the end. Her dad's speech, how he cried and turned to Monse and told her he loved her. Beth thinks of her wife's resilient strength, imagines Monse pressing it into her, warm and soft against her skin.

The man in the sheet doesn't come soaring out onto the deck. Beth hoped to add all the strength her arms could find to the momentum of his weight and send him over the railing to the gravel below. Instead he steps calmly outside past the sliding door, his head turning toward her, the fabric stretching tighter around his face as he grins.

Far away, she hears a small voice. "Nine-one-one, what is your emergency?" It's a woman, she thinks, feeling the words vibrate against the fingers holding the phone.

Beth lunges at the man in the sheet before he can raise the knife, aiming her hands at the center of his chest. The side railing is only three feet behind him, and it's low enough for his center of gravity to topple him over. She nearly falls with him, but she's shorter, the thick wooden board strikes her waist and she folds and braces her knees against it.

The Rickie lands face down on the grass beside the gravel, the air pushed out of him in a grunt. The knife jolts out of his hand.

She's torn between everything on the short list of what she can do next. If she turns to retrieve her phone and shout at the emergency dispatcher to send the police, the man in the sheet will be gone when she looks back down. Even if it weren't the slasher genre's biggest cliché, the deck is only eight feet up, maybe nine. A momentary hush will fall until she hears his boots on the porch and in the cabin again.

Her phone—she had it in her hand when she pushed him—where did it go? Then she sees it on the ground beside the man, not far from the knife, also face down. Her list of choices shrinks, and she's filling her lungs to scream at the person who may still be listening at the other end of the line when the man jerks and rolls over into a sitting position.

He lifts Beth's phone out of the grass, a white hand spattered with freckles creeping out from the green sheet, and brings it to his ear. He tilts his head up. He grins at her again—the sheet clenches around his face—and pulls the phone away and shakes it as though curious why it's not working. Then the phone slips from his fingers and falls back to the ground with all her hope.

She screams her hope anyway. "Help me!" and "I'm being attacked!" Maybe the threat of the police will do the trick. They would never get here in time, it's just remote enough to be a bad choice for someone coming to rescue a friend who's being stalked by murderous cult movie cosplayers. And for a few seconds, she lets the thought bloom in her head—that this is still just a film shoot, even if she can't see the cameras. The LARPing of obsessive fans who just won't let go.

The Rickie gets to his feet, picks up the knife, and walks back around to the porch steps with a limp. She hears boards creak under her. Beth turns and looks into the loft, wondering what's big enough to shove down onto the stairs. There's the sheet-draped desk, she walked by it earlier without picking up on the obvious imagery. It's small and probably flimsy, but it might block the stairs and slow him down.

Before she can move toward it, a pinch of agony erupts in her right foot.

The pain spreads upward through her body almost like warmth and out of her into the cloud-streaked sky. A thicker bolt replaces it, and she feels the blade of the knife slide out of the center of her foot, back through the thin sole of her moccasin, between two of the deck's boards. It seems to scrape bone on its way out.

Crying now, breaths short and whistling, she staggers over to the side of the deck and hears the door open again. He'll be on the stairs soon.

She climbs over the railing, tries to lower herself but slips, somehow with none of the liquid grace the man in the sheet had in the same fall. Her drop is short and she lands on her feet, the right bursting with fresh pain and her left ankle rolling over and maybe breaking or spraining, she has no idea.

She gets up and hobbles toward the car, thirty feet stretching out into a mile. A handful of precious seconds. One hand still has the cylinder of pepper spray. She fumbles with the safety lock as the other hand digs her keys out of her pocket. Her right foot throbs with cold fire, the shoe sopping with blood. The left ankle bears her weight but it's slowing her down even more.

The car is close enough to touch when a second green ghost comes out of the trees. Beth has to go around to the driver's side, and the Rickie will get there first. A butcher knife lifts, the bedsheet falls back from a shocking white forearm. She raises the spray as she clears the trunk, pressing the button, an orange rope arcing and bursting onto the sheet just below the hidden crown.

The Rickie grunts and folds forward but one of the pale hands grabs onto Beth's right arm. The cold line of the knife slides through her shirt and along one of her ribs before she twists away toward the tree line, limping and running for the woods.

A forest is never an escape, it's a false promise, she's seen as many horror films as Jorie. And it's what was written beside her death in the notebook. She'll stumble along and the man under the sheet will stroll, and he'll catch her somehow. She'll trip and fall. Or she'll hide behind a tree with her hand clamped over her mouth, and the Rickie will stop, listening, scenting the air like an animal.

But she staggers into the gloom anyway.

Another Rickie is already here, between two birches, the drab green of the bedsheet more vivid against the white trunks. He's pointing a video camera at her instead of a knife. The crown tearing through the cotton is different, the prongs more curved and irregular. No talent in the woodcarving, like the one she found at Jorie's house.

The camera is an Arri Alexa Mini. She's worked with them on crews, it's compact and ideal for outdoor shoots. It stuns her, even now, to see a camera filming her that costs more than any car she's ever owned.

"What the fuck?" she says, her voice between a gasp and a sob. "This really is just a reboot?" Beth thinks the first knife must have severed a tendon in her foot. The Rickie with the camera doesn't answer her, only steps forward, the sleek black lens moving into a close-up of her face. She screams and backs away from it, turns to go deeper into the trees, but there are two more crowned figures waiting.

They lift their arms to reveal long kitchen knives. The hand holding the nearest knife is mottled as dirty snow. The other's hand is darker, with a scar winding from thumb to wrist. Each of their crowns is made of three long tines that have torn nearly all the way through the sheet covering it.

Colin always loved those crowns. He said they were imperfectly the same, and deserved their place in the great fabric of horror.

Colin feels half-here with her now, as she bleeds and fights for air and tries to find somewhere to run. The way he used to laugh, how it would turn into giggles that always embarrassed him. He told her once, not long before the end, that he could never be as strong as her and Jorie.

Jorie. Oli. The notebook in Beth's pocket, *Lantman's, page 68*. She has to get back to them.

Beth rushes at the camera, grapples it away because it might be the last thing they're expecting. The Rickie seems shocked that it's not in his hands anymore. She throws it and scrambles to the right, to go around them, but he reaches out and grabs her ankle, and maybe it is broken because it swallows the pain in her other foot. She cries out and falls to the ground.

Nothing happens for a moment, but she knows they're checking the camera. There's money behind this production, not just amateurs. These are not kids. The earth under her cheek smells clean and musty at the same time.

*Don't hurt her*, she tries to say, *don't hurt her son*, but there's no breath in her. She hopes Jorie doesn't add this moment to her burden, but how could she not? Jorie put herself in the hospital for three weeks after Hannah Kim. What will this be like?

*Jorie, don't.*

*One day someone will make you pay for what you did.*

Off to the left, she sees a final Rickie watching her through low-reaching denuded limbs. Shorter than the others but with no crown, just a blank head hidden under the sheet.

She wonders if this is the true Hélène Enriquez, and even in this moment, it makes her angry to imagine a man hiding behind a woman's name in her beloved industry. She tries to call out, but only a wet wheeze will come.

Beth feels the Rickies leaning down toward her now. Her ankle is surely broken. Her arms won't push her up.

She thinks, *Please don't. I want Monse, my Monserrat, her hair down, the sunrise through the window and the city is awake.* She pictures her, Monse turning her face in the light, something about sleepyheads, and nothing bad can ever happen here.

One knife goes into her lower left side. The other rakes down her back, tearing through her jacket and shirt and opening the skin beneath them.

Someone turns her over and two of the covered faces loom. She lifts an arm up in defense. They watch her for a moment. The camera creeps closer with indifference.

"You belong," one of them says. Somehow there is cheer in the voice.

The other Rickie's knife lowers and draws a line across her throat, but Beth is trying to disperse herself into the warming air now, to a place where this isn't happening. The sun has come out from the clouds, stronger than it was.

*Run, Jorie*, she thinks. *Promise me you'll run.*

Monse.

Colin again. Colin smoking a cigarette outside a video store under stars. Then the stars themselves.

# CHAPTER SEVENTEEN

## Jorie

▶▶ "Did I tell you we missed you at the Fall Festival?" Chip leans against the counter in her checkout lane with his arms folded. Right behind her as she stocks and straightens packs of gum. She takes shallow breaths because of his cologne.

He's not working today, but he's been flitting back and forth from his office to Jorie, like she's a casserole that needs to be checked on, for the last three hours.

"Yes, I think you mentioned it." She turns to face him and adds, because she has so little patience for him right now, "I was in the deli when you told me that, about twenty minutes after I was officially back."

It's like his face fills with blood, the blush is so strong. His brown eyes dampen, as though he's going to cry. Jorie smiles to soften the moment, disappointed with herself for doing it, and turns back to the gum rack.

"Well, it was a great time," he says, his voice just a tick higher than normal. "I love this time of year. Who doesn't, right? But if you haven't done the foliage drive since you moved up here, I'm thinking I'll drive out through Stowe, all the way to Montpelier. I know a lot of places that will make your jaw drop."

Dread, that his next sentence will have her son in it. *Oli can come, too.* She knows he means well, he's decent in some sort of genuine way underneath the painful nice-guy mask he wears. She guesses that his father likely courted his mother with the same wear-her-down ritual. Leaning over a diner counter in the seventies, watching her hips work as she grabbed orders from the cook.

"We went last year," she tells him. "It was as great as everyone says."

If Chip were older, he'd probably try to corner Jorie in the office while she counted her register. If he were younger and visited the wrong internet forums, he could easily be an incel. Jorie lucked out and got something a little less awful than either.

She feels bad—sometimes—but some part of him has to know how creepy he is, and decides to keep playing this weak long game anyway. He's not too dense to tell squirming and flirting apart. She just hopes there's no anger at a low boil inside of him.

One day soon she's going to have to find another job and give him some hard truths along with her two weeks' notice.

But she almost welcomes the distraction right now. She's not just fidgeting because of him. Forty-five minutes left in her shift and Beth hasn't texted in two hours. Jorie has checked the parking lot a dozen times, hoping to see the rental car. She pulls her phone out yet again and reads Beth's last message: I'm going to check something out. Back in an hour or so. Love, Velma.

Why wasn't she more specific? The only thing that makes sense is that Beth didn't think she was doing anything risky. She could play detective from a distance, or in public.

Jorie has added five texts to the thread since that *Love, Velma,* plus two voicemails, each shorter and closer to panic than the last. She scrolls up in the messaging app and reads everything again. Saw something really weird but not a Rickie. Also. Watched teaser again. That car isn't mine.

Fucking Chip and his veiled hints and the endless droning about *Seinfeld* and the band he's always about to start. How could she have let the reference to the video and a car slip from her mind?

She has the teaser on her screen ten seconds later, but she has to watch a second time before she catches it. The front of a mint-green car, barely in the frame. Clumsy editing. Or a deliberate detail meant for her and Beth to see.

"I need you to drive me home," Jorie says, shoving her phone in her pocket. She grabs her bag and Chip straightens, his mouth dropping open. Halfway to the automatic doors, she turns back and sees that he isn't moving. "Please. It's an emergency."

She thinks of Oli as she gets into Chip's Subaru. Samantha will be picking him up from school any minute. A friend is in trouble so I'll be late getting the wolf, Jorie texts her cousin. An hour maybe. I hope. I'm sorry.

Chip climbs in and rubs his hands together, then seems to realize he's showing his excitement. "Is something wrong? Is there anything I can do?"

"No, Chip," she says. "Just home. My car's there. High Rock Road." The thought hangs in her mind, that Chip will know where she lives, he'll be able to picture her 90 percent of the time now, but it's not like her address isn't in his filing cabinet. It could already be in Google Maps on his phone.

Home is a mile and a half away, but she calls Beth six times, not leaving a voicemail after the first try, only pausing to tell Chip to take a left onto Lavigne Hill. He drives fast but not fast enough, and she's on the verge of tears when he finally turns into her driveway. The sun is caught in the tree line behind her house and it's not even four o'clock.

"Jorie, wait!" he calls after her as she spills out of his car and turns and slams the door. But she doesn't answer. Why did Beth go off on her own? Jorie's keys are out and the world has compressed itself into a roar in her ears. She comes close to scraping glossy red paint off Chip's Forester as she backs out onto the road.

There's no car at the cabin. No lights inside, just the westering light grazing the hump of mountain behind it. Jorie can't remember feeling so glad for the absence of something.

She steps onto the porch and tries the door. It opens. A chill on the back of her neck makes her turn around and scan the trees. For half a second she sees what could be a reflection, a wink of sun off a camera lens. Another trail cam strapped to a paper birch. Or an asshole with something bigger on his shoulder.

But she can't be sure, and the glint doesn't come again.

She tries to string together a train of thought, quickly because she doesn't want to linger. Beth drove here. Saw that it was vacant. Checked the trees for cameras. Left. That's as far as her mind will go without imagining a car accident, a breakdown that stranded her somewhere farther out, maybe near the state park. But these threads don't hold well unless there's no cell signal in the scenario, a wonderfully mundane reason she hasn't been able to answer Jorie's calls.

Halfway to the car, she sees a flash of color in the trees again. Red, like Beth's lumberjack shirt, hints of it like when Jorie came here to confront her about the first teaser video. An eerie loop she doesn't want to give any thought to.

Another sliver of red movement, fading back into the gloom. Beth's flannel is lying on the ground as Jorie steps into the deep cool shade of birch and maple and pine. She stops and calls out Beth's name and listens to the hush of feet running through the silence. "Shit," she whispers, and follows until she comes to an empty space twenty yards in, too tight to call a clearing.

Six light blue bedsheets are hanging from trees, fixed to the trunks with knives. The blades are of varying lengths, the handles are different, four with steel rivets and three a complete black. A scrap of brown cardboard is nailed above the display, R.I.P. 2009 written on it in heavy dark marker strokes.

"Beth?" Just a question now, low and unsure. She can't hear movement anymore. Whoever it is has either passed out of earshot or stopped to wait for her decision about what comes next. She doesn't know what comes next, that's their whole point, isn't it?

Someone laughs from deeper in the trees. Jorie strains her ears, she looks from tree to endless tree. The laugh comes again, more of a mutter, but unmistakably amused. The birches stand out in the fading light like ribs picked clean. Then the footsteps begin again, moving toward her.

Jorie turns back to the last of the daylight. It's not far, she's in the cabin's dooryard in ten seconds, but her heart is in her throat and she's sweating in the cool air. She sprints to her car but veers away at the last second, a desperation to find Beth urging her up onto the porch and through the door that's still open in an invitation that feels weighted now.

There are only minimalist furniture pieces, a chandelier with real half-melted candles and hammered metal rims to catch the wax. But there's a wide smear of red between the wicker area rug and the raw wood steps that lead to the loft.

She follows the blood up the stairs, committed now, free for a disembodied moment of all her sins and hesitancies and mistakes. She's liberated from caring and only Oli could call her back now, but even the thought of him waiting at Sam's, probably watching TV with Cara and Carter, is not enough.

He tips out of her mind easily. She's not herself for the eight seconds of these stairs, and there's enough time to wish she could be locked into this other person. She could keep climbing into someone else's story.

The space opens out at the top, the stained planks of the ceiling angled in a peak above her. She sees a desk and an antique wooden chair and a person draped with yet another ugly green sheet sitting in the chair. The figure is slumped with the head tipped back, blood soaking through the sheet at the neck. Streaks of it lead to the chair from Jorie's shoes. Drips of it have fallen to the floor.

Strained noises are leaking from Jorie because she won't let the real sounds out, the sobs or an anguished moan that would stretch into a scream.

A wooden crown sits upright on the sheeted figure's lap, two of the three long tapered points broken off. A clump of white paper, folded and folded like a note passed in a classroom, is beside the crown. Jorie would have left it open, if it were her film, and impaled it on the remaining tine.

Then she sees the camcorder, behind and to the left of the body on a bookshelf, its boxy eye pulling at her.

There's no sound below, no one storming into the cabin in pursuit. She's being directed, given information that will move the story forward. It feels like following a script, but she reaches down and takes the paper and unfolds it. *Will you believe in what you made?* is typed in the center of the sheet. A smear of blood below the words, like a signature. The paper falls from her hand to the floor.

Jorie pulls the sheet down off the face. She doesn't think she could spare herself this, and she wonders if there's a second camera angled behind her. Enriquez—someone—will want the revelation of Beth but also Jorie's reaction to it.

Beth's eyes are open and staring, burst blood vessels filling the right one, a dark tear trailing a diagonal to her mouth. She is steeped in red below the grinning cut across her throat.

But Jorie doesn't turn to look for another camcorder. She tries not to react on her surface. The roil of what feels like the end of that past life and who she has been—she's only a mother now, she thinks, everything before that is officially gone—is hidden away from the lens, in a stubborn beat where the camera will only show the wet gleams of her eyes. The rawness of her.

Let them have their long take of grief trembling in its cage. Jorie won't unlock it now, she will hold it with the guilt until she is alone.

"I'm so sorry," she tells her friend. "I'm so sorry, Beth." She whispers it without moving her mouth, so that the words are only for the two of them.

Then she steps around the desk, lifts the camera from the bookshelf, and smashes it on the floor. Her shaking arms pick the camera up and hurl it down again. She stumbles back across the loft and down the stairs.

She calls Samantha, nearly tripping on the steps down from the front porch, her phone pressed against her ear, hard enough to warp her cousin's voice when she answers.

"Is Oli okay?" Jorie says. "Can you see him right now?"

"Yeah, he's fine." Sam's voice jumps at once, alarmed, in mom mode. "Why?"

"There's been a—" Jorie tries to compress her voice into something like calm. "There's been a killing. Get Oli right now and keep everyone safe until the police get there. I'll explain later."

She hangs up and calls 911 to report the murder and beg someone to go to her son. He could be taken, she hardly has the breath to tell them. The stolen children in *Proof of Demons* are looping in her mind.

The dispatcher tells her to stay where she is, officers are en route to her location and her cousin's home, remain calm, is it safe where she currently is?

But she needs the fresh bracing air, and she wants to show them she knows they won't hurt her. They've made her their fallen star. The last of the sun is going, a peach-yellow stain across the bulwark of clouds over the trees.

She sees the figure in the bedsheet filming her only when it creeps closer to the edge of the tree line, the camera on its shoulder, the head above misshapen by a hidden crown. The camera is much nicer than the one in the loft, something professional, she thinks, the kind she long ago ruined her chances of standing behind.

The two of them stare at each other across the gravel and grass, their faces blank in different ways, until she finishes the call and drops her arm.

"Don't you dare touch my son," she says, just strong enough to carry.

Something appears to the right of the camera, a few feet back in the trees, like shadows pooling themselves together. A long man-shape, willowy, only moving when she lets her eyes start to drift away. It emerges from the foliage and fades in a slow repeating flicker, as though someone is caught in a loop of forever stepping forward to confront her. For a moment the shape is naked and white, clearly human, she can see the lines of arms and an elongated torso and a face high in the foliage.

It could be the face she saw in Oli's closet, the same round thing muddled by fear. Then it's only the column of lumpy shadow she once lied to the world about. The air snaps and clicks like the same branch breaking over and over.

It's a special effect. It's just a movie she and Beth never auditioned for.

The Rickie—maybe Hélène Enriquez herself, in all her obscured glory—turns and fades into the forest, toward the distant lake. The shape, Jorie's thought of a shape, wavers.

She stares at it, unable to crash into the woods and tackle the murderer in the green sheet and funnel all her rage into smashing a video camera into a face. The shape's arm lifts out into the open, something like a hand, something like fingers opening and pulling the air toward it. Beckoning, just as it did on the tape she found in her mailbox.

What's that line she wrote about the *Proof of Demons* film haunt? She thinks she remembers most of her words that have reached across all the years, full of young passion, to open that awful smiling wound in Beth's throat. She makes herself say the line out loud, bitter and heavy with shame and lies and truth, but it's just a whisper, and she knows she's leaving some of the words out: "What the three of us long for, in October and every other month: to be in a horror movie."

It took a long time, but here she is. Colin and Beth are gone, her son is vulnerable to what suddenly feels much closer to a mad cult than fandom, and October is creeping onto the doorstep. The old pebble that lodged in her mind at the age of seven—sneaking down to watch *The Exorcist* after her parents had gone to bed, sowing herself with the wonder and pursuit of terror—refuses to loosen and fall out, but it has eroded into such a small thing.

The tall shape in the trees breaks apart into the constituent gloom.

Jorie wills the scene to become a film set after the last take. The production crew sets out for the next location. Up in the cabin loft, Beth pulls off the sheet, wipes the theater blood off her neck, peels the gaping latex cut from her smooth sweaty skin. She pictures Beth grinning, asking if they got the scene, if Jorie was freaked out enough.

But muted warbling sirens come on the breeze, not close yet, but uninterested in anyone's daydreams.

Here is where low mournful strings might spill into the background. A drone camera would lift and drag itself into the westward sky at their cue, Jorie would recede beneath the quilt of treetops pulled onto the screen like a bed being made.

She doesn't see the actual drone. Its steady arc of altitude, the shot widening to show four green figures passing in and out of glimpses in the foliage, away from the spent cabin, then six of them, then ten, eleven, thirteen running through the trees.

The muddled kaleidoscope of the forest, its colors caught between seasons and species and in the crease of dusk. Two hundred yards to the south of the green stream of figures, a ribbon of road, and two flashing police cars. The smear of sunset on the lens and the glimmer of lake in the distance, broad as a sea.

Jorie is alone for a moment, her car waiting beside her, her oldest friend growing cold above her. She wants her mother, who's been gone so long, and her father, who's wasting away in a bed in a care facility a thousand miles south. More than anything, she wants her son burrowed safe inside her arms.

She finally hears the angry crunch of gravel out toward the road, then the single bleat of a siren. The noise of the world seeking her out. Red light begins to pulse across the trees. She turns away from the strange shadows it makes and calls her cousin again.

# CHAPTER EIGHTEEN

## Trevor

▶▶ "You know what it's like to belong? Somewhere that nothing hurts?"

The POV of the TikTok video looks up into a man's face. Mid-twenties, maybe, with long dark hair he twitches out of his eyes every few seconds. Blood is smeared high on one side of his forehead. The phone he's speaking into is shaky. His voice is too loud, almost breathless.

"It's hard to find hope in the world," he says. His eyes won't stop moving around the room. "Like, being at peace, where you can look at the news and people aren't talking about genocide and climate change and people's rights being taken away and just shit and more shit, you know? I think I can feel that peace now, like, near me in this room. A—like a future that isn't scary."

After a moment, he pulls the phone away from his face. A blurred sweep of a small room, a sofa with a wet red stripe on the wall behind it, streaks of chandelier lights. "I saw on Reddit that it helps to draw a line of blood on the wall. Scalp wounds bleed good, so I did that. Listen. Hear it? The trees have come inside with me. I'm haunted, man. It worked."

He laughs. Something in the sound tilts into a lower register. Trevor feels a cold tingle spread up his arms, that soft visceral breath he's felt so rarely in his life.

Back on the screen, the man whips his head back and forth and goes on. "So anyway, some lady saw me filming her dad's funeral and complained, but I got all six minutes, and I did the 'I belong with you' like the video said. And it's brought this peace and a belonging. Not in me, but like I can see it reflected in windows, like stains in pictures I take with my phone. It's getting closer and—"

The voice stops and the camera turns. It pans across the room, to a column of slow shadow standing by a picture window.

It's wonderfully hard to see at first, a tall cylinder beside a curtain, a misshapen head and shoulders bent over below the ceiling, until its arms lift up. Then it becomes a creature, a presence, an entity wearing a heat mirage for skin.

The jerking gasps of the man's breaths fill Nils's high-end desk speakers. The camera shudders. The light in the room in the video clicks on and off, stays out for several seconds.

When it blinks back, the dark smudge is moving closer with eerie stop-motion judders. It's more humanoid, pale inside the smoke color and almost fleshy, like an insubstantial, enormous corpse. There's a sort of hole in the center of it, an obscured autopsy cavity dragging at the camera, which roughly tips up to find the corpse's upper body, its head and the staring holes of its eyes, still folded over under the ceiling. Looking down at the camera.

The video's sound seems to dip beneath water and grind slowly, moans and wet chewing. Pixelated static drifts across the screen like dandelion seeds. "Yes," a voice says, half-garbled and almost certainly the man's, and the POV moves toward the hole and the reaching arms. Something is moving inside the hole.

A crumbled voice says, "You belong," and the clip is cut off.

This is creeping across social media. Hundreds of shares since this morning.

The effects in the video are incredible. Trevor watches it again, on YouTube this time, where it has six thousand views. He's eager to see the Pine Arch Creature—if that's what it is—inside the walls of a house, beyond its expected environment. It's not the same creature as the one from the original film, the one he drew for Hélène Enriquez in 2007, that one never had eyes or what he would call skin, but it's close.

The Pine Arch Creature 2.0 is more organic. Amateur effects software has come a long way.

Still. He feels a rush of pride and envy and a what-if blur in his thoughts, that it could be real, what if it's real, whether he wants it to be real. He knows it's not, it's a movie, but the grim reverie is still there.

He backs it up and pauses when the creature is still by the window. Its arms waver down toward the floor, long-fingered and fingerless at the same time, and the contradiction makes as little sense now as it did the unknown number of times he froze the screen during *Proof of Demons* to stare at it all those years ago. Back then it astonished him that something he had made was in a film and being talked about with awe, in voices that felt hushed even in text on a computer screen.

The video unpauses and he watches the light stutter before the creature moves across the man's living room. He turns and looks over at the apartment door again, listening. For a moment he thinks he smells smoke.

It seems obvious that Enriquez is paying actors to stage these found-footage scenes, then disappear for a few days to cause a public stir. He had his fill of *Proof of Demons* the first time around, when people pushed too hard to make it real. They ruined the movie, as far as he's concerned, they diminished his art, and they killed a real person not long after.

So the new ritual Enriquez is setting up seems to start with "I belong" at a funeral and finish with "You belong" in some other place. In between, for an unknown length of time, the person messing with things they don't understand is haunted by the Pine Arch Creature, or some new leveled-up version of it.

The director has brought the six minutes into it, too, really pushing the idea forward that a film can itself be an occult object of power. Trevor likes the symmetry, the call and response. He has to admire the crowdsourced perspectives, or at least the pretense of them, a new way to go viral as a fictional framework.

But there are elements of these videos that he can't pick apart from a technical effects angle. How is Enriquez managing such incredible Pine Arch Creature animation in handheld phone video? There's a grainy authenticity here that Trevor has never quite seen in found footage. The thing in these people's homes looks genuinely organic. Hours of combing through his own software and the editing tools he's heard of haven't gotten him closer to understanding.

He drums his fingers on the pale wood of the desk, thinking of how to word a social media statement asking people to be horror-minded—they would expect nothing less of him, and neither would he—but also to be careful and stay grounded in fiction, and not believe everything they see, and to hell with the inevitable trolls that will climb into his mentions.

A few years ago—after the Slender Man stabbing verdicts, when urban legends were in the news again, painted as a North American affliction—he gave a quote to a *Vice* journalist who was connecting the Wisconsin case to the girl who died in the Pine Arch Creature woods. Trevor remembers asking the writer if she worried about jamming a stick into a hornet's nest, and wasn't it edging too close to the Satanic Panic of the eighties?

He was exaggerating then, just a little, a defensive gesture against his beloved genre—and subgenre, and even sub-subgenre—being dragged out into the town square to be gawked at by God-addicted parents on school boards and other people who didn't read for pleasure. The types of people who reach for stones without much prompting.

This, on his screen, is more of a hornet's nest.

He searches for Jorie Stroud but already knows she's not in the usual places, she was chased off by pitchforks and torches a long time ago. If she still has that ancient email address, he could try to find out if she's involved with all this. Trevor always admired Jorie, enough to make a piece for the October Film Haunt site. He traded a couple of rare films with her, too.

Why would she have that address all this time later? Why give the past a doormat? There are already numerous posts, even a few hashtags pulling her name back through the mud, condemning her for more deaths before there's a body count.

But he looks up Beth Kowalczyk and is stunned to see that she was murdered just two days ago, apparently by people dressed in sheets who were acting out a new *Proof of Demons* scene. At least one person is claiming the killers brought cameras with them.

A deeper coldness creeps over him, pocked with hot pinpricks. Grainy stars wash across his vision. He leans back in the chair, his hand to his mouth, everything changing. This isn't just a movie. He never knew Beth outside of the occasional message, but there's a welling sting in his eyes.

"What the fuck," he whispers. The snippet of news he clicked on—too thin on detail to be called an article—hangs there in the white gulf of the screen. But the text wavers and he can't read past the fact of her death. His eyes feel like they're crawling through the words to the blank pixels behind them.

Switching to email, Trevor searches "helene enriquez" and opens the single thread of communication between him and the director in the fall of 2007, where they briefly hashed out what she had in mind for a demon she wanted him to draw. *Something very tall, incomplete, something that has just been summoned, a clay hardening, a moment away from its true form,* she wrote.

One of the first monsters Trevor ever dreamed up comes into his mind, a horrifying thing taller than his ceiling that would watch him after his mother turned the lights out and he was supposed to go to sleep. He embellished it for Enriquez, but it wasn't so different from the one that lived in his memory. After he attached the hi-res image file a week later, a few hundred dollars appeared in his PayPal account.

He never heard from her again, until this week:

> *The demon has to evolve.*
> *The demon has to speak louder.*
> *A film has to speak louder.*
> *Will you believe in what you made?*

Maybe he'll send a cease and desist. He never had ownership rights to the Pine Arch Creature, would never have thought to want any back then, but he has an agent. She might know if he can take legal action and whether Enriquez can use his art beyond the original film.

Hi Kristin, he starts in a new email window. His fingertips brush the keyboard, waiting for a way to word his request that isn't too steeped in the language of horror. She's gotten used to the hideous things his brain makes up, but she isn't exactly a genre connoisseur.

He hears something at the apartment door. A small, dry scrape, like fingernails on the wood. For a few confused seconds he thinks Calloway has gotten out into the hallway, but the noise comes again, measured, too human.

Trevor stands and creeps up to the door to press his eye against the peephole. There's the same irregular pulse of light from the other day, just before Jenn came home. The opposite door bows forward in the fish-eye.

But something is standing in the hall, almost out of frame to the left, close enough to reveal a presence but nothing more. Perfectly still, curving away in the distortion. He sees the cheek of a vampire-white face, only an inch or two, and the greenish edge of clothing below it.

The shape moves suddenly, pulling out of view.

He steps back and says, "Who's there?" and the sound of his voice has the same tenor, that uncertain rawness, that he's heard a thousand times in movies he's hunted down in old video shops and across the internet. He's heard that rising waver in most of the world's languages. The quiet weaves itself back into the space where his voice was.

He looks through the peephole again. Empty. With a frustrated sigh, he opens the door and leans out.

The white face is at the end of the hallway, half-hidden behind the corner with one giant charcoal eye glaring at him. The figure could be something he created, he's sure it *is* something he created but can't place. A reenactment of one of his pieces. The light above him keeps cutting on and off and throwing shadows behind the oversized white head, painting the grinning mouth. It's wearing a green dress—or a curtain or bedsheet—and Trevor pulls himself back inside the apartment and slams the door shut. He locks it and slides the chain back into the guard.

He's not taking chances, not after what he just read about Beth Kowalczyk.

"What the fuck?" Pacing the shape of a smile—that evil idiot grin in the white face—between the desk and the door, back and forth. "What the fuck *is* this?"

Nils's cat slinks out from under the sofa. Her eyes are just cat's eyes. She stares at him, holding him to the promise of dinner. Trevor can't just hide in here, it's the second time in the past week that he's been trapped in an apartment.

When Calloway is hunched and eating, tail swishing, he walks back toward the door, caught in a loop of investigation and retreat. *Come on*, he tells himself, but somehow he senses that the empty space has filled up on the other side of the door.

He looks again and there is only the white face now, nearly filling the lens. Its grin is gone at this new angle, there are only the two huge eyes and the top edges of a few teeth. It doesn't move. The hallway becomes hazy, as though a mist is rising.

"Fuck you," he tells the face, "no autograph," and slams a fist against the door. The chain rattles. Smoke begins to leak into the apartment, not mist, grasping at his ankles. A high groaning noise climbs up his throat as he jumps back.

He slips his shoes on, goes through the living area and into Nils's room to find something big to hold in his hands. A hockey stick leans against the wall. Nils played guard at university, before Trevor knew him. It feels solid, the thick tape grips his fingers. He squares his shoulders, plants his feet, lifts the stick up before him like a Canadian zombie hunter.

A horror artist setting out to deal with an unhinged arsonist fan dressed up like one of his own pieces. That's never been on his bingo card, but he's been threatened online before. It comes with the territory no matter how creepy your art is, but he's usually okay with admitting he might be more prone to this. He returns to the open space of the apartment, the long wall and the hall door.

He checks the hallway one last time and sees nothing. The light up in the ceiling has burned out, and only a dimness, gray with an orange tinge, remains. Orange because of a fire. His hand reaches out, twists the dead bolt, slides the chain back out. He opens the door and steps back in a smooth glide, wielding the stick.

A waste bin sits in front of the doorway, flames licking over its rim. Trevor grabs his water bottle from the desk and empties it onto the burning paper inside. Stick figures writhe and char.

Beyond it, the huge white head lies on the carpeted floor, face down. He nudges it with his foot—it's not some papier-mâché thing someone would make for a comics convention. This is latex, the kind of reinforced mask a film effects artist would labor over for hours. When it comes to his characters, it's mostly Siren Head merchandise that people make. And nothing this elaborate.

He leans the hockey stick against the wall and picks the head up. He can't stop himself. It slides down over his face until it meets his shoulders, snug and moist and smelling of something—menthol cigarettes, maybe. He peers through a fine mesh in the eyes, down to where he first saw the person wearing it.

Nothing. But a faint mechanical noise comes from behind him, down the other half of the hallway. He lifts the head off and turns to sees a drone hanging in the air at eye level. An expensive one. It hovers like something out of an old sci-fi film, the round eye of its camera catching a gleam in the near dark. Its blades whine in a blur of motion.

The tinny voice of its speaker says, "You belong," loud in the silence.

The words tremble in the air, and he notices broken shards of wood on the floor below the drone. He imagines a foot coming down on a long tapered crown. A crown that looks too familiar. He imagines himself gluing the pieces back together and—what? He doesn't know, because he also imagines a figure in a bedsheet stepping into the hallway, holding up a knife to cross Trevor off some inscrutable kill list.

"Fuck that," he says, "I never said the 'I belong' part." He drops the rubber head and grabs the stick, a delirious weight pressing on him. A rush and a species of madness. He charges the camera. It jerks into movement, retracting itself away from him, slowing, then turning right.

The next hallway is empty when Trevor reaches it, his momentum carrying him almost into the wall at the intersection. He watches the drone escape through an open window, sailing out over the courtyard of the building, toward Ellesmere Road and Lake Ontario beyond.

The light comes back on behind him, steady and as precious as air. The normal world starts up again, a filter is removed from the scene. The latex mask stares at him from the floor down the hall.

Trevor walks back to his door and pauses there. Not to clean up the mess but because something feels wrong. It feels cut off, like a scene that isn't done yet. He stares at the elegant wood grain, the bold 857 etched into the brass plaque.

As if the thought is a stage cue, he senses a presence and turns. A figure is closing the distance on him, long strides billowing the sheet draped over it. The dull green cloth stretches tight around the face and the strange shape of the crown. One hand raises a tapered kitchen knife.

In the same moment, he sees another Rickie in a sheet behind the first, a sleek black video camera on their shoulder.

If he hadn't paused, if he had turned around to see the Rickies three seconds earlier, he would be able to stumble back into Nils's apartment and slam the door, but he finds himself sprinting down the hall instead. Another giant white head lunges around the corner at him when he reaches the end, a block-toothed grinning mouth and awful scribbled eyes, and for a moment the hands beneath the head have him. The creak of leather gloves, pain clamping his forearm.

Trevor screams and twists away and runs to the left down the next hall, with thudding boots behind him. He turns again—a third corridor, before long he'll loop around to where he started—and pushes through a door near the stairs, into a narrow electrical room. A classic horror movie dead end, but he commits to it and finds an alcove at the back of the space. Most of him is hidden. He stands with the hockey stick pressed against his cheek and waits.

Footsteps storm by, but he's not sure, the slamming of his heart has swallowed the ambient sound of the world. Gasping for air. He's not sure he would hear the snick of the metal door opening.

Five minutes later, he's tempted to embrace the anticlimax of this and return to the apartment. He doesn't have his phone, he can't call Jenn and tell her to stay at her office. Two more minutes and he's itching to leave this room.

"Trevor," someone says from the hallway. The door lever shakes, sending a thrill through him until he remembers there's no lock, this is just for show.

He stays in the alcove, squeezing the hockey stick and wishing it were something heavier.

"Trevor, don't worry," the voice says through the door. It's a little flat, nasal, something like a midwestern accent. It aims for conversational but only manages amusement. "You have one more scene. Get ready for it. Believe in what you made."

"And say hi to Jorie Stroud for us." This is a new voice, deeper.

Trevor says nothing. His hair is damp with sweat. He waits and waits and finally decides the voices are gone. He thinks he can feel an emptiness seeping in from the hallway.

He finishes the loop he nearly ran earlier, creeping along the walls, hunched with the hockey stick raised over his shoulder. The doorways measure his pace like background animation in an old cartoon.

He thinks of Jorie and Beth from the October Film Haunt, still unable to believe that one of them has been killed for a movie. He thinks of kids filming funerals and wonders what could possibly follow them home. He thinks about sequels, reboots, slashers, demons, cults, all his wheelhouses, and his relief breaks apart. It feels like a brittle thing.

No one is inside the apartment. Nothing is disturbed, but ash from the waste bin fire has been scattered across the floor between the kitchen and Nils's desk. The door is locked and chained again. Calloway is cradled reluctantly in his arms.

Soon he will call the police, he'll start reaching out to the handful of directors and producers he knows and the much longer list of horror film obsessives. But for now he calls Jenn and can't speak for several seconds when she answers.

# CHAPTER NINETEEN

## Jorie

▶▶ "Do you or Ms. Kowalczyk have any enemies, anyone who would want to cause you harm?"

"How long had you two been estranged, exactly?"

"Why would you say someone would put you in one of these horror movies?"

"Have you had contact with anyone in this 'cult'?"

These questions the police keep asking her. The answers are complicated, they exist out on the edge of a niche.

Two days since she found Beth under the sheet. Constant motion, even when she isn't moving. The skin under her eyes bruising. Pots of coffee in the middle of the night. Checking the windows, looking over her shoulder, shapes behind every tree, hunched inches beyond the corner of the house with poised knives. Green bedsheets floating through the woods.

Watching eyes. Camera eyes. In the eye of the second act, what happens next.

She keeps her son close. No school, no work.

The first night, after Beth's body was placed in a quiet ambulance, Jorie sat through hours of questions at the Hinesburg Police Department, a modest gray house on a residential street that could hold maybe a dozen cops at once. She walked Officer Shelby through the October Film Haunt and Hannah Kim, doubling back to clarify every other point. Some of it was in the police report from her house, but most of the story went over his head. He had kind eyes, at least, and gave her time to cry.

"What did you touch inside the cabin?"

"What exactly do these people believe?"

"You're saying nobody knows what this Enriquez woman looks like?"

"Do you have somewhere you and your son can go?"

She had to tell him twice that she didn't think demons were real, but these people were. And they had knives. Hours of pale and bloodless exhaustion, just to be told that the state police would be handling the investigation, they were the ones with the resources, and she would have to repeat everything to them the next morning.

Shelby looked like the police chief in Sam Marzioli's *Notte Rossa*, a florid, soft man who would die early in this reel because he didn't believe what Isabella had told him about the killer, couldn't be expected to buy into such a *giallo* premise. She sat there thinking that Hinesburg wasn't so different from an Italian village in 1979, quiet and cozy and oblivious, and that her mind was still an encyclopedia of horror films that she would never empty out.

There was always a physical resemblance to call upon. She had always been able to find a reference to some movie character in the crevice between bloody plot points.

Sam was waiting with Oli and a uniformed officer when Jorie finally got home. Shelby followed her the two miles and came in to check all the rooms, and still Jorie snapped at her son because he had put the mirror back up on his closet door.

"I like it there, Mama," he said, using the name he had stopped calling her more than a year ago. He was crying, Agatha's dry black eyes stared up at her from under his arm, and Jorie hugged him hard enough to make him gasp in pain.

She left the mirror up for now, pressing her nails hard into her palms, telling herself to stop trying to make this movie supernatural. The Rickies had her looking for Enriquez's proof in her own home. How to create psychological horror, chapter one.

The irrational fear of the Pine Arch Creature appearing in the trees at the cabin—it wasn't real, but it was also the kind of thing that is added in postproduction—was swallowed up by grief for Beth. The grief was washed over by guilt. The anger always came after, a sort of freeze crawling over her mind and clenching her teeth. A slow and sour rage. The grim vendetta she needed, a promise to finish what she and Beth started.

Yesterday, three more hours giving a statement to the Vermont State Police out at their barracks in Williston. She came home and tried to decide what to do with her quiet, sullen son as four cops tromped through the woods around her property, finding no evidence of recent "occupancy," as one of them put it.

Then a terrible hour with Oli, finally telling him what happened to Beth. She let herself be honest enough to give him the PG-rated version. It opened a new vista for him, the fact of death itself and the fact that it happens to people who are still young.

"Is someone going to hurt you, Mom?" he asked after his tears worked themselves out. Her own child, having to ask this. A stone down a well in her chest.

"No way, buddy," she told him. "Your mom is working on that, and working on keeping you safe most of all."

He sulked when he overheard Jorie on the phone with her father, debating whether to fly to Atlanta with Oli and leave him with Eric's parents. Her dad joked that Oli could stay with him in his room at the assisted living center not far north of the city, and for a full minute, maybe longer, she thought about it. She could talk to the staff and explain the emergency—only a few days, it's unconventional, yes, but she'll be back to get him as soon as it's safe.

"You still there, Gory?" he had asked, using the nickname that had stuck when he caught her watching *My Bloody Valentine* when she was twelve. His osteoporosis is sinking its teeth in now that he's approaching eighty, but his mind is still clear as lake water. Every cent of his money goes into his bed in that place.

"I'm here, Dad," she said, crying, furious with the tears. "I'm sorry. I'll figure something out."

But Eric still has both his parents, and they're ten years younger than Daniel Stroud. They live in a townhome with life teeming around it. Eric is there, too, which is exactly what Oli would want.

And what about the money to fly there and back? She has a hundred other uses for it, like new windows and probably a furnace replacement soon. Better snow tires. School and work would have to be missed. Impossible variables spilling over into the mouselike life she has built around them.

In the end she called Eric anyway, leaving a cryptic and alarming voicemail, the bitter part of her wondering if even that would be enough for him to call back. Not too much detail because she couldn't bring herself to jeopardize the permanent custody arrangement, but mentioning a murder on the periphery of Oli's life.

Deep in the crease of last night, she woke hearing someone in the hallway, the floorboard near Oli's room groaning. Then her son's voice, sleep-thick. The hall was empty, Oli was a lump under his comforter where Beth should have been.

Eric calls at nine this morning. Jorie goes into her bedroom and learns that he and his parents are in Scotland for three weeks, meandering from castle to castle to get close to their Paterson heritage. Jorie does the math and guesses that it's two in the afternoon over there. Father of the Year material. She wants to scream at him.

"That must be nice," she says instead, squeezing her phone hard enough to make the plastic case creak.

"We're driving up to a cottage on the moors," he says. "It'll be awesome. It's beside a loch."

He asks the right questions about the situation, how Oli's handling it, for the bare minimum, but Jorie can't believe the lack of concern. It takes away any appeals she could make, anything she might be able to say to make him feel worry for his only kid.

She visualizes a dozen foggy horror movies finding him in that setting. She pictures him wandering half-lost through the thick woolen air. His flashlight—his "torch," he would call it, he always wished he had been born over there—flickers, the batteries dying, the light going a pale yellow before the black dark closes its throat around his hand. A bleached white figure approaches, glimpsed in the last grains of light.

She shakes her head, reluctant to part with the daydream but needing to think straight and get off the phone. It's been months since she heard his voice. She used to think it was rumbling and disarming, it felt like the only thing that could protect her. Now her left eye seems to ache with the old specter of his fist.

"Thanks, anyway, Eric," she says as he starts into some local legend, and hangs up.

So Georgia isn't an option. She is frustrated and relieved.

Oli tries to be brave for her when she tells him. "It's okay, I want to stay with you," he says. "You need me and Agatha. Mom, let go, you're hurting me."

She can't let go.

Monse texts, telling her that Beth's funeral will be a private affair, family only. I know how much you meant to her, but it's just too hard. I couldn't bring myself to call and tell you.

Jorie stands at the dining nook window with the phone in her hand. She watches the empty tree line and the bright, chilled Vermont sun pouring onto the house.

Threaded through these days are hours on social media and Reddit. She scans and skims and begins to see the awful shape this sequel is taking.

The two videos from The *Original* October Film Haunt are everywhere, gaining traction, at least by the old standards Jorie once measured everything she did by. Hundreds of thousands of views across the platforms, but worse, she finds more and more videos filmed at cemeteries with "I belong with you!" shouted at the end, all posted with the hashtag #funeralwatching. She sees #hauntme and #filmhaunted scattered through posts. In a couple of the clips, the heads of mourners turn to see who is interrupting the service, and

Jorie's heart hurts for them, even as they remind her of the awful creepy actors on the VHS tape.

All the horror forums and cliques are talking about the funerals, the Pine Arch Creature, *Proof of Demons*. Inevitably, they're talking about Jorie, too.

"It's gotta be her she brought October Film Haunt back right?"
"Totally sick to team up with enriquez"
"Of course she would be anonymous about it!"
"Stay buried, Stroud."

This is nauseating enough for her, but there's crossover, too many other people turning it all into memes and TikTok videos. A couple of them look like genuine footage being sourced for the film.

She tries to tweak the statement she and Beth worked out together but is unable to change Beth to past tense in it.

"I can't find Agatha!" Oli's voice cuts through the house and through her doomscrolling. It's not easy to drag her eyes away from the hate on her screen, but his voice is shaking with misery and fear. "She was here," he says when she goes into his room and kneels by the bed. "She was under the blanket."

It's almost cold in the room. Jorie looks to the closet, its mouth half-yawning, the mirror reflecting Oli's shirts and his new parka. But the curtains near the door breathe in with a sigh. The window is open.

"Did you do that?" she asks, pointing.

"Agatha wanted to look outside," Oli says, and leans against his mom. "I forgot to shut it."

Half an hour of searching and Agatha is still missing. Jorie suggests a nap and hears him start crying softly into his pillow when she closes the door.

More new *Proof* footage is unfolding on social media, pushing this new spin on the old—elderly in internet years—legend. Like the other clips making the rounds, the one posted less than an hour ago was shot on a phone, but the production values are clever and surely expensive.

She watches the black-haired girl in her bedroom speaking of an entity coming for her, and the monstrous elongated thing appears, its torso and head bent horizontal behind a ceiling fan. Its body somehow turning whitish and more human, like a pale colony of mold sprouting on a corpse. It's even more appalling because it has eyes and a vague mouth that clicks and rattles in the cheap microphone. It has something that is almost skin.

The girl seems to decide to climb into this thing—it's so close to Enriquez's film until it isn't—and Jorie stands up and stumbles back from the table, out of the dining nook, and down onto the floor. She pushes herself backward on the seat of her jeans with her palms and feet, she hits the wall beside the doorway to the den. Her eyes staring across at the laptop screen. The window light soft and streaming around it.

"I want to belong," the girl says, just before her phone camera spins to reveal the dark column folded under the ceiling. The words spreading across the world. They can only sound foul to Jorie after all this time, and she still wonders sometimes if Hannah Kim said them before she lay down in the hole that was dug for her.

The camera moves toward the creature, which looks real enough to send Jorie back to when she almost believed her own lie. A different kind of hole opens in the thing's torso, a crackling voice says, "You belong," and in the chaos of camera movement, this echo of Hannah is taken into it.

The video sticks in her. It weights her lungs. This is like the months after the final film haunt, if they were dialed up and broadcast from a more powerful antenna. How long before people start believing this marketing gimmick?

She thinks it might be too late. After Beth, the line of fiction has been crossed.

The girl in the video is from California, one of six missing "funeral watchers" across the country—and a seventh in Spain. Maybe the sequel, reboot, rehash has left her behind. She could be free of it—just run and hide with her son, anyplace she can afford for a few weeks. They've killed Beth, let them be content and move on like a virus with their footage.

Oli could be her excuse again. To just let go, even when the grief and guilt and anger well up. The anger feels biggest sometimes, and she wants to scream at the computer, on the computer, that she knows better than almost anyone how easy it is to get someone killed.

She looks out the window, tracing the clean lines of the paper birches for a shape hiding behind them, and the doorbell rings.

"Mrs. Stroud?" the woman at the door asks.

"Not married anymore," Jorie says, "but yes," and she suddenly finds herself inviting two FBI agents into her grandparents' house. Their coats are warm from the sun as she hangs them up. Cold air and a dozen plotlines leak in behind them. Horror movies have to stretch beyond state lines to cast the FBI.

An exhaustion settles over her, that she's going to have to tell the old story again.

The senior agent, a Black woman with hair grayer and even shorter than Jorie's, sets a small notebook down on the dining nook table. The other, a pale, long-limbed guy who can't be thirty yet, holds an iPad in one huge palm, the TikTok app open to the *Original* October Film Haunt's profile.

They sit on Jorie's uncomfortable chairs. She wades through it all, listing the scars she made in other people's lives. Starting a simple blog in 2007, sliding a sheet off her best friend's dead face all these years later. She covers everything she knows and the much longer list of what she doesn't, all the gaps of her exile.

"Have you been involved with any films in recent years, Ms. Stroud?" the woman, Agent Fuller, asks. "Any message boards, film classes, professional or personal relationships, anything that could connect you and your past to this without you being aware of it? Or do you know if Ms. Kowalczyk might have been?"

"Beth worked in film," Jorie says, "but not with horror. She left that behind like I did. I basically got her blacklisted, too." She looks down at her hands, which are clutching each other, and forces them flat onto her thighs. "As for me, horror movies, books, blogs, magazines, TV, everything, none of it's been in my life for a long time. I haven't had contact with Hélène Enriquez ever, and not with anyone else who makes movies since 2013. I'm almost a recluse these days. I haven't even seen *Get Out*."

The younger agent, Campras, leans forward. "Do you know anything about these..." He swipes and taps on the tablet. "These 'Rickies' outside of their online personas?"

"No, I'm sorry," Jorie says. "Well, I'm not sorry, I'm glad I've never known any of them, as far as I know. I could point out the usernames I remember from Reddit and places like that. I already told the police about the new ones I saw, 'pinedemon' and 'helenelives.' They're the ones who used Beth's initials. And mine."

She told Oli to stay in his room, but she thinks she hears him shuffling out in the hallway, lured toward the mystique of the agents like any eight-year-old would be. All the movies he'll watch one day. The absence of Agatha's face tapping his bedroom wall, his nervous tic, is louder than his movements.

Agent Fuller takes the lead back. Her face is blank and softly lined. "I'm sorry to ask this. I know you were asked already by the local police. But do you believe someone would target you or Ms. Kowalczyk because of revenge for what happened back then?"

Jorie's eyes are burning. She blinks tears away. "I don't know. I told the police I didn't know. I don't. I'm sorry. I think revenge could be *used* as a motive but not as the *real* motive, you know? Because it would really be about tying in all that old stuff to generate public interest. Making the movie about Hannah Kim and me and Beth in some way to give it more marketing momentum."

Back to Campras. "Did you ever get the impression of anything like an actual cult back then? We're looking for structure, religious tenets, a central living space, recruitment, things along those lines."

"No, never. It was just a harmless story until it caused harm." She presses her lips together to hold back the little anguished noise that wants out of her. "And they were just fans, that's all I ever thought. Die-hard fans, sure, but just fans of some movie. Until now, apparently."

They leave with Beth's VHS tape and Jorie's shaky insistence that she's figuring out what to do. She's taking her son somewhere, she believes her part in this is over. She has to give up her laptop, too—she was almost certainly at work when Beth was killed, but there's no hiding the need to scour her activity and cross her off the list.

The agents don't strike Jorie as horror buffs, but they recognize wishful thinking when they hear it, and they know there's a reason she was left alive as a witness. Jorie tells them about Oli's open window, the doll going missing, how she doesn't know what is a threat and what is coincidence.

"We can arrange for a car from the local precinct," Fuller says at the door, "to watch over your home for a week or so. Night and day, if needed."

Jorie says yes, and she does cry then, as she shuts the door and leans against it. She still thinks these videos could be nothing more than teasers for Enriquez's sequel. Beth hangs heavy over that thought, but there's still room to hope that Enriquez isn't aware her fans have murdered someone, and the director will come out of the woodwork at long last and make a statement condemning it all.

That is some deep wood, though, and Jorie doesn't know where to start looking for the rot.

"That was like TV, Mom." Oli is standing at the front of the hallway. Jorie watches his hand shape itself as though it's circled around Agatha's waist. "Are they going to catch the bad guys?"

"I think so, buddy." She wipes her eyes and makes sure her smile looks real. "We'll be okay."

But even if a police car swings into her driveway and never leaves, whether a state trooper or a Hinesburg PD kid a year out of high school, she still won't feel safe here with Oli. She thinks of how that worked out in *Scream*, murderers slipping in and out of the house while Dewey's SUV was parked fifty yards away.

The windows are still empty and cold with condensation. The mirrors are mirrors. No one is filming her from the paper birches as September winds down.

Why demons again? There are no demons. There are only weapons. There is only snake oil.

Nothing is haunting her house except herself.

# INTERLUDE

[Excerpt from "Hell Is Just a Word: Secularism and Belief in Hélène Enriquez's *Proof of Demons*," by Colin Davies, *The Witch Tapes* #6, Fall 2011]

**What even *is* a demon in today's world?** Traditionally, it is a spiritual creature by definition, but *spiritual* has become a slippery word. Does the crowded history of demonology have meaning in the shadows outside Carl Sagan's shrinking candlelight of faith? What if the literature is thrown away? How would something crawling out of a traditional Hell entertain us in the secular now?

*Proof of Demons* (dir. Hélène Enriquez, 2009) has earned a reputation as a "bipolar" horror film due to its oil-and-water blend of the occult and slasher subgenres, which cross paths obliquely in the infamous "Transfigurations." There is also the Pine Arch Creature—a tall malformed thing that could be a dominant demon or a submissive familiar. It's not an easy movie to pick apart.

To make picking even harder, a third of its running time is spent not moving the camera. Five plot-dragging shots of precisely six minutes each, four of which are purported by a subset of fans to alter the world's fabric and open some terrible Door. These scenes are rumored to be the "Proof" of the title: a legitimate ritual disguised by the plot elements arranged around it—a kind of entertainment camouflage.

(The first six-minute scene, in which the Pine Arch Creature makes its awful, already iconic entrance, is discounted because neither "I belong with you" is spoken to open the alleged doorway nor "You belong" to permit entrance.)

Two years after it hit niche video stores, a rabid fan base seems to be congregating around the film and its alleged occult architecture. The term "Rickie"—presumably an affectionate shortening of "Enriquez"—is cropping up in certain chat forums. I am certainly no Rickie myself, but I admit the film has something. As though it gets close to Some Thing. However, in the two years since the film's release, nothing has occurred to suggest that it is in any way truly occult, leading these so-called Rickies back into fiction, like an ouroboros caught on tape eating its own tail.

Despite the film's title, demons are discussed sparingly. In what is perhaps a red herring of a scene, a voice (assumed to be the unnamed, de facto leader of the cult, portrayed by former Oscar nominee Roger Eilertsen) shares this chilling secret with Jackson Smith (Kip Corliss) in a Catholic church's confessional booth: "The Bible is no place to look for demons." He briefly expounds upon this notion, concluding with, "You may find demons with the small light in a child's room, but not with the light of any Christ."

The meaning here is clear: belief, not faith. Knowing something rather than being told. In this way, we are our own gods, we commune with ourselves. We summon our own demons.

I use the word *chilling* above not because Smith expected a priest to be on the other side of the privacy screen—though this does deliver quite a chill, built upon a dreadful pause in which Enriquez subtly creeps the camera toward the screen and the unseen speaker—and not because a hole appears in the booth, revealing a wild, peering eye. I use it because the world of *Proof of Demons* is a world without God.

Stories that traffic with devils and demons employ Christianity as counterweights. Novelists and screenwriters tend to pluck a historical/biblical demon from scriptures and grimoires to claim a sense of authenticity, to give their audiences footholds. A downtrodden priest locks with the unholy in a contest of faith. The unwavering church provides a sanctuary whose boundary can be breached by no satanic evil. The very iconography of religious belief is often sufficient for even a non-cleric to at least fight a demon to a draw. And the word *satanic* itself, of course, denotes that Satan stands behind every entity fouler than a ghost in the majority of folklore, literature, and cinema.

But Enriquez's demon—if demon it is; the filmmaker has no apparent interest in holding hands—is unencumbered by the hallowed ground of the church. Wherever it comes from, the Christian Hell or "another green world," it is able to cross the barrier of sanctity because that barrier is not there.

It can be set loose, an answer without a question, a starved mosquito from a jar.

But how did this mosquito—this *demon*—get into the storytelling jar, if not by the hand of God? Who, or what, will set it loose?

# CHAPTER TWENTY

## Jorie

▶▶ She helps Oli look for Agatha again. He still has his brave face on, trying not to show his desperation or let on how much he needs the doll. But Agatha is gone. Jorie isn't all the way here, either. Washes of anxiety flush heat across her skin, frequent enough to make their own rhythm. She glances at the dining nook table where her laptop should be.

The sense of being watched is stronger. Terrible thoughts grow extra teeth in her mind—a plan to break in and take Oli, leaving Jorie bloody under a sheet, a voice calling "Cut!" over some grand, awful finale.

But she feels a lightness to her that wasn't possible a few hours ago. The federal government is involved. There's a proactive edge to the fear now, like this is a thing that can be managed. Part of it has been taken out of her hands.

Someone from the Hinesburg Police Department calls. An officer will be sent over at six, just before dark. A few more panic cobwebs are brushed out of her mind. She finally feels a little like Sidney Prescott from *Scream*.

She keeps pulling her phone out and opening the only two photos she took of Beth while she was here. The horrifying weight those words have now, *while she was here.* One is a selfie she almost deletes because the cabin is in the background. The other is of Beth sitting in the same chair Agent Campras used, her arms around Oli. His smile is exaggerated, but his face is different. There is an open, simple softness she might not have seen since he was five or six.

It's because three people were in the house, she thinks. He was happy.

And the anger comes again.

"I meant what I said the other night," Jorie tells Sam.

Oli has dragged Cara and Carter into the den to watch TV. Jorie's dinner invitation—spaghetti, Pixar, a little too much wine—was an excuse to put pressure on her cousin.

"Meant what?" Sam says. The twins' jackets are still dangling from her hands.

"I want you guys to go off somewhere for a week or two."

But Sam just smiles, a crooked one that holds an apology. "We can't afford it," she tells Jorie. "Not unless you're talking about a motel off the interstate or something. I talked with Jeff and we feel okay. What I'm worried about is you."

"Hiding is the backup plan, Sam." Jorie isn't sure how to explain what's taking root in her. Her cousin knows some of what happened. She already knew about Hannah and the implosion of Jorie's old dreams, the guilt. She knows about Beth and the police crawling everywhere. But explaining this half-sketched final girl mentality Jorie's trying to embrace isn't easy.

They go into the kitchen and lean against the counter. Jorie pours a ten-dollar Malbec into glasses. "I can't just let my life fall apart again," she goes on, gathering her thoughts along the way. "It still has its old Band-Aids all over it. They offered us police protection—a car would be stationed outside for a while—but I don't know if that's hiding, and I still wouldn't want Oli here. But I'm broke. There's no breathing room on my credit cards."

"Hey, what about Leah Compton? She's babysat a lot for you. No one would have a clue Oli was there." Sam says this through the corners of her mouth because there are four bobby pins pressed between her lips. She twists her yellow hair into a sloppy, harried-mom shape and slides the pins into the roots she likes to keep dark, a sort of ghost of Rachel from *Friends*.

"I don't know," Jorie says, and turns to the dark outside the window. She thinks for the twentieth time today that whatever Enriquez is up to, it hasn't involved any young children. The sequel seems to have an older focal point, the magic teen years of slasher movies.

She faces Sam again. "Babysitting isn't exactly the same as 'Hey, can my kid live with you while the police try to catch a bunch of murderers,' is it? I forgot her name was Leah until you said it just now. She's just Mrs. Compton. We're close but not that close."

Sam's face tightens. "Sure, but if you're determined to not hide, it could work. All three of our kids like her. Oli would be right down the road, and Leah's son and her grandkids are in town, too. I met him at Lantman's, actually. Short guy, stocky. Almost bleached hair that's too long, probably to hide a bald spot. He seems nice, and he dotes on his mom. I feel like you could trust—you two cut it out right now!"

The voices in the den have lifted into bitter squeals as Cara and Carter fight over something. Jorie can't hear if Oli is part of it, but the other two burst into the kitchen. "Oli says something lives here," Cara tells her mom. "In his *closet*. Will you tell him to stop it?"

Sam looks over at Jorie, who goes into the living room to find Oliver sitting on the sofa, staring at the TV's frozen image of Lurch from *The Addams Family*. For a moment Jorie feels as though this is how horror has crawled back into her life, not through the unwelcome VHS tapes she played on this screen, not Beth's murder or being filmed in its aftermath, not her grandparents' graves being gently desecrated with bedsheets. It's in this beloved ghoul paused in black and white, gazing down at Wednesday.

Because here is her son, letting her fear and paranoia in. He's caught in the grim fascination, processing more than he should ever be responsible for. It's now his dread, too, worse than any film haunt.

"Buddy, are you trying to scare your cousins?" She sits down beside him and touches his shoulder.

He turns and looks at her, and his face makes her skin go cold. She realizes she was bracing herself for something from that encyclopedia of references, the pale blankness of Aiden from *The Ring*, or—what is wrong with her?—the quiet secret-keeping of Damien in *The Omen*. Horror films are littered with kids, fans expect them, and again her mind hinges on that thought, that Enriquez has moved on from the tired child-snatching trope.

But this is only Oli's normal face, the soft and open pleasantness of it. Unhappy, unsure, but full of faith in Jorie. That whatever is wrong, this thing she's keeping from him, she'll get to the bottom of it.

"I didn't mean it, sorry, Mom," he says. "You think a monster lives here, though."

"I have never said that once," she tells him, pushing his shoulder. He doesn't flop down with exaggerated force like he normally does. His body is rigid and doesn't yield to her. It's maybe the first time she's sensed the teenager that will come out of him one day.

"Something scared you." He says it in such a soft voice, she has to lean down to hear it.

Jorie wants him out of this house, even if she's right and this fucking reboot has fled to some other state or corner of the internet. Yes, something has scared her. She can't stop him from seeing her eyes go from window to window, waiting to see a green sheet shifting between gray curtains. And she's scared because she has to work tomorrow instead of keeping him tucked under her wing.

She hasn't figured out how she could take time off to tread water through this emergency. Not with her credit. It's like she said to Beth—in movies, the typical frightened protagonist doesn't have finances to worry about.

"Never mind that," is all she can say. She cups the side of his face in her hand. "What would you think about spending a couple of days with Mrs. Compton? Since your dad's still out of the country? I'm sure he'd drive up here if he could." The last part might be a lie, but she tends to cave and soften his disappointment in Eric when she can.

He looks down at his lap, then up at Lurch on the television. Even in the pixels of streaming video, the source material is so old that the Addams butler seems to be degrading on the screen, the digital fuzz squirming like distant moths on a light. This suggestion of movement makes it seem like Lurch is shifting his face to his left, toward the 1960s camera with eternal patience. If she sits here long enough, pushing her problems away, his eyes will reach hers across time.

It's fitting that Enriquez's tape would mix with Jorie's brain to infect all the media around her.

Oli mumbles something. She tips his chin up and he says, "Why can't I stay here with you if there's no monster?" His fingers twist in his lap, restless without his doll to hold.

"Look," she says, and fills herself with breath. "It's not about monsters. Just . . . just people who make pretend monsters. Like Uncle Fester, kind of, only not as nice. A long time ago, before you were born, I wrote stuff about them. And I don't know if it made them mad or what, but one of them hurt somebody, so the police want to talk to them."

"You mean Beth." His voice is small again.

"Yes. I mean Beth."

Here she is, on the verge of telling her eight-year-old more about the murder and wanting to hide it all from him at the same time—but how can she give him any of the truth? "I'll be working with the police," she settles for, "and while I do that, you'll stay somewhere close that only me and your cousins know about. Does that work?"

"I guess." Nearly whispered, and he shuts her out by pressing play on the remote. Wednesday Addams judders back into her dance as Lurch waits for comprehension to seep into his head. Jorie waits for her own understanding, or at least a hint of peace, that she is making the least wrong choice from a list that proves how small her world is.

When it's just her and Oli again, she puts him to bed, reading him a story for the first time in months. He chooses the one from *Scary Stories to Tell in the Dark* about the babysitter, and she doesn't let on that she knows what he's trying to do. *It's just in case*, she wishes she could tell him, if nothing else, but she can't trust him to know the depth and texture those words can have.

The doorbell rings, the old two-note chime decaying through the rooms. Most of her grandparents' furniture is still here, knitted throws over the sofa and armchairs, Gram's wooden owl collection scattered across bookcases. Deep-pile area rugs drowning the beautiful old red oak planks. The house eats sound.

Jorie hopes Oli doesn't see the fear on her face. She tells herself it's not a killer, then walks down the hall and opens the door. It's a man in full uniform, thirty-ish, on the short side with blond hair curling out under what she thinks of as a trooper hat.

"Sorry to bother you so late, Ms. Stroud," he says, her name steaming out of his mouth. "I'm Officer Willard, from the Hinesburg department. I'll be parked just over there till daybreak." He points toward the driveway, as though she might think he left his car in the woods.

"'Jorie' is fine." She tries to smile but it's too hard. "Come in, I'll make some coffee."

"I have some in the car already." He has no trouble grinning, and the single dimple on the left side makes her wary. "I'm a night owl. But some backup couldn't hurt. Lot of hours to go."

She leads him into the kitchen. No small talk comes to her, just an empty clang of spoons and the coffeepot on the marble counter. She can't remember the last time a man under the age of fifty was in this house before today. Now there have been two, and it almost surprises her how little that seems to mean to her.

"They told you what these guys look like?" she asks him, starting the old Braun machine. It came with the kitchen, and it wheezes like a grandparent as it brews.

"Green ghosts or blue ghosts, I was told. State police haven't said much to us yet." He leans back gently against the counter and crosses his arms. It makes him look like a teenager. "Carrying cameras. I watched some of that movie on my phone. I guess they're going with some cult look, huh?"

"Something like that. But carrying knives, too."

The smile he's had for most of the four minutes he's been inside fades. "Yeah. I mean, it's just some messed-up movie, right?" He sees Jorie turn, her mouth opening, and holds his hands up to ward her off. "Except your friend got killed, I know, so I can't just pass it off. I'm not."

She stares at him, absorbs the fact that he's not trying to be callous or masculine or any of those cop things. She doesn't think so, at least. He seems soft, like—she lets herself think of Dewey from *Scream* again, and it fits. "Well, thanks," she says, pouring coffee into a travel mug. "You take cream and sugar?"

"I like my coffee like I like my assignments," Willard says, the dimple appearing beside his grin. "Whatever keeps me awake. Just sugar is fine."

He steps outside with a thread of steam winding out of the mug's mouthpiece, and Jorie takes her old brick of a laptop into the dining nook, dreading its performance, resigned to being stuck with it for weeks. She stays away from social media and its traps of bitterness and anger. All she does at first is stare out at the night, the yellow tinge of the birches, the phosphorescent white of their trunks. Yellow is too easy to see in the dark, her eyes can turn the patterns of the leaves into other things.

She pictures FBI agents sitting in sterile rooms or in cubicle farms—her movie context is rusty—with bad coffee and headache lighting. Watching the new footage, the Pine Arch creatures, whatever Enriquez is calling this new iteration, gliding out of the trees. Phones ringing and clipped voices.

This image gives everything weight in a way that even Beth somehow couldn't, the simple fact that the government is involved, grounding it in heavy reality. She can see the agents telling each other that there are hardly any killers in bedsheets in this stuff, not on the tape and not in any Facebook posts. *What the hell even is this shit?* one of them says, maybe the tall guy, Campras, from earlier today. *I think we got separate things going on.*

Officer Willard's cruiser is parked on the gravel just out of her angle of sight. She would have to go out the front door and a dozen paces to the right to see the shape of him in the front seat. He's only a phone call away, and she would see the blue and red strobes light up the trees if he turned them on, but the house is an unmoored island floating off from safety.

Though her son is even closer, twenty feet down the hall, he feels like an itch she can't reach, exposed and vulnerable every moment he's here.

She opens her old email account, the one linked to the dead October Film Haunt site, and has to convince the server it's her, it's been so long. It shouldn't be surprising to see a handful of media requests from the past few days—*The Eldritch Vault, IndieWire, Witch List*—but it is anyway. There's a message from Sadie Hartmann. Jorie remembers her with a brief smile that almost turns into a sob. They used to talk about how hard it was for women to gain traction in the horror world. They lifted each other up. Another pang from a lifetime ago. Sadie wants to write something supportive about Jorie for her Night Worms blog, but it's too much right now.

The newest email, not even an hour old, is from someone named Mollie

Dryden at *CinemaBlend*, with the subject line "Looking for comment on recent Proof of Demons disappearances for web story."

She ignores them all. She'll panic when she sees something truly viral like *TMZ* in her inbox, but for now, she hopes, it's just the timing. Halloween season will be upon the world soon, and Enriquez's brash marketing is giving people something to cash in on. They'll be digging up Hannah from her second grave yet again.

All the old email data is gone: videos, photographs, mock-ups, PDFs, store invoices, half the guts of the blog's archives. This was the half she didn't delete herself that one blackout night, dragging the cursor across her desktop to highlight her life and dumping it all in the trash bin.

That was the month her apartment was broken into, she remembers, not long after Hannah died, and the laptop before this one was stolen. Their neighborhood hadn't been the safest, but she took it as a sign. She salvaged a lot of material from emails and Dropbox accounts until eventually deciding it all deserved to go.

But she still has her contacts.

She starts by emailing one of the first people she ever talked to about *Proof of Demons*. Trevor Henderson knows more about horror movies than anyone else she's ever met, and it doesn't hurt that he's the creator of the Pine Arch Creature. He's on the short list of those who might still trust her.

Halfway into the third paragraph to Trevor—*looking for anything you know about Enriquez and the Rickies obsessed with her, especially in the last few years*—she stops and looks up, sure she saw a shape approaching the window across the lawn, from the yellowing trees. A minute fades by. It's nothing, not even one of the barn cats from the Mills house down the road. Not so much as a jump scare.

And her phone is right here. She taps it awake to prove it and swipes the lock screen photo of Oli's scrunched-up face away. The cop's number is programmed in.

She won't call unless she sees something, so she lets her mind drift back to the unreal. What would the Pine Arch Creature look like in the dark? Would it be a part of the dark? Would the dark be a part of it, the same skin and the same hole that draws all the colors in? Would it trigger the motion light at the corner of the house? Would the front stoop creak if it put its unknowable weight on the old boards?

Once upon a time, in other trees, she pretended to know these answers. She wrote about the crunch of dead leaves when there was only silence. Now she knows better, but there are still real things out there. There are mundane kitchen knives and cameras looking for blood.

And because she is staring out across the grass, toward the dark-eaten trees for long enough, she picks out what could be a camera lens. The dull crescent of a handheld moon shifting between birch trunks, the barest shine of glass. After a moment, a small yellow light appears beside it, unsteady, a cigarette lighter or a hidden candle that's only there for a few seconds.

She stares into the night for a full minute, imagining what she must look like in her box of lamplight, displayed like an artifact. The thought makes her get up and turn the light off over the table, brightening the ambient glow of appliances through the kitchen doorway, the microwave and oven clocks, the coffee maker's red eye.

She goes back to the window and watches her dark bleed into theirs.

A flashlight cuts on, a gray-white line across the trees. For an instant she can see a ghost-shaped figure, one of those awful bedsheets standing on the edge of her lawn, a black box on its shoulder. Filming her silhouette at the window. The flashlight bounces, drags toward the house, motioning something at Jorie, then clicks off.

Two pale shapes detach from the tree line. Jorie can almost make out the crowns on their heads, pushing against the fabric of the sheets.

She grabs her phone off the table and calls Officer Willard. Her thumb swipes the speakerphone button by mistake, and three, five, seven hollow rings burr into the quiet room. He's not answering.

Outside, after these silent years, the film haunt turns around on her.

# CHAPTER TWENTY-ONE

## Coleman

▶▶ The way the light goes out of Evie's eyes hurts him more than anything a doctor has said about his lungs. More than Gloria's tears or even the time he heard her sobbing in the shower the morning after they found out.

"Daddy, stage *four*? Really?" If he weren't her father, he doesn't think he would be able to parse the words, they're so blurred and wet. "Only six months? On top of someone *stabbing* you?"

He insisted on small talk, asking questions about Charlotte and Liam, on the ride home from the airport. He kept checking the rearview mirror, making sure his eyes had not turned to black coals again. But mostly he stole glances at the passenger seat. It was just too wonderful to see her, as profound as magic, and he wanted to stretch the moments out to some impossible length.

Coleman remembers how small Evie was the year the three of them drove out to the Buncombe County fair that set up shop for a week every October, backdropped by the quilted mountains. An electrical issue had closed the whole operation down for the day. The mini-coaster and Ferris wheel stood like new ruins in the fading light.

Evie looked something like this when they pulled into the grass lot and absorbed the sparse silence across the field, and the thought seems to pull him back to that late afternoon, back through every mistake he ever made. Through every random dark cloud. His mind skips the moments of joy that overwhelmed those clouds. His stubborn fatalism veers around all the dad jokes and the tight lifted-up hugs when he came through the garage door after work and the excited squeals for animals and birthdays scattered through their time together, and this can't be what dying is supposed to be like.

The smells of faded popcorn and sugar seem to hang in the air. Coleman is doing everything he can not to cough in front of her. It's hard to stop once he gets started, even if it seems the thing stalking him has somehow cleared his lungs a little.

Gloria is bookending their daughter, her hand gliding up and down Evie's back like a paintbrush, soothing. Her eyes are glassy and unfocused.

He remembers the phase with the long-boned thing under Evie's bed, not long after the closed fair. How her face crumpled at the end of every bedtime story for weeks when he moved to turn out the light. The thing's bones were soft like mushy arms, she told him, and they were long with so many elbows to help it reach all the way out and up and onto her mattress, the exact length to make it to the center where she lay shouting until they came back to comfort her.

Eventually, they had to let her cry alone until the bones got shorter and withered back into the dark.

She's making that face now, these seconds before the tears feel as long as the thing under her childhood bed. Her father is in the room with her this time, but he's still leaving her to face an awful thing. A light is still being turned off. Coleman gets ready to put his arms around her, to catch her or hold her, he's not sure. Gloria is looking away from them now. The brush of her hand is still gliding up and down Evie's back.

"Stage four," Evie whispers.

He nods and looks down at the hands in his lap. He has to lift them to feel the blood pushing through the fingers and palms, to know they're his hands. The same blood that cycles through his lungs. "I'm sorry, angel," he whispers. Angels, what use does he have for those? What proof of them is there? He thinks of his brother. He thinks of the DVD he slid back into his laptop earlier. He nods again.

"You're starting treatment, though, right?" Her voice beginning to calm for a moment, at least, because she needs to ask this and hear his answer. "You're going to. When is it?"

"Yes, honey. Soon." Thinking the word *no* until it picks up an echo of itself. Evie tries to smile but her mouth makes the sweetest and most grotesque shape he's ever seen.

Coleman sees the thing from the woods creep up behind Evie in the kitchen, after the dishes have been cleared away. The thing he's almost certain has been living inside of him, at least some of the time. She's beside the sink, talking to her mother in a low voice as he comes out of the living room. *Smudge* is still the closest word he can find, a long stain dirtying the air across the room in shaky flickers until it reaches her.

He is frozen between rooms until a lock of Evie's dark hair lifts up from the back of her head as though on a string, then drops back. The smudge gains just enough mass or substance to be called a figure, a person-shaped suggestion with arms that might span the narrow room. The reach of a long-boned thing. The top of it bends from the ceiling, curving down toward her head, and Coleman shouts, "Don't!"

His wife and daughter look more alike than they ever have, turning to him with their mouths slightly open. Coleman is so struck by this that he almost doesn't see the smudge turn with them, the movement of its head smearing across the air.

Gloria nearly runs over to him at the living room doorway, and the thing takes the opportunity outside of her line of vision to solidify further, into the thought that was just forming in Coleman's mind. It's the thing from the movie, in the graveyard.

Then Gloria's hands are on him, patting and fussing. For a moment she absently straightens a tie that isn't there, that probably won't be there anymore until he's lying in a casket. He thinks about cremation again, his organs breaking down in an oven, his eyes caving in like sinkholes.

"Feeling up for dessert?" she asks, but he hardly touched his dinner.

He looks over her head to Evie, but she's standing alone now, whatever calm she found beginning to tremble apart. The rasps and briars are filling his breaths again, the soupy air congealing in his throat, and soon he'll have to cough them all out.

The smudge, the child stealer from *Proof of Demons*, comes back. It leaks out of the trees along the south side of their property the next afternoon, moving like woodsmoke that has turned to jelly. It towers over his wife as she tries to dig the worries from her mind in the garden outside their bedroom. The thing is more visible in the sunlight. Its hands are shifting, half-fingered stumps.

He watches from a window as it stretches down to her, and the brim of her sun hat lifts until it tumbles from her head. Gloria looks up, and Coleman doesn't understand why she can't see what he sees, even as the half-liquid shape of its hand touches her.

Her body goes rigid and is shoved to the side, the red spade flung across the grass.

Coleman collapses on his way out the door to her, retching in their small foyer, his lungs on fire, and has to be driven to the hospital.

Dr. Banchhod comes in after hours, his dinner forgotten at home, to finally get the appointment in stone, for first thing next Monday, expedited. Evie hears her father promise, this time formally, that he'll start aggressive treatment right away.

Gloria is fine, she's there holding his hand. "You lied to me, Coleman. You lied and watched me mark the calendar. No, don't apologize, I'm just relieved to hear a doctor say it. You get some rest."

A perk of dying is to be forgiven for everything—or almost everything. All Coleman has done is bring his unmade decision into the foreground. Gloria must suspect that he's thinking of cheating the cancer out of its endgame. He could never tell her about the smudge haunting their house and threatening her and Evie, and she would never understand his temptation to draw it away with him to Vermont.

The gown he's wearing is nearly the same shade of green he saw in the woods. It's a coincidence. He doesn't want to know if it means something, but he has to protect his family and follow this course that started with the blond man's knife or even earlier, when the first cancer cells bloomed into rotten life.

Or when he was a boy tumbling out of a tree, he thinks, like some deep bell tolling behind his heart.

"I'm taking a leave of absence," Evie tells him, squeezing his other hand. "For a few weeks. Char and Liam can stay with their other grandparents."

*No, your mother is already taking too much time off work,* his mouth opens to say. He doesn't trust himself to speak, but Evie can read the look on his face well enough. "We have to try," she says, and he's so tired.

The darkness and the silence are too heavy.

Coleman wakes from a dream of his brother, the lake again, the sun dragging a path to the canoe. He's tipped into the pitch black of the hospital room. The doctor wanted him here overnight. Just in case, he told him, and also because three of the stitches tore in his stab wound when he tried to reach up for the doorknob after falling. It's humiliating that he couldn't even get to Gloria when she was in danger.

The machines that were on and humming when he last went to sleep are dark now. No hospital is allowed to be this lightless, is it? There's no ribbon of hallway light leaking through the gap under the closed door. The curtains must be clamped shut against the night. He hears footsteps fading away from the woolen quiet of the room.

But he's not alone. A sense is around him in the air, somewhere between a smell and a taste, coating his tongue. He lies in the bed for what seems like minutes, feeling a tube pinching his left forearm. He tries to identify the odor and can only think of musty burning leaves, wet with a texture of bitter ash. The wound in his side is a distant shouted argument under an opioid cloud.

Something shifts and leans over him in the blackness. It lowers itself to his face. The smell in his mouth doesn't get stronger, but his awareness of it grows, he can feel the wheeze of it in his lungs now. Metal shavings in saliva, the tang of copper. Sour dirt.

His eyes adjust to the dark and he begins to see a reluctant shape, black felt on black paper, at a great height and folding itself over. It comes close enough for Coleman to feel its heat. An almost electric static along the skin of his cheeks, in the hairs of his nostrils, in the air of his rapid breaths. The shape makes a low, dragging sound over and over, like dust on a record's needle at the end of side one.

He barks out a strangled sob and begins to cough, the deep moist hacking that feels like the start of vomiting. The thing lifts a few inches away from him, and the respiratory monitor blinks back on to his left, throwing threads of light along the vague contours of the smudge. The air above the bed is a black pill dissolving in dirty water.

Something touches the wound in his left side, it feels like a nub, hot and thriving and horrible. Its counterpart, the other handless hand, brushes against his face and drags itself down to his lips. Coleman is being taken into an embrace. He squeezes his mouth shut, coughing against his teeth and groaning with the strain of his lungs as the thing tries to get inside and bloody mucus tries to get out.

A second shape appears to his left, near the rolling nightstand. "We will clean you out," a voice says, thick and wet but very human, genderless. Coleman sees the gleam of eyes in the rumor of light from the monitor. "You will be free of this."

He says nothing as the shape—the person—turns and passes back through the dark soup of the room and opens the door. The hallway is its own lightless void.

Another machine wakes with a beep, the wide monitor with its ubiquitous jagged lines reading the book of his heart. The smudge is suddenly gone, the warmth and weight of its presence leaving a hole in the room that normalcy rushes back in to fill.

That heavy black lump in his throat again, as the smudge pries its way in. His eyes burn. He imagines them filling with blood, the blood turning black with decay.

He opens his mouth wide and surely these wet heaves and gasps will tear him apart, but the ceiling lights stutter on and someone is saying, "Mr. Smith? Mr. Smith?" like a strange bird's call. "Mr. Smith, stay with us."

And he knows before he turns his head and sees the nightstand, the white business card he found in the woods—where the crypt was or should be, he can't decide—lying on its fake mahogany, that he will have to find a way to tell Gloria and Evie that he is going to Vermont.

# CHAPTER TWENTY-TWO

## Jorie

▶▶ It's 12:02 A.M. and October has two more days to wait.

She stares at her phone instead of leaving a voicemail. The digital light saturates her vision and turns the view through the window into VHS darkness, a vague haze that reminds her of low-budget slashers. It's fitting.

Jorie taps Officer Willard's name on the phone again and squeezes her eyes shut, tries to reboot them as the rings come through the tiny speaker. The rough trill of them sounds almost vintage, and she thinks of that old movie, the cop telling the babysitter that the prank caller was inside the house.

When she looks out the window again, the two Rickies she saw creeping across the grass are gone. She wonders if they're the ones she saw on Reddit with their clever little shorthand, *JS in VT confirmed* and *BK en route*. Some of her anger comes back, a taste of what she'll need in the final reel.

All the doors are locked. She checked the windows earlier. Willard must be sleeping on the job or draped over his steering wheel with blood pattering on the floorboard.

The phone screen times out, its fan of light blinking off and pushing Jorie back into the dark. She moves toward the front door, steeling herself for the don't-go-out-there moment, but then swivels and half-runs down the hallway to Oli's bedroom. His hair, the pale rind of an ear are visible above his blanket. The closet door is open and dark, the mirror hanging with only the edge of Jorie inside it.

She doesn't know whether to hide him somewhere or hope—what kind of a word is that right now—the Rickies are only gathering footage. Establishing shots, EXT. JORIE STROUD'S HOME, HINESBURG-NIGHT.

After too many seconds spool out, she goes to his bed and shakes him awake. She shushes his sleep-thick "Mom?" and tells him he has to get in the closet, all the way back against the deeper left wall. He goes without protesting but starts to cry as she pushes shirts on hangers against him, then his wicker laundry basket to hide his legs.

"Please, buddy, be as quiet as you can," she whispers, hating herself for letting him be a part of this. Saving most of the heartburn rage for Hélène Enriquez. "Fucking asshole, I will find you," but she doesn't say it far enough under her breath. "No, Oli, not you. It'll be okay, we just have to be quiet. I'll be right back in here, I promise."

Then to the kitchen, where she pulls her own Rickie knife out of the block. She stands and listens to the dark. A scratching comes at the back door that opens out onto the redbrick patio, her wayward garden.

She walks deeper into the room. The panes of glass in the door angle into view and someone is standing there, looking in, the blank face cocked and the crown straining under the sheet. The shape of the face is a grin, or high gaunt cheekbones are stretching the fabric.

Jorie watches him—or her, the figure isn't that tall and cults don't have to be a fraternity—peer through the door, unaware that she's right here. She watches until the figure steps away and passes across the window, a gliding ghost, toward the driveway.

The silence that settles is hard to wait through. Eventually, all she can hear is Gram's electric clock above the door to the laundry room. Two minutes, and Jorie thinks the Rickies must have left, passing by the murdered officer or melting back into the trees to keep from waking him.

She crosses the width of the house and steps outside with the knife flashing cloudy moonlight. There's nothing, just a swollen calm. The suggestions of the trees, the colors of gourds murky in the dark.

The left taillight of the police cruiser is just visible up ahead, where the driveway bends right to the road around the trees that lead to Mrs. Compton's house.

The front door is open behind her. She doesn't want to move away from it and leave Oli in the closet alone, but she has to check on Willard. She has to walk out into the open for their cameras, show them she's scared but will give them some fight to make their narrative sing. The blood will shine brighter if she makes them work for it.

If they're filming her right now, they're using night vision, which means this is a found-footage film. She feels that mote in her heart again, the one that loved this. It was always wide-eyed at horror's altar. It's there, but it's never been smaller, so shriveled. It has never wanted the sun more.

Walking beside the gravel to avoid the squeak of stones, triggering the motion light up on the corner eave, she sees the shape of Willard in the driver's seat, not moving. Her monstrous shadow elongates in front of her. The moon slides out from clouds as thin as rice paper, as though it's reading script cues along with Jorie. All she knows is that she doesn't see blood yet.

The veiled colors of fall to her left, bloated with silence, no snapped twig or footsteps, but something makes her look into the trees. The white birches like the bars of a cage. The night between them is so black that it swims, that analog grit again, she can see the particles inside her eyes drifting along the dense backdrop. Then movement, a green-draped shape leaning into sight, a white arm lifting up to a face.

"You killed her," something whispers at Jorie out of the dark. Her first thought isn't to run. Her first thought is, *Beth or Hannah?* Tears come burning into her eyes. A weightless cold sinks through her body.

"Who are you?" she hisses, and takes a step forward, raising the knife.

But the Rickie is gone in a rasp of leaves, and she's not about to run, alone, through the half-acre of woods toward the road.

She squeezes the knife's handle, the textured plastic rough and damp with sweat, and crosses the driveway to look into the car. Willard is slumped toward her. She raps on the window and he jerks up with a small muffled scream. Jorie can only laugh, twice and harsh, as he wipes the sleep off his face.

"I'll keep you safe," Oli tells her just before his breathing changes. "But I need Agatha."

"I know, buddy," she whispers into his hair.

It's his first time sleeping in her bed since Beth was here. Before then, it was the week they moved into the house. She promises him she's making everything okay, and that seems enough for him to fade into sleep.

She only feels her little spoon trembling once in the night.

Later, she extracts herself from the tangle of Oli and sneaks out of the bed. The officer sits in the dining nook. She avoids him. As far as she knows, he has stayed awake all night after calling in the "disturbance," as she heard him phrase it on his radio.

There is stillness around the house. The Rickies have moved ahead into her future.

Willard doesn't really believe anyone was here in the night, it's all over his face. As though no intruder would dare step onto this property when a man, a badge, a gun—these supreme assurances—are in the driveway. She wants to ask him how he can doubt that, after what she saw and heard, after Beth. The worst possible things could have happened while he snored in his car. Sometimes women in horror movies jump at the right shadows. Even when they aren't final girls.

But she keeps it to herself. He leaves an hour past first light, not quite sheepishly enough, with a promise that someone will be back before dark. At least it answers the question of whether police protection will be enough to keep Oli safe. Her Dewey is a letdown. Another Dewey might be, too.

That leaves Mrs. Compton. Jorie needs to make the decision, it's like something held in her hand and turned at every angle for more and more scrutiny. Putting Oli somewhere only Sam, the police, and she would know about. Separating herself from her son, where anything could happen and it would be too late by the time she found out.

Or keeping him with her, together, and going into hiding. Living off money she doesn't have—the narrow space left on her credit cards? A personal loan? It could mean letting someone else die. It would mean Beth was killed for nothing, it would turn her into a delayed footnote on the page of what Jorie did in 2012.

She can at least float the idea. She finds the number in her phone and calls before the swarm of second guesses can descend.

Mrs. Compton answers after several rings. "Well, if it isn't the mama bear," she says from the other side of the woods. "Hello, Jorie. How's our young Oliver?"

"Hi, Mrs. Compton," Jorie says, ignoring the strong desire to hang up. "He's okay. We had a long night. I'm sorry but I have to ask you a favor. A pretty big one."

Enough time passes for Jorie to think the call has dropped. She walks with the phone down the hallway to peek in at Oli, the top of his head just visible under her grandmother's blanket.

"The favor must be for a good reason," Mrs. Compton finally says, "if it must be asked."

"It is," Jorie says, and speeds through the slimmest nutshell of the story. "I have a stalker, and it's gotten serious. A friend who came up to help has been—she's been killed, and I need to make sure Oli is safe. Not with me is probably the safest he's going to get right now, and it has to be somewhere no one would know about. I can't afford to just leave, so I was wondering..."

"If I could keep him? Hide him away in my old-lady bungalow?" Someone laughs in the background, and the older woman's voice gets distant for a few seconds, as though she's moved the phone away from her face. "This is just terrible, Jorie. A stalker. It's like one of those awful movies. How long would this be?"

Pops of static crease the line, filling the silence as Jorie decides what the answer to that could be. As *one of those awful movies* hovers like its own kind of static. "Two days," she says. "Or three, maybe. I really don't know, but if it's longer than that, I'll come get him and figure something out."

"My son is visiting. He could help keep him company. I guess this could work."

"Thank you," Jorie says, then has to stop. Her throat wants to close up. A fierce heat comes into her face. "How about I call you back in an hour? It'll give you some time to think about it. Oli's only spent the one night with you before. We don't want to impose."

The line goes dead. Jorie checks the screen but the phone app is gone.

She almost calls back, but she wants to push away the reservations and the nagging thought—that she has no idea what she's doing, she's a clueless mother. The truth of it aches. She wants to cover it up by going online and finding out more about the sequel. Look for new funeral-watching videos on social media, see if Trevor has written her back.

Unearth something. Maybe not an answer, that's too easy, but there must be a clue. She's no Miss Marple, but surely there is a path laid out for her, a list of directions she's supposed to stumble across. She can stop the next Hannah from dying.

But Oli is in the way of these thoughts. Every thought. The idea of the possibility of anything happening to him—she just can't.

Sam's right. If these people want her son, for the movie or to get to Jorie, they know to look for him here, at his cousins' house, at his school. But Jorie and Oli haven't been to Mrs. Compton's house in months. She could tuck him away, closer than anywhere that's not here, like a squirrel burying an acorn at the roots of the tree it nests in.

Finally, the decision made, a few ounces ease from the weight on her shoulders. She goes to her bedroom. He's still sleeping, but she shakes him gently until his warm brown eyes open.

They both have to move forward now. Jorie's heart breaks a little more, and she gives herself one minute to lie down with him and feel the heat of his small, thriving body.

# INTERLUDE

[Excerpt from "Horror Film Marketing Campaign Linked to Possible Disappearances," by Mollie Dryden, *CinemaBlend*]

[FEATURE] The FBI, alongside police departments as far-flung as Rhode Island, California, and Florida, is asking the public for information regarding disappearances that have been connected with an obscure horror movie and a troubling online trend.

In less than a week since the appearance of a teaser promoting an apparent sequel to the film *Proof of Demons* on social media, the hashtags #funeralwatching and #filmhaunted have led to hundreds of shared videos of a viral challenge. At the time of this writing, five people ranging in age from 16 to 31 have posted clips seeming to reveal a strange presence in their homes. In each case, a missing person report has been filed by their family.

Federal and local authorities advise extreme caution regarding these incidents but also stress the possibility that the disappearances are part of an attempt at viral marketing, coinciding with numerous suggestions that a sequel to the film is in production. However, the murder of film editor Beth Kowalczyk (*Greenest Pastures*, *The Lion of Idaho*) near Burlington, Vermont, this week has also been linked to the alleged film, sparking heated rumors that the project could involve a real killing.

Hélène Enriquez, the director of *Proof of Demons*, is a suspected pseudonym and could not be reached for comment.

Kowalczyk rose to minor prominence as a member of the October Film Haunt, a popular blogger/media group that was dissolved in 2013 following the death of North Carolina high school student Hannah Kim and the trial of two of Kim's peers implicated in the ritualistic burial that led to the teenager's asphyxiation. A controversial blog post written by fellow October Film Haunt member Jorie Stroud was purported to have played a role in the group's decision to perform the ritual.

A source involved with the Vermont murder investigation states that Stroud is a local resident and that Kowalczyk was visiting the area. Authorities have declined to comment on Stroud's status in the investigation, though one person familiar with the FBI's operation says Stroud has cooperated and is not considered a suspect. This person also revealed that Stroud is not believed to be responsible for accounts named The *Original* October Film Haunt on TikTok and other platforms, which have posted the videos around which the "Funeral Watching" challenge is centered.

Stroud did not respond to requests for comment.

There has also been police activity outside the upstate New York home of Roger Eilertsen, former Academy Award nominee (Supporting Actor, *Came Down the Mountain*, 1978) and cast member of *Proof of Demons*. Two people familiar with the investigation said a 911 call was placed after several fans of the film were seen attempting to climb the gates onto Eilertsen's property last week. No other criminal acts have been reported, and neither Mr. Eilertsen, who has reportedly never spoken on the record about Enriquez's film, nor his representatives responded to requests for comment.

Meanwhile, Providence, Rhode Island, police continue to search for 19-year-old Brandon Mares, the supposed first to perform the video ritual and share it on social media. On Instagram, Mares's sister shared a since-deleted image of his bedroom wall, on which a thin vertical line had been painted in what many assumed to be blood, though no physical evidence of violence was found at the scene. However, one person familiar with the search for Mares revealed that investigators have reason to believe the teenager was paid to film the video, though this has not been verified.

**RELATED:** Are Urban Legends Dangerous in the Post-Truth Era? One Redditor Says Definitely Yes

# CHAPTER TWENTY-THREE

## Coleman

▶▶ "Coleman, no," Gloria says, "you can't leave, I won't let you." She blocks the door to the garage with her body, the only shape in his life that he could draw from memory.

"Please, honey," he says, "it's Jackson. I think he's contacting me. I'd do anything to see him again, you can understand that, can't you?"

"Jackson?" The name disarms her, and for just a second her outstretched arms relax. "Your brother contacted you?"

He waited until Evie was at the market, but he is so weak these days, Gloria is almost able to overpower him and get him back into their bed. "And I'm going to be cured," he tells her. "This will protect you and Evie. Those bedsheets the grandkids found. I have to go."

"What do you mean, 'cured'?" Her voice, trembling. He's breaking her. She wants that word, *cured*, more than he does. "Coleman, talk to me, we're not in any danger. You not being here is our only danger. Please talk to me."

She could never begin to understand. He takes a single leather duffel bag out into the garage as she calls someone, Dr. Banchhod's office probably, and wails again—*wails* is the only word that comes close—into the phone. "He's leaving us, he's going to go die somewhere, he's leaving us, stop him."

Coleman manages to enclose himself in the car before the coughing fit starts. He wipes the speckled droplets from the steering wheel, spit and blood on his palm, as the garage door drags itself open. His wife's voice carries out to him, through the seams of the car, begging someone to come.

He checks the mirror to make sure his eyes are his eyes. He presses a finger against his forehead, but no black bruise spreads there.

Coleman backs up the driveway and imagines a trail of his bright red life, all their memories and touches in the dark and their fingers lacing together through everything, spattering a trail from his mouth, along the oil-stained concrete, through the side door onto the terra-cotta porcelain tiles to where Gloria is standing in her terror in the strong kitchen light.

The idea of leaving them is its own cancer.

He wavered on a thin line until today, the inertia of his sickness and his wife and daughter holding him here. He slept through three nights after the hospital. No changes to his face, no blood pooling just beneath his skin. No smudges or stains in the air around his family. The house felt almost safe, not a reprieve, but a sense that he could imagine one. The first chemo after the weekend. The rest of his life, rolled out in a short fraying line.

Until the other grandparents mentioned something strange to Evie. Charlotte and Liam had gone out to the Rusins' front yard to play in the thin Denver air and found pale green sheets pooled on the lawn. Carla glimpsed two small ghosts twirling, almost blending with the grass, through an upstairs window.

The color of the gown they put him in at the hospital, Coleman thought when Evie told him, the color those strange men wore in the woods. They made his grandchildren little trick-or-treat versions of *them*, and he couldn't swallow past the horror in his throat.

Evie came up behind him not long after, before his pretense of asking her to go to the store. She slipped her arms around his belly. Her cheek warm against his back. His lungs seething against her cheek.

Something unlocked in him. "Did I ever tell you my brother disappeared when I was a boy?"

With only the kitchen to look at, it was easier to feel his way into the thing he couldn't say to her or her mother.

"Of course you did." He felt the warmth of her voice spreading like dampness through his shirt. "Uncle Jackson. You were ten, or maybe twelve."

"Twelve, yeah. I've always wondered—" He started to take a deep breath of preparation but stopped because Evie would hear the wet clog of his lungs. "I've always wanted to know if he's still out there, and lately, some things have happened that give me hope."

The weight of her head lifted away from his body. She was listening, wary with her own hope. "What do you mean, Daddy? Have you found him?"

"Something has found me," Coleman said, and there it was, the beginning of the truth, spoken, out in the open. But he couldn't go on to the next sentence. He didn't know what it would be yet. "I'm just scared," he told her instead, and sewed the conversation up with such insufficient stitching, the wrong color and texture.

The message that came in the mail from Vermont, chanting in his head. *There Is Jorie → Jackson ← Jorie Is There.*

For another hour, his inertia stuttered in its stubborn track, even as the strain of momentum pulled at him. How long it would take him to drive up there, how he could tell Gloria, how he could ever give her the burden of telling their daughter. How he could make them believe he'd be back soon and would gladly sit in a chair as hours of poison seep into his veins out of a bag. How much he loves them and how sorry he is.

He stops at the corner of Blythe Street and Sweeten Creek Road, and a woman comes out from behind one of the tall hedges bracketing the neighborhood entrance. It's the young mother from the ice cream family, the one who told her daughter about the crypt in the woods before Coleman went into the video store.

He powers his window down but doesn't say anything. A new cough is stretching itself up his throat, and the vibrations of his vocal cords would cause it to break open. Soon he'll have to reach back for the prescription syrup in the duffel bag behind him.

"I've been waiting for hours," she says, leaning down to peer in at him from the curb. "Yesterday, too. You know the crypt was moved, right? You were out looking for it. You know, the 'coven.'" Her hands come up and hook quotes around the last word.

The need to cough fades to an ominous tickle, and he thinks he can trust his voice. "Where is it? How did you know I would—" But the coughing does come, heaves full of wetness. He bends down and puts his forehead against the wheel for a moment. Stars swim in his eyes.

The mother is waiting patiently when he sits back up. A breeze lifts her dark hair and pulls it around her face as she says, "I think this is my only other scene." Her face looks warped and inhuman, wrapped in the sheet of her hair. Her words are muffled. She laughs and brushes it away. "The crypt, though, it's in Vermont. I figured you would know that. Everything else is up there. Most of the cameras left yesterday morning."

"Cameras," he says, and stares ahead through the windshield, as though expecting to see a rig clamped to the hood of his Accord. "I don't get this. Another movie?"

"Something," the woman says. "I'm just supposed to remind you that you belong. You have sort of a growing fan base." She hands him a business card through the window, a duplicate of the Hélène Enriquez one that was left for him near the cemetery and in the hospital. He turns it over but there is no haiku. The woman walks off, away from the main road and back the way Coleman came.

"Wait!" he calls after her, but his breaths are shallow, a tickle of warning is in his throat.

He watches her in the rearview, feeling no threat in her. He doesn't worry that she'll stop by his home or wait for Evie to return. He doesn't worry that this is only his instinct.

A small figure runs, almost lopes out of some white pines between two front yards. He thinks it's an animal for a second, but it straightens and the woman extends her arm to it. The figure grasps her hand, and in an instant they're mother and daughter. He forgot to ask if they ever got their ice cream, or if that was just a line she memorized.

Three hours to Greensboro, the hum of tires instead of music, his wife's pleading underneath the hum. How is Evie reacting, and how can his heart stay whole for much longer? His phone is turned off, hidden in the glove box.

He finds his childhood home after only a few wrong turns and corrections. He feels compelled to stop here, like something on an itinerary he hasn't been given.

But the house has changed, the brick ranch torn to its bones at some point and built into something with a two-car garage and bay windows. He can nearly see the ghost of the old place trapped in its amber.

The tree that broke Jackson's arm and opened a window onto the afterlife—onto somewhere—is entirely gone. It could have been struck by lightning or disease, or the people who live here now wanted it gone to let the sun spill into the bowl of this backyard. There's no depression in the earth to say it was ever here.

He stands near the place where he landed almost half a century ago and looked into another world. Another green world, maybe, as the old man in the cult says in *Proof of Demons*. What happened that day? How did it stretch across all these years? He only remembers glimpses of people moving in light, how the light swallowed the colors. The only green thing was the eye that looked down at him, darker than his child eyes, framed by oak leaves full of shadow.

There are scenes he's noticed in the film during his multiple viewings, where nothing happens for uncomfortable stretches of time. Where the camera is waiting. Or the film itself is waiting. Coleman waits.

Out past the remade house and across the narrow street, he sees a few trees tangled together. Two branches, a young pine and what might be a hickory, seem to reach for each other with a patience humans could never know. There's a sort of arch, if he wants to believe in it enough.

He looks up into the sky, without an oak crown to crosshatch the sun, and tries to bring back the memory of the impossible window. He remembers being in the woods last week, sitting by the lake from the movie, and he says, "I belong with you," just like he did then. The minutes start to trickle away.

"The hell you think you're doing?" a voice calls from the house. Coleman sees a large man come out of a door in the expanse of bricks, below what he thinks was once his bedroom window. Ten paces farther to the right was Jackson's. "This is private property."

"Sorry!" Coleman shouts across the lawn at the man, and has to bend down and grip his knees to catch his breath. "I used to live here as a kid," he goes on, staring at the lush grass, the man's shadow stretching across it. This spot was once dirt packed hard by the endless shoes of boys.

"You all right, mister?" the guy says. Coleman looks up at him. He's in his early thirties, taller than the man who stabbed him but just as thick. A sun haze washes across the day, and for less than a second, gone before Coleman recognizes it, there's a knife in the man's hand, the wrist rotating to flatten the blade in the light.

But it's only a man. He has a manicured beard, and there are children's toys littered across the property, an almost hidden green toddler pool, a small yellow bicycle. It's just a young family with the best parts of Coleman's past ahead of them.

"I don't know," Coleman answers. "I used to live here. I wanted to see it one more time. I thought maybe I could feel something of it."

The bearded man squints at the sky, then off toward the south. Small birds draw chaotic patterns in the air over the western trees, out where the sun is trying to get to. Coleman sees pity on the man's face, the way he won't look back at him. For a moment he pretends there's a knife in his own hand, heavy and cold.

There are still thirteen hours between his birthplace and the part of Vermont where he thinks he's supposed to be, and his body makes it nearly halfway. The car leaves the denser forests behind in Virginia, and he sees the suggestion of the land opening up somewhere in the distance, the ocean over a far horizon. He wonders if he's close enough to smell salt in the air but can't breathe deeply enough to know for sure.

He drives in a long curve around D.C. and draws even closer to water through Baltimore, these places he's never been and hardly sees now. At one point distant gulls scratch the gray gloss of the sky. He pushes himself a little farther.

Something Gloria kept sobbing, "You're not coming back," whirs and whirs and loops in his mind, a livid spirit pursuing him north. The heartbreak of it hangs in the car with him. But even as he cries silently in the droning rhythm of the highways, thinking of what he's doing to her and Evie—what his daughter's face must have looked like when she came home with the fixings for breakfast—his thoughts turn more and more to Jackson.

He has had forty-six years to get used to his absence, the only thing in his life longer than his marriage. He has wondered, imagined, he has left him behind. His brother's face has faded until he's not sure when he stopped having a clear picture of what he looked like. Forty-six years, but Jackson is still the one string that could be picked at to unravel Coleman.

"Why now?" he asks the loneliness inside the car. But it seems obvious to him. "Because it can't be later," he answers. A wheeze has been building up in his breaths. Pain slowly radiates through the axis of his bones. The car drifts onto the shoulder twice, and he finally pulls over two miles inside Pennsylvania, at a single-story box of a motel called The Way Inn.

Later, the syrup numbs his throat. A low dose of tapentadol swims through him until his skin could be fusing with the scratchy sheets under the heavy rose-patterned comforter. He doesn't enjoy the fierce and mute undertow of opioids. It feels like drowning in someone else's body.

It's cold in the room even though he dialed the shaky AC down. The sodium light from the parking lot pushes at the gap between the blackout curtains. If he turned his phone on, the room would fill with the desperate vibrations of his family, but he doesn't, and the world is soft and scentless and lulled by passing cars. He drifts with the lamp on, and he wakes at the end of a chain of moments in the night, a black space with only the faintest rinds of the room's furniture visible.

The seam of light between the curtains is gone. His eyes sharpen as he stares at where it should be and begins to realize the lights outside are still there. They are limning the edges of something huge standing inside the room, in front of the window.

There is a paleness to the shape, behind or under the dark of it, that slowly becomes the brightest thing in the room. It's different than it was in the hospital room. It reminds him of Evie's long-boned thing.

"What do you want?" he asks. "I'm going up there."

The shape steps forward, closer to the bed. He could still call it a smudge, but it is something else now, thin and so tall that it has to hinge at the chest and wedge itself into the room. The textured plaster ceiling rasps against it as it moves, the glinting suggestions of eyes looking down at Coleman. It has the ghost of a mouth, or its mouth is the vague hole in its torso, puckered with fleshy tissue. The parking lot lamps push between the curtains and into the space it has left behind.

"What do you want?" he says again. "I'm almost there. I'm doing it."

Its voice, at last, is cold and clotted and deep. "You belong." It is a voice that has never been used, but inside of it, like the bloodless white in the shadow of its body, he hears his brother. "I did the hole," it says. "In the air. The tree. The eye. When you saw. It saw me." There is no breath between these broken sentences, only clicks and blank pauses on an old tape.

The lamp on the bedside table blinks back on and he sees the thing for a moment. He sees Jackson's face pressed against the ceiling. His brother's eyes stretched wide and glaring. A full mouth with threads of light between the hints of teeth. It could be the face Jackson would have grown into, at the moment of his death after raising a family, suffering, breaking into joy, lifting grandchildren into the air.

"She read your words," Jackson's face says. "She wanted to see. The hole. The eye." Then the face is formless again, and the rest of its body is an open shell. Something is shifting inside, a curdled light that is a gas and a liquid and neither, only light. Coleman thinks he could wear the thing as a suit. Pass through it as a door. He feels warmth between his legs as his bladder surrenders.

"She wanted me," it says. Brief clicks and pops. "Inside the camera. Her eye." It begins to fold its great length down to the bed.

# CHAPTER TWENTY-FOUR

## Jorie

▶▶ "What if the bad guys find me there?" Oli asks after a few minutes in the trees, not looking up at her, and her heart splinters. He sounds frightened again. His feet swish through last year's leaves.

"They won't," she says, and it takes too long for her to go on. She doesn't want to be honest. "If they do, even though there's no one who would tell them that, Leah will call the police and protect you, okay?"

There's a sense of actual relief—because the choice is made and because she's making Oli walk through the woods instead of driving him. She's almost sure they aren't being watched, but absolutely no one can see what happens in the next twenty minutes.

This is after Jorie spent an hour combing her property for more trail cams, anything that might suggest the house is still under surveillance. The leavings of Rickies, traces like candy wrappers. She stood in the dry swell of trees and listened to the hushed noise of the world, tracking trunk to trunk for a flash of pale green.

Midmorning they snuck out the back door with Oli's pack strapped to his back and his overnight bag on Jorie's shoulder—four changes of clothes, she told him, not letting herself think past that many days—and slipped into the pines and maples.

Now she scans the treetops for cameras as they go. She rakes the sky for drones. There's no one out here. Oli will be safe.

After several minutes of walking away from High Rock Road, parallel to Lavigne Hill, toward almost true wilderness, they hook back in a direction that thins out halfway to Mrs. Compton's house. There are fewer birches on this side of her grandparents' property.

"I don't want to stay with Mrs. Compton," he says. His shoulders slump so much the straps of the backpack nearly slide off. The air smells dusty and the sun falls through a strainer to reach them in the trees.

"I know, buddy. I don't want you to either." Pieces of their neighbor's house appear in the foliage ahead. "But it's only a few days, the police know you're there, and I'll be close. Missing you."

Mrs. Compton called back yesterday after barely an hour and said she'd be delighted to watch over "such a poet of a boy." Jorie wrestled with a heavy, many-limbed urge to say no, she would figure something out that kept Oli with her. A shameful corner of her heart was half-ready to make a move on Chip just so Oli could come to work with her.

But she's been over it with Sam. She talked to an officer at the Burlington station. Everyone agrees this is a smart compromise.

The house is a soft yellow Cape Cod that's even smaller than her own, with cedar shake siding and a bright brick chimney that's too tall for the greenish roof. The cornflower blue shutters nearly make the place ugly. A stamp of lawn fades into gravel, which curves briefly through skinny pines to the road. A compact Subaru wagon sits coated in road salt dust.

They climb onto the stoop, under a white-painted trellis tangled with dying morning glories, and Jorie knocks on the door.

"Here's my little Oliver Twist!" a voice says the moment the inner door opens, slowly swinging back to reveal the tall shape of Mrs. Compton, veiled through the screen. She laughs and pretends to stagger back. "Oh, but you're not so little anymore! You've grown another foot since just the other day. We'll have to think up a new name."

Oli smiles, and it almost looks real. He's going to be fine, Jorie tells herself. He has a month's worth of books and a new jigsaw puzzle she was saving for Christmas Eve.

"I've got plenty of stewed cabbage and kale and all those kinds of things growing boys love so much," Mrs. Compton says, and he smiles again, a few more watts of it finding his eyes. Jorie notices again that he needs a haircut. "And I made sure to get rid of all the ice cream. We're safe."

Oli goes in first and Jorie follows, looking at her savior with a shame that burns in her cheeks. She has to tilt her head up, and the warmth she sees in the honey-colored eyes eases her heart. "Thank you, Leah. I just—I can't tell you how much."

"No need for that. I told you I missed him, and I really did make him a pie. Might even have some vanilla ice cream for it." The two women stand in the narrow throat of the foyer while Oli puts his pack down beside the sofa, just through the doorway on the left.

It's dim inside, and Mrs. Compton seems to take up so much of the space, her height and her round thinness, the baggy dark cardigan hanging off her. She stares at Jorie almost too intently, brightly, and years seem to have faded from her skin, nothing like when she came to the house the other evening. It's like she's wearing makeup, something Jorie wouldn't expect her to even have in her home. Or maybe it's just that her hair, wadded tight into a gray bun, is smoothing the fine wrinkles from her face.

Oli is talking to someone, and a moment later a man fills the frame, a good five inches shorter than his mother. His pale hair could use a cut, too, but it adds something older to the boyish face.

"Paul," he says, but doesn't step forward with his hand out. Jorie's not sure why she expected him to. "Mom's been telling me about Oliver. It's good to meet you two."

"How old are your children?" Jorie is aware of the strained rudeness under her voice. She doesn't like it, but she's glad it's there. Her son will be sleeping under the same roof as this man. She can just see Oli behind Paul, picking books up off a coffee table and flipping through them.

"No, they're not here yet," Mrs. Compton says, smiling at her son. "Paulie's wife is bringing them. It's just him today—he has a fear of flying, so he drove up early. I've had him chopping wood, getting my snow tires on, all sorts of things. I keep a running list for when he comes up. They're good boys, four and six. Oliver will be like a king to them."

Jorie finds herself staring at Mrs. Compton's son, trying to x-ray him for any reason why she should snatch Oli back. He seems uncomfortable being stared at, his eyebrows up and unsure, a crooked smile on his mouth. But his mother is a port in a storm, and nothing about him rubs Jorie the wrong way. He doesn't have to rub her the right way.

She turns back to Mrs. Compton. "I hope this will be just a couple of days. Two or maybe three. He'll be skipping school. God forbid it's longer, but I'll figure out where we can go if it comes to that. And I'll pay you as soon as I can."

The hallway bisecting the house is full of shadows until the last doorway, which glows like only kitchens can glow. She remembers it as a minimal space, not much like a grandmother's kitchen. How can she explain the situation without selling it short or terrifying them? Everything except the sharp ache of Beth feels like a gray area, cloudy and hard to quantify.

She almost wishes she had a copy of Enriquez's script to know when the last act can start. *Proof of Demons 2: The Final Evidence.* She wishes she could laugh at the absurdity of it, the stark wildness of all this, and Mrs. Compton tilts her head in confusion. "Everything all right, Jorie?"

"It's nothing." Jorie rubs her eyes, pushes a knuckle and thumb into them as the past week swarms over her for a moment. "It's just that there aren't many people I can trust up here. I'm kind of at my wits' end. I don't know if these people want to"—she drops her voice close to a whisper—"kill me or film me. And I need to find that out. Thank you. Thank you for doing this. Watching him."

These staccato sentences like beads on a string, clacking together. Mrs. Compton slips an arm around her and pats her back. "You go rest and let the police do their jobs," she says. "We'll keep him under lock and key. The boys will be here soon, and they'll tire him out so much, he'll barely have time to be homesick. Paul will keep one eye outdoors."

It's kind of Mrs. Compton to say that, such a normal way to phrase it, and Jorie keeps nodding to delay the moment of her leaving. But she finally steps around Paul, crouches down beside the sofa where Oli has been half-listening and half-reading *Scary Stories to Tell in the Dark*. She didn't notice him put that one in his bag. At least it's not open to the one about the babysitter.

"I'm sorry, buddy," she says, pulling him against her. "I'll call over here in a couple of hours. And after I finish at the market, too."

"Okay," he murmurs against her neck. His arms slide around Jorie's neck. "Will you find Agatha and bring her?"

"I'll look everywhere twice." She squeezes harder. "I'll find her."

"But what if the monster gets you?"

"Oh, honey. It won't. I promise it won't." Being stabbed by a Rickie must feel something like this moment. Burying herself alive. She can't hold her son tightly enough. "Just a couple of days. And then I was thinking, we could go get you a phone. Early Christmas."

She pulls away and watches his face soften at that. A bit of light comes back into his eyes. He's thinking of Eric and how they'll be able to talk more. Only eight years old, but wise enough to know his dad is much more likely to commit to something as low maintenance as text messages.

He gives her a smile that's more honest and not unbearably far from cheerful, and she kisses his hair and steps out onto the stoop and stands looking toward where the road is. She dragged it out as long as she could, and now her little wolf is somewhere else.

She thinks again that characters in movies only have to go to work in the first reel, they spend the rest of their stories trying to stay alive and get to the bottoms of mysteries, not stopping to eat or take care of bodily functions unless those mundane actions serve the plot. Helen's husband hiding in the bathroom at the end of *Candyman*, any kitchen set piece that makes the cut only because the cabinets and drawers are going to fly open at any second. The restroom stall in *Ju-On*.

Jorie has to live out the deleted scenes.

There's nothing here to buoy her. She likes nearly everyone she works with, but she hasn't made a single real friend in thirteen months. Linda is a sweetheart, and Jorie doesn't even care that she's older than her mother would be if she were still alive, but Jorie has to play the daughter whenever they work together.

Not counting Sam, with Beth gone, Mrs. Compton might be the only thing close to a friend she has in the world, and Jorie hardly knows her. What does that say about her new Vermont life so far? What does it say about the last decade?

But the thought of Mrs. Compton makes her doubt her decision again, and she pushes it away. She'll make friends when this is all over. Sam knows other Hinesburg moms. Jorie will drink red wine and join a book club, if people in early middle age still do that.

The inside of Lantman's is the last thing she wants to look at as her head spins with thoughts. The tall windows at the front of the store. Too much fluorescent light, sticky light that seems to crawl along the floor as slow as the next six hours.

She starts off on register, but as the day winds toward the busy hour before dinner, she ends up in the back of the store, stocking yogurt and sour cream and sweating jugs of milk. Chip is the shift manager, of course he is. He makes the schedule, so he's nearly always here on Jorie's days. He's brought up the ride he gave her three times already.

"Hey, I forgot to ask," he says on one of his circuits, his shadow draped over her, cut out of the harsh light. "How many typos did you find in that book?"

"The usual number," she answers, not letting herself roll her eyes. It's not quite his fault. Most people think editing is only hunting down stray commas.

He tries for another opening. "You seem tired. But that's okay!" Mock defensiveness, his hands raised to show he's on her side. "It makes you look sweet."

His subtext feels like cold fingers on her skin. She wishes she could go into the back and cry.

"I am very tired, Chip." She drags a new box over and cuts it open. It's full of skyr, which she's never tasted, in elegant white tubs. She stares down at the blade of the cutter. "My head hurts from all those typos."

"Well, take a break and come into the office when you're done with those," he says, pointing at the box. He takes a step back and his shadow slides off her like dirty silk. "I got some Advil with your name on it. And I'll make us some coffee, the good kind. Hope I don't have to drive you home again." He actually winks at her.

Make that four times. "I'll see how this goes," she says. Finally she looks up at him, squinting, and gives him a sickly smile.

She steals moments to look at her phone and wants to check on Oli. But she called when she got here. "I'm bored," he said, "and I miss you. I miss Agatha. What if I don't like those kids?" She heard the resilience in his voice, though, and hugged the phone to her chest when she hung up.

Moving along the back of the store, the meat cooler, the cold cuts, ice cream, frozen waffles. The trick is to zone out and let her thoughts settle onto each item she takes out of the cardboard boxes, let her mind follow her hand to the shelf or the peg or the bed of ice.

Her phone buzzes with an email from Trevor Henderson. It's nicer than she feels she has a right to hope for. He offers any help he can give, but the only thing truly salient is a detail from several years ago.

> Back when Siren Head was kind of blowing up, this guy (assuming it was a guy, he felt a bit mansplainy) "Avery E." pitched a project to me about PROOF OF DEMONS that he said was fiction but contained more clues about the actual proof from the movie. He was DEEP into it and thought Enriquez was a genius and maybe a god too. The story was crazy and had the creature from the movie eating horror writers (ending with Stephen King, major eye roll), but it would have been an intellectual property headache even if I'd been into it.
>
> I passed and got a nasty email back, something about me maybe getting a visit from the demon one night. But I ignored it and that was that. (I deleted everything he sent, or I'd forward it to you. I checked my block list and the email address was pinedemon@j.j—that can't be a real address, though, right?)

Pine Demon. Avery E. She can guess the first—she's already seen it on Reddit—but wants to scream because the other sounds a chime in some far corner of her mind. That last name, that *E.*, is the one she really wants. "Please don't let it be a fake name," she asks Lantman's fiberboard ceiling. This information could be a grain of sand from Hélène Enriquez's shoreline. It could be nothing, a speck of lint. But it's more than she had yesterday.

She taps out a quick reply: Is there any way you can get his last name? Can anybody you know help? Please get back to me with a last name. I'm at work but will keep an eye on my email. Thank you. I owe you.

When the message is sent, she tells herself again, *It's more than you had yesterday.*

As she works, moving away from the cold stuff into aisle 3, she sifts through everyone she could ask about someone with that name hidden in a horror niche—Lovecraft, Marble Hornets, weird fiction, cult films, "real" hauntings. Everyone who might have crossed her path.

She still remembers a handful of these people, and one of them could have been an Avery, crouched in the hundreds of private messages on Reddit or Facebook, emails sent through the October Film Haunt site's contact form, the uncountable tweets she was mentioned in at the height of her potential, when she had a movie deal and the earth seemed so far below her.

Maybe someone remembers someone. It feels like a dead end.

She checks her watch and it's 6:15, over two hours to go. The time isn't flying by, but it's not crawling and gasping anymore. She's barely registered the subtle swell of noise in the store as people stop in on their way home from work, or the night lowering through the front windows.

Now that she's coming out of her haze and her cycling thoughts, she hears children laughing somewhere near the breakfast cereals. More cans of soup go on shelves, she turns each can so that the label faces out for all the obsessive-compulsive folks in Chittenden County but really for herself.

Something hits the floor down the aisle she's kneeling in, then the sound of a metal can rolling. She doesn't look up until she hears the same noises again. An older man is standing at the end, backlit by rows of milk jugs and fluorescent tubing. A Red Sox cap blacks his eyes out in shadow.

His hand is held out in front of him, the fingers still forming the shape of the can that has rolled out of Jorie's line of sight. He stands that way, loosely inert, seeming to watch something ahead of him.

A middle-aged woman enters the frame of shelving and slows to a stop a few feet from the man, her cart pointed at his back. Red hair frizzes down onto her shoulders, wild as though the wind is up outside. She stands motionless, too, as though caught by the same unknown vision over by the bakery area.

The two of them are a tableau, the harsh light on the verge of flickering above them, the colored plastic caps of the milk containers making sight lines. Jorie's eyes are a camera positioned just so by a cinematographer.

They're turning their heads toward Jorie, so gradually that she doesn't realize it at first. The tendons in their necks could be creaking, they must be full of rust and determination to swivel with such dreadful slowness. It feels as against nature, even as unholy, as the people at the funeral on the VHS tape that showed up in her mailbox.

Another shopper enters the frame of the aisle but doesn't stop. The man gives the first two a strange glance, then veers around them, holding a basket with a French loaf peeking out.

The children stop laughing and bickering two aisles over, and this lets a voice rise up to the ceiling and drift over to Jorie as she kneels on the polished white floor with a box of organic soups open at her waist. She can't quite make out what the voice is saying, it's a hushed river that doesn't let a single word break through the current, but she recognizes the muddled tone and cadence of the supposed minister in *Proof of Demons*, the male voice that reprised its role in Enriquez's new footage.

The woman and the old man continue to turn their heads obscenely, almost too slowly to track with the eye. They're frozen, they're a haunted photograph. Jorie tries to stand but sits down hard on the floor instead and scoots herself backward.

She checks behind her and sees another woman standing motionless about twenty feet away. Her hand is on a box of baking soda, the mustard-yellow box at the edge of the shelf, tilting, about to slide its weight off into her palm. She's younger, a brown ponytail folded inside a high blue coat collar. Her face is absorbed in the yellow box but beginning to rotate toward Jorie. An inch every ten, fifteen seconds.

The movement—the threat, the regard, the marking of her, whatever its intention—is so strange outside the screen. The ill choreography has no expectations without a horror movie scene to fit into. But it feels even more awful because it's so mundane. Jorie can almost laugh at them. She thinks again that it's the opposite of a jump scare.

The ends of the aisles are otherwise empty of customers. Jorie's eyes roam the ceiling, the top shelves, looking for cameras. The voice is still droning its possible eulogy on the edge of comprehension. At the far end of the white tiled floor, the first two heads continue their agonizing pivots, the limbs and postures immobile.

She gets to her feet and faces the woman with the baking soda. "What are you doing?" she says, letting herself step to within five feet of her. "What is this?"

The woman doesn't react to Jorie's voice. Her face is still trying to break from its stillness, like the paused video of Lurch, or a stroke victim pushing her way back. Behind Jorie, someone says to the first two frozen people, "Could you move? I'm trying to get home."

"What the fuck do you want?" Jorie is almost shouting at the woman with the yellow box now, in a moment she'll lose the *almost*. "Is this a movie? Did Enriquez send you? Who's filming this?"

Jorie has a hundred more questions, but the woman says something, the words buried in her mouth. Her head has completed maybe twenty degrees of its dragging arc.

"What?" Jorie asks her. "What did you say?" She moves closer, ready to dodge away if an arm shoots out, if a knife swings around in the hand not gripping the box.

The woman speaks again, but it's still too soft. Jorie crosses some threshold of frustration. She moves all the way into knife range and shakes her. The third time, Jorie is sure the words are, "Will you believe in what you made?"

Jorie looks back down the aisle. The old man and the woman have almost turned their heads to face her. Their expressions are inscrutable but not blank. The man's face is still shaded by the brim of his cap, but there's something resentful and hard in the wideness of the woman's eyes, the skin tight around them.

And as Jorie stares, part of a third figure steps into view next to them, the green bedsheet stark against the bright row of milk. Half a smooth cotton face, the crown hidden above it. The sheet lifts until it slides down along the arm to reveal a long tapered knife, a fluorescent gleam trailing down to a black handle and a white hand.

The man and woman are finally staring right at her. They begin to walk down the aisle.

Jorie turns and runs, her shoulder colliding with the baking soda woman, who spins and slams against the shelf. The box hits the floor, a small cloud of powder blooming. Jorie hears a shout, and someone else screams in a register above it.

She rights herself in time to see a Rickie step into the aisle, at the end that leads to the checkout lanes. The right arm raises, the green sheet pools against the elbow to show the same kind of plain kitchen knife they all carry around with them. The hand holding it is pale and splotched with pink, almost like a cheek flushed with embarrassment.

But this blade wears a dusting of old blood, as though it was washed poorly, and Jorie knows the blood once belonged to Beth. She knows, somehow, that she is meant to recognize it. The same blood that coursed through her best friend and brought her back to Jorie and this awful, undead past.

The Rickie's mouth sucks the cotton in, forming a shallow dent so that Jorie can see the grin open up in the blank face.

She glances behind her—the first Rickie in front of the dairy cooler, the two starers halfway to her now, not in slow motion anymore. She's walled in. So she holds Oliver tightly in her mind, her little Oli lifting his eyebrow at one of her hundreds of dumb jokes, looking too grown-up for her liking, and runs forward.

The Rickie braces, turning the knife hilt to stab downward with a kill shot, but Jorie drops to her hands and knees just outside arm's length. She uses her size to plunge forward and between the Rickie's legs, where she half-stands and slams her head upward with every atom of force she can gather.

There's a huge grunt of pain, expelled breath. The knife arcs down past her, no more than three inches from her face, and the Rickie follows, crumpled and rolling on the glossy tile floor with his—for once, she was praying it was a man—hands cupping his groin. He groans through the sheet over his face, dotting the fabric with a pointillist mist of saliva.

Another scream. The sound of slapping shoes just behind her.

Then she's back on her feet, pushing between registers 2 and 3, a crying toddler and a mother saying, "Excuse me," the automatic door ratcheting open, and the cold belly of the last of the day, the sun leaking orange into the trees to her left, away from Oli and away from home.

# CHAPTER TWENTY-FIVE
## Coleman

▶▶ Is he having a stroke? Is this how his mother felt the night that put her in the nursing home?

The beige room phone sits miles away on the nightstand. He doesn't want to lie awake and aware on his back, feeling his brain short out, regions of his identity dying like a feeble power grid. But even if he could stretch his hand across those miles, he can't call his family, and there is no one else.

Hours pass after the withered, elongated thing that looked like his brother. Coleman lies cold and sweating on the motel bed. Fever creases into fever. He can't speak. The parking lot light fades and the pink sun builds up in its place, blurring the gap between the curtains. His breaths hover like ghosts over his face, with no coughs to dispel them.

At first he bends his neck back and hinges his mouth open. His chin shifts side to side as he strains his vocal cords inside his throat. Only scratching clicks and his clean hanging breaths. Slowly, the opioid wears off, but there is little pain waiting.

He tries to decide if a stroke cheating the cancer would be a more frustrating end.

He is finally able to lift his right arm and make a slow fist. His left arm follows and makes a second fist. He squeezes them both tight. His legs fold up into angles when he tells them to. So not a stroke, probably.

But he is so weak. He wonders if the smudge—his brother—is a vampire. He traces that thought out to its edges for a while. It would make as much sense as the rest. At least he's seen vampires in more than just the one movie. But wouldn't Jackson have been preserved in his youth? *I'm no vampirologist,* he would have told Gloria in his former life. She would roll her eyes because it was one of his favorite joke templates. Almost a leitmotif.

The thing that visited Coleman was an old man. He can't remember if it had teeth.

With his head tilted back on the pillow, Coleman can see the perfect red line drawn on the wall behind the bed, from near the ceiling to the headboard. He watches four flies crawl on the paint that he knows isn't paint. He thinks the blood came from the wound in his side.

A memory slips away, of his mouth saying in Jackson's voice that Christ was pierced in the side, but only to make sure he was dead. That this story has nothing to do with him.

*The Bible is no place to look for demons,* Coleman says in this memory, *that's from the movie.*

He thinks he said this as he smeared the line down the wall, standing on the mattress. Before the wall opened along this new seam. He remembers it parting like thin bloody lips. Did tendrils of light seep out? Did his brother worm through, even though he—it—was already in the room with Coleman?

At the same time, these things were only a dream. Did he dip his fingers into his own body to wet them with blood? He is confused, the inside of his head has been washed in oily water. When the light gets stronger, he will check his hands and his wound.

He wonders what color his eyes are.

"Gloria," he is able to say at last, and it is his own voice. His mouth is numb and dry as paper. "I'm sorry. I'm going to keep going north. I'm sorry, Evie." He sleeps for the first time as the light gets in through the crack and crawls up the bed, up the wall, onto the stripe of blood.

It is darker than he expects in the room when he wakes. The sun is hovering over the motel. The plastic clock on the nightstand reads 11:29. Checkout was at ten, so he must be paying for another night. But he is fully himself.

He proves it by sitting up and turning on the bedside lamp. His left hand is clean, but the right is coated in what he tries to tell himself again is dried red paint. The room phone feels like it's taking in a breath so that it can ring. He stares at it for a minute, slowly remembering that the mother of the ice cream family gave him another of Hélène Enriquez's cards as he was leaving Arden. The woman who made *Proof of Demons*. What would he say to her?

He reaches for the phone and lifts it from its old cradle.

The line rings nearly twenty times, he's lost count, before noise answers it. Wind across a receiver, voices in the background. What might be wheels clacking across floorboards. "Yes?" someone says into the phone, and all the ambient sounds cease, as though the person has stepped into a room with thick walls.

He clears his throat. "I'm calling for, I don't know how to say the first name. Hélène Enriquez."

There is only breathing for a moment, then a laugh. The laugh is pitched high and bright, but then slows and draws itself out into more breath, a rattling sort of wheeze. He would swear it didn't come from the person on the phone, and it bothers him that he could know that.

"The *H* is silent. Is this Mr. Coleman Smith?" the voice says, and it seems normal, not like a cassette tape. It could be a woman's voice, he thinks, and he's almost sure it's the voice that spoke to him in the hospital room. Any accent suggested by the name—if this is Enriquez he's speaking with—has long been sanded away.

"It is," he says. He is sitting on the motel bed, holding the phone with his bloody hand.

"I exalt you, Mr. Smith." Someone laughs again, farther away, behind her voice. "I extol you. I celebrate you. There will be a funeral, of sorts, in northwestern Vermont. Not for you, not really. The cemetery's name is Maple Walk, you know the zip code. If you could be there at eleven A.M. tomorrow. We'll talk."

A click sounds in his ear, and the line is dead. He asks, "Was that my brother?" anyway.

He puts the phone back in its cradle and thinks about how long he lay on his back this morning without coughing. The prescription syrup is still too unfamiliar to know how much of a grace period he has left. Grace—that is a fine word for the simple state of not needing to cough and not feeling the next one coiling like an infected spring.

He had grace his entire life and never recognized it until it was gone.

The knife wound above the waistband of his boxer shorts is still stitched up tight. The blood came from somewhere else. He pushes the covers down and there is a red stain on the mattress between his legs. It is still damp. He smells urine in the sheets, too, and feels the shame of wetting himself.

A small mass lies on the stain. The size of a tongue or part of a kidney. A tiny diseased lung. It glistens. Bending closer, he thinks it's a small animal that has been turned inside out. Tufts of gray fur clinging to the blood. Like a gift brought by a cat.

He wants to stop thinking of the smudge as Jackson. In the end, it was on him, pressed against him with a wet, unpleasant weight, and he fought it for a moment. He pushed at it. It smelled like tree sap and sour earth.

Then—he's not sure. The room was dark and the thing's weight seemed to dissipate all at once. Jackson's voice was speaking to him, telling him to be calm, did he not want to know where his brother has been all this time? Coleman's brief sea of time?

He breathed the thing in, he's pretty sure, it became incorporeal and sank through his pores and leaked through his gritted teeth. A knot in his throat, sinking to his lungs. He couldn't cough it out, and his mind detuned, like a radio between stations, and the world turned itself toward the sun.

Standing on the bed and using Jackson's voice, dragging bloody fingers down the wall. Stooping to dip his fingers in the well of the animal's remains. Discussing Christ. These are impressions, like hearsay with only himself as a source. There is blood between his teeth in the mirror over the dresser.

There is a face under the bed in the mirror.

Coleman watches it grin at him.

He finally admits to himself that it wasn't a stroke at all. He is possessed. The movie is called *Proof of Demons*, isn't it? What else would they want him for? He never thought it would be such an organic process, with so much grit and tissue.

This is why his eyes turned black in the kitchen, back at home. This is why his entire body has been a bruise waiting for the gentlest touch. He is the proof.

Cleaning the room feels beyond him. He leaves a note asking the staff to bill his credit card for the damages to the wall and the bed linen. He flings the dead animal, wrapped in toilet paper, into the parking lot and gets into his car and drives north.

Two hours pass before he coughs again. It's a brief fit, as minor as a tickle in his throat. When he pulls the tissue away from his mouth, there is grainy black saliva mixed in with the blood.

Burlington is too far to reach before dark, but he is able to fill himself with the splashes of yellows and reds in thousands of trees along the way, as the sun seeps into the rearview and the Green Mountains climb out of the horizon ahead.

He pretends Gloria is beside him, saying again and again how beautiful it is up here, how old and untouched by man if you ignore the power lines. "Oh, Coleman, just look at the colors," he says for her. "Our mountains aren't like these somehow, and it's not even peak foliage yet."

Sometimes it's Gloria in her twenties, her rich brown hair, her open face smiling, edging Jackson to the corner of his heart. Sometimes he feels her hand on his thigh.

For a few minutes he lets himself imagine the ancient car seat in the back, Evie kicking her legs and asking questions hooked onto questions. But even she goes silent in this vast painting.

He apologizes to them over and over.

His hips and back ache from the driving. He stops every hundred miles or so and walks some of the stiffness out of his legs. But he only coughs enough to pull over once, in an interstate breakdown lane. Four tissues wet with black mucus and threads of blood, clumps of something like compressed ash. Like a campfire coming out of him.

"You got here just early enough to get lucky," the woman at the bed-and-breakfast tells him.

Coleman has made it as far as Shelburne, Vermont. His throat has been filling with this new presence again, distracting enough that he felt the car roll onto the shoulder of the highway a few times. He keeps trying to make himself cough it out, but the mucus and the pain seem to be gone.

"Lucky how?" he says. His eyes feel like they're burning around the edges. He wants sleep.

"With a vacancy." The woman takes a step back from the desk. "Next week the leaf peepers start showing up by the carload. We got a nice porch out back with a view of Lake Champlain. It's heaven."

Coleman thanks her and goes out with his room key and stands looking at the open darkness of the water for a minute. It just might be heaven, but his fatigue is deep in his joints, like sluggish oil.

A malevolent quilt drops onto Coleman when he steps into his room. Its profound dark weight wraps him, squeezes him, tries to pin him to the wall and crush him to the floor. The light thins to a dirty smudge, and the ambient sound of the world flattens in his ears before vanishing. Coleman begins to drown in the thrumming thick water of it. The lake outside, the lake stretching decades back into his youth, the lake in Arden and the horror film, everything recedes like a sleek tide until it is just a hotel room.

The demon is standing in the corner, at the edge of the lamp's reach. It must be using Coleman like a suit, coming and going, leaking out and crawling in. Leaving him draped across the bed or crumpled on the floor.

It looks even more like Jackson tonight. A Jackson that could be ten feet tall if it didn't have to bow itself under the ceiling, its body hinged and full of creases.

Its bloodless lips are new and clumsy, and a long tongue keeps coming out to wet them. Sometimes its chest opens up. It speaks for a while, but half the words are lost in its muddy clicking speech. Everything sounds like it was prerecorded and copied onto an old cassette. "Yes, we saw him. Fell from the tree. We took him. We wore him. We saw us."

It tells Coleman shards of stories about when they were children, and he has to pick out names—Chris Deloitte, Sarah Layton, old Mr. Hugh from down their street—from the clipped fragments of sentences and context clues to patch the memories together.

"Remember. The fox den? Don't you. Want to know? What will. Come out?" Its warped voice cresting on the waves of the question marks. The fox den, whether the demon has plucked it from the fabric of Coleman's mind or from the essence of his brother, convinces him that this is all real. Jackson was not taken by anything like an angel.

The younger brother sits on the bed, his feet on the floor, occasionally glancing up at the demon's head pressed against the ceiling. Mostly staring at the floor. He doesn't speak until he begins to wonder why he hasn't, how he has become this diseased vessel that things are being done to. A dying puppet.

"Did I summon you from the movie?" he asks it finally. "Why are you here? What did you see when we fell out of the tree that day?"

Instead of answers there is only a deeper silence, and he thinks Jackson is gone. He lifts his head and sees it—far from a smudge now—crossing the small room to him, bent over so that its head reaches the bed before its arms do. It seems to move by shuddering in and out of materiality. Coleman notices that it has something close to fingers now, white growths like mushroom stems.

He tries to get up and lunge to his left, but his brother's awful old face is on him. Then the rest of the demon is there and pushing him back onto the bed. The dead weight of it is cold, and what feels almost like skin is slick and moist. Corpse wax, Coleman remembers, the soapy substance he has read about when researching his coming death. When bacteria break down the fat in the body inside the grave.

"I saw us," it says. A stench of soil and pine resin, the stickiness of its touch. The silty grain of its voice. "I came for you. You never stopped. Hoping for me." Coleman clenches his mouth shut, squeezes his eyes closed, but there are so many ways into him.

# CHAPTER TWENTY-SIX

## Jorie

▶▶ She's just as restless at home, veering around to the backyard and stopping herself from sprinting into the trees. She needs to know Oli is okay, but the whole reason he's with Mrs. Compton is exactly this, so the movie folding around her can't get to him. Jorie has to stay away and keep the script, whatever scenes are waiting in it, on this side of the woods.

The thrum of adrenaline from Lantman's is more of an itch now. Her skin crawls with it, and it doesn't help that she can still feel Chip's hand on her shoulder, kneading.

"Go get everyone out of there!" she screamed at him after he followed her outside, her eyes on the windows. Customers streamed through the automatic doors, wailing, streaking to their cars and causing an immediate chaos of brake lights. "You didn't see the guy wearing a bedsheet with a knife? Trying to kill me? The police need to be here." She pulled her phone out and dialed.

"I want you to go home and get some rest," he told her. She hated the *I want you* tacked on, the casual ownership of it. "Anybody with a knife is probably halfway to Burlington by now. You can call me tomorrow and let me know about your next shift. Or if you need anything from me."

And his hand loosened and slipped down to her collarbone, making tight circles of what only he would call comfort.

"Chip—" But she didn't trust herself to speak. She just ran to her car and babbled at the 911 dispatcher as she drove home. She refused to stay at the scene and said they could come to her house and get a statement. Apparently, someone was already on the way to High Rock Road.

She left a message for Agent Fuller, a few sentences that couldn't hope to summarize what had just happened. Particles of stars swam in her vision, like the birth of a migraine.

Back in her horror movie days, she was too ambivalent about the scenes where no one believes the protagonist, late in act two when it's still to the bad guys' advantage to stay shrouded on the periphery of all the secondary characters.

This part of the story is a mean sequence of paranoia, a storytelling trick meant to break the protagonist down, isolate her from those who have always trusted her, until she's jumping at all the shadows artfully placed around her. Until her nerves give out, the audience is a little frayed, the well of unease spills over.

If Enriquez's third act is to kill Jorie—the default final girl—then they should go ahead and get to the climax. She doesn't like this dragged-out middle. It's too much like gaslighting, and she's already had one breakdown in her life.

But then, the Rickie in Lantman's seemed to want to skip ahead in the screenplay, too.

The trees turn into lumps around her as full dark pools in every hollow place. A dark like syrup the moon has drowned in. A deeper kind of cold comes with it. She shouldn't even be out here, where the Rickies might see her and wonder why she's not hiding in her nest. *Go inside and call Oli,* she tells herself.

Gravel crunches somewhere up the driveway. A fan of light thickens around the side of the house. *It's only the police, Jorie.* She goes to the corner and peers around a downspout until a black SUV appears along the curve. She has to squint to see the light bar on the roof.

Jorie walks up and says hello. It's Officer Willard again. "They let me take the big car," he says. The corduroy collar of his jacket is turned up. "It's real easy to nap in here, but I've been sleeping since this afternoon, so I'm on the ball tonight. Seen anything since you got home that I should know about?"

*Like walking away from my son when he could be in danger?* But she only says, "Just two of them showing up at Lantman's. Maybe more than two. I told your dispatch about it."

"I heard on the radio, and they called me. I don't have any information for you, either. Nothing from the feds. I'm sorry." Willard props his forearm on the doorframe. "Not like they'd tell us anything. You know how it is with federal agents and country cops, right?"

"Sure. They throw elbows and treat you like kids. In the movies, anyway."

"State troopers don't really tell us anything, either. It's their investigation. We just get the DUIs and domestic stuff. Nothing like this ever happens here, thank goodness."

She manages a sad, crooked smile. "Let me know if you want coffee or anything to eat in the next couple of hours."

"Stay safe, Ms. Stroud," he says. "We'll catch these guys. And I'm sorry about last night. It won't happen again."

In the kitchen she calls Mrs. Compton, who says Oli is getting ready for bed. "He told me he gets half an hour for his books. He's been a veritable angel all evening. My grandsons will be so happy." That *veritable* feels like the first normal, good thing in Jorie's day. A pound of anxiety exhales and unwinds itself from her chest.

"Reading time is good," Jorie says into the phone, moving into the dining area and checking the window. She's glad Willard has parked closer tonight. She can see the entire length of the SUV, the dull metal of the wheels and the windshield catching gleams of light from the house.

The motion sensor times out as she watches, draping the car with shadow. She's not sure if it should have already clicked off.

"Can I talk to him for a minute?" Jorie says. Only that bright voice, still years from breaking and sounding too grown up, can settle her heart tonight.

There's no response. Jorie pulls the phone away and sees that the call was dropped. Just like yesterday. She calls back and gets Mrs. Compton's voicemail. "I know service can get spotty out here," Jorie says after the recording starts, "but if you could call me back. I'd love to talk to my little guy before he falls asleep. Thanks again."

An itch, all over her, the sense that everything is wrong.

She decides to brew some coffee for her and Officer Willard. Then she spends the next hour looking for Agatha, checking the same rooms, the same corners and shadows under furniture, even the attic in case the doll came to life—it might not be the strangest thing to happen this month—and crawled back up to her old cardboard box.

At the edge of her mind is the idea that one of Enriquez's awful acolytes broke in and stole Agatha. There was the open window in Oli's room. She won't let the thought all the way in, though, because who would do that? What would it mean? The thought of one of them *inside the house*, breaching their sanctuary, taking a boy's comfort away from him, is too much.

The thought of them intending it as a warning.

"Thank you, Mrs. Compton," she says to no one, to the universe. Her heart is worn raw. Something is chewing at the edges of her thoughts, some kind of memory that might slot into this blurry puzzle.

She walks through the house again. "Agatha!" she calls out, and the desperate, liquid waver in her voice scares her.

Out of all her finished and mid-draft screenplays, even the two she was writing when Hannah died, only a single scene has had the strength to draw her back during this silent decade. It was from something she was planning to call *Walpurgis, West Virginia*, something old, when there was no such thing as *Proof of Demons*, not even an *Under the House* yet, she's pretty sure. When she couldn't hurt anyone with horror stories.

She stops pacing and sits down in the dining nook. Long, slow breaths with her eyes closed before she lets herself pull the scratched laptop toward her. She pushes at the lid but doesn't use enough force to lift it, because it's unclear what it would mean if she opens a Word doc and starts typing out that scene. Not from memory, exactly, but from something like retrospect.

She wonders how this Jorie, the one with the cut-out tongue, would write it.

The urge is so strong it makes her want a cigarette, it makes her twenty-three again with the sun full on her face. The sun sinking and a swollen moon coming up to push her to fill pages. Chain-smoking long enough to make her cough the next morning. Beth would call or come over and compare notes and make plans. Their easy laughter. Another weird rabbit hole Colin found online, his defense that the internet needed more weird rabbit holes.

Not long after, the first film haunt, then the next film haunt, rising over them like all those moons.

An inevitable feeling came to her then, fame and film slates and lights. Her name on people's lips. By the time she was ten, she realized she already had a horror pedigree: her parents had accidentally named her after Laurie Strode from *Halloween*. She adored that echo. She adored these pure things, before her greed took them away.

She remembers that one scene from *Walpurgis*. She wrote skeins of dust inside an abandoned house, rotting sheets over furniture. The dead eyes of its windows.

She made up a circle of friends to join hands in a circle of tall candles. The pages were filled with circles. There was a game where everyone invents something about an evil spirit, taking turns until there were eleven "known attributes," then a ritual involving their blood and hair and saliva in a stone bowl. Her characters would build and knit the spirit into a sort of physical form. It was called a tulpa, and they would all be bound by oath to spread stories about it.

A camera filming the ritual. Candles blowing out in a rush. Blurs of voices and thumps, the staccato rhythm of stomping, running feet through the house. Night vision lighting up green and white like a sulfur flare just as a scream swelled and elongated in another room. Faces smeared by camera movement.

Jorie remembers writing a strange, uneven black shape. She textured the air around it with a clicking noise. She knew it couldn't have influenced the Pine Arch Creature, only Beth and Colin ever read any of the pages. But she would revel, later, in an imagined kinship with Enriquez. They sought out similar aesthetics beyond the male gaze.

The memory of that kinship, the warmth it once held for her, shouldn't hurt after all the huge things in this endless week. Her son is in hiding, her friend is dead after just two breakfasts at this table. But the memory is still here in the fabric of Jorie. It still hurts.

She wonders—for the first time—if the *Walpurgis* scene led her to make the blog post what it ended up being, if some desire to spread her lore got blended into the love of *Proof of Demons* that followed it.

Eventually, she lost the screenplay draft when her computer was stolen, when she was on her way toward rock bottom and then Oli. But now the laptop is open. Her finger is near the power button. What is she doing?

"Everything I can to not think about how scared my son is right now," she answers the empty house. "Or all those trees between us."

But there's something she's not remembering here, inside the scene. She thinks what she's really doing is trying to retrieve a detail. Something that might lead her a step closer to Enriquez. She had it in 2007, when she was writing, and she thought of it when she saw *Proof of Demons* for the first time. It might have been something she mentioned in her blog post, but she's not ready to find it online and read it.

She's waiting for it to crawl to the tip of her tongue when she hears a thump down the hall, the sound of something falling over. Oli's room. *Of course it's Oli's room*, she thinks. The police SUV is still exactly where it was, Jorie can see a hint of the dashboard lights suspended in the distance. Willard could be listening to the radio. Maybe a podcast, but in a movie it would be rock music loud enough to drown out her screams from inside the house.

She gets up and goes down the hallway, reaches blindly into Oli's room to flip the light switch on the wall.

His closet door is almost all the way open, the mirror hanging there with an angle of Jorie wedged inside the glass. She can't swear the door was closed earlier, but she thinks she remembers pushing it shut until she heard the click of the knob after she packed his bag.

Even standing in the wake of an unwelcome sound—the possibility of an intruder in her home, with Willard parked outside nodding his head to heavy metal that's turned up louder than it should be—she's more troubled by the urge to write that came over her at the table and the laptop.

She's given over the responsibility of her son to another person, however temporary. Is this supposed to be symbolic? Has a door opened fully onto her past? There's even a mirror for her to see that self, small and small-boned, a face that looks too drawn. Her nine gray hairs have probably been breeding lately. Could she step over Hannah's grave and finally come find herself?

She wants to. She wants to be the quiet new Jorie she's still figuring out how to put together. 2007, 2012, that was a happier Jorie, but a weaker one under all the bravado.

Her face changes in the mirror, only for a second. It grows fuller like the moon she was thinking of before, her mouth forming words, the flesh of her cheeks sagging. Almost someone else's face. Someone else's arms are about to reach out of the dark.

She steps into the room and it's gone, it's her face and her wide eyes. Checking the inside of the closet, there's nothing behind the clothes or crouched at either side. She lifts the mirror off the door and slides it under Oli's bed, then closes the door again. She makes sure it clicks.

When she turns back, she notices that three books have fallen off the bookcase near the door. Those could have made the thump she heard, especially the hardcover one about dinosaurs. "Encyclopediasaurus," Oli calls it—or used to, he cycles through interests so fast these days. But he's like her, they both have more books than space, and there are always a few stacked on the edges of shelves.

She goes into her bedroom and the door to her own closet is shut tight. She thinks it's supposed to be. The laptop and the circle of candles call to her from down the hall. She can almost see the movement of the inconstant light and the puddles of wax spilling over the bowls of the candles.

Jorie's not a writer anymore. She's not even a fan. I'm turning in early, she texts Willard. Look alive out there. That's probably much too familiar a tone to take with him, but she's past caring.

She wakes in a profound velvet dark. The small sound of hinges creaking. Someone is opening her closet door, an inch at a time, with a slowness as awful as the people turning their heads toward her in Lantman's last night.

There is no light, even the blurry red of the alarm clock is gone. She can't see the window or the hands she lifts up from under the covers. The creaking stops and all the noises of her home drop away like the light. She hears the insides of her body, the quick pulls of her breath, the covered drum of her heart, and nothing else.

The closet door has a tendency to swing back a few inches after opening with a last mutter of hinges, so a hand must be holding it in place while the silence thickens around Jorie. She lies there, her mind gaping, a thought looping, that she brought a carving knife to bed with her.

Finally, there is one sound that isn't made by her body: the soft whir of a machine. It could be anything, but she knows it's a lens adjusting, finding her with its eye. She imagines herself glowing black-eyed in the camera's night vision.

Then the quiet seeps back around her, until she hears a different creak. She tries to make the sound come from the person standing in the closet, but it doesn't fit.

It's the wooden floor, and when one of the old boards sighs again, she realizes it's coming from under the bed. A man is lying on his back, shrouded in green and grinning up at her. Imagining the shape of her up here, and what he will do to it.

She feels the blanket slide down her body toward the closet, and footsteps move toward the bed. Jorie rolls over to the nightstand, her fingers spidering across it for the knife, but it's not there. Her phone is gone, too. She reaches up into the shade of her grandfather's old lamp, but a gloved hand seizes her leg and yanks her down the mattress. The footboard scrapes her back and then she's crumpled on the floor, screaming.

Someone steps around her, clumps that sound like heavy boots now.

She slides herself backward and feels the mouth of the closet doorway around her. One hand touches the old millwork of the frame, the comfort of hundred-year-old wood, and she remembers the baseball bat leaning in a corner of the closet. She lunges back, feels around until the bat falls over, then it's in her hand and she's pushing herself up, moving forward into the room and swinging it at nothing and everything in the dark.

The bat connects with an arm or hip, a dull and glancing blow. Some part of her notices she's still screaming, but she hears more heavy steps. The bedroom door opens, and the small red glare of the alarm clock is back on the shelf across the room. 2:08, October is here, it couldn't have been scripted any better.

A pounding starts somewhere at the front of the house. Her name is shouted, Officer Willard trying to get in and save the day. She thanks everything in heaven that Oli's not here. She cocks the bat and stumbles her way around the bed to the lamp Granddad made.

Just before she twists the light on, someone laughs under the bed. It's just a low chuckle, a small private amusement, and then cold fingers slide around her ankle.

Jorie screams again and pulls her leg away as the person slithers out from under the bed frame, their bulk pushing against her. She falls back to the floor and scrambles away, swinging the bat at the rising figure limned in red by the clock's light.

The head, misshapen by the covered crown, turns to her. She sees a red gleam on metal, but the Rickie pauses when the pounding at the front door comes again. An arm lowers, the silhouette becomes a ghost again, and the shape follows the first Rickie out of the room.

She gets to her feet and switches the lamp on. The room is empty and defiled. The smell of unwashed male bodies hangs in the air. She's gasping, her body is shaking, she doesn't know if she can go out into the hall to let Willard in.

*They're already gone*, she tells herself. Out through the kitchen. Into the trees, halfway to wherever their twisted little horror camp is, to laugh about crossing *in the closet* and *under the bed* off their creepy scene list in a single home invasion.

The corner of something black is sticking out from under her pillow in the yellow spill of lamplight. She slides a VHS tape out. PROOF OF DEMONS: OCTOBER FILM HAUNT is printed on the white sticker along its spine, the UNT lightly smudged as though the ink isn't quite dry.

# INTERLUDE

[Excerpt from "Hell Is Just a Word: Secularism and Belief in Hélène Enriquez's *Proof of Demons*," by Colin Davies, *The Witch Tapes* #6, Fall 2011]

**Looking at faith from an angle** not burdened by the religiosity of the demon, there is the *tulpa*, an entity given life by intense mental concentration. It's an unwieldy theosophic concept typically relating to powerful minds in deep states of thought. In a demonic context, one can't help but think of black magic and new age occultists. Or something more clinical, such as the Philip experiment in early 1970s Toronto.

But strip away the wind chimes and candles and synthesizer chords, the lab coats and clipboards, and you're left with simple *belief*—belief as creator.

There's some compelling food for thought here for sociologists and folklorists, the potential for a profound comment on mass hysteria. After all, part of the thrill of Slender Man, an urban legend born shortly before the Pine Arch Creature, is that some claim he is a tulpa that exists tangibly through the collective fear of those who wish to believe in him. These entities are birthed through the modern campfire stories of pop culture.

Even if *Proof of Tulpas* doesn't exactly roll off the tongue.

Here is our opportunity to separate faith from religion. To have the former under supernatural circumstances without needing to adhere to the latter. I will argue that modern horror fans and movie audiences are beginning to look for stories that aren't so concerned with propping up the Good vs. Evil paradigm that has long pumped blood through Hollywood's dollar-sign heart.

Beyond this simple point, the idea of the occult as a personal construct is thrilling for the horror genre. Call it *Demonology for Dummies* if you must, but there is a fascination in detaching the devil from heaven and hell and giving him to us, to do what we will. Dissolving the pagan, Abrahamic, and whitewashed Jesus lines until it's one deeply creepy horror melting pot.

Earlier, I mentioned being our own gods, at least in the context of fiction. In a world without much to believe in, the tulpa holds great allure. This could be the idea of the Transfiguration. The *I belong* and the answering *you belong*.

*Proof of Demons* is a way in, perhaps. It's why so many are drawn to it. If Enriquez intended her audience to take the film's simple title at face value, it's only one step further to argue that *belief*—and its attendant *fear*—could weave the Pine Arch Creature and the eye and the portal into things that could be seen and touched.

But my mind comes back to the word *proof* again and again, contrasting the concept of the tulpa like a preacher climbing into the vampire's den. Even if belief could hold such power, it must still be earned, and the film is so sincerely secular, so content without an *-ism* or *-ology*, that it infuses conjecture with uncertainty, even abstraction.

So what *is* a demon in the world of Hélène Enriquez? What does her *proof* point to? Why did she push away the literature and its precedents? What does her film want?

Perhaps she is hiding behind a clear love of ambiguity and oblique puzzle-making, something to do with erasing those lines, returning demons to the wild of their pagan days, before Christianity rewrote their natures across the globe and made them gaudy soul collectors. Once freed, they can now wear us for skin, drive us mad, or crouch just ahead in the dark, dragging their fingers across our nightmares.

However the director would answer these questions, I would be first in line if she ever decides to make a sequel.

My conclusion, shaky and hardly helpful, is that Enriquez simply uses the word *demon* in a broader sense here: an inhuman, nonhuman, never-been-human entity. Almost certainly not a fallen angel, and something that has never met the devil.

I believe it's something—lowercase *s*—that lives in the fissure between one belief and another, or between the earth and the air. In whatever strange hole we tell ourselves not to get too close to. In the puncture of the proboscis before the mosquito drinks our blood. Whether her demons or our own, they are unknowable, and anything beyond this is just calling out into the dark without a candle,

"I belong with you."

# CHAPTER TWENTY-SEVEN

## Coleman

▶▶ He buys gas for the car. A woman at the next pump opens a pack of cigarettes, a breeze touches his face, and it all feels so strongly of another life that for a moment he thinks he will sink to his knees. He takes a staggering deep breath but can't make himself cough.

Last night is a stain on his memory. Coleman remembers the demon pretending to be his brother—but that's not quite right. It somehow had his brother inside of it, or it was the other way around. Jackson has spent these decades communing with the demon. Or else the movie has pulled the idea of Jackson into it.

A long sleep. Normal green eyes when he woke. An overcast sky low over the bed-and-breakfast. The pillow speckled with black mucus. The lake blue and gray out to the horizon. His heart on the verge of reunion.

And Gloria and Evie a thousand miles away.

He finds Maple Walk Cemetery on a dense forested road. The wrought iron gates look like a movie set, and two hundred yards past them, the acreage opening up on a vista of tombstones and flat lawn, he sees a camera crew and actors. The actors are lying face down around a redwood casket that sits directly on the grass. Strands of sunlight begin to pry the clouds apart.

Coleman passes through the gates and sees four people with cameras, two of them on complicated tripods, the other two on shoulders, spread out at corners around the actors playing dead. None of them are wearing sheets, and he's not sure why this surprises him.

He's too far away to be sure, but one of the people holding a camera looks like the man who stabbed him in the video store. The same wisps of blond hair lift in the faint chilled wind.

The demon is gesturing from the trees across the grass. It wears Jackson's face between two bright white trunks, one of its long disturbing arms bending upward and pulling back. Coleman walks across the gentle rolling lawn, feeling two dozen eyes pretending he's not here, and reaches the sun-dappled alcove among the birches. It is empty.

Then a swelling sensation in his mouth. Something slides past his tongue and into his throat. Coleman chokes for a few seconds, his eyes go blurry, but each time it enters him is less painful.

"Look at them," a voice says from Coleman's mouth.

He does as he is told and watches the people lying on the ground around the casket. "Who is Jorie?" he asks, and inside of these words he says, "Jorie is not here."

The demon says nothing else, so he stares across the lawn until someone walks into his field of vision, stops thirty feet or so from the casket, and sits in a small chair facing the trees.

"The director," the voice says, and now he can feel the coldness of Jackson in his mouth. The person is genderless from this distance, on the tall side and wearing a baseball cap, but it must be Hélène Enriquez, it's the type of chair he's seen on film sets on TV. The person begins to speak. He can see the mouth move, the arms lift and punctuate, but the words come from Jackson.

"It is an honor to meet you, Mr. Smith. Your life is a benediction." The cadence is clearer. It is almost the voice he heard through the phone. "I struggled in my film career for some time. I struggled in my personal pursuits. One night I was looking for the kinds of things I tend to look for, and I happened upon the website you created for your lost brother. I was inexplicably moved. I was transfixed. There was—something there, touching me. It resonated and rang out, like a finger on the wet rim of a wineglass."

A hole opens, ragged, in the clouds. The sun leaks through onto the cemetery.

"It reminded me of a summoning I had read and then forgotten in an old book," the director goes on. "A simple thing, an incantation opening a door, an emergence of an idea, a response granting the summoner ideation. Blood left as a token offering. The ritual, for lack of a better word, had not stuck with me, all the years until I found you. Then the shock of you and your brother, children coming to it organically, with authenticity. Jackson could not have known to smear his blood on that bedroom wall. But there he was, inventing an incantation. 'I belong with you.' He created the words. His door was the first of my doors."

The actors lie waiting with their faces pressed into the grass. Blackbirds rise up like confetti over the trees beyond the graves and across the road. The ceiling of clouds knits itself shut again, turning the sun to a white smudge.

The director shifts in the chair. "When I was younger, I wondered if demons and hell were perhaps not mutually exclusive after all. It was a passion, that an entity could exist in and of itself. I had the training, so to speak, to see what you two boys had done. Something more elemental than religious rite, like an accidental seam in the world. I felt you were right that Jackson went somewhere. I had to write my way toward that place."

A truck grinds between gears on a nearby hill. Its air brakes sigh.

"*Proof of Demons* was only ever a film, no matter what my little detectives wanted to think. My creature was effects, I paid someone to dream it up, my eye from another green world was more smoke and mirrors. I was curious, but I never presumed otherwise on location or in editing. I wanted it to have the attributes of a ritual, so I arranged the scenes into an equation. But it was only ever a film.

"After . . ." The voice pauses for several seconds before going on, as the actors continue to lie motionless in the grass and the cameras film them. "My little detectives had been cogent. The film began to tell me they were right, it was as much exploration as narrative. Somehow, Mr. Smith, you had put something in my film. You and Jorie Stroud and the viewers. An entity. Well, the *idea* of an entity. I was not sure then. But what I perceived, and more crucially, what my *fans* perceived, had to be taken deeper. There was unexpected belief, but not yet proof."

The arms lift and stretch out to indicate the scene around the casket, the graves everywhere else.

"Social media exponentializes belief. It is a new alchemy of fact. I am almost certain that until now, our entity has only been a concept, a *potential*, drifting from ideator to ideator. Waiting to become fact. It seems to have tried with your brother, it's why I used his name in my film, but I'm afraid he was never the suitable vessel. It was you. You were the one who saw its great eye. You saw the idea, you knew it as truth. And now your sickness has cleaned you out. Our entity has eaten it. Used it, subsisted on it. Your vessel is at the fulcrum of life and death, like a door starting to open to what comes after. Imagine what existence could be like between the two. It will be different this time."

Coleman realizes the demon is no longer inside his throat. He turns to look behind him, but something that is not quite a hand grips the back of his head and holds it in place. The actors rise from their feigned sleep or death and kneel on the lawn, turning their heads toward where he stands in the trees.

The voice continues, cupped in his ear now.

"You feel your sickness leaving you. You don't have to die. This entity has peeked through a keyhole at you, it comes into our noisy world from—somewhere. It wants to make more of itself. It needs a vessel to spread, that much the folklore gets right. In a manner of speaking, it wrote the folklore. It wrote the belief."

The voice stops again, but Coleman can hear it humming, softly, a melody he doesn't know. "And with belief can come proof," it goes on, almost in that same tune. "And with proof, there is faith. Soon you can live forever, on the internet, inside of media, in the trees, in the air seeping through closed windows. You will appear in corners and in mouths because you have always belonged here, and those voices are calling out to belong. They long for a peace the world won't give them. Jackson saw the picture of a vampire in your mind. It is not so different, it is a form of eating and continuing and living in consciousness."

He tries to turn again but isn't allowed. "Maybe I didn't see anything that day," he says, suddenly close to panic. "I was a kid. I was coping with trauma. I had a concussion."

He doesn't know if the person hears him across the hundred feet of lawn, if Jackson is a transmitter in each direction. "We have come too far and proved too much," the voice says, an edge in it now. "The means of calling the entity are spreading through the veins of the internet as we speak. You know where to go. To complete your, to borrow a word, transfiguration. We love you, Coleman. You belong."

The director stands and walks away from the chair, leaving an open and incomplete space behind. He realizes the director was a counterpoint in the scene, anchoring the actors playing dead off to the right. The cameras were framing the entire vista as they spoke.

The departure unlocks the actors. They fall onto their hands and feet and scuttle across the grass like spiders. Their elbows and knees make bent angles as they approach Coleman and his knot of trees, and he turns and runs, his lungs filling and wheezing themselves empty like a younger man's.

The demon nestles in Coleman's swollen throat, roots seeking through his lungs. It guides him inland along gentle wooded curves, past a mossy barn and a rust-stained silo, until his foot slips from the gas pedal and the car coasts to a stop before a gravel road. Coleman opens the door with a trembling arm and climbs out between two crowded walls of trees. The demon slips out of his mouth. Wet clouds pack the sky like attic insulation.

Jackson is there in front of him, the dark smudge trying to look like a man. It fumbles at Coleman's mouth. The world loses its definition. Muddled sounds. The younger brother opens his mouth in an awful yawn and breathes the demon back in, and the sensation is more forceful than it was before. He gags. He retches, folding over and squeezing his kneecaps with his hands.

But then he and his brother are boys lying on their backs in milky light, an eye opening above to watch them, and Coleman reaches out and takes Jackson's warm, whole fingers. They begin to laugh. The future unravels ahead of them. Lost years rewrite themselves, and he finally begins to understand where his brother went that morning.

Standing on the rim of the forest, he feels his body reach up, stretching tendons and knitting bone. His sinuses swell with pressure. His eyes gloss over with bright shadow. The pain is immense and distant.

"I'm so glad you're not gone," he tells Jackson, but stops speaking when he understands that the looping clicks scraping the air are his voice.

He drives for miles through the soft woods, Jackson twitching inside him, or as him. He is no longer sure where he ends and it begins. *Possessed,* he thinks, *possessed by a demon. Possessed by the angel who stole my brother.*

Coleman still has some of his thoughts, but they waver, spliced with images of their childhood in Greensboro, the sun setting over the house, their mother hanging laundry on a line. A decade of their life shutters through his mind. These, too, warp as other things are shuffled in like a strange deck of cards. An old man hunched and pulling something across a dark room, a young woman holding a cell phone toward him—toward it—like a weapon, fog and trees and streaks of clouds, a small boy sleeping with an antique doll curled in the crook of an arm.

A shadow stretches up a wall and bends at a right angle.

A shadow stretches up another wall, this one powder blue, and folds over on itself, blending with the silhouette of a ceiling fan.

Threads of screams and laughter and grunting moans sewn into the images.

The car drifts. At some point, by accident, Coleman comes out on a main road. He stops and inhales as deeply as he can, trying to make himself cough. He feels his lungs inflate and clench like powerful fists. The cancer might be nearly gone.

The director, Hélène Enriquez, whoever it was, said he knows where to go. "One fourteen," he says in clicks and dry pops. He pauses, concentrates before speaking in something like a normal voice. "High Rock Road." The address on the final envelope he received in Arden.

Five minutes later he's parked at a gas pump, standing with a breeze in his face. He can't feel his hair moving in the wind, which is strange because it's gotten so wispy the last few years. But he keeps remembering, he is different now. He is being remade. The beautiful cure in the paper birches of Vermont.

He pulls the nozzle away from the pump and looks down at it. His hands are still his hands, but they're swollen, glossy things, stuffed too full. The skin looks diseased. "They're wrapped in my lung tissue," he says, and is glad to hear only faint crackles in his voice, like a needle building up dust on a record player.

Then it comes to him that he already bought gas today, before he went to the cemetery. Why did he come here?

"Is something wrong, sir?" a voice says, and Coleman looks up. "Do you need—" The man at the neighboring pump stops speaking and staggers back against his old Volvo, his face twisting into a grimace when Coleman's eyes find him.

The man's shirt is black, long-sleeved, with a stark white clerical collar at the throat. He is short and thin, and his hair is graying.

*Possessed*, Coleman thinks again, *possessed by a demon. And here is a priest.*

"Will you help me?" Coleman says to the man. He tries to think of Gloria and Evie when he asks. Gloria tugging on his arm as he left the house with his suitcase and his promise of being cured. What was she wearing? Did she have her glasses on?

The man raises the gas nozzle like a gun, then seems to realize what he's doing and lowers it. "What happened to you? Do you need a hospital?"

"I've been to one of those." He fills his lungs with breath, and it seems he could go on filling them for minutes, without a single cough. With his head tipped back, sucking the wind into his throat, he sees someone by the gas station wall, filming him with a boxy camera on their shoulder. "The demon found me there, too. Where is your church?"

"It's just down the road. Saint Jude the Apostle. Do you need God? Your face is—" He can hardly bring himself to look at Coleman. "It's not right. What is this about a demon?"

Coleman goes quiet so that Jackson can speak. But Jackson has crawled into one of the holes inside him. "I'm possessed. Don't you see it? I could tell when I looked at you."

And before the man can respond, Coleman opens his mouth and feels tendons crack. His chin presses hard against his sternum. His tongue twitches out of its new cave. His eyes burn. He thinks he feels blood running from them down his cheeks, hot but cooling in the breeze.

The priest moans and makes a choking sound, but Coleman can't see him for a moment. The demon has swarmed into his head, a sensation like moth wings, and liquid is splashing onto him. He smells the ripe tang of gasoline. The priest is spraying him with the nozzle.

Coleman moves toward him.

Someone, maybe a woman, screams, high and ringing and somehow angelic. The splatter of gasoline ceases, the stink of it thick, and Coleman sees the priest fumbling in a pocket of his black pants. A trembling hand pulls a small brass box out and flips part of it open with a neat snick and a small clean note of struck metal.

A lighter. The man's thumb strikes it, hurls it at Coleman with an ugly shout. For an instant the air is an iridescent swirl of fumes, and Coleman watches the flame open up like a bedsheet around him, soft and slow.

Then there is heat, a pressing anger of heat, and the world is heat, and Jackson is there, breathing the heat into their lungs. An endless inhale.

Somehow the fire retreats, he sees it pull away from the pump and away from his own gas nozzle, which he dropped to the concrete at some point. The fire sinks into his hands. When it's gone, he only feels a terrible cold.

"Our Father, who art in heaven," the priest shouts somewhere close, "hallowed be thy name." He's tugging his small crucifix out of his shirt, between two buttons. Its chain breaks as he lifts it and presses it against Coleman's face.

"I guess you can't help me, Father," Coleman says, and nudges the priest away, almost gentle. But the man won't give up, he's blubbering something from the Bible at Coleman. They're just half-enunciated words. They're the barest edge of the lifting wind.

The air is still crackling and muffled. The man is still filming them. The woman is still screaming like an angel.

Coleman gets back into his car. A lumpy creature, a clouded shadow of skin and clay, meets his black eyes in the rearview mirror.

His body elongates inside the moving Accord. Bones stretching, segmenting, softening to mush. He reclines the driver seat and folds himself in half behind the wheel.

High Rock Road is close, laid on a curve between tree-bunched rural pockets. White streaks of paper birches skimming by. He looks for 114, Jorie

Stroud's address, but Jackson slows the car and turns into a gravel driveway with a numberless mailbox. If Gloria were here, she would say she's never seen so many gravel driveways, it must be to help with the snow and ice.

Coleman tries again to hold on to her.

The Cape Cod at the end is small and faded yellow with a green roof. He parks next to a dirty Subaru. The gravel crunches under his feet as he approaches the house. At the window he has to duck down to see, which makes him realize again that he is growing so tall. There is a kitchen, a wash of light.

The blond man who stabbed him is standing at the counter.

Coleman feels a terror clutch him, watching the man pick up a knife. He steps back and shambles around the house, not knowing where he is going, carried by the demon. A small wooden door reveals a crawl space, and he urges the long weight of his body into its restful grave.

Later, in the dark beneath the blond man's house, he fumbles at his phone until it turns on and trembles with dozens of notifications that try to bury the image of Gloria's face. He waits for them to clear and stares at the photo until he remembers who she is. The phone's light glistens on damp spiderwebs.

I hope to be home soon, he texts her with the new stumps of fingers he is learning to use. The cancer is leaving and I love the life we had. He can't be Coleman anymore. Why is he lying to Coleman's wife? He turns the phone off.

The demon thickens in him. It coagulates and ripens. It must sleep and dream and drift and emerge in rooms at the ends of tunnels of voices. It is summoned. Coleman is summoned. People—young, fresh and vital as herbs broken from their stems—are terrified and elated to see him, they don't know which emotion to put on top. They hold their phones up and he tells them they belong. He believes he eats them, or something like eating.

"You're the fucking Pine Arch Creature," one of them says, gazing up at him. His drooping mouth takes her into the space that once held his lungs. He doesn't know what has replaced his organs, or where his heart might be.

Room to room to room, time passing. Screams and wet noises. He is in the trees and a vast lake stretches out to the right. A young man with a beard comes around the path and he eats him, or something like eating.

Then he is in a large house with a ceiling higher than even his looming head, and an old man is tucked into a hallway. He goes to him and eats him, or something like eating.

Something like creation.

These moments are voices like leaves calling to him from trees etched along mountains. A chorus of voices trembling on boughs. The voices want to belong. He finds the right curve of the right peak. He finds the right tree and he finds the leaf.

He brings the peace they ask of him.

Through it all, he can't find his old body, even on the way back from the voices, when Jackson tells him Jorie is coming to visit them under the house. He no longer feels his brother near because he is his brother. Or neither of them is here. They are the great mass of the demon. They are the vessel.

"You belong," Coleman says, his voice a syrup of clicks and gasps, and pushes out of the crawl space into tepid daylight. A tall green sheet stands at the tree line, long tines of a wooden crown reaching up with the pine trunks. The camera on its shoulder watches.

# CHAPTER TWENTY-EIGHT

## Jorie

▶▶ "It's a lot of your house on the tape," Willard says when he finally calls, not long after dawn. He sounds as exhausted as Jorie feels. "But not you. Then, uh, there's also some footage with your friend. Before she—before the end. And during. I'm sorry."

She looks up at the ceiling of the little gray Hinesburg Police house. Her eyes are wet, but she doesn't have the time or the headspace to cry. "Is that it?" she says.

"And there's this other part," he tells her, with his own pause. "At the end. There's someone sitting on the couch in your living room. Not wearing a sheet. Could be a woman. She's looking at the camera for several minutes, that's it. Holding some kind of doll, looks like, but it's washed out with static."

"Is Oli on the tape?"

"No, he's not."

"Say it again—he's not on the tape. Mrs. Compton's house isn't on the tape." Her phone is pressed hard against her ear, the cartilage sharp and painful against the plastic case.

"Oli isn't anywhere on the tape, Ms. Stroud. Not that house, either."

She feels relief, a cresting wave of warm calm, just for a moment.

Jorie spent the rest of the night in the station because her house was full of officers. Forensics from the state trooper barracks. The FBI was called back. Willard—Ryan, she'd finally asked him his first name—offered to take her to the station, and she said no, not even looking at him.

She called and woke Mrs. Compton before they brought her here and almost asked her to wake Oli up, too. Instead, she settled for bringing his favorite old blanket with her, cotton wolves howling at cotton moons, and clenched it in both hands as she lay awake, half-feverish, on a cot someone dragged into the interview room.

"The cops are gone, but you shouldn't get your hopes up," Willard says. "Those guys were wearing gloves. The tape they left under your pillow is evidence, you can watch it later."

"Someone else is going to die," she tells him. "Someone in these funeral videos online probably already has. There's a guy named Avery, last name starts with an *E*, who might have been involved in this stuff a few years ago. I already told the FBI about him, too. You have to find this guy. I don't have many feelers to put out there, but I'm trying to get his last name, at least."

"That shadow thing you saw, whatever it is, it's not real, Ms. Stroud. It's special effects. Your friend Ms. Kowalczyk, these were hopped-up kids wearing sheets, maybe, getting caught up and elevating a situation."

*Elevating a situation.* She wants to tell him he's not the authority on what's real or not, but she can't find the energy.

"I have to get my son somewhere far away," she says instead. "I'm picking him up and leaving, like I should have done in the first place. I wish I could lure these assholes out, let them finish the movie, whatever. But you guys are the final girls now."

"We can protect—" he says, but she disconnects and doesn't hear the rest. She grabs Oli's blanket and holds it close to her face all the way home.

A trailer shows up online.

The laptop is open on the table in her dining nook. It's after nine already. She wakes it up and cycles through social media platforms while packing the one good suitcase she owns. There are more videos filmed at funerals and of the supposed Pine Arch Creature appearing in people's homes.

She finds major news reports about disappearances, tech companies trying to ban all related content. Hashtags like #funeralplanning and #doyoubelong circumvent algorithms and make it impossible to know how fast it's spreading. But it's spreading, not with the staggering rush of the airborne pandemic but more like something that has to be touched or fondled.

She calls Mrs. Compton again but there's no answer. The phone rings the second she hangs up, but it's Willard. She lets it go to voicemail. She wants to start thinking of him as Ryan, in someone else's plot there might even be something there between them, never mind that she's at least five years older.

This isn't that movie, and when she sees the trailer for the one she's trapped in, the thought is wiped from her mind by bright red terror for her son.

\* \* \*

It starts with a fade-in of Beth, filmed from inside the attic loft of the cabin. She's on the deck with a cup of coffee and a laptop, and the camera catches her pausing to look up and out toward the trees.

Fade out, then Jorie pulling a curtain aside to look into her yard.

"It happens at funerals," someone, probably a young woman, says in voice-over as Jorie is filmed from somewhere in the paper birches.

"Wasn't there a movie that killed somebody in real life?" another young voice asks.

A second exterior shot of Jorie at the same window, the curtains raked apart, this time she's sitting at the laptop that's in an FBI field office by now. "It only started in the movie," the first voice answers. "She died because no one understood. It will be different this time. This time there will be belief."

A cemetery now. The camera creeps toward a dark wood casket poised above a hole in the earth, its lid open, the trees out of focus behind it.

Then it's moving toward Jorie's house again, accompanied by a rising distorted cello.

The trailer jumps to a Rickie standing in the middle ground of a wide shot, in long grass before a wall of reddening trees. Wind tears at the green bedsheet, ripples the fabric like breath on tea that's too hot. The blank face stares across the swaying grass at the camera. The crown is held in white hands, near the waist. Without it, the head is such a mundane shape, a draped bulge waiting for a child to cut the eyeholes.

Jorie feels the dread of something terrible approaching. It's cold on her skin. She wants to stop the video, but the chill is all over her, she knows the coming moments are for her to see.

Her dining nook window a third time, but someone in a green sheet is looking out of it now, inside the house. Then Jorie a few hours ago, filmed from her closet doorway in the glaring wash of night vision, her black eyes rising up from the bed.

Beth on the cabin's deck again, shot from the woods below, she's looking down at a Rickie holding a knife in the foreground. The shot is angled up past the Rickie's back, the shape of the hidden crown tearing through the sheet, silhouetted against the leaden sky. Beth shifts from blurred to in-focus over the right shoulder and above the blade.

Cut to an older man with pale red hair approaching pine trees, gravestones to his right. It's Pinewood Cemetery in Arden, not a birch in sight. Cut to a middle-aged woman coming out of a garage with a wide hat and a slender spade, perhaps her voice saying, "You belong. You have always belonged here. It will be different this time." A hand moves a small branch out of the camera frame. The shot zooms in on the woman.

Cut to the three strange watchers from Lantman's in a decrepit house, standing around a small figure under a sheet, but it's filmed through a dirty window that smudges them. The size of the covered figure makes her heart stop.

Cut to the redwood casket again, closer now, a drifting, slow approach. The light brightens, the scene changes to the vantage of the cabin's front door, Beth limping toward the tree line, sobbing.

"Then one of the haunt died," the first voice from the opening says. "Colin. And the other two forgot the rest."

Jorie's breaths are shallow. Her eyes are wide. The cello drone plays continuously, rising and falling in counterpoint to the sparse dialogue and voice-overs, creeping and breathing. It sounds infected.

Cut to an old Colonial house that strikes a frayed, distracted chord of recognition in her.

Then the mirror hanging in Oli's room, a reflection of a pale green shoulder tucked back in the dark of his closet.

A living room on fire, two blazing curtains framing gray and glass buildings. A hallway lined with doors in stuttering light, a figure with a huge white head standing in shadows watching the camera.

Officer Willard getting out of the SUV at dusk and looking around.

A man and woman eating ice cream with a girl around Oli's age. The mother says, "They practiced witchcraft underground, where the colonial cemetery used to be. There was a crypt and they would take children there, to change them." The girl smiles with vanilla smears around her mouth and asks, "What did they change into?"

Jorie from behind at her grandparents' graves, the original film's blue sheets spread out like tired ghosts.

"Will you believe in what you made?" a woman's voice asks, and Jorie remembers the tension that knotted her shoulders as she imagined someone there in the cemetery, watching.

An old man walks down a marble hallway with a cane. He stops as a strange clipped laugh repeats, but he doesn't turn around.

The woods, a palette of fall colors, the glimmer of water, the camera turning onto a trail where a tall corrupted shape stands in the trees.

Cut to the mourners from the first tape in the middle of the slow arcs of their heads, their eyes beginning to reach the camera. Cut to a familiar bearded man turning and running, pursued by the camera down a hallway, past numbered apartment doors. Cut to someone setting a man on fire beside a gas pump.

"What happens when they don't believe?" a deeper voice says. The figure with the oversized head steps into view in the background and reaches for the bearded man. The trailer jumps to the shape in the trees again.

The first voice answers, "The demon has to speak louder."

Cut to a large room of an abandoned house, windows without curtains and bleary light pouring inside. Eight seconds pass, a long moment in the context of all these sliced images, and a human shape that is somehow dark and pale is stretching up to the ceiling, like mold growing on the air.

A rapid series of phone videos that nearly overlap, faces staring down into lenses. "I want to belong." "We're a part of this." "I've never felt like I belonged." "To finally belong to something bigger than me." In some of them, a huge gray smear, similar but more distinct, fills half the background.

A garbled voice answers, "You belong."

The wooden casket, nearly filling the frame now. White satin lining is visible, there is a hint of clothing. There are the top few inches of a cardboard sign propped inside against the lining, what could be the name HANNAH rising into view.

Cut to the exterior of Mrs. Compton's house, a Rickie standing at a front window, the wooden crown torn completely through the sheet, and Jorie's throat closes, her heart begins to seize.

Cut to Oli crawling like a spider across Mrs. Compton's living room. His elbows and knees are bent out at sharp angles. He stares at the floor, silent except for the somehow graceful impacts of his hands and feet, his head swinging from side to side.

A body on the floor at the top of the frame, slippered feet sticking out from the other side of the sofa. The bunched hem of a long blue cardigan. Oli's missing doll is propped against the body, dead porcelain eyes staring at the camera.

"Will you believe in what you made?" someone says, a little louder, closer to the microphone than before.

Cut to the cemetery from the *Funeral Watching* tape, Maple Walk, where her grandparents are buried, several long distorted arms waving out of the paper birches. "Then Beth died. The second of the haunt," the voice from the beginning says. "Will the last one left belong?"

And finally, Oli outside Mrs. Compton's house, holding hands with a Rickie. Oli is wearing one of the crowns. They're walking toward the left foreground, neither looking at the other. Less than two seconds of tender, obscene devastation.

Jorie screams at the laptop.

Cut to the title screen, shifting black with a simple white serif font, *PROOF OF DEMONS: OCTOBER FILM HAUNT*, and a small sea of attributing text nearly illegible below it. But Jorie can see, even as her body pivots out of the chair, her momentum carrying her toward panic and out the front door, the words *AN HÉLÈNE ENRIQUEZ FILM*.

It takes her twenty seconds to reach Mrs. Compton's driveway and wrench the car into its curve, her tires spinning in gravel. The house swings into view, in almost the same light as the video, as though Oli walked through the front door seconds ago.

But it has a dead look. Her heart has been torn out of it.

The door is ajar and she runs inside, scanning every room, empty, empty. She can't stop seeing her son scuttling across the floor and then walking with his docile hand reaching up, held loosely by a killer.

A wooden crown sits upright on the kitchen counter. She shouts Mrs. Compton's name, thinking of those feet in their slippers behind the sofa in the trailer. Oli's not here, no one is here, but she runs through the house a second time.

She passes the crown on the counter again and notices a sheet of paper beneath it. *I'M UNDER THE HOUSE* has been written on it in green crayon. Oli wrote this, she would recognize his careful block printing anywhere.

Jorie grabs a knife from the dish rack beside the sink.

Mrs. Compton doesn't have a basement, though Jorie does another lap to make sure before stumbling back into the narrow yard and circling the house. She finds the crawl space, a small fairy-tale door with peeling yellow paint. It wrenches open and there's enough light to see through to the other side, the rich smell of musty earth, cobwebs glistening in the damp.

She drags her phone from her pocket and sweeps its flashlight into every corner. "Oli! Are you in here?"

"Here," something says, more like a wet gasp full of clicking noises, and part of the crawl space's dark moves into her light. A shifting glare of white teeth, a huge oily shadow sliding on its belly. "Jorie." The last syllable of her name wheezes like dying breaths.

Jorie stumbles back as it gathers against the small doorway. The lump of a head tilts up, eyes like blackened cataracts find her. Its color bleeds from gray to speckled white, and for a moment it's just a man, sixty or so, thin reddish hair full of broken leaves.

This man was in the trailer she watched five minutes ago. She takes another step away, a groan leaking out of her, because it's also the man she saw staring out of Oli's closet. The thing Oli told his cousins about.

"Jorie," he says again, but there are two voices, taped together. "Found you." Something in its hollowed, sick face is begging her. Its eyes are green now, and half-filled with blood.

"Where is he?" she says. "Where is he?" She says it again, she screams it.

"Under the house," he says, and the whites of his eyes are gone again into dark clouds. "Not. Time yet."

"Please." Her voice breaks open into a sob, stretching the words. "Where is he? Please tell me."

"Help me." The voice turns to a mess of cracked looping shards. A swollen hand reaches out and tries to grab her leg, but she falls and pushes herself back. The face changes again as the thing—or man, she doesn't know how to think of it—crawls out into the light and falls, soft-limbed onto Jorie's legs.

She lunges out with the knife from the kitchen. It sinks into the mottled flesh with no resistance, like stabbing an already open wound. "Where is my son?" Shouting the words over and over, swiping at it blindly. "Where is he? Where is he?"

With a rhythmic strand of clicks and moans, the thing staggers up onto the wet shadows of its legs and lopes into the trees toward town.

Jorie loses it quickly in the woods.

She goes back to the crawl space, slips halfway in and fills each corner with her phone's light, dreading a small crumpled shape at every movement of her hand. But it's only sour dirt scattered with leaves.

The drowning silence of the property, adrenaline pushing her around the other side of the house to Mrs. Compton's front yard. She calls the police. It's the first instant they've entered her mind since watching the trailer. She hardly knows what she says, just a rush of tear-choked words, begging, and then waiting for the sirens.

Her phone rings in her hand as she's ending the call. She doesn't recognize the number. "Where is my son?" she says almost before she can answer.

"Is this Jorie Stroud?"

"Who is this?" It's not what she thought a Rickie's voice would sound like. Human and hesitant and wavering with warmth. Please let this just be a ransom, something mundanely awful. Don't let it be what she's thinking.

"It's Trevor Henderson." There's a distant hissing sound over the line, like an old modem breathing. The voice goes on in a rush. "It's been a while. You gave me your number when you emailed, right? I—I think something is happening to me, too. I saw the trailer and you and I are *in* it. What did you say about your son?"

Even though she heard from him just yesterday, it takes a moment to plug the name in. The artist. Her kindred horror obsessive. She only met him in person once, at a convention in Toronto, but he was an unofficial October Film Haunt member toward the end, during those best years of her life.

"Trevor, they took my son." Each word feels swollen and blaring as it comes. The panic rises, the overcast sky is too bright. "Enriquez and her—whatever they are, the Rickies with the bedsheets. They took him. I think they killed my neighbor. I tried to hide him and they took him."

How could she let him out of her sight? The air is unsteady with tension, like strings whining on a soundstage, but the entire world is silent. There are no sirens yet. An echelon of snow geese spell the letter *J* in the sky, black-tipped wings and white bodies, but their calls don't carry in the thin October air. The sun is caught behind a film of plastic clouds.

*It's October*, she thinks. *It's October now.* How could she?

"Jorie?" Trevor says, and static crackles through the phone speaker. "Are you there? Is your son's name Oliver?"

For a long moment, the world still empty, she doesn't think she can answer. There are only the mute receding geese. But she finds herself. "I'm here. How did you know that?"

"I was given a message for you. About Oliver."

# CHAPTER TWENTY-NINE
## Roger

▶▶ Faber's man is late. There is supposed to be a security presence inside the house at all times now, someone experienced with unpleasantness, gun strapped to hip like an extra in a cartel film. Roger is paying dearly for the privilege, but he's been horribly exposed the last fourteen minutes.

He checks the alarm system to make sure it's armed. He stands in the entrance hall, one hand on the walnut railing of the stairs, and wishes he hadn't told the thick slab of a day shift guard that he could do a sweep around the house and sign off for the day.

Roger hasn't heard the taped laugh—"haha ha, haha ha"—in three days, but still he has stopped playing music. No TV, no sounds of any kind in the big house, save for the occasional sleek whoosh of the heat coming on. The tap of his cane on the elegant floor tiles. He wants to hear anything, down to the faintest chime of glass breaking. Not all of the 112 windows have alarms on them.

In the meantime, he has grown increasingly fixated on the pentagram he chalked and greased onto the library floor.

He has taken to standing in the library doorway, staring in, the books shifting in and out of focus around him. "Hélène," he whispers at the pentagram, and sometimes he stands and watches it for six minutes, thinking of her, counting, his internal clock still sharp. Waiting for the thing Hélène will send him.

There is no desire to meet it, whether it is the wet green eye from her film rolling in its huge socket or something from her supposed sequel, the thing the internet is making a fuss about in cheap footage. But he also aches to meet it, like oil and water in his heart, a contradiction he can't put into words.

Maybe he is simply at the age where a man turns around and lets his life catch up to him.

There is no belief in Hélène, not really, or her creatures, either. The last time he was wide open to the faith of drawing symbols on a floor, the agoraphobia only had its long fingernails in him, not its teeth. Why did he draw this one?

Another memory of those old late phone calls with Hélène. Lying back on the sofa like a virile young thing, his heart knocking harder than it had any right to. He remembers she had started mapping out *Proof of Demons* then. Roger had agreed to play a part—he was willing to traverse the gulf between this house and a chartered plane, stuffed with Zoloft to keep the panic at arm's length, just for the chance to meet her. As disappointing as that turned out to be.

"Just imagine it, Roger." She would always breathe dusk into his ear. Sometimes her voice would spread chills on his skin. "Moving images hold moving hinges. A keyhole in stillness. *God*, can you imagine it? To open a door with a film, any door, really."

"I can imagine it," he sighed. There was no dusk in his voice. He didn't need her to feel any.

"I have my five blank spaces in the script. If they could be five valleys, five stepping stones across some other place. Five cups to fill up. The rest would be just tendons connecting muscles, Roger. A current around the stones. Do you see?"

"I see." But he never saw, no matter how he coveted sight. He was too old, then, already.

Hélène almost felt close that night. The prickle on Roger's skin. Later, the dusk cleared, her voice grew brisk and light and logistical. The film shoot, and it faded altogether.

*Will we finish, dear Roger?* her email read two months ago. *Will we believe in what we made?*

He moves from the entrance hall toward the library to check on the pentagram again. Like peeking in at a new pet. His cane clacks on the floor. He calls Faber on the way.

"Your guy isn't here. There's no one keeping the house safe." His voice slips into a high whiny register on the last few words, but he's only embarrassed for a second. He's old enough to know feebleness will catch up with him, too, any day now.

"I've got Jim Buehrle on tonight," Faber says. He sounds surprised, even concerned. "He wouldn't no-show. He should be there."

"Well, he's not, so find him." Roger swipes the call away and watches the library doorway swim toward him. His eyes are strong, but they are in their eighties. He stoops to massage pain out of his left knee as he arrives, then tips himself forward to look into the room.

The pentagram is smudged into a pointless blur, the black chalk ruined. Someone has dragged their hands through it like a sulking child.

Roger is staring at it, realizing someone could be in the house right now, when a dark shape moves in the far corner. It folds under the ceiling. A shadow leaking upward. The house breathes with quiet as he remembers being young and wanting to peek behind the world's veils.

There is something here, like a great lung straining against him, not so different from what he felt inside of Hélène's plywood crypt years ago. What he imagined in the crypt, he reminds himself.

Has she brought him proof? Has she found it for herself?

He leans into the room's dimness. The bent shadow is gone. There is only the corner, the door to the sitting room with its own books. There are only the angles of the smeared-apart pentagram, the books slowly crumbling.

Roger nearly screams when a pounding comes from the front of the house. Someone at the door. Then a low groan, stretched out somewhere down the hall. A pretend ghost.

"Stop it," he hisses at no one, maybe at himself, and shuffles back the way he came. He is weary of his weariness, of this thing hanging over him. He is tired of his tiresome thoughts sifting through his life, dredging up the fame and the arcane.

Most of all, this prison. The house, its poisoned thresholds. The first time the light and the air and the unending eyelid of the sky triggered a panic attack was 1986. He had loved the outdoors as a child, it was necessary in Erwin, Tennessee, when home was one large room in a farmer's pasture, no plumbing, but something changed as a young man in his ascent toward stardom. He began to feel comfort on closed sets, anxiety when he shot open-air scenes. After his early retirement, on trips to buy cursed things for his collection, the agoraphobia began to open in him like starvation.

Within a year he was like a vampire without a sunset. Close to four decades, eight million dollars, six thousand square feet shrinking down to the size of a coffin, until he wasn't allowed to feel the grass under his feet and had to rely on hot humming UV bulbs to remind his body that it was supposed to crave the elements like a good animal.

Three dozen acres in this sprawling pocket Eden. Woods full of red spruce, fir, a narrow creek trickling like a secret toward Lake Placid. Paper birches white as litters of bones. The lush fields of grass that have never known picnics, every year new quilts of snow unbroken by galoshes. All this land teeming of its own accord, manicured for no one, only Roger's eyes through the house's tall windows.

It might as well be a postcard sent from some far restorative place, because his mind will squeeze him in a vice if he steps foot on it.

Back in the entrance hall again, he stops and listens in the crystalline silence. Only the main porch lamps are on, but even from inside, the night seems to pull at the light. Eating it. And still no security guard.

The doorbell sounds, amplified by the high ceiling. Roger cries out and staggers as a face appears in the sidelight window, pale on the dark porch.

But it's only Beatriz. Her black silvered hair and severe, kindly eyes, wide tonight. The worry lines drawn down from her thin lips are deeper than usual.

The only person he has felt warm regard for since Hélène.

He rushes to let her in, his left knee flaring again with age. His finger stabs the wrong code into the security panel twice. "What is it?" he says when he finally gets the door open. "What's wrong?"

She lifts a shaking hand to her mouth. He has never seen her hair down before. "Mr. Eilertsen, someone was near my cottage," she says. "She has a knife."

"She? How do you know it was a woman?" The word *knife* takes its time sinking in. Is Hélène here? His body doesn't know how to react to the thought. He feels his face grow hot, but cold traces down his back.

"A woman, or someone in a dress." Why does the dark seem swollen behind Beatriz? It could creep up onto the porch and touch her at any moment. "Mr. Eilertsen, you must call the police."

A dress, or a blue bedsheet draped over one of those movie fanatics. Beatriz would not know the difference, looking out her window into the night. "I'll call them. You go back to your cottage and lock the doors. I'll call Faber, too, he'll move you into a hotel in the morning."

"I don't like to think of you here, alone, and someone with a knife."

He reaches over and flips all the switches beside the door. Along the circular driveway, the gravel path out to the guest house, islands of light flare like stars behind dissolving clouds. The cottage is a white smudge against the crowded trees three hundred yards away. "Someone may have already broken in, so you should go back."

"I'm glad we have the security men," she says.

"Not at the moment. But there's some light for you now. Go on. I want to make sure you're safe. The police aren't far."

She says good night and turns and descends the steps. Roger sometimes thinks of those fourteen planks of wood as a portal to another world. He does so now as he watches Beatriz pass from white blur of light to woolen dark to white blur of light along the lawn. She looks young with her hair down, a pale yellow blouse, loose jeans like scissors cutting the shadows.

His heart is aching, not from anything like romantic love, though he would be lucky to love such kindness. This is only bland, sharp shame, that he cannot walk her back to her little house across the grass.

He feels the worn bone of his cane against his palm. Richard Bonbridge once set this walking stick to the side and cut a man's throat. Useless knowledge of useless men. *I have wasted my life*, Roger thinks.

Out on the endless lawn, a bedsheet unfolds from the dark and glides toward Beatriz.

How could Roger not have known? Why did he let her go? These people were outside the house just the other day, goading him on, did he think they had packed up and slithered back to whatever basements they lived in?

The light makes the tall rippled thing look green instead of blue. Roger can see the boxy edges of a crown on its head.

Then another of them, sidling in an arc around Beatrix and the first figure. A camera held out, sweeping them into its lens. This one looks shrouded in green, too, and Roger realizes they're not blue sheets like those from the film and the handful of idiots at his gate. These have separated themselves from the past.

Roger steps through the front door onto the porch. The impact of his foot against the varnished wood hums up his ankle. He takes another step, and he is fully outside, dizzy campfire sparks whirling across his eyes.

Beatriz screams and turns to her left, running now, but the first of the bedsheets catches her easily, lifting an arm to expose the flash of a knife blade.

Roger doesn't think, he sets his right foot on the first of the fourteen steps. The left, then down, thirteen steps, twelve, ten, terror waking fully in his head.

His slippers touch the ground, the unsteady surface of the world, the mutter of gravel under the soles. The fourteen steps are behind him.

But he can't move. He can only watch the glimmer of knife lunge out and into Beatriz, high in her chest, the shoulder, he thinks. He can only hear the grunt she makes beneath the roar of panic in his ears. She stumbles to the grass. White hands drag her into the dark. But his legs will not move.

*Go to her, goddamn you*, he thinks. He finds Reverend Spide in *Came Down the Mountain*, the role that lit the first grand fuse of his life. He becomes this broken, vile, arrogant villain on the other side of this gulf of time. "Come on and get me!" he shouts, a line he still remembers the cadence of, down to the deep hole of the *own* and the phlegm of the *git*.

His right leg lifts, rusty and shaking, and steps forward. He needs the cane but it keeps slipping, betraying him on the gravel.

"Don't worry, I'm right here," someone says from behind him. Roger spins around to find a third man, shorter and stockier than the others inside his green sheet, his tall crowned head behind the viewfinder of a video camera.

Roger swings his cane. The man dodges and the camera takes the blow. A piece of something jolts off it into the dark. Roger turns the cane around in his hand and swings again as the man closes the distance. This time the bone grip connects with bone, the skull, and the feel of something giving sings through the wood.

The man drops, and a line of pain slides down Roger's arm. A knife wound has opened the sleeve of his black robe, blood already soaking the silk and pattering down. The shape of the man's crown is askew. Petals of blood are spreading on the fabric below it.

He looks back to where Beatriz was but only sees the first two men. They turn to him and simply watch for a moment, one slowly lifting a knife that is smeared with red, the other filming everything with the camera.

Roger groans and runs to the house. Something starts to buckle in his left knee, but still his legs almost remember being young in the Tennessee hills. The steps to the porch reach out for him, his lungs are heaving for air, and he's up and inside, slamming the door and locking it.

He doesn't pause to reset the alarm. The study. Red spatters follow him down the east hall toward the ancient revolver moldering in his desk. His knee is swelling, bright splinters of pain as something inside it rubs against something else. He tries to listen to the house over the gasps in his throat.

His shadow melts across the wall as he enters the study. A swath of something red has been swiped down the wallpaper to the left of his bookcases. Another echo of Hélène's film, and almost certainly blood. He ignores it and opens the top right desk drawer, fighting an urge like drowning to just slide down into this chair for a minute, until they find him, anywhere that eases the agony of his left leg.

Beatriz falling, her body sliding out of the light on the grass, looping in his mind.

He opens a worn wooden box and lifts the gun out of it. He can see the bullets waiting inside the chamber. His hand reaches out for the desk phone.

"Haha ha, haha ha." Click. Not too close. The library, maybe. The laugh needles at his memory again. Is it Hélène's?

Roger stands, wavers, waits for a wash of dizziness to fade. "Fucking murdering children," he says, and limps out into the hallway.

At the first corner, he sees movement to the left, a long pale shape fading through the doorway into the smaller sitting room next to the library. A sweep of fabric, as though a sheet has stood up from one of the pieces of furniture upstairs and is flitting through the house.

But the sheets upstairs are white, not Hélène's new pale green.

His hearing is still mostly fine, but whatever he saw, it is standing as still as he is. The quiet expands until a voice leaks out toward him, "Haha ha, haha ha, haha ha." And that click again, like a tape being shut off.

A scratching noise follows this, and Roger lifts the gun and pulls the hammer back. He moves down the hall, as far as the library doorway. The same green shape appears across the room, at the adjoining sitting room entrance, only the barest edge of its face, a shoulder.

"Hell is just a word," a voice says, and is cut off with the hollow click. It is Roger's voice, and it sounds so young to him now, even flattened in the small speaker. "You may find demons with the small light in a child's room, but not with the light of any Christ." The click again. "They are in another green world." Click. "They are transfiguring as we speak." Click.

He has no interest in hearing lines that have lost all their resonance. He doesn't want to listen to the desire of belief in that voice. "Proof, damn it," he mutters, then louder, "Get out of my house! I have a gun!"

There's a shimmer of light above the ruined pentagram, gone before Roger can move his eyes to it. The spines of the books brighten for an instant. The pentagram is still smudged into a pointless blur.

"Haha ha, haha ha, haha ha." Click.

When a voice says, "You belong," he waits for the tape player to be turned off again. A thump comes instead, the sound of sliding. Then a grunt, and a shape plunges through the doorway across the room. Roger shrinks back as the shape falls to the floor. A man, a pistol strapped around his torso, his neck and white button-up shirt a splotched red mess. Jim Buehrle, Faber's security guy, dead eyes wide and still.

Roger turns and hobbles back the way he came, his cane knocking against the polished floor, meaning to shut himself inside the den. But something is standing back in the darkness of that room, the contours of a person draped in the same pale green sheet.

From somewhere behind him, the tape again, "Haha ha, haha ha."

*Not like this*, he thinks, *not one of these foolish Hélène acolytes.*

Roger puts his arms out in a warding-off gesture, the cane gripped in his left fist, the gun raised in his right. The figure moves toward him, and Roger sees the camera on its shoulder, the dull glass of its eye watching him. Above it, the shape of a crown hidden under the sheet.

He turns to find the other pretend ghost, the one from the sitting room, striding toward him. A fist with a knife streaked with drying bloodstains. The sheet has been tugged down over the crown, the wooden tines piercing all the way through like horns. Roger remembers what it was like to wear one of those. He still has it in a glass case in one of the second-floor rooms. There is likely a sheet over that crown as well.

Roger points the revolver at the one with the knife and pulls the trigger. Nothing happens. Then he remembers noticing the empty chamber under the hammer, once upon a time, and pulls the trigger again.

A hole appears in the left shoulder of the approaching green sheet, just before a crumpled roar of sound slams his ears. His arm jerks with the gun. The man is knocked back, too, staggering, blood seeping through the green cotton.

But he keeps coming. The blade catches Roger in the stomach. It is pulled away quickly, and Roger's hands fold around the wound exactly the way he was told to do it on the *Gunsmoke* set, his first speaking part, when his eyes were full of stars and he was radiant as an angel even though they had smeared grease in his hair and dirt on his face for the scene.

He hardly feels himself hit the floor, the cane rattling away. The gun slides across the expensive tile.

He fell to a church floor just past the climax of *Came Down the Mountain*, as Robert Duvall glared down with blood spackling his knuckles. Roger remembers the pebbled leather of Reverend Spide's Bible, Roger held it upward like a shield against Duvall. There were still some stars in his eyes then.

Above him, a dark, long-fingered hand peeks out from under the sheet holding a tape recorder, a bulky black thing from decades ago. It clicks on. "Roger," Hélène's lightly accented, deep, contagious voice says. "I'm regretful to make you reconsider. Something tells me you said, 'I belong with you,' just as I asked in my email. And you do. But it will be different this time. You always wanted proof, isn't that right?"

The thumb slides over the recorder and presses a button, cutting her off.

The figure from the den appears, looming, inverted above Roger's head, the camera tilting to film him. The two of them go still, standing and looking down at him, as Roger gasps at the blood that seems to pool in his throat. The burning ice in his belly, the gravity of pain beginning to thread out from it. He stares up at them, his vision blearing.

"Please," Roger says.

At some point, he is aware that time is passing. He realizes what they must be doing. They are in the six minutes, waiting, the blank spot in the narrative. [x6:00x]

Then both of the covered faces turn toward the front of the house, toward the entrance hall and the staircase, the sheets stretching tight across their noses and cheekbones. The air fills with a clicking sound that echoes, decaying under the high ceilings.

"Please," he says again. His lips feel wet but he can't see if it's blood. In films, blood will make its way into the mouth no matter where a person is wounded, so that the dying words are red. It always felt unrealistic, but look where he is now. "Please don't do this. I'll do the movie."

The wound in his stomach is full of agony and cold shock. His slashed forearm is stuck to its blood on the floor.

He moves his head to see what the figures are seeing, and what is there makes him feel for a moment like meeting Simeon Gott in 1983, when the occultist's long finger reached out and touched the ridge of bone between Roger's eyes and left a smear of goat blood. The stars in those eyes dialed up to the brightest they would ever be, they could have sparked liquid white like a welder's torch.

A magnificent thing is inside his home. It is approaching the hallway. It is the cusp of what Roger once believed was the path of his life.

He recognizes the approaching mass from his viewings of *Proof of Demons*, when he had some sense that Hélène had truly meant the film's title and intended her art to realize all the conversations they had shared. That moving pictures could frame a door and hold a key. All that dusk she poured into his ears.

But this is reality coming toward him, even as it passes in and out of reality in its unnatural movement. It is Hélène's creation caught in some amalgam of puberty and death, a towering corpse made of tissue and shadow and sinew. Its skin is not quite skin, both dark and bloodless white. An autopsy cavity flexes open like a mouth.

It is taller than it seemed on film, and when it reaches the meeting of the vaulted ceiling and the hallway that curves through the rear of the house, it bends its uncertain head down and drags it inside toward Roger. It wedges itself in, a grating, looping noise coming from the hole in it, crackling pops filling the air like an old television.

"Don't," Roger says.

The sheeted figures step away from the Pine Arch Creature. Roger's shirt is wet with blood, and his hands fall away to the cold tiles. The loops turn into cracked words: "She caught me. Inside the camera. Moving toward. You never stopped. Hoping for me. You belong."

It says, "You belong," many more times, until its strange half-grown eyes are close, the ruined wonder of its face is lowering to him. Roger thinks of the sycamore tree across the property, its arms like this creature's arms. He hopes Beatriz is somehow alive and back in her cottage, embraced by the sycamore, that these people and this thing will have no use for her. He likes her very much. She has made these last years kind.

"Haha ha, haha ha, haha—" The dull click is followed by another, then at last the recognition of his own recorded laughter, slowed a little and chopped into pieces from one of his films. Then the rasping sound of a tape being removed from its slot.

# CHAPTER THIRTY

## Trevor

▶▶ Once he says the name of Jorie's son out loud, everything changes.

He walks down Birchmount Road toward the lake, phone pressed to his ear, listening to the raw panic in Jorie's voice. It's the most unselfconscious thing he's ever heard, this open and naked despair shared with someone she hasn't spoken to in at least ten years. Her son is missing. Someone has murdered her friend.

Trevor doesn't want to tell her about the email he received a few minutes ago. But he has to, he has spoken Oliver's name and made all of this real in some final way.

There is his own fear, too, dilating since she answered his call. He knows he's a lifeline here, an unprepared anchor, but he can't calm her down or channel her wildness into a discussion of what they should do.

"What do you mean?" Jorie says. "What message about Oli?"

Trevor stops walking. He leans against the wall of the tapas place Jenn likes and lets the trickle of pedestrians flow by him. He recites the email. It doesn't take long. He doesn't even have to pull the phone away from his ear to make sure he has the words right.

"'Tell Jorie our names. Tell her Oliver is in the sequel.' That was all it said."

"Oh my God," Jorie says, and he lets her sob those words until she's done. "What names?"

"It was just the one name," he says. "You remember the email I sent you the other day? Avery E., the guy who was obsessed with the Pine Arch Creature? He sent me that message today, like he knew I was trying to find out who he was, and this time he signed it Avery Ellis, with a YouTube link to Lecomte's *Under the House*. Jorie, you and I are in that sequel trailer, and now your son might be in trouble—"

"I hear them!" Jorie cuts in. "The police are here. I have to go. We need roadblocks and APBs and anything I can get. I'll call you back." And she's gone before he can respond.

Trevor can't help the stiff clinch of frustration in his jaw. The trailer, he needs to talk to someone else who is in it. The fire next to his apartment was in that video. Someone tried to kill him for their half-horror, half-snuff film. He needs to know what to do. He needs to be far away from Toronto, not trapped in someone else's home with someone else's cat.

Two commissions are due this week. He tried working on one for a worthless hour, but the peephole in the apartment door grew into a huge eye daring him to look. He's been out walking, avoiding it most of the morning.

Jenn will call him soon. They're heading out of town to her parents' house when she finishes work. She has Boo at the office already, and all that's left is to swing by and grab Calloway, who will have to deal with being closed off in her own room if she and Boo can't get along. Nils won't be back for two weeks, and this trouble is a lot more than a couple of guys with a drone camera and an unstable sense of fandom haunting the hallways of his apartment building.

He misses Boo enough to feel the ache of her in his chest.

*Tell Jorie our names. Tell her Oliver is in the sequel.*

It's not warm out, here in the slim bright window before winter crawls over Ontario, but the sun gives the cool air some texture. The light feels good on his face. Maybe he'll walk to the trees and the lake before taking a Lyft to Jenn's office.

There are more and more funeral videos on Instagram and TikTok and all the rest, more disappearances, this slow-motion cascade of a horror movie. People have gotten the idea that they're supposed to streak dark lines of blood on their walls, to welcome the Pine Arch Creature. One young woman says she's been seeing her best friend hiding in the shadows all around her family's home, except that the best friend died in a hospital two years ago.

Another guy said on Instagram that someone was watching him in the mirror when he turned the bathroom light out, a weird face growing layer on top of layer. He has since been added to the list of the missing in the #funeralwatching tally.

Trevor is tired of seeing the kind of content he should love but can only feel sick and worried about.

He's watched the trailer at least twenty times. Whenever his name appears in the credits, he tells himself that if the trailer's out, his part in the movie has been wrapped up, all his scenes have been filmed. It's a nice thought that shivers apart as he reaches for it.

Either way, nothing will happen to him in broad daylight, out in the world.

But when he reaches Birchmount Park, he sees two men in woolen hats across the intersection. Each is holding a phone out, possibly toward Trevor. *Maybe they're taking selfies*, an assurance that lasts through the crosswalk, as they turn to track his progress.

He sees the first Rickie of the day less than a minute later, tucked in the rear of an alley across Birchmount, between a salon and a solicitor. A sleek video camera is perched on the shoulder of the green sheet. Trevor runs toward the alley, the air brakes of a bus and a single whining car horn following him into the gap between the buildings.

"Hey!" he calls after the Rickie, but the bedsheet whips back and around the corner. Still too far away to see clearly. Trevor plunges out the far end and scans the new street. No one draped in green, no running figure carrying a camera. No one gathering Trevor up into footage.

But now he knows he is still a character in the story.

The bluffs aren't far now. The unending lake and the sun cut into smeared coins by branches and turning leaves. He'll walk where the land is thinning, autumn barren as it drops down to the lake, the wind off the water screened by the trees.

No one seems to be following him, but he takes a senseless route the rest of the way, through a parking lot, down and over two extra blocks, then into the eastern side of the park. Past a rock fountain and through a garden of red pines and rosebushes.

By the time he's on the trail to the bluffs, he has decided to rent a cabin far from the city. Peterborough or even Barrie, a place on a smaller lake. Then what, a flight to Vermont to team up with Jorie? He pictures the two of them poring over webpages and emails and DMs, tracing shards of modern folklore to Enriquez's doorstep, uncovering a nest full of huddled green-sheeted lunatics for the police.

These daydream fragments feel more like a montage of recycled footage than the pieces of a plan snapping into place. Straightforward scenes from safer films, comfort food with final girls and old priests who know the backstories. But the thought of Vermont feels like forward motion, and he leans into it, flipping his jacket's collar up as the shade deepens.

He remembers a day when he was little, five or six, on a nature trail somewhere with his mother. Late in the year, after the trees turned to skeletons. He told her a ghost came into his room at night, so tall it had to curl itself under the ceiling. It was black and went all fuzzy when he looked. It watched him as he tried to go to sleep.

His mother picked her way through five minutes of words explaining that it wasn't real, how she had seen something in her own bedroom when she was his age, though maybe not quite so scary. He would tell her sometimes, giggling, that she talked too much, and she would pretend to be angry, but that day Trevor waited until she was done and told her he liked the ghost. It scared him and he needed his seashell light sometimes, it wasn't his friend and it would eat him if he let it. But he liked falling asleep with it in the room.

She crouched down on all the fallen leaves and looked at him until it hurt, but finally she nodded and told him to tell her if he ever stopped liking it.

He doesn't remember when the folded-over ghost was replaced by something else, and then something else, monsters that got better at hiding in corners and behind furniture, but he never stopped loving the terror of any of them. They were the birth of the Pine Arch Creature and Siren Head and all the rest of the things that lived in him. He started drawing and painting not long after that.

The line between then and now used to feel nice.

"Hey!" he shouts into the park. "I belong with you! Is that what I'm supposed to say? I don't fucking *want* to belong. I'm good, thanks." Far ahead, at a curve in the trail, he sees someone disappear into some undergrowth.

He comes to a widening of the path, and there are no longer trees behind the trees, only a wide and empty blue space bisected by the surface of Lake Ontario, the sunlight glinting and the hint of chaotic America lost in the hazy distance. He looks out at the water, wondering what to do. Would just hiding in a cabin be enough? **[x6:00x]**

The minutes filter through the pines and sugar maples, but he doesn't think to count them. This park was in the trailer, the Pine Arch Creature hiding in the frame like something from one of his own pieces. A part of him was admiring it, too distracted to pay attention to where it was.

A faint whine comes from the left. He turns his head and the drone camera he saw in the hall outside Nils's apartment is dragging itself through the air toward him.

"Will you believe in what you made?" The voice crackling out of the small speaker is genderless and cold. The camera's eye flexes, dialing in on him.

Of course. The Rickies were able to follow him, it didn't matter how smart he thought he was. He was cooped up too long, they wouldn't want his next scene to take place in the same hallway with the same scares. The woods are vintage found-footage land.

Trevor runs, and the drone whirs into motion.

A bend in the trail, the trees leaning toward him and the lake from the right. Pools of sun shake on the dirt path. Something is standing in his way, a tall column of shadow, the top of it hidden in the reaching red branches of a maple. A bloodless seam is opening its torso into a hole, and something he can't find the words for is moving inside. Open hands or milky clouds, eyes with cataracts, tongues, all of these and none of them at all.

He spins around and the drone is there, filming him, nudging him through the scene. "You belong," it says, then with a click, "Will you believe in what you made?" Another click, "What did they change into?" A woman's voice, he thinks. Sound bites from the trailer.

The slow shadow thing is still there when he turns back. This is not the Pine Arch Creature in the trees above the Scarborough Bluffs, because the Pine Arch Creature is nowhere, it's not a real thing. His overactive imagination dreamed it up and drew the lines of it in the dark of his childhood bedroom. He grew up to paint it on a computer screen and give it a blank slate of a mythos, unknowable, because it has always been scarier that way in his mind.

This is just a projection, an AI rendering, a technology he has never heard of. The Pine Arch Creature is not here with him, the red leaves of the wrong kind of tree hiding its face.

He moves forward, daring it, and the charcoal smudge bleeds of color. It grows pale and wet, and it takes its own step toward Trevor, shaking the maple as it pushes through its limbs. It stutters out for a moment, like an image, then returns. Its arms lift up, making it person-shaped, and a branch whips away behind it as the head appears. Holes melting into eye sockets, a small opening mouth with half-drawn teeth.

Trevor's life has been, however abstractly, training for this moment, and he trembles on the edge of accepting it. The Pine Arch Creature, the flesh of it. The presence of it. "The proof," he says, but he doesn't hear his own voice.

It's almost exactly the thing from the most recent video he saw online, the thing a girl who couldn't have been more than seventeen walked toward until her phone fell to the floor. But paler, even more corpselike now, its face elderly, somehow, and rounded by the promise of cheekbones. Nubs on the arms that want to be fingers.

*More organic with every summoning,* Trevor thinks. It's moving past cryptid and legend and CGI and anything he has ever slipped into the darkness of a photograph.

Part of him is five again, or six, he doesn't remember anything that can fix the exact age, but he remembers the beginning of this thing towering over him. Before it found the door of a story.

"She caught me. Inside the camera," a voice says, as though finding his thought, but now it's not the drone with its propellers churning the air behind him. It is the Pine Arch Creature speaking. "You belong," the last syllable wearing out into a hushed clicking cloud like a dying speaker.

*A dying speaker*—he has seen those words used to describe it before. Recently. Jorie's blog post all those years ago, the one that caused all the shit and heartbreak. He reread an archive of it yesterday. How could she have known its voice, if she made it all up? The Pine Arch Creature is silent in the movie.

"No, I made you up," Trevor tells it. "You were the start."

The elongated thing takes another step toward Trevor and stops. Its head doesn't move, there are no ears emerging from the dark pale smudge of it, but Trevor can sense it listening. If he reaches out, he will almost touch it. Red and brown and yellow leaves from the earth cling to the stumps where its feet should be. Its new musculature is moist.

The *-long* at the end of its last word is still fading into the air, a looping snap of breath.

"You didn't come out of me." Trevor rubs both hands over his face. "You were there already. Somehow. Weren't you?"

"You belong," it says again, muddy and harsh. "You have. Always belonged."

The hole in the middle of it doesn't move. It is not a mouth, not a cave or a container. Trevor doesn't know what it is. There's movement in the trees beyond the creature, a video camera and a green sheet. A blank cotton face. The drone still hovers behind him, filming the rear angle. He wants to go to the hole in the thing's torso and find out what it is, but he can't, instead his center of gravity recoils and he staggers back.

As he falls, the thing's arms reach down and catch him. Trevor's glasses tumble to the dirt but his eyes are closed. He clenches them shut. He holds Boo's face in his mind and feels the tickle of her whiskers under his nose. They're almost real enough to make him sneeze.

He thinks of Jenn, the first time he made something for her, a photo of their third date with a red-eyed man inserted under the next table in the restaurant, hiding and watching them fall in love. He adored the way her scrunched-up mouth didn't match up with the joy in her eyes as she held the picture.

He thinks of the first time Jenn shared her own art with him. The first comic with her name on the cover. The day she came home with a Siren Head plushie and asked him how this was their life.

Jenn laughing, hot sauce smeared on her nose.

Boo's deep rumbling purr.

Then something breaks inside Trevor. Bones squeeze against other bones. He is lifted, he thinks he opens his eyes but it is dark. Who will feed Calloway, but Calloway and Boo and his love are gone. All his beautiful creatures are gone.

Only a strange pain is left, something like teeth, a great green lake of pain. It swells and dims and turns into endless chattering voices. Drawings he can't see. Then nothing.

# CHAPTER THIRTY-ONE

## Jorie

▶▶ "This is punishment for what I did to Hannah." She sits on her sofa in the den with Sam, rocking back and forth in tight jerks with her hands locked around her knees. Her breaths are short, gasping sips of air. She can't keep her voice steady. "They took Oli because of what I did to Hannah."

An hour ago Jorie stood in another house, in another ant farm of cops. Officer Willard and the chief, whose name she has already forgotten. Extra forensics technicians with powders and lights from Waterbury. More statements. They watched the new trailer. She told them someone hiding in the crawl space had escaped into the woods. Questions darting through the air, the answers nowhere, voices rising and softening in the background.

Some of the officers brought Jorie home and are stationed outside. Willard said he'll be here later. An APB was put out on the waves. The FBI en route. She fainted at one point.

"You have to stop." Sam's voice, Sam's hand on her arm is warm. "This is not your fault."

Jorie looks around until she finds her cousin's face. It blurs and the world goes dark again.

Later, after all the bootsteps and voices have left her with the greater noise inside her head, after screaming and crying, after Sam forces her to take a pill and she sleeps through the last half of the night, she is able to look for her son. Except she can only do this through a blank browser window on the old laptop, her hands fidgeting over the keyboard, while the police are out there chasing ghosts with bloodhounds and fingerprint dust.

Hopelessness and hunger feel the same in her stomach, like clenching fists.

She actually finds herself typing "where is oliver paterson" and has to make herself clear the search bar.

The spread of the #funeralwatching videos continues, #filmhaunted and #youbelong and #hauntme and a dozen other hashtags, and more of the world is paying attention. Thirty-seven disappearances across four countries, in a single week. At least one suicide and a heart attack recorded live. All of them telling a camera they want to belong.

Appeals to the public, pressure to ban anything associated with the film, networks beginning to invite academics to talk about mass hysteria and social media terrorism. "The vein of anxiety and dejection about the world that is so concerning in today's youth has been tapped into," says one professor of cinema studies on CNN, and he might as well be drafting his next paper on live TV.

*Proof of Demons: October Film Haunt* is trending worldwide. Jorie sees someone wearing a T-shirt in an Instagram reel, a red vertical line with YOU printed on one side and BELONG on the other. Enriquez is racking up viewers, and the release date hasn't even been announced.

Some are convinced Jorie is involved with the sequel, which feels like a reheated 2013 until she learns she's named in the trailer credits. *WRITTEN BY HÉLÈNE ENRIQUEZ & JORIE STROUD & COLEMAN SMITH*. A few people attempt to vindicate her—"october film haunt taught us this is dangerous years ago, leave jorie alone"—but this feels just as cruel, somehow. There's no way to take it all in.

She's more interested in finding every video she can, scrutinizing the backgrounds for clues that aren't there, ignoring the actors because she still can't think of these as real summonings, the Pine Arch Creature stepping out of fiction, like it did in her own lies. She's not at that threshold of acceptance.

But she remembers the impossible shape in the trees outside Beth's cabin, the man and not-man, and the belief she could gather from it if she wanted, and this leads her mind to the original film, the moving hole with its eye and its doorway and her son being taken to a place where he's changed into something that has no answer yet.

She does get closer to something. A wicked tension headache, calling Trevor Henderson and leaving voicemail after voicemail. Useless research. She sits back and closes her eyes. She pictures the two FBI agents who took her computer, one of them holding the envelope the first VHS tape was mailed in. The thumb drive was in the envelope, too, and she remembers the words PINE ARCH RESEARCH scratched into the black plastic.

She hasn't googled *pine arch* without the *creature*, but now she tries with *research* instead. The first result is a YouTube video called *The Pine Arch Collection* from 2018. An obvious Enriquez connection, and the channel's name is pinedemon, which also matches the email address Trevor told her about and one of the Reddit handles that mentioned her and Beth.

The short found-footage film mostly consists of a weird, vaguely human "lump," as it's called in an on-screen series of emails between a group of insidious filmmakers and two friends. The lump looks like tar that is trying to be a person. In the beginning it's reaching an arm up to the high window of a house, and later it seems to have assimilated itself with a woman, who is crawling out of a bedroom into a hallway.

It's enough like the Pine Arch Creature to resonate, and that makes the human-lump hybrid even more disturbing.

First-person POVs lurch and flee through the woods, names are shouted, and it's surely an example of some great creepy stuff Jorie has missed during her long exile. Making movies has never been so easy. But she feels that Enriquez must be behind this film, too, it's like a dry run for the new *Proof of Demons* in the way it forces a narrative upon those who don't want it. The comments below the video argue about whether this is Enriquez canon.

She looks up the names of the victims and learns that they're not fictional. Both were reported missing in January of 2019.

Everything, from the afternoon she pulled the tape out of the mailbox until this moment, becomes tighter around her. Losing her son, losing Beth, staring at the screen, struggling to breathe. But she doesn't see how this can point her to where Enriquez is now, and the desperate hope that this will help her find Oli.

In one of the emails that serves as scene breaks in the video, *Under the House* and the impostor October Film Haunt group are referenced, so this must take place in the same story universe. Jorie looks up the older film and sees that the original is still online, with four and a half million views. A comment from yesterday reads, "When is Enriquez/Lecomte going to make a sequel to this one? My heart is ready." She glances up at the channel name: lecomte.

Something comes close to her thoughts, maddening as an insect, but she can't grasp it. Something to do with Colin. And Sam, too, though she can't imagine why.

She closes her eyes again and sees her cousin standing in the kitchen, but the words she's saying aren't quite there. Samantha is the connection she just felt, though. The two of them at the counter by the sink, Cara and Carter in the den with Oli watching *The Addams Family*, Sam talking about how Jorie can keep

Oli safe without dismantling her life—if only she *had* dismantled her life, Oli would be okay, she would be clinging to him—but none of this can have anything to do with *Under the House*.

The dining nook window is her lens, it's how she thinks, the paper birches like fresh scrolls with the answers written inside. She stares out at the tree line for two minutes, three and then four minutes, her thoughts sluggish with panic, and sees a pale face appear in the last tatters of the morning ground fog. It pulls at her, too far away, but why wouldn't it be the thing in Mrs. Compton's crawl space? The face in Oli's closet? At this point, why wouldn't it?

As she's leaning toward the cold glass, it changes into a much taller thing, a dark streak with impossible limbs stretching out. The Pine Arch Creature, it must be, something in her finally wraps its arms around the idea of it.

She runs out the front door and sprints across the yard, but it's gone by the time she's close enough to know. The patches of peeling bark could have arranged themselves into a face from her angle inside the house.

But Jorie is at the point of the movie where she doesn't want to deny the supernatural anymore—these instances are too much like rituals, the videos on social media look too real for such amateurish contexts—and she is too tired. The final blink of the final girl, and it all feels different. Enriquez has proved her demon, somehow.

She wonders if she should push all her chips in and go find a funeral to film, and shout at the trees out past the gathered mourners. Instead, she pictures Hannah. The thought of her, a kind of summoning of her face. Hannah has always been more real than the Pine Arch Creature. She has come to define reality.

"Some of you may remember me." She pauses, lets herself think she's being foolish for just a second. "For the rest of you, my name is Jorie Stroud, and I've been hiding for years. Hiding from the world, but mostly hiding from myself and what I did in the year 2012. I helped make people believe something that wasn't true. It doesn't matter if I thought people would believe me. I wanted to believe it myself. I know it would've been more awful if I'd done it out of some troll mindset, out of conspiracy or meanness, but the fact that I wanted to believe my story has felt worse over all these years of sitting alone with my thoughts."

Her phone is braced against a stack of books. She looks as small on its video screen as she feels, her dark eyes too round for her face. One of her gray hairs, above the right temple, catches a glint of morning sun from the window.

She starts crying but clenches her jaw against the emotion. *Just enunciate*, she tells herself, *who cares about the rest*.

"Now I'm the only one left of the three of us in the October Film Haunt. Colin died not long after I told the lie. I helped put him in a place where he turned to addiction. Beth was murdered by whoever's making this new movie, but she might not have died if she hadn't come to help me when I asked. Many of you out there are thinking that I should be next, and I won't comment on that.

"Mostly I've thought of Hannah Kim and her family. I know in my heart that she would be alive if not for me. She died wearing the October Film Haunt shirt I sold her. I wrote her name on the package I mailed her. And it's in the spirit of what happened to Hannah, all these regrets I have, that I want to talk about the *Proof of Demons* sequel. I don't know if Enriquez is really behind this movie. I don't know if she's honestly trying to prove the existence of demons, but she or some people pretending to be her have been terrorizing me, and now they've kidnapped my son. And I don't know what to do."

She stops to wipe her nose and eyes with her sleeve, looks at the window again but doesn't even see the trees.

"I have not been cowriting this film or participating in its production willingly. People with cameras are following me around, they've broken into my home, but I have nothing to do with any of it. Please don't make these funeral videos. They might not be fake anymore. They're not fake like me. I think they are harming people. I think—I don't know if there's something supernatural going on, and I'm not going to say the Pine Arch Creature is real. But please, let's slow down the spread of this movie. Or even more people are going to die."

Her voice crumbles in the last sentence, and she has to stop again, build herself back up to get through the next part. She takes a deep shaky breath.

"The other reason I'm here is to ask that if anyone watching this knows where Enriquez is, please message me or call the police or FBI. If you don't want to do it for me, please do it for my son. He's eight years old and he must be so scared right now. I need him back with me. Please. Thank you."

She taps the stop button on her phone screen and opens all the social apps. She gets her hashtags ready. Before posting the video, she changes the names on all her accounts from Wilt Flowers to Jorie Stroud. The handle she's been using ever since Hannah, @notaredemptionarc, stays. It has never felt more appropriate.

Within an hour, the video has been shared nearly five thousand times. She ignores the hundreds of comments. She has no choice but to sift through her inbox, the messages of support and nasty sentiments, none of them with anything helpful.

She's called Trevor a dozen times. He's still not answering, but her last voicemail makes something he said yesterday finally click through her terror for Oli. *This time he signed it Avery Ellis, with a YouTube link to Lecomte's* Under the House. Avery E., the writer Trevor told her about, the name she gave to the police.

She knows the name but in a dim way that won't come to her. There are several Avery Ellises on Facebook, most of them young women, but scrolling down she sees *Associate at Cult Horror* and clicks on the profile's glaring male face. And the nagging memory breaks through, this man following her around at the last convention she ever attended, CryptidCon in March of 2013.

Her fake blog post had been spreading for months by then. Jorie remembers that time before Hannah as a slowly mounting regret and dread, a feeling that too many of the wrong people believed her. When asked directly about it, she had started to backpedal, claiming the post had been a metafictional exercise.

But it was half-hearted damage control. The IV drip of dopamine in the likes and shares and retweets kept her too silent.

This Ellis guy kept finding her in the hotel lobby, the conference rooms between panels, in a conversation with a producer at the upstart A24 that had her blood singing with excitement. Ellis asked her what it was like seeing the Pine Arch Creature, if it was erotic at all, how the eye in the hole made her feel. He grinned at her. He touched her waist in an elevator and told her she would be a legend.

She shakes the memory off and clicks into his most recent post, various photos of a structure in the woods that Jorie recognizes at once from the opening frames of *Under the House*. There was also a glimpse of it in the new *Proof of Demons* teaser, she realizes. The same blank windows, the same air of wilderness. The peeling paint could have been preserved from the day the movie was uploaded to YouTube in 2008.

Ellis is in one picture, smiling with what might be a green sheet draped over his shoulder, nearly cropped out. The final photo is of a body of water, a silhouette standing in the trees at the shore, a crown on its head.

*There and under again*, the post's caption reads, with the location tag, *at Winona Lake, Bristol Pond Rd., Monkton, VT*. That can't be more than ten miles south of Jorie. There are only two likes, but one of them is from a Helen Enriquez with an anonymous template photo and a blank profile.

The house is a horror holy grail. In another life, Beth and Colin would be elated to see this, they would already be packing for an impromptu film haunt. Jorie would be right there with them, scrounging gas money and putting off work.

But this thought is scraped away when she remembers the note left for her in Mrs. Compton's kitchen. *I'M UNDER THE HOUSE,* in Oli's green crayon. Jorie's hand creeps into her mouth, and she bites down on her fingers. Someone would have made him write it. Someone would have made him put it beneath the crown on the counter. She pictures those rough wooden tines sliding onto Oli's head, an ugly voice coaxing him to crawl through the house like a spider, and begins to cry again.

A noise comes from the kitchen to her left, a sharp scratching at the back door. She's out of her chair and standing beside the oven almost before she's aware of moving. She slides the longest knife out of the wood block.

Someone is peering in through the dirty panes. The door begins to shake gently in its frame, and Jorie's mouth goes dry as the eyes look up and find her. Colin's dead white face, livid with its freckles gone, the dark hair matted with stray yellowed leaves from a birch tree. He smiles at her and rattles the doorknob.

Two of the panes shatter, slivers of glass ringing across the kitchen floor like bells. Jorie sees a crease of dirt along Colin's long soft neck. Blood streaks the hand that reaches through.

But the illusion breaks apart when he smiles again. His face darkens into an inkblot with two staring eyes and cheeks crawling with shadows, and Jorie can see he is the Pine Arch Creature—or one of them. This thing is too short and lopsided, it lacks the tidal draw of what she saw through the dining nook window.

It stoops down and presses its face against one of the broken panes. "You killed her," it says around a wedge of glass. "You killed her. You killed me. You belong." It sounds like his voice recorded on top of someone else's, warping and crackling.

"I know," she hears herself say. "I know, Colin. I'm so sorry." Some distant, detached part of her is wishing she could tell Colin about this copy of him. To watch his wide eyes and that self-conscious grin. *And then what did the Colin thing do*, he would ask if she could tell him, probably lighting a cigarette.

To find out, she draws back her arm to stab at the swarming face.

The thing pulls away, flickering, into the sun smeared across the patio garden, noiseless on the brick pavers, and when Jorie wrenches the door open, it's gone somewhere into the yard. Glass grits under her shoes.

She steps back to the window and sees the trees behind the house shaking with its passage.

A knock comes from the other side of the house. She swallows a scream and runs through the kitchen, across the little foyer to see Sam's hair through the window at the top of the front door.

What she was doing before the Colin apparition—doppelgänger, trick, demonic entity, whatever Enriquez has tapped into—begins to snap back into place in her mind. Leaving here, driving to Monkton, looping Winona Lake until she sees the house from Avery Ellis's Facebook post.

"I think I know where Oli is," she tells Sam before the door is all the way open. She yanks her cousin inside. "Or at least I'm close."

# INTERLUDE

[Excerpts from "REAL Proof of Demons," www.reddit.com/r/CultWeird]

**Posted by u/slenderpine 3 hours ago**

**I can feel PAC in my room**

Since I recorded a funeral yesterday:

Weird white face in closet, corner of my eye, mirrors, sometimes my dead grandmother

Wet clicking sound like a rhythm

Feeling of unbearable static electricity CLOSENESS whenever I'm alone

**Posted by u/mygoodness 5 hours ago**

**My sister is transfiguring!**

I will be soon. We don't care if these people really are being taken by a demon. We want to be part of it! Before she left she felt such peace and the world didn't feel pointless and rigged anymore. I get why they want us to say we belong with the trees on our videos. People will always remember us. We will be legends. We will be talked about in the dark forever. I feel it so close. Watch me live over on . . .

**Posted by u/shittyhellscape 6 hours ago**

**This is so great**

I think it's in the basement with me please watch this. I am a movie! ♥

youtu.be/NToh7_7ujRK

**Posted by u/lostfootage05 8 hours ago**

**The pine arch creature saved my life**

I had a bottle of my mom's pills ready when you guys introduced me to Helene Enriquez's movies. I love horror but this is so next level, for the first time in my life I feel like I belong to a community. I heard you don't have to go to a funeral to summon it, you can just stand outside and hope to belong. Just say the words. It's best in the trees. I'm going to do that now. You have given me hope.

**TAPE 3**

**YOU HAVE ALWAYS BELONGED HERE**

HI-FI VIDEO

I believe, but what is belief?

—ANNE STEVENSON,
"DREAMING OF THE DEAD"

# CHAPTER THIRTY-TWO

## Jorie

▶▶ "Are you crazy?" is the first thing Sam says. "You can't go there by yourself. You have to call the police." These could be lines from an eighties slasher. Jorie's two lives keep folding over each other.

More important, these are precious minutes that Jorie can't let slip away.

"No, listen," she tells Sam. "It's not some code of honor, I swear. It's just common sense when dealing with the supernatural. You can stay here if you want, I want you to stay here, but you're wasting *time*."

"The super—" Sam can't get the whole word out. She pulls her phone out instead, as though the argument is over. Jorie grabs it when she tries to call 911, gritted teeth and a hurt little groan from Sam as Jorie squeezes her fingers to make her let go. The possibility of violence rises and heats the space between them.

Sam steps back and surrenders the phone. "Honey," she says, massaging her right hand, her eyes wide. "Get a grip. You have to think."

"All I've done is think!" Jorie doesn't mean to shout it, nearly scream it, and it's so hard to bring her voice back down. "I know what these people are doing. They have it written down, trust me. I'm the protagonist who goes to get her son."

Gravel pops in the driveway, and Jorie is out the front door, sprinting. Officer Willard is getting out of a Ford SUV, in his street clothes, clunking the door shut. Fear spreads across his face. "What happened?"

"Did you find him?" Jorie says.

"No, we're still looking, we're—" He stops and looks behind Jorie, to where her cousin is standing on the stoop. "Did someone demand a ransom or something? What's wrong?"

"Something could be happening to him right this second!" Jorie shrieks, and something in her voice tears. There are no birds to frighten into scattered handfuls out of the trees. She takes deep breaths. Hyperventilating won't help Oli. "Ryan, I know where he is," she says. "I'm going to him now. No one is going to stop that from happening."

They take Willard's SUV because that will help him be the hero. They have all agreed, Jorie can go, but not without them. Not a single moment since she pulled the tape out of her mailbox has felt more scripted.

"Tell me one more time," he asks her in the driveway. His seat belt clicks. He puts the key in the ignition. "A movie being filmed inside an old house on Winona Lake? Why can't we have twenty cops storming this place?"

She's still holding her grandmother's kitchen knife, the handle a textured wood that was once smooth and dark. "Movie characters have my son. We do this the movie way."

It's a movie line, and she hates it. But if her two lives must overlap, she will burn the old one and use it as fuel.

They don't see many houses on their slow circumference of the lake, which is really just a glorified pond. The strip of forest is too wide and dense, the falling sun caught under the rim of the trees. But they find an old Jeep with its plastic windows buttoned up and a blank white cargo van parked on the grassy shoulder of Bristol Pond Road. A rutted driveway pushes into the woods between them, blood-orange birches and maples so red they look fake.

"These cars were left here for us to find," Jorie says. Willard pulls over beyond the Jeep and she gets out and turns to Sam. "You stay here. Please. You have to."

Sam opens her door without a word.

A hundred yards into the trees, Jorie has doubts. This area is too nice, too Vermont money to fit as the setting for *Under the House*. But soon they begin to see fragments of a building in the foliage. She can tell the paint is peeling, she can feel the abandonment pulsing at them.

It's difficult not to run toward it. It's difficult to wrench her mind away from the things Colin would say if he were able to be here. *I told you, Stroud, I told you,* Proof of Demons *and* Under the House, *and you doubted me.* Beth would squeeze her hand and tell her it's okay to be wrong, her sarcasm too happy to feel gloating.

The house seems to be searching for them, too, because it's suddenly there, through a last stand of birches tangled in viny undergrowth. It is the house from

Lecomte's film, down to the broken shutter slats and the intact windows like sleepy eyes, a faded gray Colonial box. She can't tell if it was wedged into the forest or if nature is making a patient claim on its walls.

Even the vantage mirrors the opening of the movie, when the camera creeps out of the trees at crawling height and the house has the faintest tilt on the land. In the background, pieces of Winona Lake glimmer. She feels as though she ended up in the wrong sequel.

There are no vehicles, no one is waiting on the wide porch. There are no faces at the windows.

Jorie turns to her cousin. "You have to go back to the car," she tries one last time.

"No, Jorie. You're here. Oli's here. I don't like guns, but I'm glad Ryan has one."

Willard fumbles at his belt for the radio that's not there. A dark gray pistol hangs in a holster on the other side of his waist, more plastic than metal. He looks at Jorie and tries to smile.

Jorie can't return the favor. She can only think that he's here because Enriquez needed the trope of a cop to lend some weight to the climax.

They step up onto the porch, and Jorie touches the scrolled brass doorknob. She looks at Ryan and her cousin, then down at the #hauntme carved into the boards like some ancient app. It sort of is, really. She turns the knob and pushes the door open, revealing nothing but a pale green curtain, something from an enormous hospital, hanging across the front of the house from a chrome-bright rod near the ceiling.

She goes to the left end of the curtain and peeks around it into a narrow hallway that must extend fifty feet or most of the house's length. Bare windows line the left side, but on the right is only a tall plywood wall that looks pulpy and full of splinters. A camera is positioned high on the wall at the other end.

She turns back to Sam and Ryan, but instead of speaking, she walks to the other end of the curtain. Beyond it, another plywood wall forms a small passageway along the side. A second camera watches her at the end, and what looks like a huge streak of red paint—haunted house blood—runs halfway down the back wall from it.

"This isn't a house," she says in a low voice. "It's a replica with a giant box in it." Without waiting for an answer, she pushes through the curtain into the gap. Sam follows. They only have a few inches of clearance, and when Jorie looks back at Willard, she sees his shoulders scraping the walls.

Halfway down the passage, someone laughs softly behind them. A Rickie is standing at the front of the house, the tines of their crown completely exposed so that the green sheet clings to the shape of the head. A feeling of helpless absurdity seizes Jorie, the thought that they are cattle in a chute. Willard can hardly turn around.

"Ryan, don't!" she hisses, but he's moving back the way they came, his arm searching for an angle that will let him draw his gun cleanly. The Rickie steps back behind the curtain, the green of the sheet blending perfectly with it for a second, and she calls out to Willard again, but he's gone.

Then a shout, several thumps, and the dense crack of a gunshot. And silence. Just like that, he's been removed from the script.

"What do we do, Jorie?" Sam's hands are pulling at Jorie's jacket.

Jorie is about to say they should keep going when the Rickie, or another Rickie, appears at the curtain with a video camera and begins a sideways stumble toward them, the movement awkward but fast. Sam's hand finds Jorie's and they run to the back of the house, where the wall ends and the space opens up just past the streak of sticky paint. She tells herself it doesn't look more like blood up close.

They turn the corner into a room arranged to look like a film set. It *is* a film set, Jorie realizes, of course it is. A decrepit living room bracketed by hallways, short walls with night-painted windows, a small sofa, a row of director's chairs inside a wide ring of burning candles. Someone is sitting slumped in one of the chairs, and Jorie runs over to find Mrs. Compton with her head bowed nearly to her chest.

Jorie shakes her. "Where's Oli? Leah, where's Oliver?"

Mrs. Compton lifts her face to look at Jorie. Her eyes are red. Something is wrong, terror and a strange disgust crawl on Jorie's skin as she looks back at the end of the plywood wall. Sam is standing several feet away. There's no Rickie creeping up behind her.

Names are printed on the backs of the chairs. Mrs. Compton is sitting in LECOMTE. To her left is HÉLÈNE ENRIQUEZ. JORIE STROUD is on the other side, and beyond that is COLEMAN SMITH. She feels a heavy, pressing thought come toward her and thinks of Colin again. Sam leaning on the kitchen counter. Each opposite trying to eclipse the other.

"Somewhere," Mrs. Compton says. "They took him." She gestures toward the dark opening on the left, then her hand jerks to her mouth—for an instant, Jorie thinks she's covering a smile. "So many of these green people around, Jorie. They said something. Do you think a cult must be religious in nature?"

"Did Enriquez take him?" She glances back and sees Sam closer to her now, turned to watch for the Rickie. "How many of her people are here right now?"

Mrs. Compton ignores her. "For that matter, do you think a demon summoned by a cult must be religious? What would religion have to do with it? Wouldn't it be older than a church? Couldn't it be so much younger?" Now the woman is smiling without hiding it. What did Enriquez do to her?

Jorie doesn't have time. Ambulances and all the therapy in the world can wait. She gestures to Sam and they pass through the scene, a single long-necked lamp adding to the candlelight, and go through the doorway, more plywood, into darkness. A light flickers to life, something on a motion sensor. Its stutter casts the narrow space into a horror film cliché. Fake numbered apartment doors line both walls.

Something with a grotesque white head is standing in the corridor. This thing was in the trailer, but it's more of a nightmare here, the molded head turning toward them with a familiar and awful slowness.

Another camera watches from a corner of the ceiling.

She holds up the knife she took from her kitchen. The movie monster braces its hands—pale hands, human-sized, she sees hair on the backs of them—under the head and pushes up. A face slides through the hole and grins at them inside a dark beard. Jorie stares for several seconds before she says, "Trevor?"

"Will we believe in what we made?" he says in a muddy voice that clicks on every syllable. His mouth opens wider in exaggerated cheer, but the face is rotting and remaking itself, the same way Colin's did. The skin turns the white of something hidden from the sun, then blackens until only the eyes are visible. It beckons at them and staggers away, dropping the head on the floor. The light blinks out above them.

Movement comes from behind, at the mouth of the hallway, shuffling and a soft chuckle. Jorie thinks of Willard—Ryan—but the sliver of pain is barely there before it's gone. She reaches back for Sam's hand and moves toward a faint light.

They enter a reproduction of Jorie's dining nook and Oli's den, but without the wall dividing them. Several recessed lights paint glimpses of the scene, and thick curtains hang over the windows. The pendulum clock on the wall to the left of her writing table. An almost perfect match of the sideboard just behind her office chair. Across from these are the sofa, the television, two untidy bookshelves. Just enough of the details are here.

This part of her home has been laid out like a cross section, with two large cameras on massive tripods pointed at the table and the laptop sitting on it.

There's a heavy steel desk with wide monitors and another cluster of director's chairs. Black boxy equipment in a corner. A boom mike stands waiting on a tripod. The air smells of heated dust and men who need to bathe.

Sam screams as the Pine Arch Creature—not the real one, either, Jorie's mind insists—moves out of the far corner toward them, clouding and cohering. It's bent to one side, and the top of its head lightly scrapes against the low ceiling. It's still wearing Colin's face, his high forehead and receding hairline.

It grins down at her. "Same crown," it says in the clicking voice.

"What the fuck is that, Jorie?" Sam shouts, clawing at Jorie's arm.

The lights go out.

Jorie stands in the dark, but her memory sees her cousin in warm white light, in the kitchen several days ago. Sam and Colin are still trying to tell her something. Finally she hears Colin, in the backseat on their way to a film haunt, maybe on their way to Arden, North Carolina, leaning forward with one hand on Beth's seat and the other on Jorie's. *Lecomte is Enriquez, I guarantee it. Seriously, how could you just ignore almost the exact same crown being in both movies?*

They hear the Pine Arch Colin dragging itself out of Jorie's dining nook, the set piece. A faint crackling sound follows it. Sam's grip on Jorie's arm tightens.

*The same crown.* And he pronounced it *Leh-com-tuh*. When she told him that probably wasn't right, he said that was how he had heard it in YouTube videos analyzing *Under the House*.

Then another block dissolves, and Sam's words from the kitchen seep through in Jorie's memory. *What about Leah Compton? She's babysat a lot for you. No one would have a clue Oli was there.*

"What about Leah Compton?" Jorie whispers. "What about Lecomte?" The room is empty, she is being given this moment. She doesn't know what the pronunciation would be in French, if the name truly is supposed to be French. She thinks the *-te* would be cut off.

What is she standing here reaching for? Mrs. Compton made *Under the House*? She pictures the older woman in the director's chair with LECOMTE printed across the back. Smiling too much. Mrs. Compton, her neighbor, the harmless older woman living a quiet widowhood for months just on the other side of Jorie's woods, a woman Jorie knows and spends time with, that woman is Hélène Enriquez?

But Jorie hasn't really known her. She's probably been closer to Leah than anyone up here other than Sam, but they're neighbor-close, how could she know whether she's harmless? How could Jorie know anything? Mrs. Compton moved here even more recently than she and Oli did.

And she remembers thinking she saw her in a horror movie—one of the funeral scenes on the tape that was left in her mailbox. How long were she and her son living in this sequel? Jorie has been a fool. They had to stick the movie in her face to get her to start waking up, and still she handed Oli to them.

"We have to go back to Mrs. Compton," she says to Sam, her voice rising and wavering. They're in a dark that's lined only with a distant residual glow from another space—another set, another scene. "None of this is right. It's not real."

"No shit it's not real," Sam says in a harsh whisper. "It's a movie set hidden in the woods. We have to find Ryan and call the police." A sheet of light flares out from the phone in her hand.

"I mean that Leah Compton is behind all this. She's the one who's been doing everything. She killed Beth." Jorie fumbles for Sam's arm and squeezes it, dread washing over her. Anger rising in its wake. Her voice falls into a whisper. "If we find her, we find Oli."

# CHAPTER THIRTY-THREE

## Coleman

▶▶ *Time to finish the film.*

The voice calling to him is more resonant now. A thousand Jacksons, mixed with the voices of a thousand directors who spoke to him in the cemetery. He is standing in a room when the voice comes, before a window with parted curtains. A woman is screaming in his hands.

When he is Coleman, he feels the last of the cancer trickling out of his pores. He holds Gloria and Evie and the kids in his mind, clinging to the shapes of them in desperation, memorizing the way the light hits them.

When he is his brother, when he is the thing that ate his brother, there is heat and pleasure and hunger. It tastes the air with unimaginable lungs. It feels everything but Coleman's emotions. The shape of the world is small and richly textured.

When he is both, his body is more than flesh. It breaks apart and he is movement. Seams of light, doorways. The demon has given those it will transfigure—its children, its copies? Coleman doesn't know the word—a way to reach it. *I belong*, they say. Take this funeral, take these few words as an airwave, take this heart as a beacon. *You belong*, it says. And Coleman and his brother are movement, traveling to them.

Eating and making.

He follows the voice. The whisper of the great warm distances ends in a small cave, the suggestion of scorched tunnels leading into the earth. A place the director has made to look like a cave. Coleman stands folded over until he sees a channel leading upward. He squeezes into it and climbs up its throat into a small grimy cellar with wooden stairs. Cameras stare at him from tripods across the floor.

At the top of the stairs, light from wide windows sifts through a storm of dust motes. A cracked marble slab lies on a weathered marble box. It is the crypt from the movie that marked the beginning of the end of his old life, or a room made to look like it.

He crawls out of the hole into the light and keeps crawling, not because the ceiling is low but because it hasn't yet occurred to him to stand. The seams are nearly dissolved, and Coleman and the demon are a perfect soup. They have two eyes and the remnants of a heart together.

He feels himself rotting in the way that has been fascinating him, the things that happen after death. Some part of him can smell it. But underneath, he is strong. He is coiling and hardening.

Coleman passes through rooms and sees lamps on end tables, three figures draped in green sheets and a fourth hurrying across the floor on hands and knees. The first three turn to him and lower themselves into quiet hunched shapes.

Then a hallway with chaotic light. Then an open room and the director in a chair. He sees Jackson's red line on a wall, Jackson's door to heaven.

Dirty sunlight, and he stands for a moment and reaches his strange height toward the ceiling. New bones creak. Past a doorway, out of this strange house, into monstrous pines scratching the sky. A ring of green ghosts murmur in low voices and prostrate themselves before him in the dirt and needles.

There is a hum and he tastes their fear and their wonder. He tastes his brother in his mouth and reminds himself it is his own taste.

Then he is inside, back home, and Gloria and Evie are seated on either side of him on the sofa. Picture frames hang on the half-formed walls, but empty, their art and photographs taken elsewhere. "Back to the past," he says in a wash of breaths and clicks.

A light comes on in the North Carolina kitchen, off to the left. Gloria wraps her fingers around his arm and leans against him. "My Cole, my man," she says, sighing, "my love." She used to say this to him, when they were young.

Evie stands to circle her arms around his long neck. "My daddy, my long-boned thing." She's crying and she's a little girl again but too tall. His grandchildren, Charlotte and Liam, are there with her, craning around their mother to stare at him. "Are you coming back, Grandpa?" "Come back."

Coleman surfaces to think, *Am I dreaming this?*

He thinks, *Are they dreaming me?*

He lifts just above the demon's murk and wants to go home and die in silence. He does not want to eat or create. He wants to be eroded by his cancer surrounded by these magnificent women, who made him into something special long before he saw the movie that Jackson was trapped inside of, long before the doctor sat down and spoke into that cloud of death. Before the knife slid into him, before the haiku.

"Crawl back to us, Daddy." Evie's face is stricken. "Jackson is gone. You have the choice. This is the one moment the demon is afraid of you."

"My Cole," Gloria says. "It will take that boy's mother in your place if you crawl home. Come now and we will keep your light."

He notices a hole in the center of the North Carolina living room, and through it he sees the woman from the house on High Rock Road, the woman who found him as he and his brother became one. She approaches. Her hair is cut as short as Liam's, she is looking through the hole at him with a slack mouth and wide wet eyes. Brown dark eyes.

This is not his home. This is the director's crypt. But Gloria's fingers tighten on his arm. "I got you," she whispers. Evie's arms sag with weight across him. "I'm here, Daddy," she murmurs in his ear.

"Who are you?" the woman asks. He tells her. He thinks, *She is the demon, I can pass this to her.* This burden. He is on the real side. She is on the movie side of this lens that opened over him when he was a child. Creamy light swirls through to him because she wants to come out of the film.

She says something, and Coleman hears angles and edges, *my son, give me, where is, give.*

This woman is his way home. Gloria was right. It will be different this time.

But the young boy. The woman is looking for him. Coleman can't do this to her. *You know where the boy is,* something drags across his splintering mind.

"You will be the demon," he tells her. He reaches out, through the hole in the lens. His wife's fingers slip from him. His daughter's arms fall away. He takes the woman's hands—Jorie's hands, her name swims back to him, the bond they share swells—and feels the slight bones as light as birds.

She gasps. Her mouth moves and prisms of sound spin in the air.

But Coleman pauses at this, and he thinks of his brother. Their mother's bruised eyes. Those decades Jackson was gone, lost and chewed in this demon's mouth. He can taste the mouth now. He can move the tongue.

The sweetness of reunion he never stopped waiting for, and there is something as strong as desire to be this deathless smudged thing, a desire like the dust in the failing sunshine around him and like the colors spearing in his eyes, to find and eat the voices that call him. He wants to spread through the world.

"Say it," the demon whispers to Jorie, twining through Coleman's voice. "Tell me you belong with me."

She must choose now, and he must choose now. Crawl back home as Coleman or disperse himself as spores. He is sitting in the North Carolina living room. He is crouched in a crypt in Vermont. He is breaking along a fault line.

A long clear endless breath. His lungs span the sky. He hears Jorie crying inside the pale light. Then her hands are gone. He rocks back as though pushed.

Another voice speaks, and Jorie shouts in desperate anger.

The hole still hangs in the air, and through it he sees Jorie moving across the crypt. Coleman stands, frantic and needing to complete something. Gloria and Evie and his grandchildren sit on the sofa, their heads tilted up to gaze at him across the plaster ceiling. "Come back," one of them says. He listens to them, then staggers to the hole leading back down to the false cave and worms himself into the tunnel.

Time is sticky. Jorie is there in the chamber, clinging to something, her body turned to keep it from him.

And now Coleman is the brother swimming. Jackson kneels on the shore of the lake and watches him undo the stitching of the sun's thread on the water. The canoe draws closer, the girl and her father burning black coals against the light. Soon a red line will divide the sky, from the horizon up into the dome of clouds, curtains holding heaven or hell or likely both. A closed lid holding his eye.

He will not tire. His head will not sink into the water. He will reach the canoe with his own arms.

Something changes. They are above, in the cellar. Jorie is standing again, and a new hole is opening in the air between them. He stoops and peers through it. He sees himself as a boy, lying dazed on a patch of dirt, windblown shadows rippling like water on his chest. He sees stubborn clumps of grass. This strange child turns his head and looks up at his own great blackened eye.

Coleman watches the boy on the grass, as an angel might.

It would be a fine thing, it would be right to go back to the broken oak limb and start again, to fall again and to leave his family to other lives. The pain of letting them go shines on his childhood face, it shivers on the lake and is gone into another green world.

Maybe he can set his brother free there.

He pushes at the opening but the Greensboro sky bleeds away, the helpless little Coleman in the dirt and grass is gone. There is no green world, just visual noise, the wedge between the world and whatever nudges, blank, elemental, against it.

It clears and Jorie is standing across a dark room watching him, the edge of a bed, a bookshelf, two doorways between them. He tells her what is in his heart, his Evie and her Oli, what he wants, but he only has a moment, and in a shutter of images, Jorie's son dashing through them like snow, he is back in the cellar with her.

The copies of him—the demon's children—are gliding down the stairs. He feels his mouth tear open and drip as the demon uses it to smile, but there is nothing of Jackson left there, only strange new tissue and the last of Coleman's blood.

Before the director finishes, while the demon is fixated, he pictures Gloria waiting, he pictures Evie calling out. They are clear and heavy images, and he pins them to the decaying felt of his mind.

He folds himself under the low ceiling and moves forward, into a rush of screams.

# CHAPTER THIRTY-FOUR

## Jorie

▶▶ They're about to step into the hallway leading back to the ring of candles, where they saw the fake Trevor, but Sam's arm is torn away from Jorie. Her phone's light swings up to the ceiling, painting a Rickie white-green for a moment. The sheeted figure has its arms around Sam, pulling her toward the far end of the set. Jorie glimpses another holding a video camera behind them.

She stumbles forward, reaching for her cousin, through a doorway into a pale wash of light.

CUT TO:

It's Oli's room, a perfect facsimile with his tiny bed and its unicorn comforter and his clothes waiting for the laundry on the floor. The night-light is the only thing they got wrong, he hasn't needed one since just before he turned seven.

Beth is lying on his bed, her legs hanging off the end. A vertical slash of blood or paint has been drawn on the wall above her. *It's not her*, Jorie tells herself, *like this bed isn't Oli's bed, this is a thing with her face. It's like copying a VHS tape.* Beth is elongating, its malformed body pushing down the mattress until the stumps of its feet meet the floor. "You're here," it says, insectile clicks perforating the words. "You have always belonged here."

"Where is my son?" she says, and she's filling herself up to scream it when Beth rolls off the bed and wraps its arms around her. Its touch is cold and somehow both brittle and spongy, like bones decaying in wet moss.

"He belongs." Beth's face descends, its skin wrinkling with shadow. Its body smells of rain and soil, it's lengthening again, lifting Jorie onto her tiptoes. "Will you kill him, too?" Over its shoulder, Jorie sees a Rickie filming this new scene. She pulls free and falls onto the bed.

A ticking, humming silence falls. Oli's night-light clicks off. It's the cue to proceed to the next set, the next chute in the slaughterhouse. Jorie pulls her phone out of her pocket and presses the flashlight on.

The room is empty. She lies half on the bed, panting, sweeping the light from the closet to the doorway, where the Rickie is still shooting. The crown tearing through the sheet. The blank idiot face. An elderly man appears out of the dark next to him, and she recognizes Roger Eilertsen, in his eighties now.

But he's grinning like the others, body tilted, mouth open too wide and the small teeth seeming to grow and recede in the black pocket of the face. Of course the original cult leader is a Pine Arch creature now.

She screams at them and lunges, but Eilertsen fades back—or up toward the hallway ceiling—and the Rickie slips off to the left, into a hallway that branches from the entrance to the den and dining nook. Jorie runs after the Rickie, squeezing into the passage in time to see Sam's soft red jacket disappearing through another doorway of the maze, where a thick wedge of light is pushing out.

Jorie calls out to her as she runs toward the next room.

CUT TO:

She steps into a replica of the crypt from *Proof of Demons*, she recognizes the pitted marble tomb from the film, its lid pushed several inches open. As though something has just risen from it. The look is as close to real as everything else has been. But a green screen in a metal frame has been set up in the center of the set, with an irregular hole cut into it, twenty feet from the doorway.

The half-man from under Mrs. Compton's house is on the other side, a corpse face with heavy flesh under the eyes, hollowed cheeks. Its mouth is hidden below the rim of the opening.

Is this the moving hole? Just CGI, after all the impossible things she's witnessed in this insane house? She smells thick layers of dust, as though the set designer has transferred age and decay into the air. Her body is shaking. Her eyes can't focus properly as the adrenaline sends its electricity arcing through her.

There are no other doorways. The crypt is a dead end. She's been herded. Enriquez—Leah Compton, she still can't believe it—wants to direct her to this staring thing. This is the way to find Oli and Sam, even if she has to write finding them into the script herself.

"Who are you?" she asks the dead face. "I saw you in my son's closet. Give him back to me." She moves toward it, kneeling in front of the hole. The skin of it sags from the hints of gaunt bones. Up close the face is changing, growing into a coarse dark lump, paling to bloodless flesh with thin red hair above the clouded eyes.

Again it reminds her of the white face of Pazuzu in *The Exorcist*, but softer and more recently warm and human. As though it's still deciding what it will be. She wonders what Enriquez will add to the green screen around it.

"Coleman," it says, laced with those harsh sighing clicks, and she senses the great bulk of it bunched up behind the screen.

"Where is Enriquez? Where is my son?" Her voice rising and faltering at the same time, panic clawing its way back in. The strain in her throat from back at her house, when Willard showed up, won't let her scream anymore.

In the film, in the screenplay that has never been shown to Jorie, she supposes this would be the climax. This is where she is forced to come face-to-face with the thing she lied about and gave a voice to. The Pine Arch Creature has been summoned for her. "You're the demon," she nearly hisses, "give him back."

"You will be the demon," it garbles back to her. Its hands reach through the hole, tar-soft things, and take hers. "Say it. Tell me you belong with me."

At once she smells pines around her. She is in shallow woods, and her friends are close by, Colin and Beth quiet with their thoughts, she hears their pens scratching in notebooks. She feels the first thought of fiction, the lie slinking into her mind, a thought full of restless ambition and boredom that she would ignore for days as it grew thorns, tangling with her ego. The envy of those who believed in the Pine Arch Creature.

Her body is locked in stillness.

She feels a doctor's breath on her, telling her she's pregnant, and the taste of fear and disappointment in her mouth. She doesn't want a baby. She feels Oli in her arms, she smells his milky sweet skin, and the immediate, crippling love is there. He is her way back and he is beautiful.

She feels Beth's arm around her shoulder. The road vibrating through Dave's gas pedal, Colin changing subjects and favorite horror films and rankings of monsters. Crows on power lines. Turkey vultures, and wondering what they're circling above. An interstate diner, smears of grease on chipped white plates, the smell of cooking oil. The thrill of caffeine in her blood. Cotton clouds shaped like whatever they need them to be.

Her senses soak in these moments and crevices of her life. The half-molded fingers grip her small hands. Needs and supplications, unspoken weights, wrestle between Jorie and this demon.

Something is trying to get into her, heating her skin and sparking her eyes into blurs. Something pushes against her teeth. It is riveting, almost resplendent.

It is every scary movie she ever watched, but more than that, it is the feeling of watching them. The cocoon of them. The warm and bloody oath of a chrysalis. To be a part.

Her pores sing with it. Saliva spills from her mouth. Something whispers in her head, a bloody twisting cord of words.

*Your name spoken in the dark forever*
*Your child forever*
*Almost six minutes*
*Your boy your Transfiguration*
*You have always belonged here*    [x6:00x]

But a clear soft picture of Oli pushes through, his crooked smile and the sadness in his face when he thinks she's not looking. The smell of his hair before a bath. She shoves the creature's hands away and scrambles back along the floor.

A new voice says, "Which of you is the demon, really?"

Jorie looks up to see Mrs. Compton holding up an expensive camera, black and sleek with a hand strap on top. Her face is half-hidden behind it. She's standing ten feet inside the crypt, wearing a familiar navy-blue cardigan and a white V-neck shirt, the clothes of a Vermont widow comfortable in her skin. The name *Enriquez*, the shock of it, hangs in the air between them.

"Give him back," Jorie says. But she doesn't stand. She's too weak and still too full of the smell of pine resin and dirt. The strange hum of comfort. The membrane of her that was nearly breached is aching like a migraine.

"Oliver isn't far," Mrs. Compton says. The round eye of her camera is cold. "I've been looking a long time for how these two stories end. Yours and Mr. Smith's. Which side will—let's say *volunteer*—to be proof. Which of my cowriters will go on into the world. If there will be an alternate ending. It seems obvious, but the choice had to be here, you had to find your way here. I felt sorrow when you left horror, Jorie. I became wistful, so I built all this. I combined my films and my legacy for you." She peeks around the camera at Jorie. "So much great raw footage of you today."

"Cowriters?" The pull is still there, it stuns Jorie. She remembers printing out pages after writing until the sun was ready to crawl out, smelling the heat of the paper as her tongue burned with nicotine. Seeing her name spelled out. "More like plagiarism. You took my film haunt and made it real. Even the sound your demon makes. You moved in down the road from us."

"Plagiarism? No, collaboration. It's why I credited you for the new production. Your wonderful film haunt, to borrow your famous term, of *Proof of Demons*. There was truth in those remarkable lies. Because you gave it to the fans, the young occult detectives, and they believed you, perhaps even more than they believed me. Now they're on my payroll. They've started making their own Pine Arch Research films with my nurturing. One of them had you slated to die in your supermarket. Stabbed to death. As though I would ever have allowed that! But they believed enough to spread it like truth, until it *became* truth."

Enriquez pauses, and her voice has shed its lightness when it continues. "Until it became real. I don't know if it's evolution or some Lovecraftian construct, but what is it to know something, really? Belief leads us to something more real than knowing, Jorie. Have you not noticed that everywhere lately?"

"So your name isn't Hélène Enriquez?" It wounds Jorie to ask something so rooted in mere curiosity, as though she's passing the time, waiting for some action cue.

Enriquez laughs, and the camera bounces lightly before she goes on. "Yes, it is. I was born in Spain, but I could see France from my childhood window. And your screenplays, Jorie, I've read everything you ever wrote, from *Walpurgis* to *Dead People's Things* to the documentary you started about me. The break-in years ago, when your computer was stolen. That was one of my little detectives. Paul, actually, though he's not really my son.

"I wanted your computer because I loved the way you saw horror like so few can, the way you saw through to the inscrutable nature of demons. A faith that does away with the flimsiness of faith. Not a tulpa, as you and your friend Colin wrote, but not *not* a tulpa. You were close. I was trained in the occult. You were not, but that lack made us such linked spirits, Jorie. I wanted to be near you and work with you. I wanted you to be the haunted film. I wanted you to make things again."

She turns the camera away from Jorie. "And let's not forget our cowriter, Coleman. He gave me insight before I ever shot a frame of *Proof*. And now we're close to learning what's on the other side of our door."

"I will not be your cowriter," Jorie says. "I won't be your anything. This fake truth you're chasing got a girl killed, and now you're hurting other people. I helped you kill Hannah because of a stupid movie, but there's no way I'm helping make this one. I want my son. Give him to me."

Enriquez tilts her head without moving the camera. "Oh, the schoolgirl. She's important now, for the story we're making, though she felt more like a setback at the time. You and I were such villains for that! And all for a false ritual, just some trash regurgitated on the internet. But speaking of her, have you seen the new trailer?"

"Fuck you. Where is my son?"

The director smiles, her head still tilted. "Of course you've seen the trailer. People are such interesting sponges, you know, they'll accept so easily. They believe so easily. But Jorie, it comes down to this. Will *you* believe in what you made?"

Jorie turns and looks back at the hole. The creature—Coleman Smith—is looking to its left and to its right, as though following some other conversation. The look on the aged, muddled face is so human. "It's just a movie. I don't know what you did to that man, but this is a green screen, not any proof of demons."

"The proof is writing itself as we speak, Jorie. It's coursing through servers stacked in oceans. The demon has faith now, it has been given attributes, as you once wrote. Not nearly all of them believe, so it often doesn't work. But enough do, more and more of them out there. They say, 'I belong.' They still their minds. There's some delicious haunting, then our cowriter says, 'You belong.' And we have another viral Transfiguration. The faith is so strong that a seam of blood isn't even needed as a conduit. And when our film is released! Our film will—I don't want to be melodramatic and say it will remake the world, but it will certainly change the shape of it."

Enriquez lowers herself to her knees, nearly eye level to Jorie, and pushes the camera closer, getting an intense shot of Jorie's face. "I was so fixated on the eye. I should have known the Pine Arch Creature would resonate. It was what had been calling. Calling the fans and calling *me*, Jorie, all these years. Just think, a true occult, a mystic and recondite sedimentary layer to existence. Legend becomes science. Proof, real proof. *We* did this."

"Where is my son?" Jorie screams, finding strength in her ragged voice, staggering to her feet. "I don't care about any of this. Where's Samantha?"

Enriquez ignores her. "You've met the first few of those we've captured in the lens, those lesser demons, our entity's photocopies, if you will. The faces they wore for you. The ones you love. And is it really another green world they go to?" Her voice softens, she glances away, slipping into her thoughts. Her left hand begins to fiddle with a dial on the side of the camera. "In a manner of speaking, I suppose. I had no idea a sort of demonic copy would be part of each Transfiguration, but it makes a lovely sense. It's the medium, after all, and we are rooting around in the unknown. What is more evergreen than a horror film? Anyone who ever wanted to *feel* something greater than themselves, to *belong*—"

Jorie lunges forward and pushes the older woman, who falls from her knees and rolls with the camera cradled in her arms.

"Where is he?" Jorie bends and shrieks into Enriquez's face. *"Tell me where he is!"* Her voice nearly splinters.

The camera goes on quietly sipping images of Jorie from its new angle near the floor. Jorie turns away, panicked and disgusted and steeling herself to wrench the camera from Enriquez's hands and use it as a bludgeon, for Beth and for Oli, but she sees something near the far side of the crypt. There's a mouth in the floor. She runs to it, lowers herself onto thick-painted gray stairs.

CUT TO:

Steps lead down to an empty cellar. She squints in the halogen light shining from the corner, barely seeing the bulky 1980s cameras bracketing the space on tripods, humming at her in the glare. This room is from *Under the House*, the climax of the hole that led to the title of the film, just before it ended and cheated the viewer.

At her feet is a VHS tape, the words YOU HAVE ALWAYS BELONGED HERE printed in black Sharpie along the white spine. But when she turns to look for the hole in the wall—everything else has been lovingly recreated, it's laughable to think it won't be here—her delirious thoughts break apart in a choked sob.

Sam is lying at the mouth of the opening, a channel that seems to worm below the cellar. Jorie crouches next to her and sees her chest rising and sinking. Her clothes are coated in dust and filth. A line of blood has wandered down her face from the right temple.

Jorie asks her if she can hold on. "You know I have to go—" She was about to finish the sentence with *under the house,* but she won't give Enriquez the satisfaction. "I have to go get him," she says instead.

She looks at the hole and she is trembling with exhaustion, she doesn't know where that desperate mother strength has gone. But she gets on her hands and knees and tips herself into the earthen tunnel.

CUT TO:

# CHAPTER THIRTY-FIVE

## Jorie

▶▶ The air below is cold and fermented. The floor is moist, dirt and sawdust. It's a sort of smoke-blackened cave, but recently constructed. Dozens of holes have been dug into the walls.

Fluorescent lighting panels have been strung across the hunched earthen ceiling, and the space is dominated by a long trench carved into the ground. Jorie can't see into it, and though alarms are ringing brightly in her mind, whines piercing enough to send winks of light crackling across her vision, she steps forward. A giant cockroach, one of the terrifying ones she thought she'd left behind in the subtropical south, scurries along the right edge of the hole.

The grave, she knows it's a grave.

There are more cameras, of course, set up to capture every angle of whatever is waiting. They will wring every tear from Jorie's eyes if she sees what she fears.

Just two steps and she can see Hannah Kim lying inside it. The eyes are closed. The skin is lifeless and full of vitality, like a vampire's. OFH, her dirt-smeared blue T-shirt reads in a stylized white font, the letters beginning to overlap. Beneath the logo, in smaller print, is OCTOBER FILM HAUNT.

All Jorie can do for a moment is stare at the words, until Hannah's eyes open and a small smile stretches her mouth. It's the senior photo smile that filled the corner of news broadcasts for months. It would be almost sweet, if not for the length of the grave and the length of the body filling it.

"I'm so sorry," Jorie says, and falls to her knees. "I have to find my son, but I'm so sorry."

The thing in the trench rolls Hannah's eyes to its left. Its smile grows.

Jorie takes another couple of steps forward on her knees, and there is Oliver, lying on his side and turned toward Hannah like a little brother who has had a nightmare. The thing jostles him as it folds itself up into a sitting position, but he doesn't stir.

It looks at Jorie and speaks. No sound comes out, not even clicks, not even breath. Only a stream of gentle muted words, but somehow Jorie knows they are not full of evil or corruption. It begins to waver between looking like Hannah and like the things roaming above them, between the images from the videos on TikTok and the memorial website her family set up.

The years of suffocation come out of Jorie. She shoves the first camera over on her way to Oli, breaking its lens. The second falls backward and tumbles into a corner of the space. She leaves the third because it's too far to go.

She falls to her knees again and lifts her son out of the earth, her skin bunching up with dread. But Hannah doesn't reach for her. Oli's skin is cold, he weighs nothing in her arms. She stares at his eyes until she sees them twitch under the lids, in dreaming sleep. The smallest sigh slides from his lips with a rasping pop.

A thin rattle of a voice finally comes from the corrupted thing staring at her. "You belong."

"I don't belong," she says. "I don't want to. Whatever you want me to think Hannah would have said."

A cascade of dirt sifts from the hole she came down through, and an enormous dark thing slithers into the chamber. Jorie presses Oli against her and turns her body away. The Pine Arch Creature can hardly fit down here, it was made for the woods.

There is almost nothing of Coleman Smith in it. It has to coil itself sideways into a horrible spring, but then it moves toward them like a great worm from some final implacable horror image.

Jorie screams, a flat slap of sound enclosed in this tomb. The Pine Arch Creature pauses and rears up, its head dislodging clods of earth and its arms raising to brace its contorted body against the ceiling. The opening in its torso sighs, and the idea of light blooms in its dark. People crawl into that, she remembers. Seconds pass, in which they seem to regard and search each other, until it shifts away to the wall.

"You do belong," it finally says, and clenches its face with pain. "With us in the camera. With our brother in the lake. You call it the Transfiguration." There's something else, but a looping, snapping noise swallows the words in rhythmic static, the hollowed-out room wavers, and the whole of its body expands and is gone.

Hannah is still sitting in its grave and staring at them. It continues to move the strange tendons of its mouth. Its own clicks begin to slip out like hissing vapor.

A voice could follow, but its words can't call Jorie back. She hugs Oli to her side and works her one-armed way up the crumbling tunnel, fighting for every inch, pushing him over the lip of the hole.

CUT TO:

She climbs out into the cellar and holds on to her son and her cousin, weeping and ready to kill anyone who comes near them.

Oli wakes first. He says, "Mama?" and she smiles. Sam isn't far behind, with a headache and a glazed look in her eyes. The three of them hobble up the dirty gray stairs.

CUT TO:

The end of the narrative. Jorie doesn't want to think in terms of story beats anymore. She's too weak to carry Oli but she does it anyway, his face buried in the hollow above her collarbone. She feels his eyes squeeze shut against her neck to block everything out.

Sam has the knife that Jorie held on to all the way until her first time in the cellar. There's no Enriquez. Each portion of the set they pass through is intact but vacant somehow. Then Jorie notices the cameras are gone, and closer to the front of the house, Rickies are packing them up, still in their sheets and crowns. They wrap cables into coils and collapse tripods.

From stage to stage, dark to light, Sam holds the knife out, but the Rickies only watch them from the corners of their hidden eyes. Jorie asks them where Ryan is. They pretend she isn't here as they pack away boom mics wrapped in folded-up green sheets. She sees a pile of wooden crowns on the floor like bored children's toys.

One man is sitting cross-legged, without his sheet, disconnecting a MacBook from a black box with blinking lights. He turns to look at them and she recognizes Avery Ellis. His smile is hungry. Her body doesn't have the energy to shudder.

She carries her son outside the house, into the last frames of daylight. Jorie's arms tremble with Oli's weight, so she has to put him down. He clings to her leg as she pulls her phone out and calls the police. Officer Willard is missing, she says, he tried to help them, they need an ambulance.

Rickies are streaming around them into the woods in the falling dark. Jorie counts twelve of them with equipment on their shoulders, bouncing against their hips, in packs strapped to their backs. They move quickly, as close to a run as their burdens will allow, but still she braces herself for one of them to make a sudden last-act lunge at her.

Oli is looking around at the trees. "Is this a Transfiguration, Mom?" He has to sound the word out from memory, and her heart goes cold. What other words did they teach him? What did they do to him? What will have to be unraveled?

"No, buddy," she says. "That was somebody else, I think. And we'd have to stand here a lot longer than we're going to."

The house in the trees is less than a film set now. It's a wrap. She imagines Enriquez hiding in a stand of paper birches somewhere in the near distance, cheated and bitter, gripping the trunk of one of them hard enough to turn her fingers as white as its bark.

She thinks of Márcia Smith, too, in that final scene in the crypt as the wooden crown is placed on her head, pinning the curtains of her hair around her eyes. Those eyes growing wider, the camera creeping into them, a reflection of something unknowable caught between horror and joy. Jorie used to pause the video at just the right moment to try to decide what it was.

But why is she thinking of Márcia?

Jorie finds the last gleam of evening in Sam's eyes, nothing like what Márcia saw. Oli shifts his body against her. The lake and the woods ripple, a strange segmented blur in her vision, three pinkish-blue lines warping down through the air, one after the other. Almost like an old television screen, and Sam turns to her and says

CUT TO:

# CHAPTER THIRTY-SIX

## Jorie

▶▶ "Look at me." A hand pushing and pulling her. Rocking her. She opens her eyes. Sam is the one on her knees now. "Jorie, stop it. Where's Oli?"

Jorie realizes she was speaking when her mouth ceases to move. She looks down and sees that she's sitting in the long grave in the burned-out hollow of earth. Beneath the cellar. Still under the house. She's wearing one of her old October Film Haunt shirts, blue streaked with long-dried dirt.

She lifts her head and finds her cousin. *What,* she tries to say, *what is happening?* Now she feels the movement of her jaw, her lips making shapes, but her voice is gone. It's only a croak, a sound she's terrified is too much like a series of clicks. *I just put Oli down. I was carrying him. The trees.*

"You've been like this for five minutes, at least. Come on, we have to find him." Sam helps her out of the grave. Jorie is unsteady and stiff, and she can't stop touching her face to make sure it's normal. An awful feeling is coating her like sweat, the realization that her son seems so far away.

"I saw Hannah," she says to Sam. Her voice is coming back. "I think she forgave me. I had Oli in my arms."

"Yes, okay," Sam says. "We have to go up and find him. Then get out of here."

The tunnel is steep enough to be difficult, but they reach the cellar and crawl out onto its floor. "I just did this," Jorie says, grabbing Sam's arm. "I did it with Oli."

A crackling line of static passes from the ceiling to the floor, a sort of waver in the air that bends the cellar out of its true shape. Another line follows it down. The halogen lamp is still blaring like a white sun in the far corner, but its light is somehow rich now, nearly creamy. The two vintage cameras on tripods gaze at them from opposite walls. The videotape she saw on the floor, YOU HAVE ALWAYS BELONGED HERE, is gone.

"Where is he?" Jorie asks.

Before Sam can answer, just as she's tugging Jorie forward, they hear feet at the top of the stairs along the right. Something taps against a wall, a dead rhythm of porcelain, and it's a sound Jorie would recognize anywhere. Boots appear, the stained bottoms of green sheets.

The Rickies descend into the light, three of them fitting themselves into the space where the dirty concrete floor hooks around toward Jorie and Sam. They each wear the shape of a tall crown, the points just beginning to tear through the fabric.

One of them is much shorter than the others.

"No," Jorie says, the last of the rust falling from her voice, and she goes on saying that word, "no, no, no," until Sam reaches over to clutch her shoulder.

The Rickies lift their arms, but there are no knives. They grasp their sheets and pull them away. The crowns fall and clatter on the floor.

Jorie begins to scream. Oli is looking across the cellar at her. She can't tell if the smile on his face is scared or unsure. She can't read his sweet eyes. Agatha is dangling from his right hand, her fine hair drooping. He's wearing his bear sweater and one of his new pairs of jeans.

Beth takes his other hand and stares at Jorie. Colin watches Jorie, and her old friends flex and darken and whiten, like blood coursing in and out of sponges.

"Is this a Transfiguration, Mom?" Oli asks. He has to sound the word out from memory. She can't answer, her eyes are fixed on his skin, which has paled but is still his skin, it would still smell like his pillow.

More twitching lines track down the—*the videotape*, Jorie thinks—carrying brief blue and pink and greenish stains with them. An edge of the room melts inward with distortion, there and gone in less than a second.

"That's the thing about endings," someone says, and Jorie sees legs folding above, a hip and part of a torso lowering to sit on the stairs. Enriquez, the dark blue cardigan. "Would you say what's under the house is more frightening, more pure, when we leave it up to the viewer?"

Beth and Colin are grinning now, wide enough to soon break their faces and reveal what is wearing them. They begin to stretch toward the cheap plywood rafters of the ceiling. Oli stays his same perfect height, as tall as her heart, and Jorie watches his smile. It's still a little boy's smile, but why hasn't it faded? Why are terror and tears not replacing it?

"You had to know you were the enduring mother in this story," Enriquez says from the stairs, but her voice is deeper now, washed of its faint accent. If she bent down, it might be a different face peering over the rail at Jorie. "The Final Transfiguration. Not the final girl. You're too important for the happy ending, but I wanted to let you live in it for a moment."

Something shifts in the gloom under the stairs, beneath Enriquez. An eye opens, green and wet and rotting black, rolling in its socket. A monstrous eye, but a human face draws itself around it like a clouded moon, Coleman's face returning, the one that peered out of Oli's closet that first night. Still soft and bloodless and deeply sad. Only for an instant. Only long enough to speak.

They are the words she couldn't hear in Oli's bedroom. There is no voice for the words, she senses it has been taken from him, but there is air brushing against her ears—*she caught your son in the camera get him out I want to die in Evie's arms she caught him in the camera grab him go now I can't die with my Evie*—and then Coleman is gone with a last rattle of breath. Only the demon remains.

Sam screams as the eye emerges inside a huge dark lump hissing with feedback. There is so much of it to unfold. The cellar is so small, and the Pine Arch Creature was made for the woods.

"Mom!" Jorie turns and sees Oli holding up a crown. His lost doll is inside it, like a trapped witch. His face is proud, expectant. He looked that way once when he brought home a haunted house he made out of Popsicle sticks. He still looks beautiful, he has only ever been beautiful, even when he was born and she didn't know if she wanted him.

But he has always belonged with her.

Lines ripple down the wall again, furrowing her son with static, he is Oli, he is not quite Oli. The cellar warps for a stretched-out instant, her son is lifting Agatha in jerks through a frozen smear of melting images. Beth and Colin bend and snap and writhe in their one-second loops. The sharp stench of pine swells through the stale air.

Time snaps back to clarity and fluid motion. An unpaused tape. Sam is pressing her hand into Jorie's, the kitchen knife is there, and the Pine Arch Creature rears, opening itself to her. The clicks and rasping crackles of its voice are like a dying ocean.

Jorie could see into its strange body if she wanted, a kind of light is blooming inside its hollow, a living diode in the heart of a tree. But she won't look away from her son's face. She is still waiting to see what he does with his smile.

*It's the medium*, Enriquez said in the crypt above. *What is more evergreen than a horror film?*

Around her, the hum of the halogen light, the distant whirring grind of the cameras waiting with her. One of the lenses is watching her eyes. How long has Oli been reflected in them?

"And now our ending, Jorie," Enriquez says above her. Clicking burrs rupture behind Jorie's head, wet breath on her neck.

How much time is left, muddled in a brown spool of tape?

Jorie weighs the knife. She measures the distance to her son and to the stairs. To the awful woman crouched there. Jorie squeezes the knife. She tenses her legs, thinking of the old atavistic feeling she and the real Beth and the real Colin used to long for. She feels the tremble of every hope in every moment, just before the moment comes.

# ACKNOWLEDGMENTS

Back in 2016—it feels like a week ago, it feels like a continental drift ago—I published my first book, *Greener Pastures*, a collection of short stories. Included was a love letter to found-footage horror titled "October Film Haunt: *Under the House*." It's obvious to say that this novel wouldn't exist without that story, but what's less obvious is that it might not exist without the readers who told me (and the internet) how much they enjoyed it.

Each of those readers is in the creases and between the words of this novel, and I owe them my gratitude—which is all to say, talking about the art we love can have a tangible impact, and we should all do it more often.

I have to thank Trevor Henderson by name first for being so into the idea of a fictionalized version of himself. Only he could have brought the Pine Arch Creature to life, so I had to pretend he did. Go check out his artwork and never sleep right again. Special thanks to Jenn Woodall for the same kind permission.

My agent, Ron Eckel, has provided extraordinary advocacy, stewardship, and friendship. He lurked behind the curtain and pulled levers with grace. My brilliant editor, Alexandra Sehulster, was a fierce believer in this story and saw right into the heart of it—I've greatly benefited from her wisdom and the freedom she gave me to maximize *The October Film Haunt*'s potential. The St. Martin's Press team haunts these pages, too, in indelible ways.

I know so many deeply talented authors. Adam Nevill was the first to say he wanted "October Film Haunt: *Under the House*" to be a novel, and while I took a different approach, he planted the seed. I'm forever grateful to David G. Blake, who read the first draft and kept me sane (sorry I named characters after you and Ashley and killed them within a few lines). Kristi DeMeester, Daniel Mills, and Naben Ruthnum also read that early draft and offered invaluable perspective. Ian Rogers, Matthew M. Bartlett, Simon Strantzas, Paul Tremblay, Stephen Graham

Jones, Alison Rumfitt, Eric LaRocca, Gemma Files, Richard Chizmar, Nat Cassidy, Adam Cesare, Brian Evenson, Wendy N. Wagner, Ramsey Campbell, Craig Davidson, Rachel Harrison, Josh Malerman, Clay McLeod Chapman, Andy Davidson, Nathan Ballingrud, John Langan, Andrew F. Sullivan, CG Drews, Craig DiLouie... It's stunning that this is just the start of the proper list of thanks, and how much raw talent walks this earth.

The biggest, loudest, most teary-eyed-have-to-leave-the-room gratitude to the person who supports me like no one in my life ever has: Natalia, my perfect-fit puzzle piece. Thank you, love. This book absolutely could not have been written without you. You are my forever person.

Our dog, Frida, deserves a whole page to herself, but I'll just say that she's a good, good girl, the very best girl, and she has made my life so much bigger. I love you, bear.

Thanks to my mother and father, for everything, but especially for letting me fall in love with horror when I never had a single nightmare after watching *The Exorcist* when I was seven. My brothers. My dear Aunt June. All the family I've lost. Art and Merry Vuley for unwavering enthusiasm. The same goes to Alyson Vuley, Aunt Linda, Aunt Joy, Oli and Seba, Abbey Meaker, Ethan, Monse, Leo, Olivia, Levi, all the Vuley family. Thank you for the light in my life. Lifelong love to Chris, Bobby, Robyn, Benicio, Luna, Dean, Dimara, and Farbod.

And thanks to you. Whether you read a hundred books a year or just ten, there are so many stories out there, and you chose this one. You belong.

# ABOUT THE AUTHOR

Abbey Meaker

**Michael Wehunt** has been a finalist for multiple Shirley Jackson Awards and was shortlisted for the International Association for the Fantastic in the Arts' Crawford Award. In Spain, his stories have garnered nominations for the Premio Ignotus and Premio Amaltea, winning the latter. He haunts the woods outside Atlanta with his partner and their dog. Together, they hold the horrors at bay. Find him in the digital trees at www.michaelwehunt.com.